TOUCH ANI

BY

JASPER MORLEY

Touch and Go

Chapter One

Lost for Words

'If you can hear my voice you are already dead. There's not much point beating about the bush, and there's not much point me saying don't worry about it; you are in no fit state to worry about anything right now. Besides, it is all done and dust to dusted. No, you are not in a fit state, nor are you in an anxious state, a confused state, or a state of rapture; you are in no state at all as it happens. You are certainly not in a solid-state, like a cupcake, or a lump of ice. You cannot be eaten, and you cannot be added to a glass of homemade lemonade, or put in a glass of Pimms, only to find yourself left behind, along with bits of strawberries, and chunks of cucumber, after the liquid gets happily drunk. At least you managed to get a little tipsy on your death-day. Naturally, you do not feel cold, either to the touch or as a sensation, seeing as you don't have any senses and all. Luckily, or maybe not, after your time in the sun, you didn't melt away like the lump of ice you dropped on your patio, on the last day of your life. Our lump found

3

it hard to keep things together as a liquid, though it did find it easier when it came to letting go, and going with the flow; especially as it was 'the flow', or part of it at least. And you did not evaporate and rise straight up, like most of our lump's meltwater, once it had spread itself about a bit. And you are not like the rest of our melted lump either; the fluid that soaked into the ground and then made its way via root branch, and eventually leaf, in vaporous ascendency to the heavens above. And once there, live happily in, and part of a cloud for a while, and then crystallising, being reborn as a snowflake, a perfect and unique individual snowflake. A fluttering snowflake destined to be almost immediately kicked down and out of the heavens at birth. And to go through all of that only to end up compressed and compacted with all individuality crushed and flattened. And then to become part of an ice sheet; a colossal frozen block of ice; a much bigger block of ice than the one in your Pimms, slipping and a sliding, literally glacially slowly, towards the sea. Nothing quite so straight forward or familiar for you I'm afraid. But in its way, just as simple really; in the same way as a complicated process and complex structure can be part of an overall simple form, kind of simple way; like a fly's eye.'

The narrator stopped, not happy with the way things were going. They contemplated starting over again with shorter sentences. Using the water cycle did illustrate the concept of changing states, and use to make the point that Sophie should not think of herself as part of a physical being or process, as solid, liquid or gas, but it was all a little Lemony Snicket. They put their discontent down to being unschooled in word-craft. The words, 'word-craft' bobbed about and they contemplated the word craft. Something to do with making boats; they wondered what sort of boat they were crafting. Not a problem, they thought, it doesn't have to float. They decided not to begin again, knowing they would just have to learn and improve on the job. And in the meantime, if it sounded like an incoherent stream of consciousness, or to be more accurate, unconsciousness; or if it sounded like a string of platitudinous poppycock, so be it, they had a captive audience of one, and they were dead. They pressed on. They probably wouldn't be able to improve things anyway. It was not the time to change things around.

'So what state are you in? Well it sure ain't Kansas, and you are not dreaming, as you glide merrily, merrily, merrily, gently down the stream. You may indeed, end up worrying, or perhaps preoccupied would be a better word, about the state you are in, but rest assured, your hair will not, and never did. You could consider yourself being, between two states; on a bridge between, the icy winds of North Dakota in winter, and the warm rain of a tropical downpour, on a sticky summer's day in Queensland. But that wouldn't cover it; not really. And you are not in any type of, weed opened doors of experience, California 'state of mind'. No, it isn't a trip or a dream. And you are no longer even part of the welfare state, or any other state you could think of, or care to imagine. All of this much I can state categorically. It is probably closer to the truth, but still, some way off, to say you are stateless, in the international lounge of an airport terminal, with no scheduled departures, and the duty-free is shut. Or you might say, you are balanced on an invisible borderline, like a tight rope walker, moving slowly forward, with only a

chain of random thoughts to follow. And as you place each foot, carefully in front of the other, you walk the line, you put yourself on the line, and you define the shape of things unseen. You are, walking on the outline of different states of being, but you are not in one. And, not wanting to put a foot wrong, you bare your soles to feel your way, and you carry on walking. All you have for now is that invisible thin line. You do not have a grip, and you can't get one. Just as well, because you can't get confused either; otherwise, I'm sure I would have made you so by now. It doesn't matter just yet whether you make sense of what I am saying or not. Ultimately, you will make sense of whatever sense I have made. It sounds like neither of us knows what I am going on about. But on behalf of both of us, I do. This is all still a work in progress, so you'll have to bear with me. Look, the important thing is that in the long run, it will be impossible for you not to understand. You may have lost your senses, but that won't prevent it all making sense in the end. No, for the time being, (and you are not a time being like a time lord, by the way) no, it doesn't matter if you comprehend. I guess it doesn't really matter how I put things for now; what is important now, is the tone, my tone, the undertone, and the overtone. It does not matter how I put things, as long as they're not the wrong things. It's crucial I don't hit a bum note. No bad vibes agitating the mix. I have to make a good pitch. A certain pitch can crack the glass, or whatever vessel one chooses to contain themselves in. The wrong pitch from me now could make a mess of the whole shebang. All things said and done, we will get where we are meant to be. What matters right now, is how I say what I say. So long as I stay within the bounds of decency, and within the realms of your imagination, and as long as I state what I state, with conviction, and in reassuring tones, as if to suggest you are alright, then the whole ball of wax will roll along nicely. You are of course, truly not alright in respect of the life you lived, as let me reiterate in no uncertain terms, you are indeed dead. In presenting this fact to you, I have no latitude, regardless of how compost mentis or not, it is possible for you to be. It may, however, be comforting for you to know, that apart from being dead, you are alright in every other regard.'

The narrator's soliloquy was slowing down, slowly, but not slow enough to be audible.

'Although you are not able to make out the exact words I'm saying, there is a good chance you are picking up patterns. Those patterns will change, but they must always contain, the thread of truth. So once more, for the record, you are dead, and without wishing to drift too much further into the murky waters of legalese, that fact is incontrovertible. I know under normal circumstances you could have easily plucked, well-formed articulate, erudite questions from any part of your mind, and spat them at me, like the high-velocity bullet points you were known for. I also know that those questions are there, hovering around like swarms of flying ants; swarms of inklings, desperately trying to form a question. The likelihood of you being able to herd them together, and get them to fly in unison, so they can form a word that you can't remember yet, and use that word, as part of a question, about an idea you haven't thought of before, is pretty remote. The standard advice at this point is to, ignore the flying buggy things, and they won't bother you. Otherwise, if they get agitated, they can nip you, and you could end up with an itch you can't scratch. I'm afraid you are going to have to wait until you learn to think in

*words again, and then grapple with being able to express
yourself, and then you need to learn to do it faster, a lot
faster, before you can pin those swarming thoughts down,
and ask those questions. But those may not be the questions
you will want to ask by then, so you see, you may as well
ignore them. You will end up asking questions you never
asked in, what was your life. Till then, you will drift along
like a leaf in a stream. You won't so much think your
thoughts, as they will think you. You'll be able to steer your
way, and gather your thoughts as you go. In the meantime,
when you are not gathering, and collecting your thoughts
and feelings, like beautiful shells and pebbles. and
arranging them on your beach towel; in the meantime, as I
am coasting along with you, I am going to tell you a story.
There are certain things you will want to know, and certain
things you will need to know. We would give you all the
facts that you need to know straight, neat from the teat, but
you wouldn't be able to absorb, or understand the tiniest
fraction of them; just too rich to digest I guess. So, we tell
stories instead; easier to absorb in story form at this point,
rather than a huge ball of string. Yes, a story is much better.
It's like those memory guys who remember the running
order of packs of cards by mentally pinning something
interesting to each one, and stringing those things together
on the thread of a story. Like the three of diamonds being
three carrots, you find in your pocket, and the five of clubs
being a five-story office block, with black glass, or
something like that. And then you come up with the story to
link them, like I left the five-story black glass, office block,
and put my hand in my pocket, and found the three carrots
I put there, for myself, earlier. I would rather do interesting
unusual stuff in the first place, and remember those things,
like finding three carrots in my pocket, rather than
imagining stuff to remember the running order of packs of*

cards. But at least memory guys figured out something about how to remember boring stuff, or absorb technically incomprehensible stuff, which is sort of why we employ the storytelling method in this case; in your case. Not technically difficult though, just hard to stomach. Memory and knowledge can both be slippery fish to handle, better to enjoy watching the way they swim around when you go scuba diving. So coming up with a story can make absorption easier, or at least more interesting, and understandable, as well as helping you to remember. It makes it a little less dull for me too. Plus I can adlib a little here and there. Let me state the obvious, as it is the ground on which we will construct our building of many stories; the story I am about to tell you is not the truth, but let me also say, it does contain the truth. The idea of truth was always important to you. To quote Mahatma Ghandi, 'there is no higher God than the truth'. That seems to be the way you saw things; you believed in the truth as an idea and a guiding star. However, it should be said that you did not always believe the truth when it looked you in the face, not without proof. The belief in the truth is something we can work with.'

Sophie picked up on a pause, or hesitation in the narrator's delivery, as if they had lost their place. It was some time before the narrator recommenced.

'Every story is like a container. Some are wonderfully crafted, some are rough and ready but strong, and others are like puzzle boxes. Some look very ordinary but contain great things, and others are like elegant empty vases, waiting for you to put in a bunch of flowers. The story is the

9

description and expression that makes the truth visible to the mind's eye. It is the essence of something; that which makes it what it is expressed in words and numbers. That expression is what it expresses, to the recipient. It is the quantity of milk measured and expressed in, pints and quarts. It is the description of it being a white liquid, produced by mammals, to feed their young, which can be homogenised, put in containers, and put in a fridge, just for James Dean to take it out, and drink it, after he has cooled his brow with the chilled glass bottle; the bottle that held its form. Milk is milk. A story can lead you to the truth, but you have to drink it to know for yourself. The truth is the truth, and it is what it is, whether you drink it or not. 'Go on Freddy drink it; drink it in'. Some people are convinced or contented by knowing milk contains calcium, others, with knowing it goes great with cookies. If you are trying to get someone to try something new, it helps if you know what it tastes like, and its chemical constituents'.

Though she couldn't understand a word, she could appreciate the pattern of speech. She could tell the narrator sounded puzzled, before a pause, and momentarily frustrated after it. The pause could have lasted a thousand years for all she knew. The pattern of words could have been a thumbprint, contours on a map, or a swirling grain of polished wood.

'I know what I mean if you know what I mean. Despite my problems putting it into words, and your difficulty in recognising those words, I know you know, and you know I know you know; it's a 'know-know'. Anyways, we can discuss this stuff later. Maybe you can come up with

something better, when you, know you know what I'm
talking about. Luckily we have all the time in the universe'

The Narrator was back into the groove.

'There are different ways of describing something. That
much is straight forward. It is not so easy to express
something; to express the nature of something, what it is;
the essence of something, the 'greenness of green' as a
smart cookie once said. Apropos of nothing important, as I
am using a transatlantic vocabulary, your least favourite
I'm sure, and as I mentioned a bunch of flowers, you may
be a little worried. Well, let me allay any fears you might
have about the overuse of the word bunch. I will use it in
the case of flowers and bananas but not in the manner of,
look at that interesting bunch of rocks, or there is a bunch
of trees over there' and certainly not 'there is a bunch of
interesting birds over there on the previously mentioned
bunch of rocks'. Having given that assurance I hope you
will skip over that and any other cringe-worthy pretentions,
annoying platitudes, or any other such literary irritants
that occur in the crafting of the story. It may be a little
over-engineered to start with. I suppose you don't have
much choice. I guess some stories come in crap boxes, with
everything dropping out of them before you get them home.
The packaging doesn't have to look great but it does at
least have to function. I am not the greatest storyteller
there has ever been but I should manage to get your
groceries home. I have not been doing this, that long and
you might find my voice a little nasal at first. But never fear,
you will barely hear me after a while. I find it intriguing,
the way we use the word story when referring to a level in a

thirty-story block of flats as well as something we tell.
Stories in a building are like stages on which events unfold;
maybe that's the connection if there is one. New and
different, bold and functional carpets are laid and patterns
of footsteps tell a tale. The stories are layers of events like
sediment deposited by the rivers of movement. Movement is
life. Sometimes one story is linked to another by one
organisation or individual that owns the whole building,
and sometimes they are distinct and separate like flats in an
apartment block twenty-six stories high. Form and content
I guess. A passage links one room to another. A passage is
a construction and movement. You have a passage leading
from one place to another place; from the one world to
another, from the old world to the new. You have a ship's
passage across oceans, a passage of music and you have a
passage in a book. The passage in a book connects you to
other realms, the realms of the fabricator. One passage
might lead you to the infinite kingdom of imagination and
another to the information you need in your kitchen.
Passages lead you from the writer's worlds of thought
feeling and experience to the reader's mind. Move through
passages of words to alternate perception and information
and back again. You can throw in a few corridors of the
mind while you're at it. A passage can lead to a door or
many doors. Like 'Harry Haler' in 'Steppenwolf' wandering
down the horseshoe-shaped corridor in the Magic Theatre
with innumerable doors of unknown possibilities to choose
from. Oh and whilst we are on the subject of passages, let's
not forget 'the passage of time' but we can let that take care
of itself; it's a subject that comes up now and then........ My
boss, well when she speaks, a warm gentle breeze blows
over your heart, scented with orange blossom it caresses
your soul; you could listen to my boss for hours; all hours.
She can tell stories like nobody's business. You can come

away after listening to her and be totally satisfied and content without the foggiest notion of what she was talking about. At one end there is barely any story, only beautiful words trickling like a clear mountain stream to sit by, on a rock and meditate; somewhere you can take off your hiking boots and cool your feet in. Art for art's sake, nature, the nature of nature, nurture nature Nietzsche, unpredictable creature, words spoken purely for the way they sound, for their resonance; a deep resonance that connects words to their origins. Then some thoughts feelings and ideas have no specific words to express them, only words to construct a passage from; words that tunnel through the undefinable to reach them. Endless words that tell stories, amazing stories, stories that open the mind move the soul and prompt great deeds; stories that can be told with the simplest humble words and in the discordant tones. They all do something; some seem to be about the ordinary and turn out to change your life, and perhaps even help you understand your death. So, there is the box, and the content; the language and what's said. Some people have a gift for language and not that much of anything to say of great interest; someone else may have a stutter and have the most profound things to tell you and those with the good sense and patience to listen. And there is, of course, the infinite combinations and variations of the two. And amongst all of that, there is the truth, the whole kit and caboodle. I know this preamble would be as obvious and tiresome to some people as turning the soil in a garden, but Sophie, I also know that's the way you like things put together. And the state you're in, you are going to have to take things one step at a time; from the ground floor up, dig. Dig Sophie, dig. It has always been in your favour, that you liked eating the bun to get to the cream. Well, that's just fine. Whilst I am preparing the ground and working the soil, it is worth *noting that this story is no ordinary veg plot; though plant life is a lot of what it's all about. Anyway I know you used to know and understand all this stuff, it's just that you never really knew that you knew it. Besides, I have to go through it all, one way or another; every bit of it. Every grain has to be counted. It may all be a bit patronising and dull, but we have to assume a level of disconnection. And you never know, I might just be your Father or some sort of patron, which would make some level of tedium, or moments of cringing almost unavoidable. As it happens, I'm not your father or a surrogate patron. As I have already stated, you are not thinking fast enough to notice much about what I'm saying right now. Even at your best, you wouldn't have been able to notice everything you took in. Luckily, you don't need to notice everything to get it on board. Most stuff won't register as you soak it up. It will be like the grass and gravel and everything else that flashes by as you gaze out of the window of a train daydreaming. You will notice more when you pull in to a station. Right now everything I am telling you is part of a single note; a clear exquisite note that contains all the music you have ever heard, and more. It rises and falls. We are in no hurry. Time is not something we need to concern ourselves with at the moment, at least not in the way you had to before. Being dead has its advantages. I have a little scope, but I do have to stick to what needs to be said; what needs to be gone through, that which needs to be waded through before we leave the swamp. I only have certain material for tailoring this tale. I only have certain threads to weave our bespoke spoken fabric and it must be stitched together with sturdy lines. You will fill the fabric between the lines. A story, or mathematical formulas, both made up of a collection of different characters and both can express the same truth. We're going with the story for now, though I know you*

*loved numbers and could even spot formulas in the mystical.
I am going to skip that particular numerical creativity truth
lecture for now. Some tellers like to give the whole truth,
science, faith, air, river, space and 'Loony Tunes' reality
preamble right off the bat, but I am going to go straight to
chapter one. One last thing, if you get the basics of what's
in the story, you will probably get the maths. Then you will
find the bits before chapter one more palatable and slightly
more digestible; neat eh? Seeing how you cope with things
after the story is over will be a good way for us to work out
if we are telling the right one. If you come to your senses
you won't be worried about being dead. I should say the
senses you will come to are not the ones you left behind. I
hope this introduction hasn't put you off. I suppose it could
be considered a preface as I played a part in its
composition. Or it could be considered a pre-face. The face
you were wearing before you turned on the television to
watch the news and learnt the world had changed whilst
you were sleeping or the one you had when you dropped
your last lump of ice on the patio. Or perhaps it's more like
the smiling faces of the couple in a photograph, not
realising it would be the last time they were pictured
together.'*

The narrator's voice remained upbeat even during the
melancholy conclusion to the introduction. Sophie was
unable to think in thoughts, only hear the narrator and align
herself. The narrator's voice formed were her thoughts
normally did. The narrator's voice was familiar but alien.
Almost as if to address this uncomfortable condition the
narrator continued.

'I guess it's like Frost said 'poetry is the stuff that gets lost in translation'. The important stuff is what we wrap up in the words; strings of words wound over invisible forms. We will have to be patient.'

'Patient', was the first sound that registered in Sophie's thoughts as a word.

'One more, 'one last thing', any similarity between the people and events in the story and actual people not yet born and events that have not happened yet is our greatest goal in telling this story'

Chapter Two

Hard to Stomach, Considering

Sophie could hear muffled voices talking around her but she did not attempt to make out what they were saying. She was still too weak, too groggy, and too rooted in sleep to move or even form a conscious thought. But she knew the voices were talking about her. The whispering voices played out the rhythmical pattern leading up to a small gathering of concerned individuals about to depart. The voices stopped and she was alone. She began to come to and without fully opening her eyes, and despite the Venetian Blinds being down and forming a solid barrier against the light, she could tell it was that part of the day you could safely call, the middle. A delicate chorus of sounds told her that. No deliberation was needed.

Sophie drifted off and then down into a deep sleep again. After an undiscernible length of time, she rose to the surface to the world of wakeful walkers for a moment, and then dipped under again. Over many hours she rose and fell below the surface of consciousness like a needle pulling a thread over and under oceans of fabric. One side was above, clear and vast, the outside world, and the other side was beneath, warm and infinite. The stitches shortened until they matched the rise and fall of her chest as she breathed. With the third synchronised rising, she burst into full wakefulness, and her eyes split open in a flash of alertness. The room was dark and the hall light outside her closed bedroom door drew a thin bright line around it as it seeped through the cracks. She could hear the muffled sound of the 'News at Ten' theme on the television in the lounge. She felt reassured and comforted. If fully awake, she could have determined the hour but not what day it was, or even which month. Unable to resist the weight pulling down her eyelids she slept deeply again. She plunged like a whale into the depths. There on her the sleeping sea bed she lay.

She woke one more time somewhere in what was unmistakably the middle of that night when the only sound was birdsong. Later in life, she would get to know very well the distinctive song of a nightingale but never remembered when she noticed it first; until now.

'The Peach Faced Loon', a story from the world beyond the blinds'

With those words drifting in through a window in a soothing woman's voice, Sophie left the memory she had just begun to experience. It was a different voice to the earlier one and had a rich calming tone but with a sense of anticipation running through it. It was an announcement; the title of a story about to be told. Then the other voice stepped back in; the male voice she had heard before. It seemed to be artificially rather than artfully flavoured with a slight New Jersey or New York accent, she was not sure which. And she could not be certain it was a man.

'Considering how long it took to come up with the title to this story I can't believe we didn't come up with something a little better, especially as this tale concerns the nature of existence and the destiny of humanity. Maybe that's why we couldn't think of anything better. I think it sounds pretty silly myself. But I guess silliness has its part to play in this yarn, not least the utterances of the 'ancient silly language'.

I know you weren't big on silliness but don't worry there is serious stuff in there. And I know you tended towards biographies and factual stuff on how and why rather than made up stuff, but that isn't an option here. Besides, as you well know, silliness and seriousness are not mutually exclusive. Silliness can be very serious. It can carry a serious message or have serious consequences. And seriousness can be very silly. Some of the most important truths of the universe are pretty ridiculously funny really. Humour is the sense that can perceive truths rather than simply sensory data. It can illuminate serious truths that cannot be picked up on by dry rational sensible and common sense; if that makes any sense. This is not the story by the way; this is just my little pre-amble. The amble will follow shortly. I know I have given you the preface already but you aren't quite ready for the big tamale. It could even be hot tamale, but as you don't remember what tamale is I don't suppose it matters. Ah, I see you are almost ready. The next time the announcer chimes in it will be the sound of the starting bell ringing. I promise. We need someone to flip the switch and when the light starts to flash I can start. Maybe I will grow to like the title of this long winding tail of a tale. Where does a snake's tail end and its body begin? Maybe it is just tail and head. Maybe we don't get to choose the title of things? Maybe something is just called something. No, it still bugs me. I sat down on my own and with some pretty quick-witted individuals and we tossed around some ideas but it always ends up the same. We end up beached. Either it is decided that a title will emerge naturally sometime in the future, which it never does, or the creative juices stop flowing and we decide a stiff drink might help. It seems to at first but never actually does. Drunks think they are making profound sense and give knowing smug smiles, when all they sound like, is drunks, boring drunks; especially me. So our tiny ship is tossed in another brainstorm and hits the rocks of a smooth scotch. Our particular storm in a teacup is becalmed. Thank the 'Loon' that someone came up with a hangover cure that works. Not that you were ever a drinker. I've taken care of that side of things for you. I'm killing time now. It's an odd thing to kill, time. It's like killing a part of yourself; it's like taking off a chunk of the flesh of your own life. Not that that's any concern of yours; as you are fleshless. I am not sure what else to say. I am not great at chit chat. I'm not that good at telling stories either. Maybe I'll get better as we go along. It's still a bit of a novelty for me to think in words.'

Sophie drifted away to the narrator's relief.

Each time she slept she was on the surface longer and each time she went under it was shorter. It was like she was carefully filling the last millimetres of a vessel with precious liquid of sleep with a well-aimed thin stem, flow of fluid growing thinner, as thin as a thread then thinner until it falls as drops. The drops slow. A feeling of relief and joy was almost ready to emerge and embrace her but needed just a little more time, a few more drops. She heard near-silent tiptoeing enter the room and circle her bed. Someone was checking on her. She did not move and postponed opening her eyes though the very last drop had already fallen and complete her drawn out awakening. After a moment of stillness in the room with the noises from outside clearly audible, the padding of footsteps started towards the door. Every sound had a texture, clarity and character they had never had before; her hearing had never been so acute and more appreciated. From the red Pyracantha berries in the budgie like chirps of chattering house sparrows to the waves on pebble beach rumble of distant traffic and wind through Lebanon pine trees, sounds

20

carried life-affirming peace for Sophie. She participated in her memory and it played itself back to her in its entirety. As she listened to the tiptoes stop at the door she thought, 'I'm awake'

Before the handle of the door was about to turn Sophie moved on to her back but did not open her eyes. It was a gentle communication to the person at the door not to leave. The footsteps at their unadjusted level of sounding returned to her bedside. She opened her eyes and was overcome with joy and happiness; she wasn't sick anymore. She looked up and her feelings made contact with the world. She rolled on to her back.

'Mummy' she croaked as she leaned upwards and extended her beckoning arms. Her mother, careful not to let her feelings physically overcome her or squash her recovering child, sat down on the edge of the bed beside her. With this Sophie lunged forward and the pair embraced with tears rolling down their faces.

Here goes, time comes, hear say, say some, say so, stay here, don't go, who knows, hair spray, flat nose, flat line, no shows, what goes, no no's, tune in, tunic, know knows, pencil rabbit timeline frame, match latch rat-a-tat, bullet points, shoot your mouth off, from the hip, hippie-dippie queen, buds, darling buds... You can see why it is easier to give you the information you need in story form rather than in theoretical strings of raw data. They are so stringy. You heard a bit of raw data which will carry on in the background while your mind is elsewhere. You would probably have preferred numbers but you may have found them distracting. You found it irresistible to seek patterns in numbers. There are many forms of raw data, all far too raw to digest. You shouldn't notice it again but if you do, you know what it is. Because you weren't quite ready before, some of what I am about to say may seem a little repetitious, though you won't know that unless you revisit this dialogue at some later point. Very unlikely but everything leaves a trace. You will drift off into your memories. Your will to have your memories in some sort of order before you can move on, but you will need more than memories for that. That is where the story comes in. I can't shut up I'm afraid; not until you are ready for me to start the story properly. None of what you are about to hear is the truth, the whole truth, and nothing but the truth. But it is the truth, part of the truth and bits that are there to keep the truth company; a support system. Everything is part of the truth, even stories because they exist and even lies because they are fabrications. If you are not prepared to walk through walls to hear it; try the door. The truth is not a theory. The truth is in here somewhere; kicking around. I know it was your soul mate and in some ways cellmate. Some of what you will need to know would be too vague if I told it in a way that overlapped neatly with the world you were used to. We all have our favourite genres, but you are not a genre, and if you were you, you would not choose it and it would not necessarily be one you liked. At least you lived long enough to know your mind, as much as that is possible when driven by the needs of life. The truth is so weird that it is easier to grasp in a tale rather than by the tail. Placebos still have consistent statistical success even when patients know they have been given one. There is something in that; it is not a trick. The truth is not that hard to swallow really, but it's hard to keep down. We need to chop it up and chew it before it can slip down and away. A cow needs four stomachs to digest grass; grass, not exactly spicy or fatty, just simple old grass and it needs four stomachs. The simple things can be the hardest to digest and we instinctively overlook them. Coincidently human thought needs to process information in four ways. Each of *those ways has seven phases but we don't have to worry about that right now. And information has to be processed in sequence, one bit after the other incorrect order in the cerebral celestial gut before it can be fully digested and the truth can be absorbed. This preamble is part of the sequence. Religious texts, scientific theories, experiences, imaginings and instinctive reactions are too much to digest all in one go. It doesn't help that some stomachs full of their over-importance try and separate themselves. What those believers of one stomach fail to realise is that it is a process that cannot be done completed in one neat way; by one set of ideas that is.*

The narrator's voice had slowly and unperceptively become deeper, and smoother with a whiff of an East-European intellectual resonance.

Sophie wanted to leap out of bed but her Mother cautioned her against it. She understood the idea and importance of 'taking it easy' better when she had begun to feel poorly. And she did understand when she was told after her illness, that she would need to operate on her lowest energy setting for a while and build up to full power, but it made no difference. She did not leap out of bed but she ran out of the room to find her sister. It was several hours since she had woken to find her mother in the room. After their emotional embrace, Sophie felt fully rested but her limbs were trailing behind her minds wakefulness. She made herself comfortable and began to recollect events. She remembered hearing voices. Perhaps she remembered it, or perhaps she dreamt it. 'She is going to be right as rain in a day or two. It was touch and go there for a while'. The words hung high above her like a far off bell in the misty distance ringing in deep sombre tones. But what did it mean?' she thought; 'touch and go. What did it mean? What touched me and where did it go?'

'Silence is not an option now' stated the announcer. Somewhat reluctantly the narrator continued not sure if he was expressing things in the right way but obliged to carry on.

'The intellectual and spiritual struggles of human history have been too heavily concentrated on finding the balance between heart and head alone; it would have been more fruitful to have included the stomach more and paid more attention to a balanced diet, and to digesting information properly, at the right time and in the right number of ways. If something is not absorbed properly it is discarded and pooped out and the same is true of understanding, one way of looking at something is usually not enough. Stuff gets pooped out leaving the consumer with deficiencies of vital elements; deficiencies that can manifest themselves into some pretty freaky cravings and some unsightly skin conditions. The truth, the whole food well-chewed truth, and nothing wasted out your butt truth, was a long way off for humanity when you were alive, and it's a long way off now. The best that we can hope for is that we can perceive and use that part of the truth that will help us make up our minds that, the whole truth is worth pursuing; even when it can never be fully perceived by any individual. You can't blame people for not wanting to search for something they will never find, but they should always remember that if they keep looking they will find some cool stuff on the way. I must add that this is an outcome that can only be arrived at after the appropriate intellectual digestive organs being employed. And these lie dormant in most people or have never been developed in others. The nothing but the truth, well that bit is right, there is nothing but the truth only how much of it is possible to see at any one time. Some individuals have the stomach for it but not many. 'It' is not always logical but not beyond realms of science; 'it' is

24

serious and funny, weird and simple, complex but
uncomplicated. 'It' is the beginning of the story. You
sought it all of your life like other scientists, artists and
those in search of enlightenment. Some seek it far and wide
to avoid looking too closely at themselves and their actions.
'They love the truth when it reveals 'itself' but not when it
reveals themselves' as our man from Hippo once said.

    Sophie convinced her Mum that she was well
enough to get up and she was. In a day or two, after family
and friends had stopped talking about it, Sophie had
completely forgotten ever being sick and that it was 'touch
and go there for a while'. Sophie's post-mortal unguided
thoughts had led her to those events and feelings; thoughts
and feelings that as far as she could tell, she had never
thought of again since the moment she skipped out through
the patio doors and into the garden calling out, 'I'm fine
I'm fine, stop worrying!' Sophie wondered at the vast
stores of memories there must be lying undisturbed and
unobserved in draws, in rooms, on floors of towers, in
hidden gardens of forgotten lands. Lands she now felt free
to roam. She still felt between two states. Between thinking
and being, dreaming and remembering, she was on a path
and could wander off to one side or the other. She could
sway between exploring on her own or being in the
company of the words of the narrator. In the meantime, she
was moving forward towards the unknown. The narrator's
soliloquy recommenced but she could not tell if she had
missed anything; she suspected not.

'I feel a little like a master of ceremonies killing time until
the main act hits the stage. As you are an audience of one,
it should be straight forward to stick to things you know
about; we are more or less obliged to as it happens.
Returning to the subject of animals that have four stomachs
such as the sacred cow, and the idea of how we digest

information, how we chew issues over, get gut feelings or find a story hard to swallow or the truth hard to stomach; it is worth remembering that we need more than one intellectual stomach to digest information and extract the truth. The first and the most obvious difficulty is getting something that big down our throats and of course, we can't. We need to get the pieces into our mouths first and 'chew the cud'. How big is humanity's mouth? I'll let your imagination mull over that one. For now let's say we take a sniff, a lick, a nibble and eventually a bite-sized bit of something into our mouths, and avoid spitting it out through our adherence to prejudices of taste, and what we believe is intellectually palatable. The digestive process has begun. Now lets' say for argument's sake, that one stomach is an organ of digestive rationality. It analyses and digests with theories that break things down in a particular way. Let's say that other stomachs absorb intuitive, or emotional interpretations, that provide different understandings. Most attempts to figure out the mysteries of life have either concentrated on only one, or at best two stomachs. Naturally limiting ways of digesting information means matter, and material that can only be digested by the stomachs not employed passes through or is vomited out, in a sea of putrid misunderstanding. Some people get so excited by understanding that which is absorbed by the use of one stomach, they reject the very existence of other stomachs. Others notice that too much is discarded and try and make one stomach do the job of four. If you want to digest grass you need four stomachs dudes'

Sophie had already picked up on the narrator sounds a little like a surfer dude on occasions and she was not much impressed, though unable to identify the feeling as such.

'Some wacky people spot we have other organs and try and get them to digest stuff and end up putting stuff where it

ought not to be. Apart from a few oddballs, the main problems humanity has faced are caused by huge misunderstanding brought on by poor digestion. Poor digestion of the information needed to have a proper understanding. Some see ridiculousness and dismiss it when actually ridiculousness is a necessary part of better understanding, it is only needed in a small measure like a particular mineral, but it is needed. Some things that are often discarded are needed for the absorption of something else. And others are dazzled by the possibilities they see in mere scraps of ridiculousness and create whole belief systems around them. Rather oddly they believe that's enough even though they are no nearer or further from the truth than those who rely on plates of the sensible. At least the value of following gut instinct is roundly accepted.' The narrator seemed to be testing out various tones and accents as if he were a singer warming up by exercising their vocal range. 'Some communities have an appreciation that we have much to learn from cows. They see them as sacred. They may or may not have the complete story in knowing why. You never felt the need to find out during your life, so I wouldn't know either. Anyway, we don't need to look down the menu of things that humans can't digest right now. The good news is that we are all capable over time, of knowing something of, and being part of, the truth. You will need to suspend belief to awaken understanding. That much many of the faiths got a handle on and it also lies at the heart of making scientific breakthroughs. Most scientists believe they are right before they find the proof. They are all seeking enlightenment through the use of rituals, methodologies and funny hats. It's the same deal, similar hopes, and ceremonies and passionate excitable committed rather odd behaviour; science religion sport art discos, you name it they all have something going for them. Between them, they may have provided mankind with the means and motive for striving forward and the potential for fights. It is going to take some doing before everyone realises that it is better to play nicely. We are not going to get to the bottom of matters if we cut ourselves off from other organs. This is me talking by the way, not the story; just my adlibs helping me along.'

The narrator's voice seemed to be drifting towards a sage old grizzled cowboy manner of speech. The voice was meant to be male but Sophie could not tell for sure whether the narrator was a man or a woman. Sometimes it sounded like the deep voice of a woman playing the part of a man, but then again it could be a man's voice with subtle feminine undertones. Sophie without really thinking about it wondered if it was the voice changing character naturally or her desire to pin it down that made it shift. Regardless the voice was both soothing and engaging with occasional annoying lumpiness. Sophie remembered that the voice parts of young boys in radio advertising and voice-overs were usually played by women. She could usually tell. Sophie listened to a lot of radio and was often surprised how different presenters looked compared to the image of them she had constructed in her mind's eye from listening to them. In the case of what she had just been listening to she could not tell much of anything about the teller for she had a strong sense that it was all a put on. She was not sure but, she felt she was not hearing an external voice, it felt more like listening to one in her mind. Throughout her life, she sat with her headphones on and marveled at the space created in her head by the music from a source pressed against her ears. The external sound opened up limitless internal space in her mind.

'So bare it in mind Sophie, the truth is not a theory any more than a pint is not milk. The whole historic experience

of evolution and indeed what came before is part of where humanity is at. Everything has to be experienced to be taken on board digested and passed on to gain further understanding. A life is an experience that is taken in and processed and needs to be properly digested. Even when something is understood, it is not a given that it can be acted upon. Everything you have heard is contained in the boring stuff you never read when you click and tick the 'I agree' box of the terms and conditions of some seemingly innocuous free software download. By which I mean to say that this preamble is considered by most storytellers to be useless especially as your mind's eye has glazed over by now. Just tick the box, there's nothing to worry about. And if after you have heard the story, and once you have reflected on it, and the way you were able to hear it, you 'don't agree' to the terms and conditions, you can un-tick the box. But it won't make any difference, the job will have been done. For that reason and because you are ready I have skipped some bits but I may try and squeeze them in as we go. Anything leftover can wait till the end. As it stands some parts of what I have said may make sense and others not; for now, curiosity and confusion are all you need to proceed. When you learn you are dead you tend to get curious so my warm-up act aimed at stimulating interest before the main act is pretty much done for me. I can jabber on about any of a range of recommended topics as long as I pass on the data and allow the background stuff to keep flowing. I am in no rush and what I am about to feed you won't get cold. I just have to mush it up a little to make it go down easier (better than grease eh?) and hope you don't spit it out. Open wide baby bird. Oh, and the reason why I am banging on about the truth; it's the only thing you believed in. You better believe it.'

The announcer's slightly mocking voice dispassionately gave a disclaimer
'Any people places or events in this story that are similar to anything that hasn't happened yet is intentional and everything is basically down to you.'

Chapter Three

'The Peach Faced Loon'

Sophie sensed there had been near silence for an indeterminate length of time. The silence would have been complete but for what sounded like the flow of a distant stream, or perhaps constant traffic on a busy road. No thought had formed itself and she was nowhere. She wondered if she had lost her mind or just her body. She had no sense of having a body; she was only her thoughts. She had no other feeling other than a state of mental readiness. There was nothing else, purely readiness. The teller commenced the tale without any further adlibs.
'Welder' The narrator's voice was the perfect blend of magnificent humble excited and collected. It seemed to have a soft Australian accent now. An intellectual slightly cheeky Australian accent but soothing and engaging, yet it went teasingly close to being annoying.
'Welder sat in the communal lounge of the transport ship, come survey vessel sipping a bright purple liquid from a tallboy glass. The glass had the company's logo tastefully etched in relief on it. It was literally a tasteful design as a lick would prove. Beneath the logo, a message on the glass read. 'I have good taste; lick me and see'. This was a request Welder had never responded to. Flavoured glass as part of a cocktail worked but only in rare instances. Mostly

it cheapened the experience. Welder's tallboy was not glass; it was a transparent cellular structure made from plant extracts. It was one hundred percent recyclable. Rather than being washed the used container was popped into the top of the dispenser and fresh glasses could be pulled from the bottom like a paper cup from a water cooler. The material had the added feature of forming a tough but soft impenetrable bubble if subjected to force. Hence if a cell glass fell to the floor it would become a bubble trapping the liquid inside and cutting down on mess. It also meant it was pointless trying to smash a glass and thrusting it into someone's face. The only fights that 'grass glass' contributed to were occasional bubble fights in the manner of food fights only less messy. Any positive injury and mess reducing properties 'grass glass' had were lost on Welder; at home, he used only authentic glass glasses. Welder looked at the logo and reflected that cheapness was a force of nature. Sometimes cheapness created its own innovations but mostly it cheapened other ones. Welder saw cheapness as neither a good or bad thing. The forces of cheapness he decided were necessary competition to the forces of zealots of taste and fashion in the fight for the products of innovators. Both camps had their motives and loyal followers.

Just below the lip of Welder's glass was a cloud the size and colour of a small peach hovering half an inch above the bright purple liquid. The glass was itself about ten inches tall; a serious tallboy. A thick white straw stuck out from a sandy red substance at the bottom of the glass, through the bright purple liquid and the peachy cloud, and through Welders pursed large and slobbery lips. A draught of the saturated sandy substance slowly made its way up the straw and into his receptive cavernous mouth. Welder was able to extend his lips like an insect's proboscis to

31

avoid spillage on to his trim salt and pepper goatee which he had sported since he was ten years old. Extending his lips in this way and with his eyes opened wide gave him a look of anticipation that overstated the feeling he was experiencing. It was a distinct look and as animated as Welder ever appeared. Correspondence between Welder's expression and how he genuinely felt was quite rare and usually a complete coincidence. He was a big-big man and liked a tall glass when drinking climate enhanced 'Steelberry''

The Narrator sensed that the tiny multitudes of component parts of a thought had taken flight in Sophie's awakening mind. They were attempting to swarm together into a form of words. They wanted to articulate her reaction to the elements of the story she could just about make out. The story reminded her of her father and a science fiction story. If those tiny components of a thought had formed words and the words had formed sentences they would have said, 'not science fiction Dad, you know I don't like science fiction'. But the disturbed, agitated particles had not developed a hive mind. There was no co-ordinating unifying attraction and they settled back down like flakes in a shaken snow globe. This twitch of activity was picked up on as a positive sign and the narrator continued.

'Welder preferred to sit in the lounge rather than in his more than adequate and commodious cabin. He did so in the off chance of striking up a conversation; hopefully with someone real. The lounge was empty. It was 'no biggie' he thought and the urge to talk to a stranger was flipped on its head and he decided that he preferred the open feel of the unpeopled lounge and mind anyway.

Like most lounges on most transport vessels, it gave the impression of a chilled hotel bar lounge but most of it was holograms and 'the company' did not provide guest holograms for the crew to pass time with. In fairness, only the dedicated lounge lover bothered with the lounge on a transport vessel. In this backwater of the galaxy, there were no prohibitions or inhibitions concerning drink and drugs. Cures for hangovers that work, had been around for centuries. Detox and instant come down remedies, as well as lucid oblivion pills had also been around for centuries. Most drink and drugs had remedies built into them so that you could drink and take all the drugs you wanted without aftereffects. However, the 'during effects' remained problematic so limiters were built in. They turned cocktails into fast cars capable of outrageous top speeds but virtually no fuel and cut-offs to keep them within speed limits. The rush of acceleration was exhilarating at first but soon became a frustrating tease. The effects of the third drink would just be kicking in when the effects and any side effects would begin to dissipate. What no one predicted when the painful and harmful effects of drugs and alcohol were eliminated was that they went totally out of vogue. People still went to bars and drank ever more extreme healthy elemental cocktails. Paradoxically being healthy began to be associated with a degenerate quest for natural highs and the pendulum kept swinging and so did bars to a greater or lesser degree. Whatever the fashion of the day it turned out that enough people liked to hang out in bars, that their existence continued. There were the drinking bars and the bars where the enjoyment was more apparent than real; not least when holographic patrons were included. Regular bars, coffee shops, clubs and restaurants, shops and even the office all kind of melded into one. Shopping working and pleasure became homogenised like a mall of the mind.

In many ways, Welder liked the lounge bars on transports best because it was obvious that they were sub-

standard and this at least meant they were distinct. Limiters or not Welder enjoyed an old fashioned stiff drink. The bright purple glow from the built-in table lights shone through Welder's glass-making his red, grown-up slush puppy glow like....'

The description of the lounge formed a clear picture of Sophie's thoughts. She was still only a witness but the images were more vivid than those she used to have when reading a book. Despite being a spectator she felt connected to events, though not as herself; she felt like she was someone else having their mind read while she read theirs. Throughout her life, Sophie had occasional but regular dreams in which she was someone else so the feeling did not faze her. Her mind's eye saw the transport vessel's lounge bar as described by the narrator but this was different from a dream or imaginings. She was able to look around at details in the lounge not described in the story. It was not unlike the way she might relive a story after reading it and embellish it. But that would take time. The level of detail was much greater and somehow less contrived; detail and inventiveness that would have been hard for her to imagine at all. So far as she was capable of experiencing it, this surprised her. Sophie had been a deep sleeper but for short stretches. She would wake every two hours and she credited this trait as the reason for being able to recall her dreams so clearly. She had lucid dreams, flying dreams, dreams of strange cities she would return to time and time again and dreams in which her dreaming self would force her sleeping self to wake; usually when something horrible was about to happen or had to be stopped. Memories of dreams from decades past were more easily recalled and clearer than memories of real-life events in her wakeful life.

34

Sophie had marvelous dreams in spectacular settings and vivid colour but just as often she had mundane dreams of shopping at Morrison's or cleaning the house; the latter leaving her more puzzled than the former. It left her with the feeling that banality had a troubling subtext whilst the extraordinary was almost comforting. She had studied dreams and their possible meanings but her mind had remained open on the subject, though with strong intuitions. So Sophie knew dreams, and this was not like any dream she had experienced; it was no dream.

The lounge bar in which Welder sat drinking triggered a memory that led Sophie away. The memory that she was pulled to was of the bar in a bed and breakfast in Weston-Super-Mare, some distance from the fictional bar in the transport vessel in a future time, on the other side of the galaxy, but they were strangely and soothingly similar. She had stayed in this particular B and B slash hotel in Weston Super Mare for the first time when she was still a young high flying executive. A bit of straw matting stuck to the wall, a large poster of a sunset, a miniature artificial palm tree standing in a low lit corner looking like a creepy child, and copious amounts of mirror tiles adorned the lounge section. This and a Jamaican flag and sundry other beach-related tat were meant to give the bar a 'Caribbean flavour'. Sophie wondered if any bar in the Caribbean put mud on the floor with empty take away boxes and drink bottles strewn about to create a 'Weston Super Mare' flavour.

A straw donkey and assorted seashells sat on shelves around the actual bar which boasted one octave of cheap whiskey and one of gin. A couple of confused looking empty straw-based Chianti bottles hung in tandem with some fairy lights over-head. On Sophie's first visit to the bar she looked around for more straw themed items other than those hanging, standing and stuck. Even though the 'architectural' plant in the corner was plastic it still seemed to crave the natural light that barely ever made its way into the converted basement.

There was though, almost hidden amongst the tat, dotted about the place, wondrously beautiful paintings of the sea done by one of the children of a guest that once stayed a wet week in July. Sophie loved the fact that the cheese and pickled egg British seaside town seemed to have something about it on some level; at least for her anyway.

Sophie first noticed the B and B had a bar at breakfast. In the stark artificial basement light of day thick with the smell of bacon and coffee, she peeked through the screen put in place each morning and saw the bar and its paraphernalia behind. Full English in the morning and half cut in the evening in a tacky bar. This was the polar opposite of Sophie's usual daily routine and just what she was looking for as part of one of her secret weekend getaways.

When the lights were lowered, alcohol and her imagination had worked their magic, she felt transported, something she seldom felt inexpensive sheikh minimalist metro lounge bars; the type she stayed at on her many business trips. With fairy lights and a straw donkey, she was transported but not to the Caribbean or even the Mediterranean, but she was at least transported far away from her busy team manager's life. In the office, at home and socialising she put quality before cost. All those that knew her, knew that quality of design and execution of function was almost an obsession both at work and at home. This uniform approach brought pleasure and great dividends at work. And at home created a slick 'five-star' interior that all admired. She had all the comforts which she loved and had always wanted, but contentment continued to elude her, no matter what new colour the walls became and whatever ornamentation and decoration adorned every corner nook and cranny of every room and passageway.

Sophie never found out whether it was an accident or whether it was some kind of a prank perpetrated by the team she was head of at work, but one business trip to Scarborough she was booked into a Bed and Breakfast rather than the best Hotel the town had to offer. It was late at night when her taxi pulled up outside of 'The North Bay Regency Hotel'. Sophie realised immediately that there had been some kind of a mistake but the cabby assured her that this was the correct address.

'Wait here a minute. I am just going to pop in and sort this out' Sophie told the driver. She was tired and in no mood to deal with finding alternative accommodation but the thought of actually staying at the modest three-story Hotel in a row of similar Guest Houses and B and B's did not occur to her. She felt obliged to pay for the room she would not be staying in before moving on. It was a balmy summer night and as soon as Sophie unfolded herself out of the cab she noticed a front garden the size of her living room crammed with plants, classical sculptures in cast concrete lit with coloured lights, and a tiny copy of the famous peeing boy statue from Brussels. She stopped in her tracks and was becalmed and filled with contentment. She decided to stay after all. The bed was not comfortable and the shared facilities poor, but Hazel the owner genuinely wanted her to be happy for the rest of her life. When she turned off the light moonlight flooded the room and she was comforted by the sound of the waves rolling in on the sands of the North Bay.

Sophie never told anyone where she went on holidays and mini-breaks; everyone correctly surmised that she did not want anyone from work to get hold of her. She also wanted to keep her hobby of exploring British seaside resorts, the cheesier the better, to herself. There was another attraction that resorts often possessed that had become an even greater secret; a secret she tried to keep from herself too. She compiled quite a file documenting her passion for the British seaside. Unlike most of the other guests staying at the 'Soft Sands Hotel' Weston-Super-Mare, she would not have traded it for the better showers and stylish décor of higher star rated establishments even if they were cheaper. She was at least consistent in not allowing money being the determining factor in her choices. She preferred the art on the wall at the Soft sands to any other she expressions of the seaside she had seen; even in galleries; especially in galleries.

The showers in rooms at Soft Sand had two settings; one was as like dew falling and the other was like standing under a leaky gutter. The shower in room six was so feeble that it was virtually impossible for Sophie to get her thick dark hair wet. She seriously thought of sticking her head out the window as the rain was the more efficient and reliable way of getting her hair wet. She ended up using the communal leakier gutter.

Despite the showers and shabby surroundings, the memory of her stay at the Soft Sands Hotel was in a box of beautiful oddities she slowly collected over many years. She had stayed at countless power shower enhanced forgettable hotels; they seldom had windows in the bathrooms and certainly not ones she could stick her head out of. She realised that she did not want the world to be a homogenous comfort zone, despite turning her house into one. She felt fortunate to live in a time and in a country where the experience was not cushioned by being given what she wanted all of the time. Disappointment rooted in ever greater levels of expectation and the mistaken belief that comfort leads to contentment were not issues at Soft Sands.

Though she seldom drank she shared one or two with one or two of the other guests on her first night and made a friend that she loved and never lost. It was not with another guest though; it was with the barman, gardener, and owner, Albert.

Her thoughts found a natural point of rest and the narrator's voice begun to chime back in. She experienced a sense of heightened awareness she had never experienced before. The feeling settled in her thoughts like a clean linen sheet unfurled and tucked neatly in. This feeling became an image and the image became a memory that she drifted in to before the voice of the narrator could cut the delicate connection. Had the narrator spoken or was he just about to speak? She was not sure; she only knew it was distant and then it was gone. She slid down the feeling that led directly to a moment.

She was a little girl. It was the time in her life when her Mummy would not make the bed until the evening on fresh sheet days. Sophie watched her expertly flick out the clean bottom sheet. She watched, transfixed as it billowed and drifted down in slow motion to the mattress like a parachute settling after its cargo had reached the ground. Sometimes it seemed to drift down as slowly as a cloud of dust after a white horse had galloped by. She marvelled at how accurately it landed in place. Nobody seemed to know what a clever person her Mummy was but her. The thought that nobody else knew just how amazing her Mummy was did not make Sophie happy or sad; all she felt was proud and lucky beyond words. After the bottom sheet went down Sophie would excitedly wait for her Mummy to say hop on. Then she would lie as perfectly centred on the bed and as neatly as she could, with her arms straight down to her sides. Then the top sheet would unfurl and billow over her and she was in a clean linen cloud. The smell of fresh air and fresh linen enveloped her. Her Mother then carried on making the bed as if Sophie was not there, occasionally saying out loud as if talking to herself, 'where is that Sophie? Doesn't she know its bedtime?' The warm weight of the blankets was then laid over her and she was hugged into position. Then the sheet that had been over Sophie's face was folded over the blanket in a perfectly parallel six inch folded banded lip over it and her mother said, 'there she is' and kissed her cheek softly.

There was no other way she could have had that snug feeling, without her arms by her side and being in the bed when it was made by her mother with her in it and being tucked in. Nothing in later life would ever replicate that feeling but she recalled it that night that she ended up by accident or design in an unlikely B and B in Scarborough and every night she slept at the Soft Sands Inn. She felt it again in reliving it in the pause in the narrator's story.

It took Sophie many years to get even close to making the bed and folding clothes, as quickly, neatly and effortlessly as her Mum did. When she did she felt as accomplished and satisfied as she did when she got her Master's degree in Mathematics.

The narrator began again as if aware of a natural pause in Sophie's thoughts just as Sophie had been in his. She felt like she was bobbing on top of a single sound wave. She sensed she was slowly building up to asking something like a lung slowly filling with air. But before a question could form in her mind the desire to ask it had gone.

All the obvious questions about what was happening to her; all the questions she would have normally asked were like television signals and radio transmissions that were all about her but she had no proper means of tuning in to them. When a question swelled like a growing wave, it broke on the shore and she found herself looking at a handful of pebbles and all thought of anything else had gone.

She was still warmed by the memory of her Mother's kiss; she felt shielded by the warmth of it like she was walking down the street still warmed by a hot morning bath on a cold day or like the glowing boy in the TV ad for porridge from her childhood. The memory of the first evening she spent with Albert coated her core with similar warmth and a tingling sensation of meeting someone new and getting on instantly. She was almost ready to recommence listening to 'The Peach-faced Loon' but another thought rose from her rising consciousness. She realized that throughout her life and probably most other peoples, there are moments of feeling and insight experienced that are between the words heard; there are images that flash part without recognition. These moments were not thoughts but vast amounts of thoughts and feelings condensed into the time between moments. They are important and inform the unconscious without contamination of our conscious interpretation. They are part of the bedrock of our intuition. They are the dark matter in our personal universe. It was what she thought and felt between the words of a story that was full of constantly changing shapes, colour and perception. It was like the times she had noticed something new but felt like she had always known. This realization was itself remained undefined as words. It was no more than the merest movement of air that dies away before becoming a breeze.

Sophie had often reflected during her life just how glad she was to have lived through the technological age she did. A revolution that meant she could have every photo she had taken, her entire music collection and personal writings on something she could put in her pocket. She had never ceased to be amazed at just how much information she had stored on her little memory stick, so she wasn't much fazed by the idea of vast amounts of thought and feeling being condensed into a moment.

The narrator's voice emerged from a ripple.

'Welder was happy enough with his 'Steelberry' though he never had one produced by a machine that matched the ones he mixed himself, even though they were identical in every respect. Welder was happy enough in his own company as it was all that was on offer; he had some background stuff to look through for the job he was sent to do. Our man Welder' was not your typical company man. Not in the way he acted or the way he looked, despite practically living in company overalls. He was six foot six plus a couple of inches when he filled his lungs and reared up, plus a few more inches for his hair. He had beautiful thick iron-grey hair of large tight curls that didn't move, even when he threw his head back laughing. When he tossed his head to the side or back like a model flicking their head to toss their long flowing locks, nothing moved, though the volume was just as great. His goatee was equally thick and was as white as cotton, so white it glowed. His hair and beard combo gave him the look of a roman senator crossed with a cosmic centaur, and he had a magnificent belly to match. A toga and a bushy laurel would have suited him fine. He had earned more than enough laurels to sit on and retire ten times over but he was not a retiring type in any sense of the word. His hair being like a luscious carving didn't flop over his rounded rather Neanderthal featured face. His eyebrows were thick but not bushy, well defined and they looped over his eyes

like a pair of wheel arches. He had bright blue rebellious eyes that were like sparkling jewels set in dark cavernous recesses of flesh and bone under their hairy aches. If eyes are the window to the soul then you could have looked deep enough into the blue depths of Welder's to see his soul and all the souls that made up his entire genetic history. His eyes drew people in; there was no window dressing and no signs blocking the view. People found themselves just standing and admiringly transfixed. His windows were clean and clear. No blue-tac or residues of cello tape from torn down notices; nothing so tacky. No there were no fancy funky window displays to promote Christmas or next season's fashions in his eyes, and no massive sale signs trying to persuade you. If you looked long enough into his eyes you would get a chill. It was more like his eyes were the window to your soul and not his.

Welder could have been a charismatic cult leader if he was so inclined. You won't be surprised to hear that he wasn't a saint and he had enough of a dislike for almost every leader he had come across to never want to be one himself. But in the round, he was as decent a person as you could hope to deal with. He was a brilliant communicator, I mean he would do this story more justice than I can, but I'm afraid you're stuck with me. So with those saintly eyes, a charming and engaging manner, a large physical presence and a sharp smart mind too, 'our man Welder' could pretty much get away with whatever he wanted if he chose to. And he did get want he wanted; it was just that he did not want for much. He was not acquisitive or power-hungry and his ambitions for himself did not extend much beyond a certain level of comfort and space. He could have made his way to the top of the company, he could have started his own company, but that wasn't Welder. Everyone could see his potential and imagined what they would do with it if they had it. Oh yes, everybody had plenty of suggestions and advice for Welder and what he should do with his gifts but he would brush them off like snowflakes on his broad shoulders or let them blow off or melt away. He was honest but not judgemental. It meant that he did not always keep the best of company but he instinctively avoided danger and could handle himself pretty well if he faced any. He was in some ways fantastically lazy and liked his sauces but he did not like sitting around or being idle. He was so lazy he did not bother to employ his charm unless he had to. There were rare occasions when it was automatically triggered. Most of the time, his decent nature was hidden by the demeanour of a curmudgeon. Only those who truly knew Welder was aware of his true persona. Welder didn't see himself as lazy or grumpy, just efficient and a realist; I mean why bother acting all nice if you don't need to. If people get upset that's their problem. Sometimes when the effort of being pleasant and reasonable got too great he could flip in an instant and become a real old grizzly bear. But it was all show, looking like a grizzly when it stands on its hind legs. When Welder stood up straight and stuck out his inflated barrel chest and growled he was pretty scary. At least he could not access his cutting wit when he was mad; that was the truly dangerous weapon in his armoury. He could slice someone up with it. He always wore much the same clothes. A baggy set of ferrous red coloured overalls that hid his large belly by making him look bigger all over. He did not have one of those bellies that look like half a fleshy beach ball stuck on an otherwise normal body, it was one of those that started from just below the collar bones and grows slowly as it makes its way to his belly button and drops back down with little overhang. His form would be perfectly defined by the lines of a weight lifters mankini. His overalls were from the

44

smartly dressed company range but looked incredibly comfortable on Welder, and they were. His 'grow bags' as he called them were always clean and his name was embroidered in gold letters across his back like those on a bowling shirt. There was also the catchphrase from the company's earliest yet unused ad campaigns, 'it's the company you keep' in small cursive text on his right breast pocket. Overall, Welder was like a massive company teddy bear souvenir; though at times he could be a naughty teddy. Welder was the only drinker and conversationalist on board the transport. He usually sought out conversation but he rarely found anything anyone said that interesting; conversation was simply a function of who he was. His mind being freed from dialogue drifted on to thoughts of what lay ahead. He stared into space through a large rim lit porthole. His was a trouble-shooting mission though it was officially listed as an assessment and preparation of asset transfer co-ordination type of a deal. He was being sent in to clean out the cupboards. He was to make sure there wasn't anything not agreed to, left behind on the planet before it was handed over to its new owners. The planet had been in the possession of the company from the early days and was one of its most remote outposts. It was a research centre way back before the 'big dipper'. 'The big dipper' was a galaxy-wide economic and spiritual depression that lasted almost two centuries and followed the disastrous 'double-dipper'. Anyway, the research facility was abandoned and so was the planet. It was a marble that rolled behind a chest of drawers and remained uninhabited and overlooked for centuries. It was Welders job to make sure anything out of the ordinary was discreetly dealt with and all was left in a fit state to be handed over to the new owners. It sounded like a straight

forward job but Welder knew deep down that it wasn't;
otherwise, they wouldn't be sending him.

Chapter Four

The Company You Keep

'Let me tell you something about 'The Company'. This is
the stuff Welder knew about before he arrived on
Chippenham 5. Most of this stuff was in the intro-info-orb
that every new employee was handed when they joined the
organization. When Welder got his, he put it in his mouth
and jokingly pretended to swallow it. In the process, he
laughed and then proceeded to choke on it and in what
looked like a planned finale of rebellious disdain, coughed
it up. It flew out of his mouth with great velocity and over
the balcony rail of the penthouse roof-garden where he was
part of the party held for all the new recruits. He was
meant to put it into his wrist band to activate it. He never

got to watch through the company's intro-info-orb's, or fob's as it was more commonly known holographic presentation, but he assimilated all the information he needed from the party. He did, however, hold on to one or two misconceptions about the company that were never challenged. It was always assumed he was joking when his ignorance surfaced. The story of the company started with its founder Ben Crammer being attracted to an advertisement in an old comic book from the 1960s. It was in a comic that was part of a collection his granddad had given him and he found them fascinating, not least the ads aimed at children, even though he was in his sixties at the time. He reflected that the sixties he was living through were not as interesting and exciting as the sixties of the twentieth-century others had got to live through. On one page of advertisements, amongst those for X-ray glasses and packs of huge Eastern European, butterfly and astronaut stamps, was an advert for

'Amazing Sea Monkeys'. The man who was to become the founder of the most powerful galactic business empire ever known was a heating engineer from a small market town in the West-country of England. He had heard of sea monkeys from various film and TV references and knew they were some kind of 'grow your own' pet shrimp thing. He saw from the ad that you could send off and get a 'hatching kit'. All you needed to do was sprinkle the dried contents of the sachet of life to an aquarium and these amazing wee-beasties would come to life. It was like instant life, just add water. As it happened Ben's grandfather, the one who had given him the comics had bought some of these so-called aquatic primates. Ben mentioned his interest in the advertisement to his Grandfather, and his Grandfather told Ben how he too had been attracted to it. So much so that he responded to it. From what he told Ben it is fair to say he *had been left feeling more than a little bit cheated by the whole episode. Ben could hear the pain of a child's disappointment in the voice of his Grandfather, 'the Grand Poopa'. His Grandfather who was about to turn one hundred and one years old sounded as if he was a ten-year-old again, suffering that first profound realisation that, many things don't live up to their billing and usually fall well short of our expectations. It would take Poopa a remarkable number of such disappointments to reinforce the lesson that advertising could be deceptive. This propensity for advertising to at best to mislead and at worst to cheat was especially true in the early days of mass media, but surprisingly all too common in the centuries that followed. The disappointment that the Poopa felt with his wet pets was his first. It was also perhaps his greatest disappointment resulting from things he sent away for in response to the claims made by advertisements in his favourite comics. Close runner up was the spy kit with x-ray glasses, followed by the, teach yourself magic kit. Somehow Poopa had believed that the publishers of such a great about the excitement and sweet anticipation of getting a package through the post that kept the young Poopa going back for more. Waiting for the post gave his imagination time to roam free over fertile lands of exciting adventures as a spy, or having low maintenance pets to entertain and amuse him. The Poopa never lost that slight feeling of excitement of anticipation at the arrival of the morning post despite it almost always being followed by deflating disappointment. When Poopa the boy, tore open the sachet that contained the beginnings of his sea monkey family, as so alluringly illustrated, his only concern as he sprinkled the contents on to the surface of the water was whether his aquarium was going to be big enough. He watched as what looked like flakes of fish food floated*

48

about and noticed some were wriggling about and began to submerge. Most of the flakes sank to the bottom of the tank right away, along with young Poopa's dreams. He held out hope until the last shrimp drifted downwards about an hour later.

What really grabbed Ben about the whole sad tale was the actual advertisement? The actual shrimp things had tails, but monkeys have tails; that's where any comparison ended. They weren't even a little bit like monkeys. They were a minute to create and minute in size. What they were not was the humanoid shrimp family that the advertisement's illustration showed. Ben's grandfather was an original thinker but by his own admission, a sucker and in his child's mind he thought he was going to create his own people-like aquatic pets. The picture seemed to indicate that they would probably be about six inches high, and capable of basic communications through a bubbly language of some kind. The young Poopa was prepared to put in the hours necessary to learn it.

Ben was fascinated by the appearance of the sea monkeys in the advert. In the illustration, the sea monkeys were naked with no visible signs of genitalia. They had normally shaped and proportioned human bodies except that their limbs were thinner and their tummies were large and well-rounded. And let's not forget the all-important tails that marked them out as monkeys. Their tails were the continuation of a reptilian-like ridge that ran down their backs and culminated in a standard fishtail rather than a point. From the shoulders up they were shaped like elegant wine glasses, their necks being the stem. The bottom of their heads were rounded then tapered inwards towards the top which formed into a cartoon shaped crown with three ball topped uprights. Their faces were more or less human, in so far as they had two eyes a nose and a mouth, except the mouth was larger than usual and the nose smaller. Their eyes were large and oriental looking with huge baby cute lashes. They also had a patch of large but subtle scales on their chests like a patch of chest hair; even on the male and female juvenile shrimps. They may have been drawn that way to indicate their whole body is covered in scales but that's not how the Poopah imagined them.

Regardless of the product, Ben found the vision of the illustrator captured the aspirations of those who produced the product, as well as the unrealistic expectations of the purchaser. It occurred to Ben that with all the advances in genetic engineering that had come about since the Poopa's childhood, that an improved version of 'amazing sea monkeys' could be possible. He was sure that a market for a new instant pet, sea monkeys that were not quite so shrimp-like still existed. The gut feeling became a thought and the thought became an idea, and the idea became a plan. One drawback to Ben's plan was that he knew nothing about genetics. He knew that people love their pets and like things to be instant. There was something intriguing too about the idea of sending off for a bag of dried pet, adding water and 'hey presto'! Maybe the features of the pets could be controlled and various options could be available, he thought in wild imaginings. Create creatures, be the creator. Ben was full of fantastic ideas but still knew nothing about what was possible on the genetic engineering front. Ethical questions did not hinder his private brainstorming, and moral ones did not trump what he saw as the virtuous pursuit of giving people what they want and making some money. As can sometimes happen in cases of great success, good fortune played a part in what would have otherwise remained another unrealised plan in the bits and pieces draw of Ben's mind. The happy coincidence, in this case, was that there happened to be a genius of genetic engineering living down the street; well according to the eccentric, timid as a door mouse, old lady who had the flat opposite to Ben. She often complimented Ben on having 'lovely teeth', and for that reason alone he took her at her word and went in search of this genius. The old lady was the only person in Ben's entire life to compliment him on his teeth and her appreciation was sincere. Eccentric she may well have been, but she was right about there being a genuine genius, geneticist, albeit of a botanical persuasion, down the road. Local people only knew his as the 'grower', whose unusual plants were well appreciated. His name was Robert Randolph Roundway, but he liked to introduce himself as the Bubble headed Booby. He was on the young side for a crazy scientist and dressed in a non-descript way which he called his M and S camouflage. 'Robby' which his parents called him, was a fan of 'Lost in Space', and had also always been fascinated by bubbles. He was quite happy to be called the 'Boob' by friends and foe alike. He seldom if ever made a boob in his studies, except inadvertently as a parabolic curve. He didn't like being called Bob, but Bobby wasn't too bad. It became apparent very early on in Ben Crammer's initial investigations, before meeting the Boob, that genetic engineering had indeed moved on a pace since the Poopa's childhood. Ben was already aware that at the very least regenerative genetics had played a part in the Poopa's extended life. If you could cultivate human tissue and create organs, surely that's enough to get started within developing the next stage in the evolution of sea monkeys. Ben thought, 'we only need a starting point!' Then followed up by saying, 'but first we need a 'we'', as he went in search of his genius. But Ben also soon learnt that just as the science of genetics had moved on, so too had the ethical, legal, moral, and safety framework they were limited by.

Ben feared that the 'sea monkeys two, the descendants' project were going to be more problematic than he imagined; he usually had a bit of a blind spot when it came to imagining negatives. But having initiated Ben's doubts, Bobby threw him a life presented a way forward. The Boob's genius lay in the field of plant life. The doubts Ben harboured were set free on to the open sea and sailed away. He quickly saw that the potential to realise the idea in plant form was far less limited by socio-ethical, and most importantly, legal restraints than animal form. 'Research into green stuff? I like it' he told Robby, 'it will be cheaper too. I'll probably get a grant if we could come up with some ethically green spin-offs!'

But more important than the legal, ethical and moral concerns, indeed as important as the actual idea that had brought them together, was the start of the dynamic life-long partnership between two peculiarly well-suited individuals, Ben Crammer and Robert Roundway. There was instant chemistry between them from the moment Robby opened the door and Ben walked in with his proposition. Robby was only mildly impressed with Ben's idea from a science point of view, he already had plenty of ideas; he had an idea to fill the empty thoughts of every member of the entire population of the backwater country town the pair found themselves marooned in. What struck the Boob about Ben was his restless hunger and a commitment to making things happen. To put it another way, Ben Crammer was committed to the idea of making money.

Robby was mad about making his ideas manifest. He assumed that funding would always turn up from somewhere or someone, as soon as the potential significance of his work was understood. Ben pointed out to Robby, that even a genius like Fox-Talbot did not make any money from the studio he set up to exploit his breakthrough in photographic printing. Robby could see that Ben could get money or make money from his work and this would enable him to pursue more work. Ben could see he could make money from Robby's work and enable him to make more money and do less work. And so they became partners.

They thought the idea of the genetic pet still had legs, but the updated version of sea monkeys would take years to get to the point that they could live up to the advertising of the originals. They decided to keep sea monkeys as their secret 'pet project'. They saw potential in developing a product along the lines of science-related kits or vegetables that grew with smiley faces. Having thoroughly looked at Robby's research, Ben had one or two ideas on products that could be marketable.

When it came to naming the company that would produce and sell their products, they wanted it to reflect their deeper purpose of producing their own 'amazing' sea monkeys. They did not want to be too obvious so they could have a working name for all of their future business interests.

'Pets keep you company don't they?' insisted Ben. Robby nodded in agreement. 'Then why don't we call it the 'the company for the company?'

Robby with playful sarcasm then suggested. 'Or we could shorten it to 'comcom' and then we could be comcom.com'. The pair then continued to teeter between contempt and amusement for their word plays stemming from 'Company' for the name of their company. They did not come up with any particular gems and the enjoyment they got from playing was more to do with hitting it off as friends rather *than the quality of what resulted. Their amusement was enough of a reason to seek to register their company name as 'The Company company', at least until they could come up with something better. 'Company' the company. There were plenty of other companies and organisations and even individuals with the same name but they went with 'the company you keep'*

Much of the groundwork of their joint enterprise was laid down in the first frenetic dizzying hours of ideas bursting out. They immediately got into a rhythm. There would be a couple of minutes during which the material of new ideas burst forth. Then there would be a ten minute period of assessing and coming up with inventive ways of using the ideas. It was like they were emptying things out of their shoeboxes, bags and bits and bobs draws of ideas, laying them on the table and seeing what they had. There was an instant trust between them, a trust they had sought to build with others over the decades but never attained. They saw in each other kindred spirits longing to share but what sealed the deal was they could see the quality of what was in the other stores and thoughts. No convincing was required. With the pieces they put on the table existing ideas were developed and new ones formed. They lost track of which bags the pieces came out of. When the play and excitement naturally burnt out the editing began. Editing and documenting took a further ten minutes, and their half-hour cycle was over. A pot of tea was made and they were off again.

Once they got set up 'sea monkeys, generations' became only one of a baker's dozen of ideas that they chose to pursue. Ben looked through all the experiments and lines of enquiry that Robby was already pursuing, and his head turned in to a volcano spewing out money making products and commercial applications for them. The sea monkey project still somehow stayed at the hub.

 Certain ideas had the right fit for the times and the right conditions to germinate and grow. There was, the decorative sculptural fruits that looked like little heads, and a grow bag that was a bag you grew. They were amongst a dozen ideas that were an instant financial success. The rest, as they say, will become history. In all their excitement and buzz of activity, they never changed the name of their company. They did not mind the mysterious and sinister CIA slash Mafia anonymity of the name; the 'you keep' part was seldom used. It was an odour neither of them naturally exuded. Besides they couldn't think of anything better even when they put their minds to it and they never really truly decided whether they liked it or not. They liked a degree of randomness such as the occasional use of the imperial system of measurement they sometimes reverted to. They couldn't think of any good reason why they should use it but they used it anyway; maybe it was appealing because no one else used it anymore or knew why it existed in that form in the first place, or maybe it was because it amused Ben's Grandfather. They kept the full name 'the company you keep' as a catchphrase and tag line. The story of the sm2's is more significant than explaining the catchphrase embroidered on Welder's overalls. It is important to our story because amazingly the quest for sea monkeys was at the heart of what lay in store for Welder on Chippenham 5 so many centuries into the future.

 Ever since the mention of aquariums, parallel thoughts formed in Sophie's mind as she listened. As the word 'five' was still vibrating her thoughts, her focus shifted. It took her back to the 'Soft Sands' once again. The narrator noticed Sophie had drifted away from him but was not in the least bit put out; her reminisces had equal billing to the story and time was not an issue.

It was the talk of fish tanks that created a passage through which Sophie walked. She was standing before the amazing collection of tropical fish Albert had in his private parlour as it was known. Albert's wife and total soul mate had died ten years before Sophie stayed at the hotel for the first time. Albert was a one-woman man and that woman was gone. Whenever Albert talked of 'Mo', 'The Mighty Mo' or the 'amazing Mo Mo' there was a sparkle in his eyes and more often than not, if she remained present in the conversation the sparkle bloomed into a tear. And as he forced out the words choking him, those tears would seep through the cracks in his voice. Through those cracks, you could see his tender heart beneath. It was the news of Mo's cancer that had made them quit their teaching jobs, sell-up and buy the 'Soft Sands'. They both loved teaching, but it wasn't like it was when they started, and they always wanted to live by the seaside. And as the town of Weston Super Mare confidently boasted in its name a super sea and as it was not far from Bristol for Mo's treatment, that's where they went. Mo was born in Jamaica and moved to Bristol as a child with her parents. She was short and slim, one might even say petite, but her smile stretched a mile and her strong personality gave people the impression of her being larger and more robust than she was; certainly not petite. This illusionary enlargement of her physical being brought about by the radiance and projection of her vital personality continued to the end. Only when people filed passed her open coffin did anyone notice just how small she was. Albert wished that Mo had not specified that she wanted an open coffin in keeping with the custom of her catholic family. Never did a dead body look so unlike it had when filled with a sparkling life. Amongst their many shared passions were collecting tropical fish and their collection was unsurpassed in the town, possibly even the county.

Albert had set up the parlous as a room for the children of guests to paint and draw on those more than occasional rainy days, and the fish was a perfect subject. It was so much fun for some families that they returned year after year, and the children would be disappointed if it did not rain at least two days during a weeklong stay. Albert made guests promise not to tell anyone that they had had a good stay with him.

'I don't want lots of guests; only nice ones' he would say in his smooth soothing soft voice. His voice gave everything Albert said the sound of great profundity; a quality he perfected in his teaching days. Mo and Albert could have run a successful school in a cowshed.

Albert had a way of saying things that people accepted without question but he did not have the desire or inclination to exploit this talent beyond the pleasure he got from imparting knowledge and facilitating others pleasure. His subject was chemistry but his passion was fish. As Sophie recalled the wall length Aquarium she seemed to be swimming amongst giant angelfish and passed coral outcrops with lush aquatic plants moving as if in slow motion.

'Sophie it's me again. I know it can be a bit of weird way to order things, going back and forth from memories to a story and back again, but it is how your mind has always worked so I don't mind butting in. It is just that the back of your mind and the front of your mind are not going at the same speed and that can give things a fuzzy edge. The transition was never that obvious when you were alive. The front of your mind is speeding up gradually but you can only handle so much. The back of your mind has been

slowed down big time and will take longer to get aligned. As things were, and as you well know, you didn't have time to deal with everything around you at once in your day to day life. So whilst you were listening or looking at one thing, part of your mind was always working away at lots of other things. Accessing memories and analysing them whilst thinking about something else is one example. Different parts of your thinking operated at different speeds at the same time. Because time is not an issue here you will experience memories in the round; you are one. The part most people don't realise is how big part-time plays in the unconscious and our ability to access it. We don't call it the unconscious anymore and neither will anyone else once they understand how all the wheels and planets and plates are spinning. That is to say, once they realise that the driver looking ahead and the passengers looking out the window taking everything in and the other passenger looking at maps and planning the journey, and the sister left at home are all part of the same ride. And when you are on that ride everything else on it is part of you. Even the kids messing around in the back seats are part of it. That's for later. I need to move things along a little. I want to clarify things enough to steer you away from worrying as you synchronise. We have to keep everything in balance and the best way is to tell you the story and let your memory uncoil at your own pace. You are not in a coma listening to someone jabber away at your bedside by the way, though I may have a similar inane insane or accidental profundity at times. You would not be hearing my voice if you were still alive but the good news is that death is not the end of the story, though for some people....never mind. I am here to step in and keep you on track. You will hear me plenty until you get the hang of things and less and less as things unfold. I am going to

58

remind you of some bits and pieces but I don't want you to try and put them together yet; we'll take them home and build something with them there. They are not facts or fiction they are simply parts of something we are going to build together. Then we switch it on and you will know what all the pieces do. So to start with, remember the arrow being shot at a target thing that you worked out when the green shoots of your love of maths first surfaced. When you first heard about the concept of infinity? You remarked to your mother and father that the only three things you could think of that are infinite are space, numbers and love.' Sophie was looking out of the car window as they passed through a forest of oak, beech and birch. She closed her eyes and the shadows of the branches cast by the winter sun swept over her and complex moving patterns were projected on the inside of her eyelids.
'I can't think of anything else that is infinite' was Sophie's mother's response to her observation given several minutes before.
'Here's something to think about Soph' suggested her father. He knew fractions were something she had no problem with even though she had not done much about them at school.
'At a point on its way to a target, an arrow reaches halfway. Now think of that halfway as being halfway still to go. That distance expressed as a fraction is one over two'. Sophie did not respond or move but he could tell she was listening.
'Okay, I can tell this is going to be straight forward with you as you are a smart cookie. So you have the arrow halfway to the target. It now has half the distance still to travel; one over two as we know. It goes on a way further and reaches a point where it has a quarter of the distance still to travel right; one over four. Then a little more and it has an eighth of the way still left which as you also know

and eighth is expressed as one over eight. So the arrow keeps on getting closer to the target and the fraction gets smaller and smaller. And as it does so, the number at the bottom of the fraction gets bigger and bigger ad-infinitum. Numbers are infinite so the bottom number goes on forever and the arrow theoretically never hits the target; it only gets infinitely closer to it. It is one over infinity and beyond. That's just something for you to chew over while you listen to a story. I'll put one on.' With that Sophie's father reached for a Raol Dahl tape.

'It is only a bit of fun really but it did help you to get a clearer picture of how time works in different ways at different times with different types of thought. Wait till they all flow together then you'll be cooking on gas. Chewing over stuff is an important early stage of digesting what you need to. Even the toughest truths can be swallowed if you chew over them long enough'

Up until this point Sophie was interested in her memories but mostly indifferent as to what was happening.

'A kitchen compost bin the generates power as it composts its contents, a plant that consumes your organic wait then produces edible fruit, vegetables that grow into sculptural forms, grow your own shampoo (the type that's made from plant extracts), grow your own furniture, fruit bowls, etc. etc. For each of a stream of products, the company produced a material derived from a plant. They produced an organic alternative to plastic. It grew flat with interlocking fibres the made it tough but it was easy to cut and biodegradable. The material was a sort of bark from a plant shaped like a flat-sided rectangular pillar. It shed its bark and hey presto, a usable material. The bark needed no processing after being gathered. The plant continued to produce even consistent grade material for thirty years and required little more than light and water and soil with

natural compost. It was easily grown and it was ideal for packaging. And what's more, it worked better than plastic in microwave ovens. The material broke down into usable compost or fuel, by being placed in the company's living compost bin. The bin digested and converted the packaging into energy and produced fragrant vapours in the process. These vapours could be selected by choosing the particular variation of packaging and were distinguishable by colour. The vapours included ones with properties for good health and the treatment of 'whatever ails thee'. The compost bin that broke down the company's homegrown cardboard and generated warmth, and a pleasant aroma, was a template for other innovatory materials derived from plant life. Robby was a big fan of maple syrup from which he drew sustenance and inspiration.

The Company went through four main manifestations in the millennium that followed it bursting into life. The first incarnation was the shortest; it was the spark that established the flame. It was a spark created by Ben and Robby knocking their heads together; something both of their Mother's would have suggested if they had witnessed the degree of silliness the pair generated in each other.

'I didn't know that numbers are expressions. So you can express yourself and numbers. And you can shoot an arrow in the air and when it lands I won't be there' Sophie was playing in the garden on the first warm day of the year. She noted that the first warm day of the year often bloomed on her sister's birthday.

Chapter Five

Sophie and the crystal tree

Sophie was standing looking at her sister aged four sitting at the end of her bed crying. She was holding something in her hands. Sophie looked at her for a moment.

Time seemed to stop as if the memory she was reliving was on pause. She felt like she was in a lucid dream but more intense, more real. She was accessing raw data. She was regarding it on one level and experiencing it on another. Alice was holding something. Sophie remembered very well what it was, but she was experiencing the memory of not knowing. Then she was able to draw thought and feeling together once she decided to let go of knowing and not know once again. Something about what she knew, what she thought she knew and what she remembered did not line up. Parts of her mind did not properly register. The images and sounds did not ring true. So she let all else fall, all interpretation thought and recollection disperses and she was left with the experience and an open mind. Her sure conscious belief from memory that she was not responsible for her sister's tears was replaced by fear from recalling the moment that she was.

Seeing Lily's tears triggered intense pulses like blood rushing to the brain when standing up too quickly. These pulses were not dizzying, they were pulses of clarification. The sensation passed and feelings rushed in, filling then overflowing from the space left behind from emptying her thoughts. She started to cry; something she did not remember doing. It was an internal cry at first without tears to offer any sort of release. She felt like she was drowning in her remorse. The pressure was released as tears flowed and she gulped for air. The unadulterated experience of her childhood emotion was powerful and clear. She knew what was in Lily's hands.

Both Sophie and Alice had been given presents two days before the moment she was reliving. Their Dad had brought them each the same gift from a toy fair he had attended in Birmingham. Sophie was six and Alice was four at the time. Their Dad Alfred came back extremely excited about the range of new science-based toys and gifts at the show and added many new lines to his toy shop as a result. One line was a crystal growing kit in the shape of a tree, and each of them was given one. The kits consisted of two absorbent, white card profiles of a tree. They had three symmetrical pairs of branches that got smaller in regular proportion up the trunk, to a tapered point at the top. The two white profiles slotted together in a cross to add another dimension. The card tree then clipped into the centre of a round plastic dish that was as wide as the protrusion of the lower branches; about the size of an upturned lid to a jam jar. The dish was deep enough for about twenty millilitres of fluid. The card was sturdy and the girls excitedly put together their trees and clipped them in to place under the parentally caring, and professionally interested, watchful gaze of their Dad. Once constructed and clipped in to place, sachets of crystals that came with the kit were opened and carefully sprinkled at the base of the tree. They were like bright green uniformly sized, rock salt crystals, and they evenly covered the dish like the fluorescent green turf from the girl's favourite children's television show. Despite their young age they already had years of careful sprinkling experience, though usually with glitter, and they were well up to the task. The final step to follow was to add the water. 'Just add water' scrolled across the screen at the back of Sophie's growing mental architecture where thoughts were continually being projected whilst her attentions were elsewhere. Thoughts at the front were directed towards going carefully through the various stages of growing a crystal tree. The watering was the tricky part, but Alfred's fears that this part of the task would prove too fiddly for the girls were groundless. Drop by drop the water was added evenly about the base of the trees with the teat-pipette supplied. Each drop turned the crystals into a blue solution which spread outwards like blue blooms; quickly at first, then more slowly but not stopping until it reached the circles' edge. The blue blossoms spread and merged until all of the crystals were absorbed and became a rich azure, magical, primordial slime.

Alfred marvelled at his children's dexterity and even more at their care and concentration. The task was classified as being suitable for children twice their age.

An element of natural rivalry sometimes played a part in the girl's world but in this instance, they were so focussed on the job at hand, there was nothing but shared purpose. Their minds were on what their father feared was a potentially discouraging task; he did not like having an ulterior motive in observing them. Deep down he was aware that commercial motives sometimes latched on to a genuine desire to see his daughters enjoy themselves and subverted it. He was relieved to see his hunch about the product was good.

The girl's equal skill and care settled the debate between Alfred's two minds as to whether it was a good idea to get the girls the same gift. He had been particularly concerned that one tree may be a dud so was prepared to put the time in and deal with the emotional ramifications of crop failure. Plus he had a backup kit. As soon as the crystals had become a solution, it was drawn up the absorbent trunk of the trees like rising sap, and the girl's excitement rose with it. The initial quick progress of the rising blue tide slowed. The desire that Sophie and Alice had to keep their eyes fixed on the rising blue was not matched by their patience to do so. Their attention span began to bow and buckle. It was time for the crystal growers to go to the park and allow capillary action to draw up the rich solution and deposit crystal leaves on the tree's branches.

The absorbent card tree and the rich blue solution combined to release a distinct barely perceptible odour. None of the three made a conscious note of it but they would never forget that unique smell of sweet chemical blossoming.

'Welder turned on his shadow and stepped out into the fresh air of Chippenham 5. Welder was not a wealthy man, nor was he high ranking but his skills were so valued by some in the higher echelons of the company that he lived on a fresh air planet; which many above him in the company could not afford. It was known that he had got the company out of a particular mess after all else had failed, and was given his home as a reward. Welder was reluctant at first to leave the controlled environment of his homeworld and he had that same sense of insecurity, even anxiety before leaving the controlled environment of the transport vessel and stepping straight out into the open air of the planet. It was a little like a prisoner fearing freedom after being supported by the framework of bars that confined them. Once he was settled in his new home, Welder soon developed a love of fresh air and the unpredictability of a natural climate. He noted his apprehension as a curiosity. Before living on a fresh air planet, he had only ever drunk water from a pipe. There was no turning back for Welder once he cupped water from a clear mountain stream with his hefty hands. So it was with some relief when he stepped through the invisible curtain of the airlock and his air-conditioned apprehension and into the particularly fine fresh air of a new world, Chippenham 5; new to him at least.

There was no one to greet him. There was no one to greet him because there was no one else on the planet to greet him. The pilot of the hopper that had brought Welder from the transport ship didn't count; he wasn't technically* on the planet as long as he remained within the lit circle indicating the docking zone. There was no one and nothing other than an open potholed plain and a ring of distant maroon mountains. The truth was that Welder was not officially on the planet either. That was why there was no one else to join him in the lounge of the transport freighter; he was the only cargo but did not know it. There were several aspects of the mission that Welder did not know. The company needed someone to clean up the place before the new owners arrived and they were not sure exactly what mess there might be and whether it might spread. They had their suspicions but did not share them with Welder. They needed someone versatile pragmatic and of course discreet. Welder was their man. Those who knew the qualities needed for such a task wanted Welder, and those who knew the dangers and found Welders status in the company an irritation still wanted Welder. They knew if he took the job on either the job gets done, or Welder cops it; it was a win, win. It was not so much that he could keep a secret; it was more that he could disguise it with plausibility or under a cloud of confusion. Very rarely did anyone seek the secrets Welder kept in his company overall's many pockets. He was someone who could talk plausibly about any subject you could name, and many you couldn't, and he could do it without giving anything away. First of all, a complete survey of the planet was needed. This was conducted with the equipment Welder had on him and that aboard 'Maximum Matilda' the ship that parted as soon as it relayed data about the planet to him.

It was as far as planets go, small. It was as dry and as completely lifeless as the Atacama Desert until the Company set up a research facility there centuries before Welders arrival. Its breathable atmosphere was an untapped commodity that had no plant life drawing it in to replenish them. The research facility had to be entirely self-sustaining in every way. The planet was discovered and acquired by the company during its heyday; when it was large enough to keep such discoveries to itself. Matilda's scans revealed no sign of man nor beast. There were readings for plant life though. They were within the abandoned facility several hundred miles away that Welder was there to check out. Welder pointed to the scanner on his forearm and said out loud to himself and for the sake of the records, 'just a few leftover house plants'. Chippenham 5's lifeless status outside of the facility was confirmed as Welder wheeled around slowly to complete the scan and tally it with the information from the departed ship. The reason for the lack of life was simple; no water. 'There is more moisture in one of my farts than this whole planet' Welder said to his shadow.

The scanner was one function of a bracelet Welder had attached to his wrist. It looked like some kind of high-status Roman Centurion's bracelet, smooth and golden without any visible feature other than a fine linear pattern of geometric shapes. It suited Welder. It was activated as soon as it closed around Welder's thick left virtually hairless forearm. Once it made the satisfying sound of successful docking the growing sense of unease that Welder felt after the initial euphoria from his first draught of fresh air was instantly nullified. Being alone on a completely lifeless and unfamiliar planet was unnerving even for Welder. He was used to having some sort of life around even if it wanted to eat him. He would rather have dangerous natives, than nothing at all. The bracelet or, 'band' as they were known, monitored and communicated directly with one part of Welder's brain. The interface had no face; it was a voice in his head. Being able to use a band was not something everyone could manage and few *could do it as well as Welder. It fed him information and responded to his needs both directly and indirectly. In a way his band had it's own conscious and sub-conscious; this enabled it to have vastly greater functions. He could give it a conscious command in the form of a thought or pre-set functions to be carried out automatically. The band had picked up on his anxiety and with a series of signals directly to his brain, it nullified it; a pre-set Welder seldom needed but one he had set for this job. His Shadow was an ambient recording device that would follow and document proceedings and Welder's fart comment was directed at whoever got the job of editing his recordings for the company. Toilet humour had more or less been banned by social convention but Welder was a member of a strong and growing resistance movement whose secret sworn mission was to keep it alive. His attempts to fulfil his mission by surreptitiously include references to farts and other toilet humour staples into company records were not appreciated. He was not that fussed about double-entendres, he was a purist.*

All that could be seen of Welder's 'shadow' at work was a thin green horizontal light that remained constantly one foot above Welder's head. It could operate independently of the band but once the band was on the two were wedded. Welder rolled down the sleeves of his boiler suit once he was happy with the band's settings and was ready to get to work. Step one, 'getting to work'.

Welder dusted off and activated his ride. It was deposited on the planet along with a survival sphere near to the landing site several months back. The sphere was not much larger than him and the hopper not very much larger than that. Apart from that, there was nothing but pot-holed desert in every direction.

The pilot of the shuttle joined the Captain of the transport come survey vessel on the bridge. The Captain was watching a large screen showing Welder doing a kind of tyre kicking preliminary check of his conveyance. The Captain and the pilot could have been twins. They were elegant dark haired tall men in their nineties. 'Do you know anything about this guy?' the pilot asked.
'No, and I don't know what the fart he is up to either'
The temperature on the planet was hot but not unbearable and the 33 hour day was bright and clear as it always was.

Sophie noticed that the narrator's voice had changed a little. It had slightly lost its subtle (if that's possible) New Jersey accent altogether from the few accents employed. Although slightly less high pitched, it also sounded more feminine. However, Sophie still felt that it was the voice of a man, an older intellectual Australian man, or possibly New Zealand.
'Why do I talk this way you ask yourself? Well, it's good that you ask yourself, you are the only one who knows; it's your concoction. I know it sounds a little different to when we started. As the story unfolds my voice will shift and change; mostly you won't even notice it. It is all part of being here there and everywhere.

For a brief twenty minutes of playing in the park, that felt like hours Sophie and Alice had forgotten all about their copper sulphate plantation. Sophie saw the elongated reflection of her face on the metal slide as she ascended its slippery slope whilst Alice went for the more conventional option of the steps. Gripping its sides and pulling, and with her bare feet providing plenty of traction on the slightly cool metal, she scrambled up the slide only conscious of her weight and needing to make an effort as she reached the summit. She stood at the top feeling triumphant over gravity. She pitted herself against the physical still further by closing her eyes and putting her arms out to her side like the high divers she had seen on television. Her father noticed too late to warn her against her hubris. She swayed beyond collecting herself and started to topple. But before reaching the critical tipping point her little sister steadied her. As Sophie relived her childhood experience she reflected on the love she had for her sister that was built on countless forgotten moments of shared joy and support. The moment passed with only a mild rebuke from her father, 'watch what you're doing Soph. Anyway, it's time we headed back'. Alfred was accustomed to dealing with the frequent near calamitous accidents that punctuated any visit to the play park with his children. The passing of time without an accident only seemed to fuel his imagination more but his strength as a calm father had managed to keep ahead of his fears. 'I guess the danger is part of the test' he said to himself as the girls tumbled off the end of the slide in a giggling heap.

Normally the girls took a little persuading and knew they could get a good couple of extra slides or swings or spins by resisting. But Alfred had a trump card and his silence was enough to remind Sophie and Alice what it was. 'The trees!' they shouted out in unison as they slid down together as one form. They were as saturated with anticipation and pure excitement as their cardboard trees were with the solution; it was practically sending out crystal-like sparks from the ends of their limbs. But had leafy crystals formed on the limbs of their crystal tree. Despite not living up to the wild impossible luxuriant foliage they imagined on the way home, they were not disappointed at what they found. Alfred was prepared to deal with possible disenchantment and was almost as tense and eager to see the results as his daughters. All of them were thrilled to see the little card trees bursting with beautiful blue crystal buds. John managed to curb the girl's enthusiasm and create an imaginary barrier around the delicate blooming trees. Their excess energy brought on by their glee was directed towards a manic bed jumping session not usually allowed. Once in balance enough to control their desire to pick up, touch or even possibly eat their crystal trees. They approached carefully and cautiously, getting their little curious faces as close as they could without going beyond the invisible barrier. It was agreed that the barrier should be about a foot all the way around in order not to blow any leaves off the trees with the breath of human giants. The invisible barrier was not up for long but the trees were more robust than they imagined; certainly robust enough to withstand the careful attention and gentle breath of small children. They imagined being tiny creature sitting in the bows of the magical trees or being giants looking down at a multi-coloured crystal magic woodland. Many things in their play turned out to be magic. Sophie and Alice then got out the toy box of characters and creatures they used to give form to their fertile imaginations. It was an assortment of Playmobile, Sylvanians, Kinder egg toys and various other plastic animals and odd bods.

The crystal trees became the centre of one of their elaborate ongoing stories and had a stand-in and a stunt double made of play doe and card. The trees themselves remained safely out of danger on a shelf they shared with 'not to be touched' paint and glue drying projects. They had been left on the shelf before the girls went to the park and it was decided that they should not be moved as they looked so delicate and fragile. It was the shelf above the 'intensive care' shelf that was just below Alice's eye level. They were safe. Sophie checked on her little tree and hoped she was witnessing a spring that would never turn to summer and never be affected by fall.

She noticed that the little dish, the one that contained the solution, the solution that was drawn up the cardboard trunk, the solution that fed the limbs that grew the crystals, was empty. Sophie, who had seen her Mum and Dad dutifully water the beautiful array of houseplants that freshened up every room in the house with verdant life, naturally assumed that her crystal tree would need water to sustain and perhaps even promote growth. Carefully she refilled the tiny reservoir with the liquid dropper provided and went off to play. She was vaguely excited at the prospect of finding new perhaps even more luxurious leaf blooms on her return. She was not prepared for what she was met with when she got back. Every leaf on every part of her tree had fallen, followed closely by her tears on seeing such a calamity. She looked across at her sister's tree which was still fully crystal clad. She reckoned it was her watering that had brought on an early autumn; it had to have been. Without forethought, she embarked on a course of action that somehow lessened the heartache. She picked up the teat pipette and dipped it in the scratched up orange plastic mug of water still at hand from the original watering.

As Sophie relived the moment, she experienced anew the intensity of her childhood pain. No wonder she cried; her magical tree was dead, and by her hand. And she could not share her loss with her sister; the sister she adored, the sister with whom she shared so much. Everything needed to be equal. She brought her face close to the plastic cup which still had a faint smell of Black-current drink fused with plastic, and squeezed the rubber head of the instrument pushing air down the pipe and bubbling out and upwards to the surface of the water. She watched intently as she released her grip and allowed the water to rise up the pipe; just like the solution that rose to form the crystal leaves. Somehow the process soothed her until she was suddenly gripped by the impact of what she had planned. Her eyes opened as wide as they had ever been and her jaw dropped. She squeezed out the water back into the mug which she placed on the table with the look of disdain of someone who has discovered something fowl in their drink. She could not, would not bring about the early demise of her sister's tree; she felt an overwhelming sense of relief that she had not carried out her intended action. She looked at her Sister's tree and it was marvellous; more marvellous than ever and her love for her sister was greater than ever. Following relief shame at having conceived such a dastardly idea made her shudder like a dog shaking off water and with that action, the whole thing was over and she felt fine.

Unbeknownst to Sophie her Father had checked on the trees whilst the girls were not there and had seen what had happened to Sophie's tree. He noticed the extra water in the dish and added up the situation, using his own particular personal mental calculator. He came to the same conclusion Sophie had come to. Later, he happened to be walking past the partly open doorway of the girl's room at the very moment Sophie was dipping the teat pipette into the mug. He watched her as she watched it fill. She did not notice him there and he could not guess what she had planned. He was satisfied that she was not too upset by the demise of her tree and rather than startle her, he would wait to console her when she left the room. He continued on his way along the passage. She left the room less than a minute later. Sophie was somehow able to see herself from her Father's angle amid her recollections. It was as if she was looking over the remembered shoulder of her Father. He was wearing his favourite, about the house woven Peruvian smock type thing and she was pleased to remember its texture against her cheek and its unique thick natural odour.

Little Sophie came across her Dad sitting at the kitchen table with a cup of tea reading the Guardian as he often did on a Saturday morning. Alice was with Mummy at swimming lessons. Sophie stood next to her Father who was perched on the stool that became part of every one of her future kitchens. He was so large and so steady perched on the stool. There was only one stool in the kitchen. He put down his paper, pushed his stool back and lifted her on to his knee in anticipation of the story she had come to tell. 'My tree is dead Daddy' she lay her head against his chest and felt it slowly expand and contract, and she could hear the breath enter and leave his lungs and his heart beating.

He comforted her and she cried. But it was not the tree she cried about in particular. It was more of a general clearance of feelings that were 'better out than in'

Sophie was suddenly back where she started looking at Alice crying and holding a leafless cardboard tree in her hands.

'What's happened to my tree?' she said between her sobs.

Chapter Six

The Keem

Welder had not gone so fast in a solo hopper for years. He was seized with an exhilaration that started way down in his ample belly with a deep rounded guttural surge that had more to do with a physical response than an emotional one. The sensation then grew and rose until it filled his barrel chest making his heart pound hard and fast. It was not the kind of 'accelerated heartbeat rush' he achieved through his usual means of stimulus; it didn't stop after six seconds. The surge continued to resonate and be fuelled from the depths. It carried on rising in pitch and intensity as it ascended up his rib cage and forced its way up his neck. His neck was thick, like that on a flagon of cider, it was still a bottleneck and the pressure grew in his throat. He swallowed, he felt a little sick and drew a deep breath. But it was not enough to hold back the surge and he let out a rare exclamation 'OOF'. He had switched off all the emotional blockers on his Band in hope, rather than expectation, of experiencing just such exhilaration. He was travelling as close to the ground as he dared. He shot across the flat, still, dusty orange plain towards a ridge of mountains stretching out for hundreds of miles to the left and right of him. It was a massive natural wall a mile high. There were no foothills, shin ups, knee highs, or even first legs, of hills either. There was a flat plain, a few boulders then a vertical, naturally formed, massive wall. Below Welder were holes, countless holes spread over the entire open expanse. The landing spot Welder had been dropped at was the largest unblemished area on the entire pitted spotty looking surface of the lowland. The holes were all neat circles ranging between one and several hundred metres in diameter. Some were shallow enough so that if Welder stood in them his head would stick out like a large burrowing creature, checking that the coast is clear. Other holes were near bottomless pits. He was headed for a narrow gap in the range ahead. It ran vertically down from the top of the ridge to almost as low as the plain. He was speeding towards the gap at close to the racy little transport's terminal velocity. The sun was at his back and the shadow of his vehicle was ducking in and out of the holes like a high-speed terrier flushing out burrows for game. It would drop out of sight into darkness keen to catch up and race ahead. From the landing spot, the vertical slice had not been visible and from half the distance it was only barely discernible as a fine line.

Welder hurtled towards the range and it soon loomed up before him as he approached the gap. He did not reduce his speed, he did not go to autopilot and he did not activate his blockers. He shot from the blazing sunlight of the open plain into the darkness of a narrow corridor with walls a mile high. The interior of the mountain that had grown so steadily at first in his vision, flashed passed in the light of his craft. The walls of the fissure were only metres away on each side of him. Welder heightened his pleasure by squeezing out the last drops of speed from his craft. In the complete darkness of a deep ocean of rock he was a lone speck of light; a solitary high-speed pilot fish. He was deep within the fine black line that sliced through the mountain as seen from the outside, and he was hurtling towards a fine white line of light, as yet unseen by him from within; the way out to the other side of the mountain.

After several minutes of only absolute darkness ahead of him it took Welder a further minute or two to be convinced that he could see the line; then he was sure. From within the 'Pip' (a nickname for the particular model of personal transport he was in), he burst into light as he shot out of the geological slit. His craft emerged as a tiny spec from the vast range moving slowly away, like a lone flying ant leaving a giant carcass. The sensation of bursting out was made all the more exhilarating as the exit from the passage was halfway up the side of the mountain he was bursting out from. The ground seemed to be blown away as if he entered an explosion of light. A plain of similar extent and character to the one on the other side of the ridge lay below and before him. And there, beyond, ahead in the distance, stood another range of equal breadth, another elongated blank cliff face of dark grey solid rock a mile high. But there was no fine dark line marking a vertical cut similar to the one Welder had passed through.

Welder speculated that the slice he had exited was so neat it could have been made from space by a government engineering, or planetary landscaping vessel. The company had that sort of equipment too and the clout and influence to keep it quiet. There was plenty not known or even rumoured about the company, stuff it kept quiet; at least the stuff nestled under one wing of the company anyway.

Not distinguishable at first, Welder spotted what he had been expecting to see. Midway between the two ranges was a black sphere perched on a black cube of similar mass. 'Infinity over reason' Welder thought as the two standard ideal forms became apparent to him. At first, the dark forms were camouflaged amongst a myriad of holes. He started decelerating and did a completely unnecessary banking and looping manoeuvre then returned to his course. It was the only destination on the planet.
'I'll have to get me one of these' he said as he stuck it in automatic pilot mode and switched his band back on to full. The forms were not large compared to those that Welder was used to but being alone in the centre of a flat evenly textured potholed plain like a black pearl on a black die on

a polka dot tablecloth, gave his ant eye view a greater, more awesome aspect.

The base had a circular entrance at its centre like the snake eye of the die. It led to a tubular docking bay tunnel that went clear through to the central lobby. Welders Pip was still slowing as he entered the cube. He was moving at walking pace by the time he left the tube of the outer walls and went into the cubes cavernous interior. He had no choice about the speed as his craft was out of his control. The lowest part of the sphere above created a convex ceiling high above and rested on a black column with data floating and turning in rings of coloured light around it. The dark impenetrable walls of glass within the base hid the buildings workings and energy cells that could power the facility ad infinitum. The black no snow snow-globe had a battery that could outlast the planets sun. Despite their blankness, the walls seemed focused towards the centre. Attention was always drawn back to the column.

Welder sat for a moment in his Pip. There was no sign of life or any reason for the lack of it. Welder's band indicated no danger and Welder did not sense any either; only an irresistible curiosity. The cubes interior was evenly and comfortably lit without any noticeable signs of how. It was as if the light from the planets small hot sun was filtering and refracted through the dark glass from every direction. Welder parked up. One side of his transport opened as four supports searched downwards for the ground. His seat swivelled and tilted, presenting him outwards and on to his feet. To his surprise he virtually sprang forward; the massage and well-being infusion functions of the seating had revitalised him. Vehicles had become such a pleasant and even invigorating experience that many travellers sought traffic jams, though they still complained about them. There was one other personal transport parked in one of the three spaces allocated. On the wall above it was a sign the said 'This is not a pip'; an esoteric joke referring to a pre-space earth painting by an artist called Magritte. Ben and Robby were devotees of twentieth-century art. Such references were typical of those that once worked at the facility in homage to the founders. 'That's not many spots' Welder mused, once again sharing his thoughts with future viewers of his involuntary recordings.

Welder's steps made no sound on the gleaming black floor as if the sound was being absorbed. He circled the inner walls of the cube looking in all directions in the manner of a visitor experiencing a spectacular inspirational place of worship but not a believer. He did not appear to be in any hurry but he was going as fast as it was prudent to do so whilst assessing a new environment. He orbited the column like a satellite on its final inevitable lap before being pulled to the centre.

The column, like the inner walls of the cube that boxed it in, seemed impenetrable and seamless. Welder's ambling orbit ended as he was reeled in by the column that he estimated was about twenty-two yards in diameter. 'It's about as wide as the length of a cricket pitch' for the benefit of the records, knowing full well 'slab' was the only officially recognised system of measurement in the galaxy, 'whatever that is' he added quietly to himself for the benefit of his own amusement. Welder liked to throw in obscure ancient measurements to wind up the analysts. Everything Welder was experiencing, every object seen, every surface touched and sound heard was recorded independently of Welder by his shadow. Everything was recorded but within the limits of the shadow's sensors. Welder's shadow collected huge amounts of data and after long careful analysis, a pretty accurate picture of events could be reconstructed. However, the whole process of analysis could be sped up with IS or indicator statements from the wearer of a shadow. A simple phrase from Welder or even a word could save the analysts' days. This was particularly true when it came to deciphering smell. Welder was searching for the right way to describe a distinctive smell he noticed immediately on leaving his PIP but his deliberations were interrupted.

'Welcome Welder. We have been expecting you'. The even-toned soothing voice came from the column where a large slim vertical segment slid slowly out like a disc tray on its side. It was four metres high, just shy of a metre wide, and protruded several metres from its housing. It stopped short of where Welder was standing.

There was a recess on one side of the protrusion large enough for two people of Welder's size. It was his point of entry so Welder stepped in without thought or fear. The even light that cast no shadow was unchanged as the tray retracted and Welder was then inserted into the column. He could see out as though the black walls were the darkened glass of a stretch limo.'

By using the term 'stretch limo', the narrator had allowed Sophie to disengage from the story and she did. The impulse to return to her story held sway. Once again she was standing before her little sister Alice as she wept. Alice had the same sense of loss as Sophie had experienced at the shedding of the crystal tree's leaves. But the story seemed to run deeper than the conclusion of a trial of a science-based toy run by their father. Although both young girls experienced an early profound sense that things don't always work out the way you want them, still there was something more. As it had done with Alice moments before, the gravity of the moment made Sophie's knees buckle and she plonked herself down on the bed next to her sister.

Gravity of a different kind took over for a couple of seconds as Sophie's landing was heavier than she planned. Alice was about to rebuke her for plonking herself down and jolting her upwards, but annoyance at the possible damage Sophie's action could have caused her skeletal cardboard tree turned immediately to grief with the realisation that there was nothing left to damage. Alice cried with renewed intensity. But jointly they became aware that the remains of trees should be treated with care and disposed of thoughtfully so a suitable ceremony marking the 'great dying of the trees' was planned.

'What happened to the crystals from your tree Alice? Mine turned to mush' asked Sophie knowing it was only the card tree that Alice was holding; the dish was still on the shelf.
'I put them in the compost bin' Alice replied sniffling and pointing to a little leaf mulcher she made from Lego.
'Maybe you should keep the leaves, they could be magical'
        Suddenly Sophie was struck with a powerful sense of foreboding and her Father entered the room. And she remembered the feeling from that time. It was as if somehow the memory of what dead Sophie knew was about to follow, bled into the thoughts and feeling of Sophie from the past. All of her life Sophie had experienced feelings of foreboding or unannounced and unqualified excitement.
        Sophie's Father listened to and comforted Alice as she told her tale of woe. The three of them sat together on the bed, but Alfred's attention seemed to be directed more towards Alice. The thought that Sophie had found her tree without its leaves due to overwatering on her part and decided to give Alice's tree the same treatment took shape in Alfred's mind. His adding up was based mainly on what he had seen earlier; Sophie going through the early stages of a plan Alfred had correctly guessed, but wrongly assumed Sophie had carried out. Sophie would never have

carried out the plan; it was not in her nature to do so.
Alfred knew it too but too easily accepted his own summing
up. He wasn't often incorrect in his sums. It was hard for
Alfred to notice his own mistakes at times.

Alice dried her tears, got ready for going to her
friend's house for the afternoon and left with a final hug
from her Dad. He remained silent the whole time except to
say goodbye to Alice. Once Alice had gone Alfred
confronted his daughter with his rigid suspicions.
'Did you water your sister's tree Sophie?' he asked in a
calm and controlled voice.
'No I didn't' she replied coating her answer with a thin
hard indignant shell in preparation of whatever lay ahead.
Just for contemplating the deed, she did not carry out,
enough guilt and remorse leaked out in her voice for her
Father's wrong conclusions to be further verified in his
mind. She also had a sense of shock and alarm at being
confronted with her private thoughts.
'But I saw you Sophie' Her Father's voice remained calm,
and all the more dramatic and disturbing for it. Sophie's
blood ran cold and then it turned and ran hot with the
anger of being wrongly accused.
'But I didn't do it. Alice's tree died on its own'
'You just stay here in your room until you are ready to tell
me the truth' and with that Alfred turned his back on his
little girl and went back to the kitchen and his newspaper,
confident that he knew what had happened. Sophie was
filled with a sense of injustice and went to her leafless tree.
She recalled her intent and realised that her Dad must have
seen her dip her pipette. The young and inexperienced
pragmatist Sophie thought of her plan to water Alice's tree
and she thought of her Dad, who was convinced she had
carried it out. She remembered herself remembering events.
Part of her young self was angry and resolved; the part

83

that was telling her that she would never give in. She would stay in her room forever if necessary. The other voice that had her inner ear just wanted the whole problem to go away as quickly as possible. She contemplated telling the lie that she had done the deed just to be done with the incident; after all, she thought, she had intended to and she felt genuine remorse for that. 'Thinking about doing something is just as bad as doing it, isn't it? I have to tell a lie to be believed' she was addressing one of her collection of ceramic penguins. 'I will always know the truth and that's what counts, doesn't it Zoomie?' Zoomie stared at her with static intensity and replied, 'if you lie you will forget the truth'. Sophie was irritated at the words she had put into Zoomie's beak and turned to 'Flap Jack', whose different penguin character would give her a different take. 'What do you think Flap?' He gave an altogether more palatable answer. 'Don't worry about it. Forget about it; let's swim'.

'Maybe I will just stay in my room forever and play with you Flap'. With that Sophie pushed making the decision of what to say to her Father and indeed to Alice, to one side and started playing, summing up the postponement by saying to a baby hippo called Gloop, 'there are worse places to be; it wouldn't be much of a punishment to be stuck here with you'.

Sophie joined with her young self and revelled in her child imagination and play. There was something clear and refreshing about experiencing her young world. It felt like swimming in a clear pool constantly refreshed by a waterfall of water from a mountain stream.

After about an hour that seemed like a day, even a new day, Sophie's Father re-entered the room with an expectant expression that needed no elaboration with words. Sophie remembered the decision she needed to make and without further reflection said 'I didn't do anything to Alice's tree'

She saw that her father did not believe her; she expected as much. She plonked herself on to the bed and remembered times when she had successfully covered up mistakes with lies, yet now she felt condemned for telling the truth.

Her Dad stood there thoughtfully for a couple of long minutes and finally concluded 'I will just have to accept your word on the matter' and he walked away. He did not believe her and she knew it. She listened to his steps as he made his way down the stairs. Sophie's connection with her passed faded away with the fading sound of the footsteps. One final fading thought occurred to Sophie, what happened to Alice's tree? The leaves on Alice's tree did not turn to mush at the base of the tree like hers had; they were solid pieces. Her father did not believe the truth but would have believed a lie. For that reason she did not care whether he believed her or not, 'ever again' she heard herself whisper like a secret pledge.

Welder noticed his operational shadow was not visible as the segment moved smoothly and silently back into its place in the column. He was delivered into the column's interior. He did not detect the moment the movement of the man tray had stopped being lateral and became vertical, but he did sense movement upwards. This was confirmed by layers of earth that he could just make out through the dark glass-like material within which he was held. He put his palms flat against the container wall directly in front of him like a Marcel Marceau mime. It was not cold but gave away no heat; it was like touching wood. He imagined he was rising up the inside of a huge tree trunk.

85

'Now I know what a sperm feels like' he said out loud but he got the feeling his words were not being recorded by his shadow.

'A humorous observation Mr Welder' replied the calm and pleasing voice of what Welder assumed was the voice of an 'Oi' or, operational interface; which of course had no face. Welder was well used to interacting with programs and it stood to reason that this secret enterprise of the company would have access to the most detailed profile of him. It would be almost impossible to come up with something that the program would not have a response to. He had no doubt that it was a faceless interface of the highest order. But none the less Welder sensed something different about the voice; there was something behind it or contained within it, that suggested life. He dismissed the thought and concentrated on trying to describe the distinct fragrance that had gently engulfed him ever since he stepped out of the Pip. The odd thing was that as soon as he thought about the smell, he could no longer smell it, nor remember it. He could remember how he felt smelling it. He felt like he was being gently hugged; the same feeling he got from his herbal heroin tea. He let go of trying to identify the elusive smell, 'a wisp of the will' he said. Welder smiled as there was no response from the interface. It was a satisfying silence that he triumphantly and quite wrongly believed came about because he had bamboozled the programs ability to respond. Welder's lift was more than a lift; it was a scanner and decontamination chamber too. As he rose the chamber changed form in liquid fashion. It became a tube then clearly stopped just long enough for Welder to wonder if it was stuck. The lid of what was like a personal tub that was barely a foot above his head and began to rise. The tube above him was slightly broader than his shoulders. Welder looked up and a circle of light appeared and begun

to grow, and as it did, he began to rise. He was deposited within the heart of the enormous sphere, just as he had expected. The final stage of Welder's elevation had been on a circular platform that was not much wider than Welder's large frame. The disc of the platform neatly filled the aperture made for it in the ground within the sphere and the roof of the lift. The floor that received the laden platform completed a floor plain just below the halfway point within the sphere. Welder judged that the rounded ground on which he was standing was about the size of the Coliseum Hotel on Sudbury New World. His presentation into the hemisphere made him feel a little like an offering or an unwitting competitor dumped into an arena and triggered the memory that the word arena came from the word sand, which seemed fitting. But he felt no apprehension. The ground around him was covered with areas of differing grasses. Most was immaculately cut lawn whilst other areas were like meadows of daisies, poppies and wildflowers, though anything but wild in the artificial environment Welder found himself in.

'Welcome Welder' the same voice from the elevator slash decontamination chamber greeted him. But the voice seemed to be an internal rather than an external one as if he was wearing earphones broadcasting directly to his mind. It was certainly the best interactive program he had come across in his many years of being a space hopping troubleshooter. All the information at his disposal told him that nothing was threatening in what he was seeing and hearing. There was nothing he couldn't come up with a reasonable explanation for. His band seemed to be keeping him on an even keel emotionally; it was only his shadow that had stopped functioning as far as he could tell. Some sort of anti-industrial espionage automatic shutdown had done for his shadow he thought.

There was no indication of human or animal life indicated on his band, not even the tiniest insect. There was a strong reading for plant life but that tallied with what he could see. He decided it was safe to step off his spot which looked like a grey stepping stone in a well-kept lawn. But a feeling of anticipation and nervous energy gripped him and he hesitated before stepping off the platform. As he finally stepped forward he looked at his band once again to check and make sure his personal emotional filter settings did not need recalibrating in response to his growing unease. The emotional equaliser's readings were indicating that it was working. Welder still felt odd. Closer inspection by Welder revealed that the indicator light saying everything was alright was all that worked. It may as well have been a sticker on a toy dashboard. He checked his scanner again and that seemed to be okay; just the reading for copious verdant life but nothing more.

'Just salad' He knew there would be no recording of what he said now that his shadow was gone but the sound of his voice comforted him.

'There is no one on this planet that can walk in on me and I'm not being recorded, dicky dicky bum-bum'. His sensors told him that there was no animal life and they appeared to be working fine; nothing but plants. But his senses were reading something different.

As an uninhabited and undeveloped planet, Chippenham 5 had protected status. If it had useful mineral resources things may have been different. Nobody else wanted the dead rock with protected new world status except the company. They were restricted to one monitoring station and obliged to ensure that nothing on the planet was interfered with. To the outside worlds, this remained the case. However, Welder was sure that whatever the company had been up to on Chippenham 5 it had contravened any number of ethical and legal protocols. It didn't matter how well contained the plants were in this ball Welder thought, they shouldn't be here. Welder did a little checking during the long journey and there was worryingly little about the Company's business on Chippenham 5; virtually nothing. In truth, no one except the handful of individuals directly involved knew what had been going on there. When an outside party became interested in buying Chippenham 5 the only records the company had were hundreds of years old. After routine investigations nothing untoward was found; it was simply regarded as a forgotten planet and the sale was agreed. Sally was not alerted to the sale until it had already gone through. Countless such decisions were ground out every second by the corporate machine. It was the 'better check the place out just in case something undetected or unforeseen is lying in wait on the planet just sold protocol 4, being activated that alerted Sally. She also realised that it must have been someone within the company with enough clout to fast track the sale that was behind it. She stepped in just in the nick of time to make sure they sent Welder.

It was Welder's job to find out what had been going on and arrange for the discreet removal of anything that could cause the company embarrassment; anything messy. More importantly, from the company's point of view, nothing was to interrupt or negatively influence the sale of the planet; the price they were given was well over the odds. They knew that if even the most basic life form was found to have developed with the capability of surviving independently on the planet, the whole rock would be quarantined and no sale. Not only that the planet would no longer be saleable for generations; perhaps ever and there would be a costly maintenance bill. Whatever life formed naturally or inadvertently would be protected by forces, not

*even the company could influence. Welder had no
compunction about getting rid of a few house plants safely
sealed in the company's facilities. If necessary the whole
structure he was in could be picked up and taken into space.
It could be like a ball for the company to kick around space
for a while just as long as it didn't go over the neighbour's
fence. A hermetically sealed ball picked up by the most
powerful tractor beam in the galaxy; which happened to
belong to the company would satisfy the company's
administrators. But if it was that simple Sally would not
have insisted on him for the job.*

*'Not exactly as discreet as we would like' commented one
of Welders superiors when discussing the options before
being sent on the mission, 'there is a risk of detection, but it
can be done', then he ended emphatically, 'but only as a
last resort.*

*'To avoid any unnecessary delays its best if we deal with
this business ourselves on the planet Welder, and below the
scanners. The authorities would insist on all sorts of
pointless and counterproductive procedures if they got the
slightest whiff of anything odd.' Her lines were delivered
with more between them than on them. She knew he read
her meaning and that he would have to figure out the
greater mission on-site, and in sight of the true situation.*

*Whatever unauthorised genetic experiments
Morepeg Lugrut had conducted centuries ago when setting
up the facility were contained within the complex Welder
found himself within. However, Welder knew Lugrut was no
mad scientist; he was no monster and would never have
produced one. He may have produced a bad smell and even
kicked up a stink in his quest for new aromas and their
applications, but nothing too weird. Welder could not
imagine anything that could pose an ethical or moral*

dilemma in carrying out his official duty if Lugrut truly was the last person on the world.

'Just say he is on gardening leave if anyone asks', was what Welder's line manager, who rarely ever saw him and never managed him was told.

'Welder is there simply to double-check what the sensors were showing and deal with any loose ends. He is to 'expedite matters' by keeping the authorities out of the picture, okay?'

There was the problem of the 'plant right to life' movement to consider but so far no wind of Welder's mission had blown their way. They would make their own particular stink if they learned that plants were going to be destroyed.

Welder tapped his band again when he noticed his shadow was attempting to reactivate. He looked up and would have jumped out of his skin but either he was shocked into numbness or something else was evening him out. He assumed his emotional stabilizer was fully operational. In situations of danger, it was set to inhibit the initial release of adrenaline by three seconds, to use it as he wished. So Welder was expecting a full charge. The hit never landed.

'Don't be alarmed Welder' came the same voice that he thought was part of the building's interactive systems. Any alarm Welder would have naturally or otherwise felt would have been immediately dispelled by that soothing voice. But no voice or emotional inhibitors could hold back his amazement and awe of what confronted him.

Standing before him were twelve small figures; twelve childlike brightly coloured figures. Welder stood in stunned silence for a couple of seconds until his faculties returned to him. He looked at his band and there was still no indication of animate life; only multiple readings of *plant life. At this Welder gave the band a good shake which made no difference and his eyes lifted to meet those of the creatures standing not ten yards ahead of him. He had noted that the weapon functions on his band, like his shadow, had been deactivated. So his rough around the edges but honest and disarming charm was his only defence.*

'I'm sorry if I appear a little startled, I wasn't expecting company' Welder paused transfixed by the cartoon-like blue, pink, yellow and orange creatures. Adrenaline did kick in but it could have been triggered by anything. He recognised it. Naturally, occurring adrenaline could be useful for any physical challenge he may face but its effects could leak through his band's emotional blockers. Somehow what Welder was feeling was different. He felt euphoric and in despair simultaneously. He felt like a teenager again. He was not sure exactly how he felt but he was no longer in full control.

'It seems you already know who I am, but I am sure I don't know who or what the fuck you are'. Welder's band flickered and crackled as if the shock of such a weird and unexpected sight made it blow a fuse. Its malfunction was the reason for Welder expressing his bewilderment in such a way. Finally, the band was completely defunct. If external forces had not done it already it the beating Welder was giving it would have shut it down.

'You'll have to excuse me but my band is bust, and my thoughts and feelings may be erratic for a minute or two, but rest assured my actions are totally under control' Welder said as he inexplicably nodded his head vigorously, stopped and then started moving his jaw from side to side, and bending at the knees and moving up and down in sync with his jaw.

'Well just about under control' he continued trying to reassure the beings he was addressing that he was not a threat, though they showed no sign of concern.

There were six, more feminine looking creatures and six slightly more masculine ones. They were all wearing either, a simple vest like frock or shorts and a vest-like top. All the garments on show were bright, almost luminous. They looked like they were made of pure colour, like a bright suns shining through the petal of a flower. There was yellow-orange or blue and the frocks were sported by male and female alike. What made six of them look more feminine was their physique, facial features and incredibly long eyelashes. They were all slim and their skin was smooth and the same bright colours as their plain clothing that hung loosely on the wearer's slender frames. Their bodies were not quite as luminescent as their clothes but they were brighter than any life form Welder had ever seen. There was some variation in heights but not along gender lines and the tallest was a bright yellow more female looking individual about a metre high. They had beautifully rounded bald heads which were slightly larger in proportion to their bodies than a small child's. Their eyes were large almond-shaped and drew Welder in. All their eyes were green, bright leaf green and identical. Welder was not one for cute things and fought against describing them as such. Having a shadow so often in the past meant his impulse to describe what he saw was automatic 'cute'

He felt like he was looking at a beautiful tree, into a clear pool, and a bowl of beautifully formed exotic fruit.

Welder had no idea of how long he had been standing taking in and getting to grips with what he was seeing. He was no longer puzzling in his mind who or what these creatures were; he was simply regarding them as if

*he were seeing a beautiful flower bed of the most amazing
flowers he had ever seen. At the point that the thirst of
Welder's gaze appeared to be quenched, one figure stepped
forward and spoke.*
'We are the fucking Keem'
And they all laughed a slightly suppressed giggly laugh.

Chapter Seven

A Conversation with the Keem

As Sophie listened, the images conjured up took form and came to life to a degree she never experienced in life. It was as if she was present, even a presence in the scene, plugged in like Welder's shadow, and with the flick of a switch she could read his thoughts, or switch again and take in different viewpoints. She was there, part of the scene, in every shadow, floating with the fragrant vapours hanging over events. She could see over, under and into things; things not described in the story. It was more than being at the controls of a holographic recording or wearing a virtual reality headset. Even the most sophisticated holographic films or VR experience of Sophie's day did not come close to it. It was like walking between sensations and around them. 'Is this evidence that I am dead, evidence that I am a spirit able to drift in and out of strange worlds, even different universes? No, it is a story. I know the narrator is telling a story. I am imagining what the narrator triggers. I am being led to a place that I can see for myself. Or is it a projection? Am I a projection, a projection of information flickering on the edge of existence?'

Sophie had always kept abreast of the latest technology. The fact that technological advances in film and television were drip-fed to a captive consumer audience did not bother her. She rather enjoyed the process. From her observations and despite their protestations to the contrary, she believed the general public was more than willing to continually upgrade; like her, they liked being in the game. Far from genuinely feeling ripped off by having to purchase new equipment to take advantage of innovations, it was found that the process of upgrading was producing more excitement than the upgrades themselves. The way Sophie approached the whole question was to only play the game when she wanted to. It was like a soap opera which she found no problem dipping in and out of without losing the plot. In later life, the intervals between upgrading grew larger but she never lost the ability to catch up quickly. If a young Sophie had found herself in a holographic suite from nearer the time of her death she would have been impressed but not completely fooled by what she was seeing.

All Sophie was sure of was that her experience of the story felt real and she was somehow a part of it. Silently witnessing events like Welder's shadow was also true of the way she was taking in the memories she was reliving. She felt like an internal shadow of her remembered self. She switched from story to memory as if she was switching between two channels. Memory and the story wove around each other. At what seemed like deliberate cut off points she switched over. Anything more than a bite-sized portion would be too much. She was not absorbing what she was recalling and hearing so much as it was passing through her; she was the material and the process. The truth can be hard to swallow, especially if it is in too big a lump she thought. The lumps from her past were breaking down and the story was washing it down. Was the story a lubricant or was it an enzyme, she couldn't tell. Maybe I am a fly in a Venus-flytrap being digested. Apart from those she dipped into she was conscious that other recollections were part of a constant flow of information in the background. The same was true whilst she listened to the story.

'If I am conscious of these things, if I am conscious, I must be alive. Or maybe I just think I am conscious. Just a thought; maybe I am just a thought? Maybe I am just information, a sophisticated form of data? No that's not it, I am sure that's not it. I am convinced this has nothing to do with technology' She was beginning to itch and the swarms of confusing thoughts were closing in. The gathering cloud of biting uncertainty dispersed the instant she chose to ignore it. The question of what was truly happening to her had risen to the surface and returned to the deep once again. When she ever noticed the stream again she contented herself by imagining the stream was the one that flowed through her garden. She had a growing sense that this background stream was a strand of her gently downloading. All of her personal files, photos, films, writing; all of it was downloading in the background whilst she was going through some of them. Her memories, the story and the stream platted together and passed along. It reminded Sophie that she had been used to holding a text conversation and a spoken one as well as planning for future conversations based on what popped into her mind as a result of what she was taking in from the other two. Nothing felt muddled or rushed though; everything seemed to be flowing with ease in the same direction. She became aware that she was able to speculate more and more on the question of what was happening to her. But unlike in her life when she was confronted with a confusing puzzle, she was not in the least bit bothered. In life, a difficult puzzle could send her into a spin that circled a panic attack. She sensed that she was going in the right direction. Something lay at the end of the story. It occurred to her that the reason she was not concerned was that she really was dead or maybe it was drugs.

For the first time, her attention did not focus back on the story of her past. An indeterminate time passed. It was the first occasion since first hearing the narrator's voice that she could think for herself. They were just thoughts though; individual thought, even related thoughts, but they did not string together, they did not form into ideas or theories. They were notions, not deliberations. She was being carried along, flowing along channels. Although she slid off between the two channels, she knew there were more. They were dark circles beyond sight in all directions. Her path was set for now; she was in full flow; streaming and dreaming along, floating in memory and the familiar unknown unfolding story.

It was another perfect day and Sophie unzipped the flaps to her tent as quietly as she could whilst the campsite was still in slumber, apart from her and one or two other early-risers. She was fully dressed and ready for a day's walking along the coast. The dawning sun filtered through leaves tickled by a gentle breeze. She looked back into the tent and went through a mental checklist of what she might need and resisted the temptation to wake her boyfriend whose thick blond hair was the only thing visible sticking out of his sleeping bag. She zipped up the tent with the same steady noise reductive action as she had used opening it. Sophie stood up and slung her day pack over her shoulders in one graceful motion. It would not be long, she thought, before she would have to half fill it with her fleece once the sun's warmth had fully risen. She was keen to get to a pre-chosen café for a coffee and croissant and look out over the sea. She literally only needed to follow her nose to get there. She stood for a moment with her eyes closed and took in a draught of clear new day air followed by a gulp of cool water from her bottle which slid neatly out and back into the side pouch of her pack.

Without the blanketing of the sound of people, traffic, lawnmowers the general hubbub of the campsite, Sophie could enjoy a fine mesh of bird song cast wide across the hills that cupped the small seaside town. Threads of the song linked the territory of Sophie's range of hearing. The paths of their communications crisscrossed overhead and joined points of rich colourful song dotted over the landscape. The two-stroke engine of a moped cut through the mesh leaving a silencing wake but as the scooter's shrill monotonous straining died away the threads of bird conversation started up once more.

Having negotiated the Guy rope around her tent, she headed down the hill towards town. The terracotta tiled roofs of the whitewashed houses stepped down to the deep blue of the sea. Sophie loved the morning.

Sophie and boyfriend Daniel had spent every day of the six weeks of their Continental adventure together and even though they had been getting on amazingly well Sophie felt the need for a day off; a day off on her own. No negotiating, no joint decisions and no detailed planning. Sophie did enjoy planning researching and organising but now and then she liked to throw the brochures and maps in the air and just take off. She was the more obsessive when it came to micromanaging and Daniel was more than happy to go along for the ride. In a way, she needed a day off from herself.

'The Keem approached Welder and took him by the hand. He felt almost in a trance.' Whereas before the narrator's voice bridged between the story and Sophie's memories her mind moved seamlessly between one visualisation and another. Her mind's eye barely blinked. She was now more of a witness to events in the story with the narrator acting more as a commentator filling in during lulls in play. The narrator's voice was becoming more like an inner voice.

'There was a sweet fragrance in the air that seemed to emanate from the Keem as they huddled around Welder and directed him towards a central raised pond of some kind. The hypnotic fragrance was the same one that earlier eluded Welder's descriptive powers like a slippery fish whenever his mind sought to grab it. He realised earlier that he would have to let the fish go and wait for it to come to the surface again to get a proper look at it. It had surfaced once but it had a calming pleasure that blanketed conscious thought. Just below the surface was a feeling of chasing a thought and not even remembering why the pursuit had been started. He no longer cared what it smelled like; smelling it was enough.

He could have objected to being led but was happy to go along with these almost cartoon-like creatures. He noticed that the lofty space above him in the hemisphere was evenly interspersed with spheres hanging in space like giant static bubbles. They were not hanging, they were floating like an object suspended in fluid, too heavy to rise but too light to sink any further. There must have been hundreds of them if not more. They were of differing sizes from ones as large as a garden shed to others as small as a golf ball. They were just floating there, static balloons in a perfectly windless sky. Some were an opaque dark green and others were transparent and exotic plants could be seen within them.

Welder was led to a place on the pool's edge where the rim was wide enough for him to sit. The pool was about twenty feet across and its blue-tinted waters were contained within a grey stone ring about three feet high. It pool had darker seams in fluid lines and a rich dull shine which lured the eye to search for a bottom that could not be seen. To Welder's surprise, his seat was slightly warm like the warm rocks Welder would lie on at the seaside on a sunny day after a swim.

The Keem sat around him on the ground in a semi-circle like children at storytime. But in this instance, it was Welder who would be the listener. One of the Keem was nudged and got to his feet sheepishly asking the others humbly if they were sure that he should be given the honour of speaking first. There was an overly polite exchange between the chosen speaker and the others; it was a similar type of exchange to the chipmunks from early Warner Brothers cartoons; uncannily similar. Once the niceties were dispensed with the male looking Keem stiffened into complete assurance and confidently began.

'We are the twelve Keem. We were once thirteen and now we are twelve. You will learn of the circumstances surrounding the loss of one of our number in due course.' The speaker looked around sheepishly and the others collectively nodded indicating that he was doing well and that he should continue. He smiled broadly. It was a wide extravagant smile that seemed to draw his shoulders up with it as if they were attached to the corners of his mouth by string. A neat row of baby teeth was visible against the yellow interior of his mouth. The speaker was bright pink. 'We are the brainchildren of Ben, one of the two founders; the founders of the company. He prepared the ground from which we sprang. Though he never lived to see us bloom we grew from the seeds of his mindset upon the solar winds. It was the mighty and venerable 'Boob' that took those seeds and germinated them with his fertile intellect and love of bubbles and plants and things' the speaker's voice trailed off as if he were not sure about the quality of what he was saying. He made a peculiar giggling coughing sound as if he was clearing his throat but had no breath and resumed with renewed resolve. 'Then it was the sons and daughters

*of Ben and the followers of the Boob that made their vision
flesh. The spheres you see about you are all self-contained
perfectly balanced self-sustained environments that will
flourish as long as the real or artificial sun shines. The
sphere you are in now is one such sphere. There is only
plant life in the spheres, including our sphere and including
us.' The speaker paused, spotting Welder's perplexity and
his need for reassurance and elaboration. Welder
separated his mind from the symptoms of uncontrolled
emotion. He felt tearful and realised he was coping with
more than simply his band not working.*

*'That's correct Welder we have been genetically
engineered from plants. We are just like the plants in the
spheres about us now. We can regenerate and flourish to
the end of light in the universe. Rather like the chocolate
man that likes chocolate; if we were vegetarians we could
eat ourselves'. There was a ripple of infectious and
delightful giggling.*

*'You will have to excuse us, we have been sniffing giggle
fruit' said the speaker as he nodded backwards to indicate
the group.*

*Until the revelation that the creatures before him were
plants, Welder had assumed that the sphere had somehow
blocked or altered the signals of his, and the transport
ships scanners so that only plant life registered. As
extraordinary as the idea that the creatures were plants
and not animals was to Welder, it seemed more plausible
than the scanners being duped or thwarted; such was the
trust in certain technology in Welder's day. Welder
signalled his readiness to proceed by lifting his brow and
opening his eyes slightly wider and lifting his head as it
had drooped slightly during a moment of contemplation.
Welder's gaze returned to the assembled plants.*

'The founder Ben wanted to create 'grow your own pets'. He was inspired by amazing sea monkeys.'

'Amazing mazing monkeys' interjected the larger female and all nodded and looked at each other knowingly and enthusiastically. It was her voice that he had heard in his head earlier; the one he had mistaken for a faceless interface. She looked at Welder directly and he knew her name without hearing it. It was a name that need not be spoken. It was a name that evoked some kind of a pattern in Welder's mind. It was the visualisation of the unique odour he was trying to pin down with words. It was Keem. Her name was Keem. As Welder looked about at the others he realised they were all called Keem. The delicious and shifting fragrance was the Keem.

Welder thought to himself, 'it seems that not everything can be communicated or expressed in words. That's why I can't pin down that smell from before. Now I have a word; Keem.' The speaker continued having stopped for Welder to have his moment.

'Ben wanted pets that had the appeal and appearance of the advertisement for sea monkeys rather than tiny shrimps; though we regard shrimps with great respect and fondness.'

'FONDNESS FOR THE PONDNESS' the others shouted out in unison as a melodic chant followed by full-blooded laughter. The speaker joined in, holding his slim stomach at the point his body was folding as it bent under the weight of laughing.

The speaker then shook his head with laughter the way a dog shakes its wet body and rubbed his tearful eyes. Welder had a non-specific emotional surge combined with intellectual clarity. He felt like he was filling with liquid tickle. 'Just what the ball-bag is happy...' before Welder could finish his sentence his body tingling energetic surge took over and his controlled clarity was gone. He could not contain himself. He started to chuckle. It started at a gentle pace like a canal barge putt-putting along a canal. There was plenty of time to draw breath between his reliable engines coughs of the exhaust. The pace grew steadily until he was rattling along and rocking like an old train building up to top speed on a bumpy line. The runaway train careered through the breathing stop stations. Welder rocked in, eyes clenched silent convulsions. He was weeping and dribbling freely. The train hit the buffers and Welder took in a huge draught of air. Replenished with oxygen he started up again. Welder then performed a symphony of laughter made up of different rhythms and pitches. Wind section and percussion battled it out and combined in raptures of discord and harmony. It culminated in a near-silent sobbing. The top half of his body bobbed like a nodding dog. He got to his feet as if to leave to stop laughing.

Soon he was bent forward with his hands on his knees for support. His top half teetered but remained perched on his near motionless, knees bent lower half. His triangulated lower frame was keeping him anchored but began to weaken. As he continued uncontrollably quaking and shaking his knees gave way and he dropped with the appearance of a sobbing man genuflecting and begging for mercy. His out of control giggle fit did elicit a begging request from Welder. He sought any sort of help in stopping the asphyxiating laughter. The gaps between the barge motor putts had narrowed and compressed into nothing; what they became was a continual squeaking expulsion of all that remained in his lungs. The compression continued until total silence. He was begging for the fit to end just as he had begged his father to stop when he was a child. But whereas his father would eventually stop when he was near to passing out, this attack of the giggles did not stop and the painful pressure within his chest to gulp fresh air grew to be unbearable. It felt like and an attack too. He still had the capacity for independent thought but he knew it would not last much longer. Was this the Keem's weapon, possibly aided by the intoxicating influence of that beautiful smell.

He looked up at the Keem just in time to see them spinning around, dancing chanting and laughing but finally with a look of concern at Welder's plight. It was too late; he passed out from lack of oxygen.

Welder came around split in two. His spirits were teetering on the edge of euphoria; his whole inner being was smiling, but his physical being was cramped with the desperate need to pee. The bodily need accelerated the progress of him regaining consciousness. As he was coming to, the voluminous depths of his need were barely being held back by his renowned ability to hold on. He would have to rouse himself as his deeply engrained stubborn resistance to wetting himself would not let go and forced the pace. He was suffering from a form of urinary rather than respiratory narcolepsy. He opened his eyes and fought his way to his feet hastened by internal cattle prods of pain and pressure. He looked around, not for a toilet (unless there was one right in front of him) but for an instant improvised location to suffice as one.

Welder was proud of the capacity and strength of his 'hearty bladder' but his lack of compunction about fulfilling any urgent physical need where ever and in whatever way that need demanded came to the rescue of his pride. The ability to over-ride etiquette, social convention or anything that stood in the way of Welder dealing with a situation made him the Company's greatest trouble-shooter; ever. Within less than a second Welder had chosen a seemingly suitable bit of shrubbery to release the unsustainable pressure that was so great that it rose up his back to his neck causing a deep throbbing pain in what felt like his piss soaked brain. He had an image of a cartoon version of himself with pee rising up and visibly filling his eyeballs and then emptying with relief. The image of draining almost led him to piss himself. He groaned in pain and desperation as groaning was the only and almost completely useless release of the pressure that had by then cut off his breathing. Being a practical man with a penchant for selective laziness Welder's outfits provided ease of access for having a pee. However, his desperation made it difficult for his hands to keep up with what was being asked of them. He just managed to sort himself out before he was able to (what he called in his army days) break the seal. He tossed his head back and closed his eyes with instant relief. To his amazement and confusion, however, only a meagre trickle of dark green pee flowed out. After a second or two the pees aroma wafted upwards and entered his nostrils, 'hmm popcorn!' The tremendous pressure was gone but where was the usual volume of pee that followed its release he wondered.

Like physicians from the time of George the first of England back on Chippenham One, Welder placed a lot of store in recognising if something was not right with his health by the examination and analysis of his excretions. Welder's believed that the natural tendency to take note of whatever his body produced was the remnants of a lost art of self-diagnosis and even more, the ability to read the future. He likened the art to that of a geologist interpreting the past and making predictions of the future through looking at rocks and at the way ocean currents flow. By luck or intuitive understanding of Welder's observations of the subtle variations of his bodily produce were normally spot-on, or at least he thought so. If there was anything untoward about his toilette, then there was something wrong. The thought 'something's up' was his first reaction when seeing the colour and puny flow of his urine. It gave him greater concern than being confronted with genetically generated cartoon-like intelligent cute giggly plant people.

Once Welder had relieved himself he stood motionless enjoying the lack of pressure and concentrated on piecing together what was going on with him, and the situation overall. As he did so he became aware of several beautiful exotic soothing yet exhilarating scents. The caressing warming soft smells were different from that of the Keem or other vapours he had enjoyed up until that point. The new smells were just as completely alien and totally familiar to him as the others. They once again defied definition. He could not draw upon any smell he had ever smelled. There was something different too about the way he smelled them. He had heard that there are countless colours as yet unseen and the same, he soon learnt, was true of smells.

'No, not beautiful' he thought, 'this one is delicious'. It seemed to nourish him and he felt as if he had woken up completely free of a nasty clouding and numbing cold that had blighted him for twenty years. He felt great. He felt great in every way; great in stature, great physically, great operationally and great in being. The smell, the smell was feeding this greatness. The smell was feeding him. It was like a smell of baking cookies or bacon that you could consume and be replenished by. He drew a huge draught of delicious odour through his broadened nostrils then did so again and again. 'It's like a smell that you can eat but without that bloated feeling' he thought. With each deep intake of breath, the smell faded and as it did so his situation came into sharper focus. 'The smell' he thought, *'that's it'. A connecting thread became clear to him as if he had just spotted a tripwire. He looked up and two Keem was looking down had him with their head cocked in curiosity. They were lying face down on a glass dome that Welder was now within. It was a dome within the dome.*

They were not looking at his face, however; they were looking at his penis which had remained hanging out since he had taken a leak whilst deep in thought.

A particularly nice penis Sophie thought.

Welder without embarrassment quickly and efficiently 'adjusted his dress' as the signs in Victorian public toilets would recommend.

'We do beg your pardon. We haven't seen many willies', came a voice in Welder's head.

'We do not have genitals. We don't need them. Perhaps you will choose not to need them yourself in time' continued a different voice through this time audible externally.

'No, you may not need one and for most of the time neither do I, but I think I will keep hold of mine for now' he thought in an attempt to broadcast it to the Keem. He had been trying to figure out whether all of the Keem or just the first speaker was able to communicate telepathically. Keem had some form of telepathic sense, or device or smell induced capability, of that he was sure. He took the lack of giggling in response to his double-entendre from all but the speaker in his head to be an indication that they did not all have the gift. Followed by the thought that maybe they were not all tuned in, or maybe they were under instructions, or maybe they did not all see the humour, or maybe the speaker in his head was giggling at something else. It was clear to Welder that he would have to refine his test. More information was needed and without being too obvious in acquiring it. Welder did not allow any of these deductions to form as coherent verbal thoughts. He simply allowed the

knowledge to float on the surface. Knowing without thinking and using only unformed thoughts was a cerebral art Welder was well practised in. It meant the practitioner could deduce and reason and plan for short bursts without words. Welder found it a useful shield when attached to interrogation or monitoring devices. Almost all of the inhabitants of Welder's isolated outpost home planet of Pittysake 2 were born with the ability but it had to be nurtured. It was a skill that all from the planet knew, without being instructed, to keep to themselves. Not even the company knew he had the gift and he only partly knew himself. He had a variety of other well-honed mental processes of thought control that singled him out for intelligence work when he did his planetary service in the army. He had more than enough ability to have had a glittering career in the forces if it wasn't for the fact that he couldn't stand most of what they stood for. He was very particular about what he would stand for. The company understood his need to operate freely; they saw that his on the ground judgement had never been wrong to date; not once. He was more than a scout; he was a guide. This status was only acknowledged by two individuals at the top of the two wings of the company. There was Sally that recruited him; she was head of the wing that oversaw scientific development. The other wing that kept the company flying tried to recruit him too but Welder could not stand and refused to stand for, this other person. It was Walbran Prawnshot, head of operations.

Welder wondered if his toilet humour was too obscure or too refined for the main body of the Keem. But that didn't explain the one that did giggle. Welder deduced that despite their appearance, silliness and predisposition for laughter, the Keem were not juveniles. Their lack of genitals had no bearing on their capacity for and scope of, *toilet humour. He saw the handprints of tittering scientists in the formation of these creatures.*

'We can communicate through telepathy but don't worry. It is no different to a conversation. The same codes of conduct apply. We cannot read minds; we can hear and respond to thoughts directed towards us and others that occur in conversation. Your private thoughts will remain private as long as you wish them to be. It is the energy readings of your mind that we can pick up on. We cannot tune in to your thoughts we can only hear what your mind broadcasts. It is simply that we receive and perceive all the energy your mind emits and it just happens that some of it we can understand. Language is not an issue as it is the meaning that is inherent in a thought that is decipherable. You transmit the thought of a colour or a feeling and we in our minds find the words. With certain individuals, it works both ways. You are one such individual Welder and that may be why they sent you. Milford Lyme had been most upset that as intelligent as he was, he did not naturally possess such an ability yet his assistant did.'

'You must have known Milford or he must have known you otherwise you would not be here. We could not think together with Milford and he did not mention you by name. He only said someone will come. It was the interface that recognised you. When it said welcome Welder, we were not sure if it was Worlder or Welder. There are many ways to communicate welcome but it's the thought that counts'. The voice of the Keem anticipated a question Welder would have asked and answered himself if he had been given a second. He had time to wonder if the Keem had 'messaging' had predictive thought. He had already decided that they were a hive mind or a root system at the very least.

'Sometimes you will let something slip as if accidentally saying something out aloud to yourself in a public space. It

is completely against our nature to intrude on another's private thoughts' relayed a different Keem. Welder could tell which Keem was addressing him. It was a bright yellow male (at least male in appearance) with particularly large green eyes. It was halfway done the transparent dome and hanging on effortlessly.

Others joined the congregation and conversation. It seemed that they all could hear thoughts and take part but certain rules of etiquette applied.

Welder noticed there was something unusual about his skin. It was speckled all over with coloured dots. They began to grow and swirl about and before any alarm seized him, they were gone. Welder asked 'why the dome?' in deliberate conversational thought. He presumed in a private one that the dome would be strong enough to contain him and that if it wasn't he probably needed to be within it for his good. Then before the Keem answered he relaxed and without realising he was transmitting other thoughts and asked other questions. He was like a ten-year-old energetic enthusiastic child firing out a string of questions in quick succession. The Keem picked up on what he was thinking. Two of the questions he inadvertently placed in the public domain were 'why was my pee green and why was there so little of it?'

'Your biology is changing but don't be alarmed it is being added to give you sustenance. Your natural biology will remain unchanged and retain optimum performance' said the Keem. Although Welder could distinguish only one voice he felt it was all of the Keem speaking with it.

'The dome is for your protection until your biology has been adjusted to cope with longer spells in the home dome'

'Spells?'

The Keem's silence in response to his questioning request for further information indicated that just as when he was

in the column that he entered by, there were things that the
Keem had no response for and simply ignored.

Sophie looked down at her strong young feet. She
slowly lifted her head and she shuddered slightly as her
gaze crossed the line that marked the edge of the two
hundred foot cliff she was high upon. She was about ten
foot back and on safe ground but she wobbled slightly. The
clifftop was bare of all but a patch of tufty grass and areas
of loose fine red gravel over hard rock.

Beyond the edge of the near sheer drop was the
darkness of the shadow cast by the cliff on the beach below.
The early morning sun was still low in the sky and at her
back. The stretched-out shadow extended beyond the gentle
waves breaking on the shore and on to the sea. At the
shadows edge, she sought out and found herself. She
moved her arms as if to be signalling to a passing ship to
rescue her; a half-hearted attempt. But it meant that she was
able to confirm the bump on the cliffs shadow's outline was
her. A deep breath whilst scanning the broad bands of blue
sea and sky and she set off at a brisk pace.

She was headed for a little fishing village about two
miles along the coast and at that early stage in the day was
already contemplating venturing further. Gentle swells of
deep blue were dotted triangular snagged rips of white sails.
Three tankers were just visible silhouetted on the horizon.
A ferry from down the coast was headed its way across the
sea and a fishing boat was making its way back into the
harbour of Sophie's destination. Sophie stopped to pay
homage to the scene from on high before making her slow
descent from the clifftop to the beach. The white sands in
the shallow of the small bay were distinguishable as a patch
of shimmering light blue. It was the blue of a baby's eyes;
reflected sky, clear water and white sands fused as one

colour, blue, pure blue. She desire to swim in that blue was overwhelming.

By the time Sophie arrived at the small inoffensive municipal facility for changing and showering she was hot with the thickening heat of the mid-morning sun and from her accelerated efforts to get to the water. She was so heated that she was momentarily tempted by the three outdoor showers along the Naples yellow-painted concrete wall of the block. Changed into the tiny bikini which was the fashion of that more innocent and time of greater risk, she deliberately slowed herself down to savour her discomfort in the knowledge that relief was there on her command. She neatly arranged her beach towel and paused to stretch before heading for the water. With anticipation growing almost beyond containment she approached the water walking at a steady pace down the ten yards of warming soft sand. She did not alter her pace as she entered the water. Her hot feet tingled with delight. There were barely any waves in the sheltered bay flanked by cliffs. Very soon the force needed to continue at the same pace in the deepening water slowed her. She pushed on until she flopped forward in a half-hearted dive and submerged herself in the cool clear water.

When she emerged from the sea after ten-minute swimming about there were two young men about her age laying out their towels just tolerably close to hers. It was still early and the beach was virtually empty. Wading in the shallows there was an older man with thin white legs that were doing well to support his tanned rotund trunk. His disproportionately large torso emerged in every direction from his black speedos. Standing motionless in still water that only went halfway up his shins and with a shock of grey hair and large shark thin nose he looked like a weird prehistoric wading bird. The dark curly-haired one of the pair of young men glanced at Sophie, who was by then dried off and sitting on her towel and saw that she was looking quizzically towards the sea. Instinctively he traced the line of her gaze to the old man. For a good few minutes, they both watched the old man slowly lifting one leg then the other out of the water in the manner of a crane; each time replacing the leg back down slowly and gently. He continued to carry out a series of bird-like movements with great care and balance as the pair looked on like two curious ornithologists. Sophie and the young stranger then automatically looked at each other with expressions of wonderment which shifted quickly to grimaces of suppressed laughter. A connection was made.

After an hour or so of lying in the sun broken up by three minute swims Sophie was ready to carry on with her walk. The beach had steadily filled. Not to the point of being crowed but it had the secluded character and tranquillity of earlier. Sophie would probably have left earlier but for the presence of the two young men. She had the innate ability that many women have of knowing when a man is looking at her without witnessing them doing so. The boy's attentions were tactful rather than lecherous. In a quiet way, she felt tantalising and tantalised. Sophie did not pay much attention to her natural beauty and her sexual being.

She sat up and took in the scene one last time and just as she was about to get up to leave the dark-haired boy approached with the obvious intention of saying something. There was enough of a connection between them from earlier for neither of them to feel awkward.
'My friend and I are going up to the bar for a game of table football and wondered if you wanted a game' His voice seemed too deep and manly for his slender young frame. A French accent gave the depth of his voice an added richness.

What was soothing to Sophie's ear made him beautiful to the eye and to her surprise she said yes.

'How did you know I was English?'

'I didn't. I thought you were American. My name is Christian and my friend's name is Nick'

Sophie was suddenly aware of her firm nipples and barely covered breasts and Christian's polite determination not to look at them whilst standing above her and looking down towards her. He tilted his head to one side in a quizzical fashion. Sophie caught on.

'Oh my name is Sophie'

There was an empty moment but no unease.

'We'll wait for you on the road'

The second that the youth turned away Sophie regretted saying yes and started preparing excuses for a quick exit. Rinsed off and packed up Sophie joined Christian and Nick who were sitting on a wall in the shade on the other side of the street. The bitumen of the road radiated heat and Sophie had a hankering for a cold 'Orangina'.

Nick broke the ice with standard questions made less mundane to Sophie by his soft almost whispering German-accented voice.

'Do you like table football, Sophie?' Nick asked

'I don't think I've ever played it. It never looked that interesting to me but to be fair the lads I have seen playing it seem to enjoy it'

After two Oranginas and three tournaments, Sophie decided that she liked table football. She never reached for her well-rehearsed excuse for taking her to leave. She had found what she was looking for; an opportunity to stop making or carrying out plans, to be spontaneous. She would never have guessed what she needed and could never have planned for it to happen if she did. The bar was halfway up the slope leading out of the village. The threesome sat in the shade of vines in the courtyard out back and looked over the sheet of blue sea.

The conversation about music, politics, art and religion were similar to the ones Sophie had enjoyed over the past three years at University. Somehow hearing the points she had heard many times before in German and French accents gave them renewed gravitas. There was a true bond of liberal student solidarity between them. The voices of Christian and Nick caressed her sensibilities like the cool sea breeze. The bar only served barely passable ham baguettes but also the most wonderful cold bottles of beer Sophie had ever had.

'One more tournament?' suggested Nick once their appetites for food and the view were replete. It was whilst playing the last tournament of table football that Sophie would ever play that she found herself drawn physically to the young lean men. First, their hands as they skillfully and forcefully twisted and jerked at the handles of the game. Then she was drawn to the mechanics of their tanned slim muscular arms and then finally to their torsos which were easily visible as both of them wore short-sleeved button shirts open at the front. Their torsos looked sleek and lithe. Daniel did not come into Sophie's mind as the attraction was an innocent one that she had no intention of acting on. Nothing else other than the moment she was living came into Sophie's mind either.

Christian mentioned that there was a fort on top of the hill in the other direction to the one Sophie entered the bay. Once Nick had yet again won the table football they set off for the fort. By the time they returned to the village the sun was resting exactly on the horizon. They returned to the bar and watched it sink. This mark of time gave voice to a growing realisation in Sophie,

116

'I better head off you two' she said with genuine reluctance.
'How about one more swim before you go? You can catch the bus back' suggested Nick
'Why not Sophie the last bus is not for two hours' reinforced Christian
Sophie felt sticky from the afternoon's walk and a swim was exactly what she wanted.
'Okay why not indeed'
They eagerly made their way down to the beach. The cool beers after hours of walking in the sun had a more giddying effect than those at lunch.
Swimming at night after drinking, alone on a beach with two men, she had only met that day; Sophie was smart enough to know the warning signs of potential dangers of her situation, but they did not flash brightly enough, or ring loud enough for her to pay attention to them. She had surrendered her will to the moment for the first time on her European adventure.

The trio did not spend time discussing it beforehand and reaching a join decision about going into the water naked, they just quickly and efficiently peeled off all their clothes and ran down the beach naked laughing and crashed into the water like ungainly geese. The water was surprisingly cool and they did not stay in long.

There was no awkwardness as they ran back up the beach in an unofficial race to the towels with their sleek wet bodies shimmering in the moonlight. The breeze chilled them as they retrieved their towels. As if it was essential for their survival they huddled together with Sophie in the middle engulfed in towels and arms. She put her arms around Christian's waist and held herself tightly against him. She only really noticed at that point how much taller and larger than her they both were. She released one arm and used it to pull Nick to her so that she was sandwiched between the two of them. She did it as if she was in danger of getting hyperthermia and she had no choice; only their bodies could save her. They naturally fit together in a balanced structure that supported them. They went silent. They were comforted. All their youthful indignation at the wrongs of the world, all their teenage angst all that irritated, upset, disturbed or troubled them was gone.

Sophie pulled her head away from Christian's warm chest and kissed him softly on the lips. Simultaneously she reached behind and once again pulled Nick to her.

Chapter Eight

Projection

Welder had visited and worked on more planets than he could care to remember. He was given the exact number once, by his girlfriend of the time who worked in Operations Data and Development. She was the one relationship he had been in that lasted longer than six months. He was seldom the one to end a fledgling relationship. The type of intelligent sensitive women that found him attractive would usually sense early on that he was happier in his own company, most of the time; and he was. They were usually the one to make the first move and the last one.

Sophie never told anyone about the full story of her happy day on the coast; not even her closest friends; not even her closest confidant, her sister. Sophie was able to keep parts of her life so private because she did not even acknowledge she was doing so to herself. She would avoid confronting embarrassment, pain and most of all confusion, by keeping seemingly disparate events stored away and then neatly sealed in them saying to herself 'everybody has their secrets'. Her great mind created elaborate diversions to avoid breaking the seal containing events. Sophie's habit in life of skipping over those private or painful parts appeared to be continuing in death. But in death, it was just happened to work out that way. After all, such moments represented only a small fraction of her conscious life. There was no fear in death; only facts. There was no pain only information. To her parents, Sophie's years at university had been happy ones as evidenced by her exemplary grades and the elevated entry points she made in the organisations she worked for.

Given the choice, there was more than enough to explore in her vaults for Sophie to leave certain boxes sealed, not with the seal of approval but with her fear of the lack of it. As her memories unwound she jumped ahead many years and passed over times which only she would have considered to be blighted with blotches on a backdrop of achievement. Naturally to her independent living self at the time she didn't want anyone to see these blotches, botches and stains. This was not a factor in the lines of weave she was following. Each thread had to be pursued to the end whether the image of angst that Sophie had assigned the experience in question, was part of was true or imagined. Each line had its course. She had no choice and no box would be left unopened whether she looked into it or not.

Sophie sat in the passenger seat of her car, just to check it out for later. She got out, went around looking inside as she did so, and then got back in behind the wheel.

As Sophie joined her former self she noted that she seemed to detect something; maybe she was aware she was being watched. Often during her life, Sophie had experienced the feeling of déjà vu, or odd moments of feeling a presence, or a cold shiver. She was not alone in having such feelings and not alone in dismissing them, but not completely.

Sophie was so unaware of how long she had been sitting in quiet contemplation that she checked the clock on the dashboard. Six forty-six; not even a minute had passed. She started the car and headed to work. Sophie was well-liked and well respected by the team of office workers she was in charge of. Her almost obsessive attention to detail and her rigid systems were not universally liked but it was universally accepted that they got results. Everyone benefitted from those results, both financially and in the pride, they felt in being part of the best performing team in the division. She was considered young to hold her position at twenty-eight but she had an air of authority and a calm manner that put people at their ease in her company. Her work wardrobe perfectly communicated her efficient professionalism. Her fine brunette hair was always a shining sculptural form held tightly in place on top of her head. She had pronounced elegant dark eyebrows that were like two perfectly shaped Chinese calligraphic marks representing wings. Her hazel large eyes were darker and greener on the edge with brighter amber centres. Lipstick, barely darker pink than the tone of own lips, was surprisingly effective at defining their shapely form that was neither thin nor full. She was far prettier than most people realised but it was well known that she had a hard and fast rule not to fraternise with people from work and she steadfastly refused to join in any socializing. This was not merely in adherence to the idea of keeping her work life and her personal life separate from some sort of ethical standpoint or management maxim; she simply did not care too much for socialising.

She did hold a new year's party every year, however, and her people from work mingled happily with her people from the close, members of her book club, a country cousin who annoyingly turned up without fail each year and the occasional friend from university. She was the perfect host of the perfect party in her beautiful home. She had a passion for theatre and hiking which she shared with two other completely separate yet close groups of friends; neither of these groups were ever invited to her annual party and the separate parties never crossed paths.

These various groups all liked, loved and respected Sophie in various measures. Those that were given the chance to mingle regularly at her new-years parties but none of them saw each other in the intervening year.

There was a man; a charming erudite and cultured man that most people wrongly assumed was her love interest. There was interest but no love which seemed to suit them both, even when they occasionally slept together.

There was normally between sixteen and twenty workers in the open planned office that Sophie had a clear view of from her glass cubicle office. One side of the office was glass from floor to ceiling and opposite was a wall of notice boards with coloured pins on coloured charts that charted all the activity undertaken in the office. The first hint of anything being out of place was a polite notice that Sophie's 'hardy annual' party was cancelled. No reason was given.

The cause of the cancellation was a problem with roots that ran deep. Sophie had simply been cutting back any evidence of the problem that surfaced. But the roots remained and grew larger and spread further.

Reluctantly Sophie agreed to a request from her line manager that she knew she had to accept. She was to give a new employee from another division a lift to his new home for a couple of days and use it as an opportunity to make him feel welcome. This new employee had been sent from head office and Sophie's paranoid line manager had even less say in accepting him on board than Sophie had in becoming his ride for a few days. Sophie cringed at the ambiguous expression on her immediate superior's face when she used the term 'ride', suggesting a double entendre without committing to it. Certain layers of operational structure in the company, the ones Sophie had initiated and implemented were the most progressive and efficient in the world at that time, and for that matter in history to that point. But her revolutionary systems proved impossible to put in place in particular levels of management. The higher up in the company you went the harder it was to find people capable of using Sophie's many models. Sophie's boss wanted Sophie to give this new young man from head office a lift home and get to know him. She wanted some intelligence; she was compelled to get some intelligence; intelligence on this 'hotshot' who was sent to get some intelligence on her.

He was, in fact, a perfectly 'lovely young man'. Sophie chastised herself for using a phrase her mother would have and forgave herself. She had still not reached the point of forgiving herself for being middle class. The 'newbie' was in his early twenties who rather strangely Sophie thought, had never learnt to drive. He knew full well that Sophie's line manager had organised a lift to gather information on him and said so right off the bat. This put them both at their ease and the task became a pleasurable one for Sophie.

On the morning of the third day she found herself looking forward to the end of the day and chatting with young Richard whose looks seemed to match his Greek sounding surname. Her unostentatious silver-grey executive car was clean and comfortable. The pair glided along in conversation and Sophie was pleased when she saw a traffic-jam ahead as it would extend their time together. Her commodious climate-controlled car with its added extra of young Richard was as pleasant enough a place to be as any Sophie could think of. They slowed to a crawl behind an almost identical car. As they were discussing a shared love of Cajun music traffic had come to a standstill and, THUMP! They were jolted forward and then back with their heads hitting the padded headrests simultaneously. The sound of crunching cracking and shattering of metal and glass lasted a drawn-out second as Sophie's car was ploughed in to from behind. Fortunately, the car behind had not been travelling fast enough to be injurious to the couple, but fast enough to shunt Sophie's car into the rear of the one in front. They both noted just how loud a noise and just how great of a force even minor shunts made though neither of them said anything. The motion and sound was repeated, though less loudly and less violently three more times in a series of aftershocks as other cars were also caught out going slightly too fast to stop in time to avoid a collision. The exact sequence of who hit who first and why was definite but not obvious to those involved; especially in the fog of 'no claims' and other insurance considerations.

Sophie reached into her glove-box for her insurance papers and with remarkable calm told Richard she would be as quick as she could. In her hurry, she did not close the glove compartment fully and it fell open as she closed the car door behind her. Richard fully expected to see it filled with junk and rubbish, for he suspected (as did many of her staff) that she was a messy person in disguise. Or maybe she simply had some hidden counterpoints to the fastidious side of her nature such as a chest of drawers or a room where chaos reigned. These were only half baked suspicions and Richard was fully prepared to accept that Sophie's character, in respect of ordering her environment, was homogeneous and as it appeared, obsessively neat. The lit interior of the glove-box was as immaculate and seemed to confirm the latter view. It was as immaculate as any other observable reflection of Sophie's life. There was a torch, spare phone and charger, documents and everything you would expect, neatly stored. Her neatness and efficiency never had a hint of casualness about it; it carried her hallmark. But as Richard went to close the diorama of practicality, something caught his eye. It was a polished turquoise disc a little larger and thicker than a two-pound coin. He picked it up and it had the satisfying weight and smoothness of something of great value. It had a red rose in relief in the centre within a circle of text which read 'Clarence House Casino'. In clear dark writing beneath the rose was a pound sign followed by the number twenty thousand.

Sophie could read her past mind preparing to explain a simple matter that would none the less be easily misunderstood. She stood at the front of her car clearly stating to the driver of the car she had been pushed in to, that her doing so was a result of the car behind her shunting her car forward and that therefore the driver who was now talking to the driver of the car that hit him, the driver that had hit her, was responsible. Sophie was still reading her mind or perhaps it was being read to her. She could also see through her former vision exactly what she saw back then. As she and the other driver looked back along the line of cars she saw Roger holding the chip curiously; something at the time had not registered.

She found herself back at the wheel of that non-descript executive car that she resented liking. She could not help but like it for all its comforts and generally pleasurable ride. There beside her was Richard. She felt superimposed on the memory yet more a part of it than she had up until that point. During the built up to the incident she had been a passenger, an observer. Looking back at him sitting there, he looked so ordinary yet the warmth of her past self's attraction to him was blissful. Yet his image had no depth to it. How did he end up playing such a significant part in her life? The question did not belong to the young women driving in the warm bubble of attraction and it flickered for a moment and disappeared. God, it had been such a rare feeling in her life, she reflected; even back then when there were so many more opportunities. Why hadn't she acted on her feelings? This she could not recollect. She was eager to find out and went along for the ride. There was so much she had forgotten and missed, she couldn't wait to turn the next page.

As she coursed through her past questions randomly flashed on and off like a fluorescent light in the last sparks of life. What's happening to me? I'm dead! It's all there, but I am gone. Am I me or someone else experiencing me? Then THUMP! It was the multiple thuds of being hit from behind. She had skipped back. She wanted to stay in the car with Richard; she was scared and felt safer with him. This was another layer of the same event. Events unreeled just as they had occurred before, though she felt as if they were happening for the first time. She was once again struck by the detail of the record of moments she had long since forgotten; it was a lucid moment. As she watched her past-self dealing with the repercussions of the shunt once again she could see Richard putting the gaming token back in the glove box. He did not mention it when she got back in the car. He so accurately acted as if he had not seen it that she believed back then that he hadn't. They continued on their journey and Richard gave no clue that he had peeked into Sophie's private world too soon. It was this lack of control of circumstances between them that was the reason why Sophie never acted on her feelings for Richard. Self-preservation kicked in and kicked out any idea of making a move, though she was not aware of it at the time. Her feeling for him on that day passed into memory less than a week after she stopped giving him a lift home. She had gone off him and did not know why.

At this natural punctuation in Sophie's reminiscing the narrator's voice came in as if he had been standing behind her the whole time and waiting for an opportune moment to cut in without alarming her.

'Don't be scared. You are regaining your faculty for asking questions and your impulse to figure things out. It may get a little overwhelming at times. Being dead is not the end of the story for you, remember? I have another little something I want you to stick in the pot with the other bits I've chucked in there already. Then after a few more ingredients and when the mixture is ready, then you can have a taste; then you will get to taste the truth. And let me tell you it is a taste like nothing you ever tasted in life. You won't be able to describe it. You have no point of reference, nothing to compare it to. You will know it though, the truth that is, and that smell, you will know the smell. You will know the truth a taste and a smell, not a thought, not to begin with. The fear that comes with asking questions will fade when you cease to fear the answers. The feeling that what your life was is being chewed over? Well, how soon

that feeling passes depends on how many tough bits there are to chew on.'

There was a pause as if the narrator had plunged himself into a pool of thought; their private pool, and had got out and was drying himself off before carrying on.

'How shall I put this? Do you remember those times when you were walking done a busy street and for no apparent reason you look across the road and see a friend who at that precise moment looked up and sees you. Everyone has intuition; it is the minds way of speeding things up. It draws on unconscious and conscious data. That's why it is almost impossible to rationalise it consciously. You don't always have time to reason things out. There is nothing magical about it. There are reasons why you look up and there are reasons you choose to recognise what you do. The interesting bit is the difference between experiencing something for the first time and chewing it over later and what happens to that information in the meantime. When something is held in the unconscious waiting to be used or processed it likes to remind you it's there from time to time; good and bad. Humankind would not have survived if it stopped to reason out every decision it had to take. It would have in fact, been eaten. Apart from anything else, it takes a long time for people to reason things out beyond gut feelings and once the immediate threat or need for urgency goes mostly people don't bother. In the course of early history, many leaches died and many holes were drilled into heads before people begun to figure some basics out. Eventually, humanity relied more and more on reason and less and less on intuition; they swung too far the other way. They wouldn't let themselves believe in two things at the same time even when they did. Too often decisions were made purely on principle rather than experience. People even began to see intuition as some kind of inferior animal

*state and that ultimately enlightenment could only reveal
itself through conscious rational understanding alone.
Conscious thought is good at describing the ingredients of
cheesecake and can tell you how many calories it has but
you have to eat it to know what it tastes like. Intuition isn't
the whole answer either, it must be said; it works well
enough in life at least. It is useful in those situations where
you hear someone say afterwards, 'I didn't think about it, I
just acted. I am no hero'. It is such a sophisticated intricate
process that no one can go around with their intuition
turned up on full all the time. The good news for the living
is that intuition can be exercised and strengthened. It can
be developed to the point that not only do you look up and
see your friend across the road; you can sense them think
your name when they notice you. You just need to tune in or
tune the other stuff out to be more accurate. Not all the
energy of thought is trapped by bone heads. Think of all the
signals there are in someone's living room. The wifi, the
television, radio, and phone signals are all still there
whether you have the hardware to pick them up or not.
They are the sound vision and information about the
elephant in the room. People's brains are in constant
communication with themselves and that takes a process.
That process takes energy and it leaves traces. With enough
sensitivity, those traces can be interpreted just like sound
waves. It's all about transferring information'
The narrator sensed he was losing Sophie; not because she
was uninterested, she was being drawn. She was being
drawn like water from a well, as well as like a moth to a
flame.
'Okay I know this may seem a bit of a leap but let's try
something different. Let's say that two people are
connected, like twins for example. You sometimes hear of
one twin burning themselves and the other feeling the pain*

128

at the same time whilst oceans apart. I want to put in the pot the idea that, if two beings were to be somehow telepathically connected, and we know almost anything is bound to occur somewhere in the universe eventually, then their thoughts and sensations could occur to both parties simultaneously. It is not that thought between two telepaths is faster than the speed light relaying visually decipherable information; it is that such thoughts do not travel between two points; they happen at the same time; speed does not enter into it. It is simply two things happening at the same time. Now imagine these two beings, or indeed connected creations are many light years apart with their attentions focused on the worlds of the other. And now imagine these worlds establish a line of communication through a system of relay stations. Once set up communication is as fast as imaginable but still takes many years between; but not for our twins. They could be made aware of what was in a communique long before it arrives if their telepathic skills were honed enough. If they kept their abilities hidden they could use their forethoughts to get up to all sorts of mischief. That is a little something to taste, an exotic looking vegetable that will be more palatable once the other half is baked. There are of course more fact-based fictional vegetables but they don't have as much flavour as some of your homegrown theoretical ones. We are all leaves on the same tree and when the wind blows we sing together. We are all nourished by the same sun and rising sap. Yes, we are connected; how could we not be?'

'Welder was bewildered but holding himself together pretty well. He noticed that he had no will to break out of the dome within a dome, but did not feel under threat within it for now. He assumed that the variety of intoxicating smells he was experiencing were just that, vapours containing something to keep him intoxicated and under control.

Welder made his way to the centre of the dome which spanned twenty metres or so at its base. The floor was covered with one of the company's earliest successes, a carpet of immaculate grass. To fund their pet project the company developed a range of products and materials; all grown and all spin-off from or contributors to the development of the Keem. Beneath Welders feet was a lush thick grass that never grew longer than the perfect height for the 'lawn you want without mowing'. A variety of heights were available. The maximum height of the grass was the height required. They developed a plant that produced a container shaped leaf that was ideal as a kitchen compost bin that could be thrown into the garden compost bin and break down along with its contents. Avoiding the need to wash kitchen compost containers proved very popular. All of the company's products, even the homegrown furniture were grown in sealed hydroponic centres that were completely self-contained and self-sustaining. The centres generated their power and needed very little, other than water and light. The commercial side of the company and the personal research of the founders and their descendants fed each other throughout the company's long endless path of success and expansion during the first and second ages. But a schism grew along with the company's success. One wing was the commercial interests and the other was the research wing. The commercial administrative side was a huge but flexible organisation with connections far, wide and deep across the galaxy. It was difficult to remain ignorant of the company and its stated aim to a cohesive force of well-being for all life through the generation and distribution of wealth (the word accumulation was dropped early on) Countless billions of people, whole planets of them, were in the service of the company. The other side of the company was a small idiosyncratic association of genii and their individual support teams with no set objectives and deeply held belief in something they were yet to determine. They competed to be the truer force of goodness and light which was good news for consumers.

New talented recruits made their choice as to which wing of the company they became part of and enmity towards the other wing was pretty much compulsory. Everyone knew that both wings were necessary to keep air-born and that it was the tension between the factions that generated forward momentum. Welder had no loyalties other than to Sally and that loyalty sprang from an altogether different source.

The transparent cloche that Welder was beneath was slightly tinted for health and safety reasons; the organic glass-like living material exuded its cleaning enzyme that left the grass-glass undetectable to the naked human eye, so tinting was necessary to avoid walking into it. The self-cleaning glass was another of the company's early breakthroughs. It was developed by the Boob's eldest daughter Maple. Once the company latched on to the idea of developing new materials that could be grown rather than manufactured there was no stopping them.

Within the Dome, there was a mound-shaped like an easy chair under a covering of company uniform grass. There was a boulder slightly bigger than Welder from which water sprang, or more accurately trickled from. It flowed from veins of fine cracks and fed a circular pool a little broader than the base of the boulder. And there was the plant which Welder had personally watered earlier. It had the trunk of a tree fern with two stumpy bows which gave it human proportions and a huge closed lilac coloured bloom roughly twice the size of a human head and growing from between the two branches just where you expect to see *ahead. The greater part of the area within the hemisphere was open space and reminded Welder of the organic hotel lobbies that were in fashion two centuries earlier. Welder was calm and had completed his assessment of what had occurred thus far.*

'Now what?' thought Welder expecting an answer, and he got one.

'A short film' replied a Keem, communicating through thought.

'Here's the science' said another followed by collective chuckles.

Welder with a clamped smile puffed out a laugh in a single snort through his nose.

In the open area of the dome light flickered into a shape, then a form as the three-dimensional projection of a figure pulled itself together. Welder immediately recognised the holographic image that appeared before him as that of Milford Lyme.

'I thought I'd find you here'. Welder said this out loud, quickly aloud but to himself. He noted a feeling that the Keem did not seem to hear his thoughts if they were expressed out loud and quietly under his breath. By doing this he could cut them out of his conversations with himself.

'I knew they'd send you Welder' started the much larger than life-sized recording of Milford Lyme 'Thank god I could rely on Sally's good sense and send you. The Keem would not have fired up the tapes if it wasn't you so no it's not clever guesswork on my part; just clever planning. Anyone other than you or my Sister would have been turned in to compost and gone down the shoot and not up the column. Your historical bio scans and company profile are what was needed' Welder tingled with the idea of alarm rather than the cramped painful discomfort of the feeling of it. An image of the Company's silent CEO and sister of

Milford came into Welder's mind. Welder was attracted to Sally Lyme in every possible way one human being could be attracted to another. But as is often the case with even those with the greatest facility for communication, when it came to expressing his feelings he was struck dumb in the presence of the source of those feelings. Welder was not alone in thinking she was 'pretty hot' for a hundred and twenty-year-old. On the other hand, looking at the accurate hologram Welder thought her younger by twenty years brother looked a mess as he appeared before him. He had not kept up with his cellular regeneration payments.

'Ticking all the boxes was never going to be enough; it was my sister's gut feeling that convinced me that you would be the best person for the job, and my sister's gut feelings are as infallible as any empirically-based decisions I have ever come across. No, you are the only person other than her for the job.'

Milford was sitting on a stool at some kind of breakfast bar with a tankard of coffee and an uneaten muffin in front of him. He was surrounded by floating formulas diagrams icons of film clips and images, mostly of the Keem. He swept away the information that he had been perusing with the slightest of sweeping movements of his hand. It looked like important data that had been hurriedly browsed through at the last minute before a meeting. He left the stool and approached the recording device. The hologram of Milford grew as he did so he became like a huge and animated sculpture from the waist up. The truncated apparition was twice Welder's height and gave Milford's thin stooped and stripy pyjama clad body the grandeur of a wise ethereal deity.

'Cheap trick' thought Welder and as he looked up at Milford's sagging jowls. He noticed all the Keem lying flat and face down on the top of the dome looking in. Welder

felt like he was at the bottom of a pool and the Keem were snorkelers looking down at him. It made him feel like pond life, perhaps even a sea monkey. The visualization shrank to actual size and Welder wondered whether it was he or they (the Keem) or Milford that had changed the projections settings.

'You better take a seat Welder' said Milford gesturing Welder towards the verdant easy-chair. A seat came in to view for Milford next to Welder who wasted no time in taking his. There was a stoic calm yet warmth in Milford's voice. Milford smelled the large open purple bloom of the plant Welder had pissed on earlier whose image stood not ten feet away from the real plant. The present-day bloom had also opened and unfurled into a magnificent flower the size of a round, seats four, sized dinner table. The smell was extraordinary; not sweet, more like a cooking pizza. Welder was too engrossed in the recording to notice the delicious smell did not make him feel hungry. Most smells, even his gas made him feel hungry.

Milford put his elbows on his knees and clasped his hands together forming a triangular support on which he placed his chin. He was leaning forward in his thoughtful rigid triangulated stable structure on a low chair. The articulation of Milford's body looked as if it had been contrived by an artist's eye to give an impression of a profound discourse of depth and intimacy taking place. This measured seriousness of Milford, though still in his pyjamas needed Welder to be seated pensively opposite and leaning forward in anticipation of the words that would spring forth from the craggy rock face of the great man. Thus making the artist's composition complete. And Welder obligingly cast himself in just such a role. Welder thought, 'I think some serious shit is going to hit the fan'. When Welder first heard the expression, 'the shit is going to hit the fan' he guessed its origins and came up with a theory that satisfied him enough to feel comfortable using it and not research it any further. Despite his name, Welder had virtually no knowledge of physical engineering and the virtually obsolete piece of apparatus known as a fan. Welder thought the saying related to someone about to receive important news. Sitting in front of the great Milford Lyme, Welder's decision to use the phrase was appropriate. In Welder's peripheral vision he could see the Keem above him nodding in stern agreement with Welder's thought. The Keem did, however, know exactly what the saying truly meant.

Milford lifted his head and looked around as if afraid the secret he was about to divulge would be overheard by the wrong people. Leaning even further forward with the prop for his head lowered he looked to the place where he had calculated Welder would be sitting. His whole demean was of someone about to confess something; something huge. He was like a man with a once-only chance to pass on the great wisdom of his people to the chosen one of the new generation. He said in a calm low soft, but not whispering voice,
'You have got to destroy the Keem. They must be dealt with'

Welder had been staring at Milford's eyebrows which projected out like plate fungi from his furrowed brow. A horseshoe of long white hair circled the bald and sweaty top of Milford's head. Welder was so transfixed by a bead of sweat that was slowly making its way to the tip of Milford's large hooked nose that it took a moment or two to take on board what he had just heard. Milford's head dropped slightly after delivering his pronouncement and the droplet of sweat raced down the final part of the ridge of his nose and reached the end. It formed a droplet and

135

hung tantalisingly like a loose tooth holding on by a thread. It was not clear to Welder how it was managing to cling on. At the moment the droplet was about to drop the hologram disappeared in an instant; too quickly to catch the drop plummeting to its splattering journey's end. High Definition holograms conveyed so much more visual information than the real world; many more times more than what could be taken in by the human eye. So much so that Welder often became mesmerised by some detail or another and not concentrating on what could have been conveyed in on a tape machine. Welder assimilated information in the tangible world completely differently. This was the main reason he preferred to deal with people face to face and not because he was a technophobe as many had wrongly assumed. Failing the real thing, he found flat format visuals meant he could focus on the detail of the point at hand rather than a super real irrelevance. He was particular about where and when he chose to be impressed by anything. He did not like his responses manipulated or predetermined; a defence against being easily distracted. He loved technology really; he simply found it overpowering at times. All of these thoughts and feelings were contained in the infinitesimally small moment before the absence of the hologram and what had been said hitting him. The big picture came in to view in Welder's mind's eye as soon as the last image of Milton was channelled through his body's one.

He looked up at the Keem looking down at him. They appeared completely unconcerned by the message Welder had just received.

'Aren't you concerned?' Welder asked out aloud deciding that for now, he would retain the use of his voice.

'Is that why you have me in this dome? You know I will make up my mind about what needs to be done here. I have

not come to any conclusions yet. I should also point out that if I don't report back in person to Sally she will pop this bubble' Welder noticed his voice lacked authority. It had lost some of its depth and the richness that made it compelling. There was no threat or menace in his voice to support his intuitive negotiating and tactical nouse, which had come in to play.

There was no response and he wondered if they had understood him. Maybe they simply did not have a response. He also wondered if Milford had taken all of this into consideration and was trying to guide his thoughts. 'And maybe... maybe I should be more careful about what I think by not trying to second guess and interfere with what I have in mind'. He concluded that he would learn more and think less for the time being. 'Too late Welder' the voice of a Keem that he had not heard before cut in and snipped the thread Welder was following.

Welder was looked up and for the first time the Keem, who were looking inquisitively dispassionately down at him had a menacing air. They were spread out in random formation like giant moths on the outside of a skylight and he was the light. They reminded him of sharks circling above and he was a bottom fish. He felt it was safe so he let go and allowed these and other thoughts to drift to the surface as if they were escaping bubbles. The idea of a bottom fish made him chuckle. The Keem joined in and soon splashed around with laughter.

Chapter Nine

Milford Lyme

Each time Sophie returned and retuned to some part of her past it was clearer than before. She was experiencing it more directly, more truthfully and with a fuller understanding of events and feelings. She began to realise she could pause her recollections for purposes of reflection and then start them again at will. She noticed too, that there were chunks of time she never returned to or were missing. The thought that they were missing did not bother her, which she found curious. She returned to some events over and over until she felt she understood the truth of what had happened in a way that she would never have in a million years of living.

'What is a million miles? Many cars have driven a million miles. A million miles away, a million miles from home, a million miles from the truth, not so far really. What about a million words, ten novels, not that hard to imagine. Or a million thoughts; a million thoughts and a million more all easily contained on a memory stick; on a stick from a branch, on a tree in a grove. On a stick, in a stick, not even a stick and not even a splinter not even a speck in your eye. Yes, your one in a million and you are also one of a million; millions of millions of grains of sand. A grain that can be opened up and all the wisdom of the ages there-in unearthed, and translated into words that are in the grain of wood on another stick; transfer, transform, extrapolation, information, time and space, for the time being.'

In the background of her thoughts like the landscapes in the background of the Mona Lisa and her fellow renaissance subjects was a growing light from a distant valley. A valley far away, far ahead in the distance; a growing awareness she was moving towards something. It was the sense of having future thought. She felt she more like a pre-thought; that her life was from before. New flower beds were beginning to show the first spikes of green pricking the air. It was a sense of excitement and trepidation. It was the brightness from the energy of life so great it stunned her. She thought that nothing she could do would speed up the process of growth or passage forward. She was a watched kettle wanting to boil; wanting to turn to steam and boil away. She knew she was dead though she did not believe it. 'Maybe I am preparing or being prepared to be born again? Maybe I am coming back to life. Am I drowning? The light began to dim a little and she knew she had to stop asking too many questions. 'Not yet, it is too soon'. Looking directly at the light was making it fade she thought. But she was wrong. It was not her striving forward that made the light dim; she had no bearing on it. The impulse to progress, to strive, to move forward welled up once more. Sophie began to seek but she did not seek the light. She felt the need to listen. To progress, she had to stop and listen.

'Milford embraced his Sister Sally. She was immensely proud of her little brother and was not at all fazed by the knowledge that the feeling was not fully reciprocated. That particular brand of pride was more the preserve of an older Sibling. She saw Milford on the day he was born and watched him grow. Feelings of displacement and rivalry were pushed to one side to make room for the growing love she felt for her cute baby brother. Milford was a scientist; more than that he was an artist who practised the art of science. Milford saw that it was inevitable that Sally would be at the head of the largest commercial conglomerate the galaxy had ever known, 'The Company'. He knew because he felt it and then did the maths; it had to be her. She was not the CEO of the company, its public face, the face that the public saw and thought of when they personified the company. That individual was Wallbran Prawnshot and he had been at the helm for over a century. No one knew about Sally. Wallbran's hold of the wheel was unshakable and his authority absolute; almost. He was an unsurpassed genius in the practice of all of the administrative arts. He and he alone on his side of the fence knew the secret of the company's other brain. The division at the company's core that would separate into its two brains happened very early in its history. As soon as the company reached global dimensions the smaller brain separated from the larger one

to maintain the company's evolution along ethical, moral, and virtuous lines. But unlike the Stegosaurus who was so large that it needed an extra small brain to help with operations at the rear, like the backside of a pantomime horse, the company's smaller brain was not subservient to the larger. It was the smaller brain that was first on the scene and truly in control. It was the smaller brain that allowed the larger to grow. Sally's predecessor told her that the brain she would be in charge of was safely located up its own ass where no would look, and if they did, no one would take it seriously. Wallbran alone knew that he had a boss; that he was the number two. This was a fact that ate away at him, deep inside where the secret lay attached to his gut; near his ass, like the Stegosaurus' extra brain. If undisturbed it presented no problem and his natural gastric juices would keep it in check. But it was shots of energy from those parts of his gut connected to his ego that would make it a flare-up. It would flare up like the galaxy's own ulcer. And anytime he had dealings with the hidden brain of the company it flared up. Sure Wallbran was in charge of the day to day running of the company but Sally was the one with the power to pull the plug the strings and ultimately the rug from under him. Systems were in place that generations of 'number two's' like Wallbran sort to remove or circumvent but every possible way was locked down. All legal and other safeguards that could be conceived off were in place. It had been that way ever since Bobby Green decided to oversee the legal framework of the company to protect research and development funding and hide the 'pet project' from the world. The only world he knew about at the time anyway. A structure grew from that point that was so intertwined with all aspects of the company that any attempts to remove it would lead to the company's complete collapse. Wallbran knew the two parts of the company were like two plants that had grown wrapped around each other with each plant reliant on the other to remain standing.

Milford knew Sally's strengths, and there were many. She had interpersonal skills that were so refined there was never any awareness of them being employed. But she knew. She had the artistry of a footballer who employs amazing skills effortlessly or a musician that can pick up any instrument and play it almost instantly. She used analytical ways of thinking that Milford never used or thought to exercise. He was happy not to be in Sally's game. She had strength and skills and ways of thinking that Milford did not possess in the first place, unused or not. This two Milford knew and admired. Any sense of rivalry or innate competitiveness Milford had was reserved for those in his specialist field of genetic engineering. There was no sibling rivalry.

'How handsome he looks', thought Sally. A few weeks short of his hundredth birthday Milford was in his physical prime with a slender tall lithe physique and excellent deportment. His fine iron-grey hair made him appear stronger rather than older. Not the image that would flicker into life in front of Welder only a few years later. When Sally saw him for what she feared could be the last time he was a striking figure. He had never needed or desired much in the way of physical enhancement though he had free access to any treatment there was. Ninety-nine per-cent of the galaxy's population worked their life away in the hope of being able to afford life-extending procedures of cellular regeneration that were free to Milford. Extended longevity remained down the millennium the preserve of the better off. Sally was set to change all that and it was her secret goal since she had been struck by the gravity of life's inequities whilst watching the news at the age of seven. It dropped on her head like Newton's apple but more significantly into her lap along with the opportunity to do something about it. It became her secret mission, the secret drive that had given her the edge on all her rivals. It also eased her own conscious when it came to using procedures herself. In her case, it was longevity that would give her more of a chance to effect change as one of the few people in the galaxy that could. Superficial improvements in her appearance in her case were not sort after; it was performance that mattered to Sally. And not giving the game away by wearing any hint of her true beliefs on her face. To not use treatments would be a 'tell'.

Sally's thick black hair rippled gleamed and flowed down to the centre of her back. It was drawn away from her face with a side parting like the dark cover on a freshly made bed pulled back in preparation for a comfortable sleep and revealing the fair fresh soft sheet complexion of her face. Her face was as alluring and comforting as a comfortable bed to a weary traveller. She was twenty years older than Milford and thanks to science that Milford declined, already looked ten years younger. Sally drew back from their embrace then leaned her face close to Milford's and looked deep into his green languid eyes. Milford wriggled slightly and attempted several times to look away but was pulled back by Sally's tractor beam stare.

'What?' He said hoping that speech would disrupt the gravity of her gaze. After being reeled in, his eyes were locked into hers and he was motionless. They were connected and Sally communicated all she needed to about the importance of what they were about to discuss and her feelings for him in that intense and profoundly moving look; pay attention please my darling brother, pay attention this is big.

A tear rolled over Milford's high cheekbone and down the hollow of his cheek. Milford had no idea how long they had stood there, he was only aware of an inner warmth and security and a clear focused mind. He felt strong and ready to take on worlds.

'How did you do that?' he asked in the quiet tones of bewilderment, 'and thankyou'.

Sally had moved to behind her desk. She sat down and opened a drawer. She loved the antique desk that was once the desk of Ben Crammer himself, though no one knew he did not like it; too modern looking. She pulled out a small box from the draw and slid it across the desk's glass top. It stopped within an inch of the opposite edge of the surface. Preventing objects falling over the edge of a desk when pushed across it was controlled by a little device she had built into it though it was not deployed in that instance; it merely gave her the confidence to act in what appeared a devil may care fashion.

Milford picked up the box, looked at it and then looked up with a questioning expression towards his sister.

'Dad gave it to me before he took off. He said to check it out first and when I was done I was to pass it on to you' she explained.

'Dad took off ten years ago' stated Milford with the further question of, what took you so long, silently attached.

'There it is' Sally looked away after speaking showing signs of distress.

'It has all you need to know on it'.

Milford noted her distress and continued along the path he was on as it was Sally leading the way.

Milford opened the box and carefully picked out the pea-sized sphere from its blue velvet cushioned nest. It was smooth and cool and as he pinched it, it dropped from his grasp. It did not fall; it just hung there. Like a pet bird, it

144

moved to Milford who had instructively opened his hand and it came to rest in his palm. With his right hand, he reached into his pocket and pulled out a slim elegant band. It too responded as if alive to his command. It went around his left wrist without seeming to open. It was his band and although much smaller than Welder's was many times more powerful and had many more functions too. The tiny globe fit neatly into a receptacle and clicked satisfyingly into position. It then glowed warmly and hummed appreciatively for a moment. The band did not appear large enough to receive the sphere; a feature of all top of the range bands. Milford knew not to activate and access the contents of the pea until he had the time and space to do it. Sally never understood why Milford did not understand why Milford took off his band whenever they met but never questioned him on it.

It took Milford three weeks to make the same journey to Chippenham Five that Welder would take years later. Milford's natural impatience for long journeys was tempered by the opportunity it afforded him to begin the long task of looking through the records, data and other crucial material on the pea. Most importantly to begin with he would need the quick start guide. He wanted to salient information needed for the continuance of 'the project'. He knew his whole life and considerable talents were being honed for a project he knew very little about. He had only recently heard about the true power of R and B. He even thought that the initials R and B stood for Root and Branch, especially as he had seen the initials in conjunction with a beautiful tree with identically formed roots and branches as its symbol. The motif could be turned on its head and the role of root and branch could be reversed. One older example of the R and B symbol was circled by text in the ancient lost language of English and read, 'Branches *rooted to the sky and Roots hidden from the eye'; this matched Milford's understanding of the relationship between the two parts of the company. What the initials really stood for though was not Root and Branch, nor Rhythm and Blues; it stood for Robby and Ben.*

Being of a naturally lazy disposition when it came to the work element of his ideas, Ben was only too pleased to let Robby take charge of setting up the company's legal structures. When it came down to it Ben was more interested in making a fortune and then leading a comfortable happy existence and not so concerned with posterity. The pet project was initially his idea but he saw it as a way of making money, whereas the Boob had a deeper commitment to it. Ben was only too happy to let Robby pursue and care for the pet project and capitalise on the spinoffs from the innovations that pursuit produced. He never lost interest in the 'pet project though and being slightly removed gave him a perspective on the company. Later research was unable to conclude if the hidden second brain behind the success of the company was Robby or Ben's idea or both. Robby and Ben believed that everyone has two brains really; the one we use and the one we don't know about.

Onboard the transport ship, which was coincidently the same one that Welder would use further down the line, Milford decided to use the lowly lit lounge area to open the sphere. He took it from its recess in his bracelet and placed it in the open centre of a larger ring hovering in the horizontal in its light. It activated immediately and large letters appeared before Milford forming the words 'PROJECT into THE FUTURE'. On each of his middle fingers, Milford wore a ring. He had modified the pair of rings he was wearing so that they responded to the slightest twirl tap or quiver of his fingers. No other 'readers' were quite like his. He was the finest 'reed player' that ever picked up a bracelet since he was nine. His mastery of these controls remained unsurpassed and after a moment's pause, he stood with his feet together and arms out to his side like a conductor before an orchestra about to conduct a symphony. Then he tilted his head from side to side making audible clicks as he stretched his neck like a boxer before a title bout. Then, finally, he did cyclical breathing through alternative nostrils like a yoga master, but without using his hands to block a nostril at a time; he used control of his nose alone. His nose was grand rather than large and he could manipulate it in extraordinary ways. A final flaring of his nostrils and he was ready

The first option available was to view a personal message for him from his father. In his eagerness, and because there was a personal message from his father he acted out of character. He did what he so often criticised others for doing when confronted with a new piece of equipment that needs some assembly or awareness of safety hazards and dove straight in. Something about seeing the image of his Father returned him to his early boyhood which included the tendency to skip instructions and a yearning to not having to listen to his smarty frocks Dad.

Milford felt strangely liberated by going off-piste. Slowly at first images, texts, holograms, formulas and narration were initiated and emerged from the large central ring with the merest raising of one finger then another. The data built up bit by bit, filling the empty space around the lounge bar which had been cleared of furniture for that very reason. The range of Milford's projections was five metres in all directions. Information for his inspection gathered and overlapped on the periphery as he pushed it aside keeping his central area of vision clear for

*the next piece of data to emerge. As he proceeded he
became engaged in an editing dance.*

*He flicked his dark grey straight hair away from his
eyes with twitches of his scalp. He had the same deft
control over his scalp as he did over his nimble nose. Then
with jerks of his head and subtle movements of his foraging
snout, he opened files and started absorbing information at
an almost superhuman rate. Minds and abilities like those
of Milford and his Sister are only awakened from the
sleepwalking procession of humanity once or twice a
millennium. There had been times in humanity's
evolutionary progress when an individual of immense
intellect and insight could have guided the raft of
humanity's development to a brighter future but they were
stifled and marginalized by ignorance, self-interest and the
folly of closed systems of belief. Humanity's production of
individual variants (the key to its survival) has thrown up
rare unique specimens only for them to perish in war and
famine. There was once the rarity of a cluster of such
individuals, the like of which has never occurred since, as
the conditions for such a happening existed only at that one
moment. Unfortunately, it was in an area of the planet
earth neglected and abused and none of those individuals
reached the age of five, due to famine and slaughter in an
utterly pointless conflict. The loss to the potential
development of human evolution was incalculable. It is
beyond unlikely, beyond rare, it was almost certainly only
ever going to happen once, that minds such as Sally and
Milford's should spark into life in favourable
circumstances at the same time. And it is rarer still that
they would end up in at a time and in stations in life that
would enable them to flourish and ultimately influence
those circumstances. Sally and Milford somehow knew the
responsibility that lay with them and did their best to stay*

under the radars of close-minded powers that could find them threatening. They knew that with tragic frequency the visionary minds that found their voices in the past were completely ignored or worse; all because they were women or humble or simply because, the non-conformist or alternative nature of their insight could not be grasped, let alone embraced.

Milford and Sally were at the tiller of humanities makeshift craft that had been drifting in the currents of evolutionary backwaters. It was humankind's own ability to influence that had caused the stagnation and finally, it was humankind's influence in the shape of Sally and Milford that was going to break it loose again. They saw the chance to re-join the cosmic stream from which all life flows. They represented humanities best chance of moving forward. What's more, Milford and Sally knew it. Their profound sense of destiny and commitment to the development of human potential drove them forward, but it also threatened to end the order and structure that, despite its immobility, worked to a fashion for significant portions of the galaxy. Were they visionaries or bringers of doom? Their striving became a fragile balance between arrogance and compassion, conviction and doubt.

Over the previous fifty years, they had waited from the sidelines as the secret research on Chippenham Five went on. Their parent's position in the R and B order gave them an understanding of the way things were. It was a knowledge that sustained them. They waited patiently and not so patiently on occasion for their time to come. The death of their mother, who they had not seen in the ten years before her passing on, meant a changing of the guards. In the previous five hundred years, the family was as much like guardians as they were scientists. Part of guarding the secrets of Chippenham Five or C5 as it was

149

*known was keeping its activities a mystery even to those
who would one day become part of it.*

*The administrative wing of the company as
personified by Wallbran Prawnshot also harboured secrets.
Almost all of his secret plans revolved around his aim to
unify the authority of the company under one banner and
move one direction, with one figure at its head; one head
with one brain. To this end, he had to manipulate the
'Administry' without divulging the nature of what he was
doing.*

*The pet project became the focal point of this secret
civil war.*

*Milford and Sally's time had come. Sally was
already up to speed. She had assimilated all the
information on the sphere. The mystery and the eagerness
of Milford to uncover it meant that he went about his task
with unprecedented gusto, even uncharacteristic disorder.
He was initiating more and more discordant components.
But he was driven on. What unfolded was like one of those
ancient abstract, classical music compositions that puzzled
him, the ones where nothing seemed to go together, even by
accident. His concentration on the various elements and
on-going digging at the centre was staggering. He looked
like someone digging into a bottomless laundry basket
throwing items over his shoulder without looking yet sorted
piles resulted. However after four hours or more of
furiously looking through vast amounts of material he
became bogged down. He had failed to piece the mystery
together; he had failed to grasp what the mystery was, only
that there was one. There had to be more to it than
cultivated plant people. He knew in the back of his mind
that he would have to consult the manual; the manual
contained in the section that was accessed through his
Father's message. That knowledge and his resistance to it*

had kept him swimming in the swamp of his endeavours for at least an hour after he knew he was getting nowhere. One of his greatest strengths and greatest weaknesses was his fierce independence. He paused and went into a thoughtless uncontrolled wobbling walk amongst the images, texts, films and holograms. There was a clamour of voices like a works canteen and the lounge was filled with projections. Noticing the clamour for the first time he let go of his search. 'I've opened so many files he thought; normally each would have kept him excited for months. There were so many interesting pieces but they were not what he was expecting to find. 'Why was this pet project so important?' He was like a child anticipating some longed for and unrealistic gift at Christmas and despite an excellent haul of presents found the whole thing confusing and unsatisfying. Once he accepted he was going get what he expected, though in truth he was not quite sure what that was, he also accepted he would have to start again and look properly at what he got. He stopped his wobbly walk and started playing around mindlessly swirling and mixing images and texts and distorting them into a psychedelic soup. He was like a toddler rolling around in piles of wrapping paper after opening all his Christmas presents; presents that weren't toys and toys that weren't as interesting as swimming about in wrapping paper. Milford stood for a moment and lifted his arms straight above his head as if preparing to dive into a pool. With a circling of his arms in the manner of someone doing the breaststroke or like someone stretching after sitting at a desk for four hours, Milford swept away all that hung before him and was once again standing in an empty lounge.

Milford dropped to his knees then completed the transition from the vertical to the horizontal and lay on his back staring past the ceiling into his moment of *nothingness. He lay there until the stardust settled and he was reinvigorated. With his hands resting on his chest he twitched his ring finger and started again. The title page came to him. It was parallel to his prone body about six feet above his face. He went to the file with his initials. The top half of his father's holographic body hovered above him as if looking down at him from an invisible bunk bed. Milford found this disconcerting and sat up cross-legged. The frozen ethereal figure of his father shifted and was standing in front of him waiting to be activated. It loomed large and Milford felt and looked like a small lone child waiting to hear a story. He didn't like how that felt any more than he liked his father's face being larger than life and motionless. Pointing upwards he raised his hand and made a movement similar to a priest giving a blessing and he shrunk the image of his Dad to the size of an action man doll. He chuckled and moved himself to a lounge chair and returned his father to normal size. There he was, the great Alfros Cannings, a strikingly impressive man in his galactic senator's robe standing before Milford waiting to deliver his message.*

'I know you think I am a bit of a dick Milford, but hear me out and you will be glad you did. I am putting this 'fob' together for you and your sister. It has everything you need to know and more. It is the final part of your preparation for the project you have long guessed at, dreamed of, but could never imagine. I am just going to make myself comfortable and I hope you already are.' With this Alfros sat down and inadvertently gave Milford an unwanted view up his robes as he sat. Milford averted his gaze, lifted one end of his tightly closed mouth, rolled his eyes and jerked his head back with a twist; these actions in combination perfectly expressed the word 'typical', when related to an embarrassing parent. Naturally, this was not the first time

Milford reacted to his father this way. 'I'm almost one hundred years old and my Dad still makes me cringe' thought Milford. No matter how elevated his status or how great his achievements, Alfros knew his children were more likely to be embarrassed than impressed by him. But his children never truly doubted him and they were not even aware they didn't have any doubts; they just didn't have any. And they never experienced Alfros doubting himself either. Alfros occasionally did have doubts but only because he deliberately inflicted them upon himself just in case having doubt had a role in increasing his perceptions. He found that there was nothing of value in experiencing actual doubt during creative thinking and dealing with complex problems that could not be replicated with the use of a simple formula he calculated deliberately badly as a joke. By including his self-doubt algorithm into other formula and analytical processes his work and life had some sort of inherent solidity that he could not explain. No one could work out exactly how or why his 'doubt formula' worked, but it did. In the belief that there was a difference when the doubt quotient was included in calculations, he and others had no doubt. He asserted that by including doubt to his equations he eliminated it. It was the science community that was most open-minded about Alfros' formula and used it, though not with any great effect. The art-worlds, on the other hand, rejected 'the formula' but many artists used it anyway, and it coincided with a golden age of in all the arts, music and literature. The art-worlds claimed it was the rejection of 'the formula' that was crucial in 'the flourishing' but there were much debate and doubt in the assertion.

When it came to their Dad, Milford and Sally had no need for their father's formulas; they had no doubt how much Alfros loved them. However, Milford was tempted to

153

find a formula for calculating the embarrassment parents cause their children, the cringe factor, but decided it would only spoil the fun.

The incredibly lifelike hologram showed how Alfros had made himself comfortable in a grand black-winged back armchair with a headrest that extended high above his head and tapered to an elegant point. The ridiculous magnificence of the chair, the opulent robes and the importance of the information that Milford so long to hear created an array of anxious emotions Milford had not experienced for fifty years. But all of those feelings melted away, even curiosity and his ripe anticipation that made him feel ready to burst; every trepidation and anxious feeling, all melted away with the smile that came across a father's face for his child. The warm radiance of that simple smile then filled Milford with the inner glow of being loved. Alfros held the smile for what seemed an age but still not too long. Then Aldos began to lose control of his face. The smile was gone. The corners of his now firmly closed, contracting mouth was pulled down. His lower lip began to protrude and thrust upwards. With a determined slow nod, he took in a deep draught of air to dam in a torrent of emotion which he then swallowed with a gulp. Milford marvelled at how a holographic recording made up of lifeless dispassionate data could convey such warmth and generate such deep emotions in him. Aldos regained control of his expression; his lined face, fringed by thick fine grey hair was as neutral as he could make it but still communicated a lifetime of love and pride and more. It apologised for the years of separation between them and in the slight widening of his eyes, it explained that it had to be so. Milford returned the hologram to the smile and froze the projection. He needed to give himself a chance to deal with an unexpected surge of love and loss that was flooding

154

over him and having the trigger in shimmering light before him would hasten the process. He moved the hologram on to the point at which his father looked ready to commence but to Milford's surprise, he was still not. His body looked as if it had melted too. He had slid down his chair without realising and was close to dropping out of it.

'Silly old bugger' Milford said in a quiet voice out loud to himself. He wiped away a single tear, lifted his backside and stiffened himself; and then proceeded.

Alfros gave a brief history of how their ancestors had started the company and the original idea that sparked it into life, 'sea monkeys'. He explained that the products which brought the company instant success and rapid growth had been developed to finance research into the development of homegrown pets. Images of the original advertisement from the comic and the faces of Ben Crammer and Robby Green were in flat projections taken from original footage related to the company's early meteoric rise. They had just as much presence if not more, than the 3D ones reconstructed by the holographic program. Soon a texture of information was created that would dazzle most viewers. Very few would be able to take in what was being presented. It was well within Milford's power to absorb all of what he was seeing and hearing, despite his tiredness from his earlier unrestrained delving. Like a master chef that could taste a soup and instantly know the ingredients, Milford saw the whole and was able to note its constituent parts without conscious thought. His approach had swung completely around to careful meticulous adherence to the instruction manual or path laid out for him. He had tossed aside the guide earlier in the mistaken belief that constructing the story and finding his way would be straight forward. Constructing the story was straight forward but only if put together in the right sequence.

The years after the initial rise to prominence of the company were a story of slow, very slow but steady growth. As a sapling its growth was easily seen but once established as a mature tree its continued growth was barely discernible over an individual's lifetime.

The only attempt to genuinely find a viable marketable commercial product from the pursuit of a new generation of sea monkeys was 'pet pots'.

Pet pots were an innocent enough product but marked the beginning of revolutionary procedures that were able to tap in to and utilize the multifarious characteristics of plants; procedures that were employed in other straight forward practical cultivated materials. 'Pet pots' were sunflower-like plants that grew quicker than bamboo.

They were not instant like sea monkeys but grew fast enough to see growth after less than an hour. The plants grew to about two feet and produced a large flower with twelve pink petals. The centre of the flower grew into the shape of a face and the petals could close up and cover it. Cultivating plants into distinct forms in the same way a Bee-orchid takes the form of an insect was more 'straight forward' than Robert Green had first thought; at least to him anyway. Robby was able to incorporate the reflexes of plants to light, moisture and touch to allow the plant's keeper to elicit certain conditioned reflexes. This was done through the owner blowing and controlling amounts of water and moisture. But perhaps the biggest breakthrough and the 'pet pots' USP originally suggested by Ben, was the addition of sound. Robby was able to take what had previously been inaudible to the human ear, the sounds plants make. If the pet pots were gently blown on in a particular sequence and in a particular place, a tiny sweet giggling sound could be heard and the plant's petals would partially cover up the smiling face.

Robby was also able to cultivate and grow materials with strength, durability, lightness, colour, smell and warmth with countless uses. Not only were the materials versatile they were energy efficient to produce. After many generations of products being hugely financially successful, the company was perfectly placed to take advantage of the rapid progress of human exploration of the galaxy. Unfortunately despite their best efforts Ben and the Boob did not live long enough to see space truly open up to humanity.

Ben's great-great-great-great grand-daughter Lily was the one that took the families 'pet project' to an altogether more serious level. It was Lily's vision that saw the potential significance of creating a new form of intelligent plant life. It was Lily that understood philosophical, ethical, moral and spiritual implications of where the company's research was headed. She knew that to allow the project to flourish it had to be protected from controversy and imposed restrictions. She combined the commercial administrative division with the main body of the research branch. She did it to separate, hide and protect the project.

She saw that the dynamic processes of development used to mass-produce and market the more commercial products and the groundbreaking discoveries of the research division were vital to each other. Work on the 'pet project' was contributing less and less to the cause and she could see that it was only a matter of time before such idiosyncratic branch of faltering research would get the axe. She created the first secret research facility and is credited with the formation of the mysterious yet ubiquitous

R and B. R and B became a movement that many people said they believed in but no one was a member off. It was a movement that everyone was part of without signing up to simply by thinking in an R and B fashion; so the space myth went. You did not have to think in a prescribed way or of anything in particular; all you had to do was think and act well. It was a fluid idea of thought like sap rising and falling through the seasons. When its influence rose the authorities took measures to give the impression that it was either part of the movement or that something had been done to combat its corroding influence depending on their perception of the mood of the times. The authorities and the main body of the larger brained company were liked minded on most matters of public well-being. At times the government had to create members of R and B because none could be found. They unmasked heretics and hypocrites to placate liberals and punished traitors and subversives to satisfy conservatives. All of these placated liberals and satisfied conservatives were fully signed up members of the political elite. The general public had their own unwavering thoughts and feelings on R and B. Namely that it had nothing to do with conventional power. All of their efforts were simply part of the cycle of human seasons with the rise and fall of sap, blossoming, and shedding of leaves on to the cold ground; this despite the relatively small number of worlds whose plants and seasons had such a cycle.

At least half of those who worked for the company felt allied to the idea of R and B; much to the annoyance of its hierarchy. The established and fully visible research department was almost entirely committed to R and B belief but would have been hard-pressed to say why. There had been attempts to fill the research department with 'tangibles' which were anti R and B and strict company men and women. The result was that there were no results of any worth to come from the research department during the period of infiltration. There was serious disquiet in the corridors of the company's head office. The company began to stagnate and for the first time in its history, it shrank back a little. From that point on the research division was allowed to go its own way with its people; those who could get results and followed the idea with no words.

Whilst the push and pull between elements of the company was going on Lily established the first 'hidden from the eye' facility. The facility for the pursuit, developing and safeguarding of all life was created on Chippenham One. It remained hidden from all worlds, all authorities and all individuals except for the true head of the company and a select team. Only they knew where it was and what it did. Not the head that ran the company day to day; they were kept in the dark. It was the unknown head that was the real heart of the company. Even other research teams knew nothing, but they sensed it; they knew there was something else going on.

From that point in time till 'the incident' shortly after Sally's tenure began, the antipathy between the two factions was held in perfect balance. The company continued to grow. An awareness of mutual need kept the forces that strengthened the company in check. But it was the family descendants of Robby and Ben, small in number, ingrained with commitment and integrity to the 'idea', that held sway from behind the veil of secrecy and myth.

Milford marvelled at the unfolding story of how the idea of 'sea monkey's' became a more profound inquiry into the nature of existence and the possible future of the evolution of life in the universe.

There was so much to take in even Milford was
beginning to reel. After three solid sleepless sunless days of
opening files and following paths, his transport
approached Chippenham Five. He had barely scratched the
surface of a mass too big for him to fully appreciate.
Funnily enough, what struck Milford most from what he
had taken in on his journey was just how much 'the Boob'
and Lilly Crammer reminded him of himself and his Sister.
He did not trivialise this observation. But what also struck
him was a feeling that the two antagonistic parts of the
company were finally about to confront each other after so
much time. He could feel the balance wobbling. And what's
more, just at the point when 'the project' was on the cusp
of developments of profound significance and as fragile as
the first flickering of new life in the universe.

Alfros' formula that removed all doubt emboldened
those who felt allied to the movement and charged them
with renewed commitment. But unforeseen problems had
arisen in the research itself; problems stemming from 'the
incident' on Chippenham Five.

Milford resisted leaping ahead to finding out about
'the incident' knowing that he now must follow the path
with obedience and surrender if he was to be able to fully
understand.

Chapter Ten

Lost and Found

As a barely noticeable flash in the furthermost corner of Sophie's perception, for the briefest of moments, in the slightest possible manner, the Narrator's voice sounded to her like her own. It sounded like her voice, but her voice imitating the voice of the Narrator. 'Maybe the Narrator is doing an impression of me doing an impression of him. That's if it truly is a 'him'. If it was an important observation it did not feel like it and she passed on. Nothing had bothered her so far except one question, and even this she put to one side. It remained left behind, lodged in the recesses and cavities of her thoughts like a raspberry pip stuck in a tooth or a tiny splinter beneath healed-over skin. Whatever it was like, she knew that she would have to pick it out later.

'I have another little piece for you to puzzle over'. There was no hint of variation in the narrator's voice and it had that familiar quirky reassuring tone.

'Gooo onnnn' prompted a low monotone extruded voice. Sophie imagined the Narrator's eyebrows lifting in astonishment and then imagined it again with especially large eyebrows for added effect. She was not as shocked as she imagined she might have been. She realised she had been harbouring the idea of attempting to communicate directly with the narrator for some time but this first attempt was completely unplanned. Now her voice was

launched she could begin to ask some of the questions and other thoughts she had been harbouring. It was fitting that her first deep long words sounded like an ocean liner leaving port, starting on its passage. She felt ready for the high seas, or at least a poodle around the bay. She went to push out another extrusion of words but nothing came, the tide was out. There was no physical strain involved and there was no physical voice. There was only information arranging itself.

'So you have found your voice have you?' said the Narrator flatly. A tone which left Sophie slightly crestfallen having achieved what she thought was a major breakthrough.

'It will take you just as long to get to grips with using it; one's native tongue is a slippery thing to catch hold of. In the meantime get to grips with this little tip bit which is another angle on something you already know.'

He continued, *'you know about the speed of light and that when you are looking at a star you are looking at light that had taken years to get to your eyes. As you know what you are seeing is the past; however many years in the past that may be. Evolution of technology has meant you have been able to look deeper into space and therefore deeper into the depths of time'.* The Narrator stopped for a brief moment like a walker up a steep incline taking one last look at what lay ahead before throwing themselves into the ascent.

'Imagine then, that there is almost certainly someone viewing from Earth from the other side of the galaxy. They could have been looking towards earth for thousands of years. They could have been watching from before life on the planet. Eyes across the galaxy could have watched the history of the earth as it unfolded and for that matter yours. Everything you do leaves a trace. Your actions leave a trace, perhaps even your thoughts. With the right means, everything that leaves a trace can be read and recorded.

They could have seen your life as it happened so many
years before. Then you could be put into suspended
animation and travel to that distant star and view records
of your past. Imagine what you would see if you could look
through everything you did from every angle, including
what was on your mind. I am talking about information
about what made you, you, or anyone else's data on what
made them who they were, being held and available to
watch. I wonder what people would make of watching their
actions without the filter of their self-editing, without
selective memory. I think they would probably be shocked.
Alternatively, imagine if you could find a short cut to that
distant place. I am not talking about travelling faster than
the speed of light; I am just talking about taking a different
path and getting there before the light of your lifetime. You
could also look back at yourself and judge yourself for
yourself. Your actions leave their mark. They are etched in
the merest disturbance of space like the grooves of a vinyl
record. Everything leaves a trace. It all counts, even if it is
the tiniest number, it counts. Or maybe during that
theoretically drawn-out second before death when the
drowning man sees his life flash before him, he will see it
all, his life warts and all. Take away the vestiges of life, the
need to compete and reproduce and see what is left. Tired
egos give way and the true self stands alone in the universe.
A vessel is filled from the ocean. The vessel is our body and
when we die we return to the ocean.

Nothing about the universe and the way it functions
that was known about during your lifetime could have fully
explained it; it did not even claim to; I mean, how could it?
But everything was knowable and everything there was to
know was sensed and in that way understood. Anything
living can sense the truth because it is part of it. There are
words in many languages; there are many languages that

use words. But many languages do not use words. Some people experience information in colours. For others, mathematics can express the nature of the universe so clearly and accurately. Waves washed over you and left layers of information. Waves of broadcast information blanketed you through your life. The air was thick with information that you could tap in to. But they contained no greater truth than that communicated in music or the way something smells or feels on the skin. It is about how you connect with the truth; you just need to interpret that connection. I'm afraid words more often than not block the connection. It is no easy thing building a passage of words that breaks through the walls of words that block us in. Can you imagine the information and the means of communication that course through the depths of dark-matter. We just have to connect'

'Wwweeee?'

There was no response to Sophie's squealed croaking question. Just like the instant, just like the swirl, Milford made of projected information in his confusion and frustration Sophie's thoughts swirled. The swirling sped up as images, known and unknown spun around her. They funneled and drained towards the centre. Down they went, she felt like all words and meaning she had known were being sucked down a foreign channel.

Boof..crack crunch, sound or vision or both? Then everything was still and silent. She opened her eyes to startling grey with the dark veins of bare branches. Sophie felt the cold of snow on her face and a trickle of blood from her nose that had hit a rock hidden beneath her. She had managed to turn herself on to her back. She could hear her breath and her heart beating, strong and loud. 'Must get up' was the thought. But it was not her thought. She rose quickly but not in her body; it was someone else's. A man;

'eat or be eaten, kill or be kil..' the word was sliced as Sophie cut to another moment looking down at a women's smiling face in the orange glow of a roaring open fire. Then she was running followed by a brief moment of sunshine. Flashes, connected but not hers kept coming faster until Sophie was being pulled down the maelstrom of merging images once more. Then there was blackness and silence; whispers in the dark, first one, then another and another. Sophie could not make out what was being said or even the language being spoken. Then still in total darkness more whispers and still more. Whispers came in layers like the conversations in a huge auditorium before a concert. The whispers blended into a stream of white noise. The white noise became compressed into a ringing that became one-note. The note slowly faded and as it did so Sophie in the half-light of the Narrators voice beginning once again.

'What happened?' Sophie's voice was clearer.

'You shared a channel, had a dream, past-life, different life; take your pick.' The narrator's voice sounded 'matter of fact'. But there was no matter and only the glimpse of a fact. As if he knew Sophie would not be satisfied he continued.

'It rarely happens and only to rare individuals. It is unlikely to happen again.' Sophie realised she had more firmly ascribed a gender to the narrator but out of convenience rather than conviction.

     Sophie had had dreams from time to time throughout her life in which she was someone else, amongst people she did not recognise in places she had never seen. The dreams being dreams, she put this down to the capacity of her mind to imagine and reconstruct worlds from what she imagined and remembered. This could very well lead to strange and exotic possible permutations that could seem completely alien. This had always been a satisfactory enough explanation for her but somewhere deep in her soul, it was not enough. Now she felt like she was on the way to finding out the real reason, whatever its source. That source may still be from within her; coming from her, perceived by and defined by her; a truer picture is seen clearer in the wake of her circumstances; from her death. She stopped short of asking herself the question, am I really dead? She was not ready to reach in the pool, beckon a fish to the surface to her and look it in the eye and ask it, do you know? and get the answer. It was beyond her and she knew it. For now, all she could do was to stare into the pool and watch the fish glide serenely below. One thing she did know, she was not in total darkness; not completely and not always. Even from the point she first heard the Narrator's voice there was a light that waxed and waned and ebbed and flowed. There were moments of near darkness; when the whispers came. They came like the snow at night; snow that had been hanging above her like a shroud blocking out light. Each voice was like a flake that fell. There were just a few flakes at first then she was blanketed. Did the whispers belong to the stranger running to catch his prey or running away from a predator?

Her thoughts cleared as she once again looked upon the dancing light. It was brighter than before and ran across the surface of the pool with the sun goldfish below. She lost herself in reflections.

Sophie seemed to be acquiring some control over determining what memory she found herself amidst but mostly she went with the flow, happy to be pleasantly or unpleasantly surprised at events in her past. If a certain time came to her rather than her to it, perhaps triggered by some aspect of the story she was absorbing, and if she concentrated on that memory, she would shot to that point. She did not have a dead-eye when it came to hitting the exact target. She was not able to control her course to the point of arriving at a specific moment; it was more like being dropped from a plane over the general area and parachuting in. But she did not gently drift down and contemplate her landing; she went from jumping out of the plane to standing in the scene below with nothing between. She would find herself dropped on the correct conveyor belt of events but at a random point along it. So she sensed she had some control, but only before and after a lack of it. Some of the memories she inhabited she felt she had no part in choosing and had no trigger had been pulled. She felt simply thrust back. But after a time in each case, it seemed that she could figure out some reason for it or connection. Once the reason was understood the next time she returned the feeling of being thrust was gone. By understanding events that she was drawn back to the pull would lessen. It reminded her of her Mother flattening out the long hall carpet; carefully starting from one end and smoothing out the humps before pushing the food trolley along it for afternoon tea.

Each memory seemed to contain a lesson or several lessons. She found the prospect of finding out about the truths that lay in events of her own life could be initially painful and disturbing but ultimately exhilarating. Behaviour and actions that she had felt great shame over and filled her with self-recrimination during her life turned out to be nowhere near as dreadful as she once remembered. There were times, memories she had carried with her during life that turned out to be completely imagined and false. The memory of her fantasies and dreams were often stronger than memories of actual events. She relived times which revealed acts hurtful to others that she had never acknowledged to herself and she was able to unpick and understand them. After returning time and time again and after painful contrition and shame she eventually could forgive herself and move on. The bumps in the rug had to be pushed all the way to the edge.

Sophie sat in her car with her arms wrapped around the steering wheel and her head resting on her hands clasping it tightly in the eleventh-hour position. The life she had built up for so many years was falling down around her. Her life as it had been was over. She had deceived herself and all those around who knew her without exception. She had no confidante and no accomplices. No one had the slightest inkling of her gambling until Richard. It had only taken three years to go from occasional lottery ticket buyer via seaside casinos, to blowing everything she had and plenty she did not. She started embezzling from the company whose success she had so proudly contributed to for the last five years. The amounts rose steadily like dry rot. Her skill with figures and processes had not let her down when it came to covering her tracks. It was something else that had betrayed her nefarious activities. 'What was the 'tell', she asked herself; what twitch, what action had given the game away? There was no one better at working out figures, but she could not figure out what loose thread had been tugged on. A small but growing part of her was relieved that the deception was over, but that did not make the meeting she was about to have any easier. It was the first time the situation had brought her to tears. She did not cry when the bailiffs had pushed their way in to empty the house of all her possessions and she did not cry when she handed over the keys of the house itself to the officious sweaty little man from the bank. In a way, those material things had ceased to bring her true pleasure and were only of value to her as part of a grand façade. It was the crushing remorse for betraying the people she knew that finally broke her unflappable resolve. Her resolve and her belief that if she set her mind to it she could syphon off enough money to make good the losses and put things right. Her abilities had driven her through all adversity she faced to that point.

She suddenly jerked herself upright from the wheel with a determined expression; she was ready to face the music. There was nothing in the way she got out of the car that indicated to watching eyes from the sculpted conical office block, that there was anything untoward. Then without any premeditation, she calmly dropped the car keys down a storm drain as she strode across the car park. This too had the appearance of normality. She had no rationale for this act. It was not an act of defiance or petulance; it made no sense to her. Her life made no sense to her.

Sophie entered the board room in which she had shone out as the rising star. It was where she received praise from her admirers and respect from her rivals. To her surprise, there were only two figures in the room and they were sitting away from the large heavy grey stone slab board room table and were over by the window.

A richly patterned Persian rug defined a casual enclave and the figures sat in armchairs by an enormous circular window with its lowest point resting on the wooden floor and its highest point touching the ceiling twenty feet above them. There were three chairs facing inwards to a coffee table which was a single cylindrical piece of solid glass with trapped bubbles of various sizes within it. Sophie instantly recognised the two figures and they both rose with an almost sinister cordiality when they saw her approach, putting down their delicate china teacups carefully as they did so. The pair had both been holding cup and saucer and the sound of their fragility against the solid glass form made Sophie wince inside. They squared themselves towards Sophie. Sophie was more than a little surprised to warrant the attention of the company's CEO Gillian Meredith and she felt slightly flattered whilst at the same time girding her loins in preparation for a verbal thrashing. Gillian Meredith was legendary for her tongue lashings. Her skills at cutting down those she chose to, to the size she wanted them were unsurpassed. She could do it to her victims without them even noticing it with a few quick swipes of her rapier tongue. They would still be standing for a moment before falling into neat chunks. She could do it with a thousand small cuts, and watch as life slowing drained out of her victim.

It was the presence of Richard that Sophie was really surprised and puzzled by. She did not know about Richard finding the poker chip in the glove compartment of her car on the day of the shunt. She also had no real idea that Richard was, in fact, Gillian Meredith's son. Sophie had sensed that Richard had connections on high in the company but his surname of Brickley gave no clue to being a member of the company's founding family.

Now that the mask of always being in complete control had slipped, fallen and was about to be stamped on, Sophie had only got halfway through the ritual of making her appearance immaculate when she stopped with a sigh and a resigned exclamation of 'why bother?' She settled for a more natural look and it was an improvement. After an initial flight response to the threat of prosecution, the thought of starting afresh was a strangely liberating one for Sophie. From the letter requesting her attendance, she knew the game was up and she would have to come clean. There was no doubt in her mind that it was a summons. But just as she experienced the impulse to take flight when her cover was blown, when she looked at the two personifications of corporate power before her she was gripped with a readiness to fight. She was coming clean and it was a refreshing sensation; she had nothing to hide or to lose and that gave her the strength she needed.

However, the feeling of deep shame for letting down those she loved, her Mum, her sister and Dad, and those she respected at work was an open wound and an easy target like a cut on a boxer's cheekbone. The feeling resulting from the combination of threat and shame would build up unnoticed within Sophie's core and surface intermittently from that day forth. When the negative energy within was met with external stresses from without, it would cause a jolt that would occasionally floor her emotionally. She would need a day to recover herself.

Gillian immediately read the mix of trepidation and liberation and picked up an undertone of a rebellious sense of injustice. Gillian's ability to read these feelings in Sophie and any twinge of envy she felt did not show on her unaltered unnaturally smooth white complexion, either through tone or definition. Gillian's skill at reading people was a refined intuitive intellectual ability bordering on being a superpower. She could read and sense what people were feeling and anticipate and deduce what they were thinking as a result. She was able to see and understand elements, external and internal determining someone's behaviour. She could see things about people that they could not see about themselves. Her reputation as the verbal assassin was fully deserved but she seldom used her powers. Many of those who were at the wrong end of her lashings had it coming, and many that had been cut down benefited from it in the long run, as a result of the rebuilding necessary afterwards. It was her power that people feared as nobody truly knew her motives. The power was always there; anyone in her presence would feel it, and she knew they did. That awareness was there in Sophie as she stood before her. But Gillian felt something else; something she rarely felt. She felt a connection; a connection with a kindred spirit. Gillian's aspect change and she glanced at her son who sensed it too.

'Take a seat Sophie', for Sophie the warmth in the voice of her would-be judge and executioner sent a chill through her body that left her with noticeable goose pimples on her partly uncovered arms. Gillian's round white expressionless face, with the horizontal incision of her small mouth clearly outlined in deep red lipstick, and with its unnervingly blue eyes that tracked Sophie's slightest movement, seemed balanced on her thin cylindrical neck. Her eyebrows looked like two perfectly executed gestural arched sweeps of a Chinese calligraphic master's brush. Combined with her dark hair she looked to Sophie like the fusion between a Japanese samurai and an eastern European gipsy lawyer. Gillian did not look old but everyone could tell she was.

'I believe you have met my son Richard'

Sophie nodded with the flash of a 'light bulb of realisation' switching on over her head. Richard's expression had been deadpan until that point but a natural warm smile connected with Sophie in a way that put her strangely at ease.

'We are not going to prosecute' proclaimed Gillian looking down at a closed file on the floor next to her chair.

'Richard believes that you have qualities that may yet be useful to the company; not least a penchant for subterfuge.'

Sophie tilted her head almost imperceptibly but enough to express curiosity and a prompt for the speaker to continue. Sophie knew then that it was Richard that had found her out but she did not know how.

Sophie had managed to siphon off half a million pounds and nobody was any the wiser. Sophie's suddenly leaving the company after a mysterious meeting generated many theories, none of them having anything to do with being found out for embezzling. Some conjectured that it had to do with a secret romantic affair 'gone terribly wrong'; an affair with someone high up the corporate ladder. Some male colleagues who had had their unwanted advances repelled by Sophie suggested the affair was with Gillian Merideth herself. Gillian Merideth had been seen on Sophie's last day.

Sophie's activities would not have been discovered if Richard was not already tasked with investigating Sophie for a quite different reason and only then after he came across the chip. It was Sophie's refined intuitive and intellectual understanding of figures and systems that brought her on to Gillian Meridith's radar. Gillian was always on the lookout for unique individuals to improve the company's bloodline.

The mystery of Sophie's departure would continue to generate speculation as to the exact circumstances of the 'Sophie affair'. Shock was the persistent lingering sentiment when even years later her former colleagues would say 'I still don't quite believe she had a secret life' and 'how the hell did we not notice anything'.

Returning to that part of her past life dug up many feelings in Sophie and a question. If she was dead and had no body, where was she able to experience feelings?

Chapter Eleven

Sleepless Dreams

Welder had not slept for more than seventy-eight hours but he felt as fresh as a daisy. During most of that time, he had been looking through the records left for him by Milford Lyme. Milford had edited out much of the scientific data and technical material from the fob his father had left him and Sally. But he had added all the information Welder would need from his work since arriving on Chippenham 5. Milford had had to consume vast aggregates of material from the info-orb or 'fob' compiled by his father, Alfros. Generations of researchers had added to stores of information contained on that little sphere the size of a pea. The fob was a widely used mass storage device that could be activated when housed in a personal bracelet, pendant, broach or belt, or some other external device in contact with the skin. But the most popular by far was the bracelet or 'band'. Bands would profile the wearer from their DNA to an amazingly accurate count of the various bacteria in their stomach. The 'pea', as it was also known, could only be accessed by the correct profile. Fobs were allocated to every child born in the voluntary galaxy. It started gathering data about its allocated subject immediately. The standard fob had more than enough capacity for all the data of an average extended life span. It had various homing devices, the ability to hover if dropped and its capacity to follow and identify its match. These features made it virtually impossible to fill and almost impossible to lose. Plus it was well-nigh physically indestructible. Storage capacity was measured in lives; one life being enough for one person's lifetime of information; simple. Most people used twenty life fobs for no apparent reason other than, 'just in case' or 'you never know' and the possibility of adding family archives. Anything other than the standard-issue bands was extremely pricey but the less well-off usually had the most expensive ones. No one wore standard-issue bands, not even in emergencies. Most people would rather have lost a limb than lose their fob. They could have a new limb grown and bands could be replaced, but the information on a fob could never be fully recovered.

Wearer's desire to upgrade and get the latest band meant the galaxy was awash with perfectly brilliant bands infinitely better than standard issue. Invisible band technology was developed but not being able to see the band added to growing levels of band loss anxiety that could not be nullified by the band's emotional balancing function. The technical support staff employed by the pet project in the early days developed fobs with such a massive storage capacity that not even they knew how many 'teralives' of storage they had. They were tasked with producing fourteen, one-off special fobs; one for each Keem and one for the head of the project. The one for the project leader could uniquely incorporate many lives and be matched and re-matched by those who knew how. This meant that successive project heads could use it. After

completion, all records of the fobs were destroyed. The
materials and technology and skills needed to make them
could never be replicated and the fourteen fobs were the
only ones in the known and the 'not quite sure about'
universe. The stem within the central column of the Keem's
bubble was like one giant band and contained the thirteen
fobs allocated to individual Keem. These fobs became
known as the K-peas and looked like peas in a pod lined up
in the docking stem in the Domes column. The one
allocated to the head of the project was reallocated to
whoever succeeded them. The knowledge of how to
reconfigure the 'project pea' of 'pp' was passed down by
word of mouth; from one head to the next. Eventually, it
came to Milford and Sally's mother, Martha Maplefield.
Her technical genius was able to penetrate the workings of
the 'project pea' and she managed to reconfigure it so that
both her children could one day match with it, as well as
any other new project head. Normally only one match was
possible. Alros' job was to make sure that Milford would
one day head up the research and to see that the pea was
delivered safely to him after Sally had a chance to look
over it. Martha did not have the slightest doubt that one
day Sally would be the hidden head of the company and
fulfil her destiny. Alfros being a Political Scientist and a
rather unpredictable character was not trusted by Martha
with knowledge of the project pea's contents. All the love
respect and admiration Milford and Sally had for their
brilliant mother and all the sense of grief and despair at
her death was channelled into carrying on the work she
gave her life to. Alfros was unable to contain his grief and
broke into tears spontaneously at various points during his
recorded guide on the fob. This was not helped by the
imposed separation from his children that had been
decided to be necessary to maintain the secrecy of their

project. Almost every address Alfros recorded on the pea for his children ended with Alros welling up with love and pride for Martha, Milford and his beautiful little girl, Saly.

Milford had created an easily digested précis of the Keem's creation and evolution for Welder's mental constitution. Milford did not set up the reallocation protocol; his was the last pea in the pod and could only be assigned by the Keem themselves. But Milford told no one that he had set things up that way.

The thousands of years story of the Keem was a fascinating epic tale that kept Welder riveted throughout despite Milford's somewhat clumsy regurgitated constitution of the material. Information did not always drop into Welder hungry baby bird mind, sometimes he had to reach down mother bird Milford's gullet and search for it. Without his ruthless editing, however, the material Welder would have taken months and months just to sit through the headings and many lifetimes for Welder to make sense of a small number of them.

The Keem that met Welder and watched him also watched the records with a dispassionate quizzical concentration. These creatures were grown from organic material that still contained the original matter created by Ben Crammer and Robby Green.

The 'pet project' had separated itself from the lucrative products of the company that its research had spawned. This separation happened very early on. From the start, Robby Green had the opportunity to allow his imagination, ideas, passions, and personal loves the opportunity to roam free into new realms of discovery. Ben was a catalyst, a spark, a Paul to Robby's John. Ben protected Robby's arena of ideas and was brilliant at seeing the commercial potential in Robby's work. Sometimes Ben would develop products in a second

177

research facility so as not to bother or distract Robby. The two separate branches of a tree that the company became first diverged then. Apart from any of this, the pair were deeply bonded not least by their shared humour. Their unique, rather odd blend of silly yet abstract often had the in paroxysms of laughter. Uncontrollable giggle fits turned them to quivering tearful gelatinous heaps.

It was always plants for Robby Green, though for some unknown reason he disliked the name Green. So much so, that he almost changed it to Rhubarb; his favourite vegetable. Robby had been so impressed by a self-contained and self-sustained ecological sphere he had seen at the Smithsonian Institute as a boy, that he dedicated his life, right then and there to the principals of sustainability, harmony and balance it represented to him. He was convinced that plant life held the key to humanity's energy needs in the future; both for sustenance and power. He sensed too that the possibilities plant life offered would continue far beyond the current horizons of human imagination; even his.

The ambitions they had, that they could create a new version of sea monkeys were the starting point according to Ben, by their very nature, starting points are points of departure. For Robby the pet project was not a starting point, it was the far off destination that should never be lost sight off. Ben was unconvinced at first by Robby's commitment to plant life as the only possible route to take, but when he was met with a furious passion he relented and abandoned any future attempts to intercede on that subject, and that subject alone. Ben had recorded their first discussions and those records survived. It was obvious from the recordings that it was Robby rather than his ideas that Ben was most convinced by. Ben resolved during those initial conversations that Robert Green was something special, and he was prepared to speculate all he had on that view. He was certain that Robby's intellect and passion were capable of producing something unique, something outstanding, and he, Ben Crammer, was the man to make it happen; and of course, make some money in the process. As long as the 'grow your own pets' looked like the adverting and the packet they came in, and as long as they had some basic response mechanisms, Ben would have been willing to stop at that point. Robby, however, was not, and Ben could see that from the start. But Ben was willing to go along with whatever route or roots Robby followed. What had ultimately persuaded Ben during that early conversations was the point Robby emphasized about 'the vast untapped commercial possibilities from unlocking the properties of plants.'

The conversation was held in the spare room of Ben's basement flat which served as an office. The videos lasted many hours but were compulsive viewing. If Robby was touched by genius, Ben had the hallmark of greatness. He had a sense of destiny and had been waiting all his life for his real life to begin. He had an acute instinct that what they were embarking on was a partnership that would generate something, though he was not sure what, that would impact future generations. This was the first of many conversations between the two that he recorded.

'Our 'responsive plants' will need only light, water and the bedding that we provide to grow' said Robby enthusiastically.

'A bed that you need to wet' responded Ben. Robby noticed Ben's witticism but passed it by without a glance like a sale in a shop he never went in to.

'And we can create new materials that can be grown not manufactured; materials with properties of plants that have not yet been fully tapped.'

179

Welder felt a chill as he listened to the voices of Robby Green and Ben Crammer speaking to him from a distant time and place. Milford had included the recordings not because they had a specific bearing on what lay ahead for Welder but because they were important for a sound overview. They were part of preparing the soil.

'What sort of properties are we talking about Robby?' Ben was always aware of the camera at the start each time he turned it on. His first questions usually had a staged stiffness to them. Welder did not pick up on this; Ben and Robby were probably the last generations that did not live most of their lives being photographed or filmed knowingly or not. The idea of being a little awkward in front of a camera was alien to Welder. Ben soon relaxed after he backed himself away from the camera and on to the armchair that would be part of every subsequent office the pair shared. The Boob conversely was seldom aware of what was happening outside of the amorphous bubble of his thoughts; he was not much interested in how he appeared to others. He had the advantage though, of Heathcliff rugged good looks. He had thick black-rimmed glasses to match his thick black wavey hair.

'Take pseudo-copulation for example.' Replied Robby without attempting to tailor his answer too specifically to the question he knew was coming; there were better examples he could have used if he wanted to convince Ben straight away. He wanted to prepare the ground first before planting solid ideas. Robby, who was sitting at his desk looking at his computer screen, was talking as he was setting something up for Ben to inspect, swivelled on his chair and then looked across and slightly down at Ben. When he had finished doing what he was doing, he pushed his chair back to give Ben a better view of the screen.

Robby had pulled up a file and with a swipe of his computer's remote, the slide show began.

'You're giving me a pitch Robby; I'm impressed'. And Ben was impressed, but Robby less so at being told.

'It's the fly orchid. It's the mimicry involved in the pseudo-copulation, utilised by the fly orchid that you're looking at'

A series of images showing 'the fly orchid' appeared in rhythmical progression then stopped at a particularly good example of the fly like form of the plant.

'It grows in the shape of a female fly as part of a strategy to attract the male fly of the species of fly that it relies on for pollination.' Robby was off and running; he could see he had already hooked Ben but he wanted to take his time.

'Of course, an equally important part of the strategy of attracting through deception is the scent; without the pheromones, the visual prompt would not be enough for even the most frustrated fly. But as you have probably guessed I have shown you this plant as an example of how elaborate the form of a plant can be.'

Ben raised his eyebrows and looked up at Robby; Ben was even more genuinely impressed; in fact, he had gone beyond impressed too, mildly astonished. His expression communicated this and whilst his eyebrows were up there he added a request for more with a smaller secondary upward jerk of said eyebrows and brow combined.

The Boob's slide show went on with further examples of plants with characteristics that could be developed, adapted and used to realise the aims of their pet project and also produce materials and products of commercial potential. Robby showed how plants could move in response to touch like the Venus flytrap, change colour, sprout out of concrete and turn it to rubble, and more. The slide show ended and a film clip of jellyfish played on a loop.

'They're not plants Robby' Ben stated knowing that Robby's response was waiting for that very obvious prompt to be released.

'What's amazing about these guys it that they may not be plants but they have a symbiotic relationship with them. They have algae within them like solar panels on a house that produce energy. They are almost part plant. The algae provide all the energy the jellyfish needs and the jellyfish naturally swims to where the sun is to meet the algae's need. These jellyfish Ben, are an animal that survives on sunlight alone'

After thousands of years of human evolution and advances in technology and understanding of the nature of the universe the montage as a convenient method of skipping through the narrative, survived and Welder was the dubious benefactor of Milford's slick clichéd production of one. Welder had the option of freeze bubble or freeze-framing when the specific image had not been given an extra dimension, but he sat through the whole montage. He could go off on any tangent to fill any gaps. He was confronted with a large central bubble of visuals and connecting smaller bubbles showing material related to the central one. The orbital montage did still have its uses in presenting a lot of information in a short time.

Welder witnessed a potted history of the greatest, and yet virtually unknown story of one of humanities supreme achievements; the creation of the Keem. Robby was able to begin the process of forming what would eventually be the Keem's face just as the fly orchid had formed the elaborate form of a female fly. He then added movement in response to stimuli like the Venus flytrap closing on its prey. The fly theme ended there. The first face was at the centre of the large sunflower-like plant that responded to breath. By gently blowing the plant it

182

appeared to close its eyes and sleep and it would wake and open them when softly spayed with a mist of water. The piece de resistance was making it smile by singing sweetly to it. Gentle softly and sweetly were the watchwords. Robby's genius was finding ways to separate the qualities of individual plant species and incorporating them into the newest crop of pet plants. Movement could be controlled by using stomata that opened and closed to release gas and by doing so in varying degrees and in particular sequence movement was possible in response to sunlight or water or touch and eventually sound. Bobby found and cultivated many types of plant receptors that responded to ever more subtle and complicated triggers such as frequencies of sound waves. Surprisingly soon after Robby's lifetime, the galaxy began to be explored and each living planet offered every subsequent generation of 'Boobs' and their fellows, a greater diversity of features to harness. And every subsequent generation of 'Bens' was there to harness the advances the Robby's made and turn them into lucrative products.

     There had been plants on earth that could feel touch and move. Some plants could smell and taste. There were even plants able to hear and others that could communicate. But once the flora from distant moons and from planets whose deep seas could submerge the earth were discovered the possibilities expanded exponentially. There were plants so sensitive to direct and reflected light that for all intents and purposes they could see. No one plant had it all when it came to making the Keem's responses more and more complex and more and more human-like. In time, any thought of sea monkeys was dropped along with the idea of a commercial product. The Keem became a project concerned with the nature of life itself. Fast-growing and fast-reacting vines that responded to touch like a passion

*vine were developed into limbs. Unique plants from across
the galaxy all added to the whole and all shared one thing,
they drew there energy from the sun and the stars that
warmed the worlds they were from lubricated with that
magic elixir of life, water. Plants were discovered that
could mimic sound and copy movements. There were plants
drifted endlessly on the breeze and others that flew further
than the helicopter-like seeds of sycamores, they fly in short
repeated bursts. Welder watched as plants were held up
watched and grown in the lab. Plants that had the latent
energy to shoot cannon ball-sized seeds several miles.
Tough plants, tender plants, independently moving plants;
and plants with such complex forms of response and levels
of communication that it would not be overstating the case
if they were said to think and feel. On one planet there was
virtually no surface water and high winds. Whereas winds
are used by desert plants to move the winds of 'Leefer'
were so strong that plants needed to grip on to the planets
rocky surface to suck moisture that lay within. But the
plants needed to seek out new pockets of moisture once it
had exhausted one patch. These patches were spread over
vast windy rocky plains like giant water drops on a road
when it starts to rain. The 'Octopus creeper' moved as
independently as a tumbleweed whilst gripping on for dear
life. By contracting and expanding millions of tiny bubble
cells it crept along in search of moisture. The Octopus
creeper was responsible for getting the Keem out of their
pots for the first time. It was one in a long line of plants
that provided a major development in the Keem's mobility
and other functions. The Keem reached the operational
level of a simple Robot. They were able to move across a
room, giggle, give some sonic responses that mimicked
words and giggle some more. At first, they could only be
'active' for less than a minute every week. It was a kind of*

blooming. It was the use of stimulating plant scents that greatly increased their active time with only the minor drawback that the Keem needed to evacuate gases from their system twice a day. But it was the discovery of a sponge-like plant floating in the one small remaining ocean of the smallest moon of a giant gas planet called Alan that led to the most significant single adaptation the Keem underwent. These giant sponge plants looked and behaved very much like jellyfish from Robby Green's presentation only they were all plant. They were known as the 'Mude'. This was not their official name; the ascribed name they were given by the 'Galactic institute of biological name-calling' was so long (taking several minutes to say), was in a language that very few understood and virtually no-one could even pronounce, that it was never used. After being known as 'Floaters' for several years the name Mude was decided on but nobody knew why or who first coined it. One thought was that became popular was that it was an acronym for, Marvellous Underwater Doughnut Entities. A lesser adhered to, but perhaps a more accurate theory was that the Mude named themselves and placed it in the minds of people observing them because they did not care too much for the associations of the name 'Floaters'.

For the Mude to survive they needed to take turns being at the surface in the limited areas where there was light. They were taking turns at the trough so to speak. Each Mude was massive, as big as a Blue Whale. They were able to communicate through a combination of colour changes, vibrations and the way they came in to contact with each other. The ability to communicate and the need to cooperate meant the evolution of a sophisticated intelligence unlike any animal intelligence but in its way just as acute. The Mude appeared to spend most of their time, once energised, working in unison to create patterns of moving colour whilst making the ocean sing to tones created by collectively vibrating the water. Patterns of beautiful colours rippled and flashed and lit up the sky to a soul-soothing musical hum. Scientists, Ethicals, Spiritualists and Creatives all had their theories as to the reason Mudes acted in this way. Creatives maintained that this co-operative activity was pure artistic expression. They also believed that the pursuit of perfecting this expression had led to the Mude's evolutionary leap forward in intelligence; that their unique levels of cooperation resulted from a collective consciousness. Scientists pointed out that the behaviour exhibited by the Mude was more akin to a crowd at a football match than artists in a gallery. Spiritualist saw the behaviour more like a choir and Ethicals didn't ascribe any comparison, but saw it as basically being good. The scientist believed the role of art as a social imperative for the revelation of alternative thinking that is necessarily an individual expression; an individual pursuit. Ethicals were able to use the Mude to further the rights of plant life in the galaxy, for regardless of their similar form to jellyfish the Mude were indeed plants. Politicians secretly saw them as a threat. Many attempts were made to communicate with them, but each attempt led to the Mude sinking to the depths of their ocean home. Unbeknownst to the groups who wished to strike up a conversation with the Mude, each time, there was a sinking, vast numbers died.

Ethicals and Spirituals were given unprecedented access to the Mude once science had been unable to connect with them. Clusters of glowing vibrating jellies as big as houses continued their performances but shut down and sank in response to any form of approach. When it became apparent that their numbers were dwindling as a result of such efforts further contact was banned.

Unfortunately, the Mude were in terminal decline. Of all interested parties, it was decided that scientists, after all, had the best chance of saving the Mude and politicians by in large were relieved at the Mude's expected demise. Selected scientists were permitted to take twenty specimens into captivity as long as this could be done without any distress to them. This was virtually impossible; it was understood that losing colour and turning grey and sinking were irrefutable signs of distress and any approach caused such a reaction. No means were found to capture the Mude without loss. As had happened so often in the past, humanity could only stand on the sidelines and watch a species die.

It was a natural disaster that dramatically changed events. Planet Alan began to release gas at unprecedented levels and its moons were effectively blown off their orbits. The Mude tried to adapt their behaviour but they were unable to adapt to changing conditions. There accelerated end was unalterable. It appeared that they knew their future as they turned a profoundly deep blue and sank for the final time with the ocean vibrating in pulses of equally deep tones.

By chance, an artist who had been allowed to record the dying Mude had his teenage daughter with him. As they hovered above the sea of blue she perceived a discernable sound from within the depths of the Mude's watery song. A sound that no one else could hear and no scientific instrument had ever detected. It is well-known that teenagers hear and detect things that adults do not. She was being communicated with telepathically. The Mude had been trying to connect with their observers but any recipient of a telepathic communique could only hear it if they were around fifteen years old; something that never occurred to the scientists. It had long been believed that the *levels of cooperation achieved by the Mude had necessitated some form of telepathy and it turned out to be the case. What no expert had thought to try was having a teenage on their team. All teenagers could tune in but not because of their receptivity to certain frequencies; it was simply down to having fresher brains.*

The final communication made from the planet was made to the only human that could hear it, Rose. It was an unforgettable melody. Tears rolled down her cheeks as the moving chorus of a million sensitive intelligent organisms sunk for the final time.

It was decided that the Mude's remains, if there were any should be left in peace, which was another way of saying that funds, for whatever reasons, would not be available for research by any public body and permission would not be given to any private one.

A month had passed when the bulk of the eco roadshow had moved on to a new planet. Rose returned with her Father to the observation bubble floating just above the dying and shrinking ocean. The melody Rose had heard was indelibly etched on her soul and she was able to recite it note for note. She knew its meaning but experts were unable to match the sounds to the meaning that Rose interpreted from them. Many did not believe in what Rose claimed but she knew the Mude sung to her, 'it is our time, we have had our time, we will return to the source of all light' But Rose intuitively held back on the meaning of a series of unusual tones at the end of the melody. The musical message roughly translated to, 'come back in a month'. She only shared this knowledge with her father who knew no one else should know except Rose's mother, who was a researcher for the company on Chippenham Three.

Father and Daughter only communicated with Nasry once a month, but Rose used their emergency protocol and made contact with her. It was no surprise to learn that the company had been monitoring matters. He knew they would have to keep their return as low key as possible. The scientists working on the 'pet project' had been fighting a secret internal battle with the company's publicly known research division. Nasry had been battling to prevent the illegal extraction of Mude specimens. The code of 'no acceptance of known suffering' on longer applied if the Mude were shown to be dead. It would be Nasry's job to prove they were dead. There was a seam within the company that did not want to wait till it was sure the Mude were completely demised. As far as the hidden researchers were concerned, anything other than what could be gleaned from observation should not be entertained. The pet project had only used genetic material from plant life that had already naturally died or naturally occurred such as, the excess of excretions of liquids and gasses produced naturally. Rose and her Father Gaspare, were being followed by the sinister secret agents of the company answerable only to the CEO. They were ready to pounce if there was a chance of getting their hands on a 'Floater', dead or alive. All of this was known to Minty, the CEO's boss and head of the pet project at the time.

Welder had heard of Minty and knew the myths and rumours concerning Floaters. He had no desire to skip forward in the story. He watched the recordings of the observation bubble showing Rose and her parents as they scanned the ocean. One by one the massive forms of twenty-one Mude rose to the surface. The Mude communicated directly with Rose and she understood and started to inconsolably weep. All the Floaters were dead except the twenty-one they could see. The few remaining

Mude were volunteers chosen to stay alive as long as possible rather than join in the mass dissolving. They would suffer great pain to stay alive long enough to offer themselves to the humans that could benefit most from examining what remained of their lives and their remains after death.

The company's agent who was following events from an orbiting government observational space station was thwarted in his attempt to get a message to warn his superiors what was going on. Later it was determined that it was the Mude themselves that had somehow blocked his transmission. There was nothing the lone agent could do to prevent Nazry taking all of the remaining Mude aboard her transport and getting away.

Sophie found herself floating face down in the water, at peace and in a gentle drift.

Peals of laughter rang through the transport vessel as it carried out a zig-zag of evasive manoeuvres across vast swathes of the galaxy. The peels were made up of three distinct tones, like those of three clear bells ringing up a celebratory rhythm lasting several minutes. There was also a tone only audible to Rose which sounded in exquisite harmony with their communal laughter.

To Welder's listening ear the deeper notes were sounded by Gaspare, the mid-tones from Rose and the high notes from Nazri. He could not hear the even deeper and higher tones made by the Mude adding to the chorus. But judging by the reactions of the Keem watching and listening along with Welder they could hear. One or two were mimicking the tones silent to Welder's ear but he guessed what the Keem were doing.

The happy family were all aware of the unusual musicality of their laughter. They laughed in a distinct compositional arrangement. They rode the wave. Rose's parents were intrigued to see Rose separating from the chorus and composing herself. She was trying to say something. It took almost a minute before she was able to free herself from the grip of the song of laughter but she finally managed.

'They are laughing too!'

A sense of humour was the Mude's most cherished sense.

The remaining Mude were taken to and hidden on a new secret facility. It was in the interests of all the parties within the company to keep news of 'the twenty-one' from ever becoming public knowledge. The CEO of the company rightly did not believe the power of her throne was threatened; removal of the Mude was not necessary. The 'veggirite' movement' could be a useful tool if the hidden hand of the company became too strong.

Although the Mude looked like multi-coloured brains the size of blue whales, the part that controlled behaviour and communicated was about the size and shape of butternut squash. The Mude were held in the largest indoor tanks ever constructed and the conditions of their former watery world were accurately replicated. Despite all efforts, and they were considerable, the surviving Mude were dying. Once the fate of the twenty-one was accepted all attentions turned to communicating with them through Rose.

The Mude were told everything that there was to be told. They were told of humanities triumphs and disasters; of their great works and their follies and those joys and pains life brought and those that were self-induced. The Mude responded to selected bits of information with changes of colour and songs of laughter and tears. These *responses seemed to weaken the Mude as did communicating with through Rose who became an expert interpreter. They were also given all the information about the pet project. The Mude, who were happy to call themselves by that name, were drained of their remaining life each time they communicated with Rose. Two months after removal from their home ocean the Mude came together and in unison transmitted to Rose in no uncertain terms that they wanted to donate their bodies to science and in particular their 'nuts' to the Keem. They made it quite clear that they wished what could be described as their brains, should be called their 'nuts' and that the Keem should have them.*

The Mude transferred great knowledge to Rose. Although they expressly did not want Rose or anyone else entering the water with them, they left Rose in no doubt that they loved her; and she loved them. Tearfully she watched as the Mude lifted themselves one last time and they Rose to the surface of the tank in a blaze of psychedelic colour. Near to death, near to the extinction of their kind, the final communication, made by the last surviving Mude was, 'Don't eat me, eat him, titter. Don't eat me, eat only the light.' With that their nuts dislodged from their massive carcasses and rose to the surface of their gelatinous flesh and popped out. They bobbed on the surface of the briny solution that had been the makeshift home of their final days.

Great care was taken in handling the nuts but in fact, they were as hard as Iron but light as wood. The bodies of Mude simply dissolved away and turned the liquid they were within a kind of fluorescent peach. This solution filled a memorial pond especially made in recognition of such an amazing species of plant and the contribution they made to the project.

*It was the first memorial to plant entities
constructed. Many plaques followed to mark the demise of
forests and fields of unique plants lost forever and even for
individual plants; all much loved. Love evidenced by the
numbers of visitors to their memorial markers; plant graves.*

*Great haste was needed to insert the nuts if they
were to be successfully integrated. Welder watched
multiple clips of the hurried preparations for the procedure.
There was never any doubt that the operations should take
place for during the last days of the dying Mude it was
obvious to all that they were enlightened beings whether
they were technically plants or not.*

*An incision was made at the back of the heads of all
the Keem and the nuts inserted halfway as per the
instructions given by the Mude. None of the Keem's
receptors and delicate reflexive anatomy was interfered
with, and they felt nothing but a tingling sensation. The
nuts softened and a shoot slowly grew and attached
themselves to what had been acting as the Keem's central
nervous system.*

*The bulge at the back of the Keem's heads slowly
deflated and all that remained was a vertical crease.
Nothing of the Mude's lives or nature survived the
implantation but the basic mechanics worked, albeit slowly
at first. So slowly that it was feared during the initial years
that the implants did not succeed and the whole project was
ineffective. But like someone recovering from a stroke, bit
by bit the Keem's functions grew as the connections
between the nuts and the Keem became fused.
Telepathy was the final and still not fully developed sense
to emerge.
'That's how the Keem got their brain'
'Not brains Welder, nuts'*

193

After viewing the story of the early days of drifting slowly along the stream of development and the greatly accelerated progress of the middle year's Welder could see the Keem emerge into the creatures that looked down at him from above. They looked like swimmers on the surface of the living glass-like membrane above and all around him. Welder was given the option to skip ahead at various points and he did. He got the general idea of the rolling review of the Keem's biological history. He summed it up in his mind; Robby and those who followed were able to incorporate the properties of plants into the development of an interactive pet plant. This plant life was formed, made to move and respond to stimuli.

He also learned that all of these adaptations and every slightest modification were saved as a genetic material that had the appearance of green slime. This genetic slime was a verdant culture that was the living storehouse of the raw material of specimens that made up the Keem. From this material, any plant feature could be separated and employed in the evolution of the Keem or a future generation of their kind. Every property of plants, such as existed on Earth and then beyond was used to give the Keem form and function. Each new improved generation of Keem was grown from cuttings of the last. And each new generation was given new or refined qualities. Eventually, after centuries of development, it was no longer necessary to work from cuttings to cultivate new generations; all adaptations could be made with the thirteen specimens. These specimens then had the possibility of indefinite continual life. Like the trees of Earth that live for thousands of years, so too the Keem could live an indeterminate length of time. With the right conditions the present, individually self-regenerating Keem could theoretically live forever. Ben and Robby's vision

194

was extended beyond their horizons and had achieved all of their amazing and sometimes silly hopes and more. The one ambition that was side-lined so long that it never reached fruition was reproducing the Keem in any great number. There was always another adaption to be made first. Any mass cultivation could be safely postponed as long as the stored genetic information contained in the biomass ball of green slime was preserved.

Welder had noted that the Booby's love of bubbles, balloons and all things spherical was as strong a determining characteristic in the evolution of the pet project as any scientific parameter. Individual eccentricities and humorous traits were regularly added along the way. These were added in the form of 'funny stuff'. The hope that was finally achieved after the implant of the Mude's nuts, was giving the Keem a sense of humour. Maybe these random characteristics and humour were added to make the Keem ever more loveable and cute. Maybe it had the scientific purpose of throwing up something new and unexpected, or maybe it was just part of keeping the whole project enjoyable for the scientists working on it. Welder was all too aware that scientists are invariably the most emotional and freaky funny people he came across; at the least the good ones were. The Boob would shout out 'loons!' and point to the sky in the same way a small child still learning to speak would excitedly attempt to shout out the word balloon. He would do this for no apparent reason and at odd moments. It had the effect of making him and Ben laugh with disturbing consistency.

Knowledge gained from the development of longevity in the Keem was shared with the visible research department of the company. This gave the company a crucial edge in the development of regenerative procedures for humans. This regular research department was huge; it *had grown in size proportionately with the company. There were little known subdivisions of this department that were not so averse to working with and on animal life forms. The core of the company's science was plant-based and the public perception of the company was of an ethical jolly green giant.*

The regenerative microscopic living plant spores that came from the company's labs did work though some people would never feel right about having algae living under their skin and in their organs despite the company's reassuring advertising. They were completey honest in letting the buying public know that the microscopic forests were the same as having colonies of good bacteria crucially living in our guts. There were one or two disasters however, which produced mutations and the product line was almost given up on. The skin of one volunteer patient started to sprout leaves. One female volunteer made her fortune as the amazing green bearded woman. The problem was that the process was irreversible once initiated but soon all of the bugs in the process were ironed out and mutations were so rare as to be 'statistically negligible', as the advertising proclaimed. There was no doubt that the procedures worked as evidenced by the beneficiaries. The oldest living human to enjoy extended life was Griselda Coolant who is thought to have lived to over three hundred and sixty years old. She had a fairly active life of a moderately lazy person up until the age of two hundred and eighty. Beyond that, she retired to her couch. By the end, it would take her three days to say a single word and seldom moved off the couch, though she was physically able to. It turned out that most humans lose the appetite to live at around two hundred and sixty-seven, give or take a month or two. Not so with plant life, it would seem. With the company's growth assured by the discoveries and innovations, the future of 'the project' was guaranteed, though kept out of sight.

Once Lily Crammer, who was the last researcher to bear the name of either of the founders had separated 'the project' from mainstream research fewer and fewer people at one time ever knew of its existence. Welder was one person that did know about the existence of the project but had known nothing of its nature. The focus of the project evolved alongside that of the Keem. The idea of, 'grow your own pets' as a product for mass marketing evolved into a pure study of the nature of life itself with the possibility of influencing the evolution of humanity itself. Progress of the project was slow but steady with a wealth of adaptations coming from a better understanding of the earth's multifarious plant life; from the Venus flytrap to vast fields of singing wheat, breakthroughs occurred at regular intervals. Progress was made like a walker through the landscape rather than someone on a quad bike bombing their way to the good bits. Developments were made in; movement, collective connectivity, life being sustainable through minimal amounts of light and water and response mechanisms. But it was the opening up of the galaxy to human exploration and the discovery of ever new plant life that produced the greatest evolutionary jumps forward for the Keem.

By the time of Welder's birth on a café table on a remote inhospitable mining planet humanity had centuries in the past, given up what was considered the barbaric practice of eating animal flesh. Initially more for reasons of economic efficiency but as time went on the very idea of eating the bodies of animals became as disgusting a prospect to humankind as voluntary cannibalism.

The eating of animal eggs and the drinking of animal's milk almost completely died out as a result of cheaper plant substitutes rather than for strictly ethical reasons. The animals that were reared to produce eggs and milk had better, freer and more comfortable lives than at least twenty percent of the human population.

However, once species of plant life on new worlds were shown to have varying degrees of intelligence, new ethical and moral boundaries needed to be drawn. All but a few of the 'smart plants', or 'smarty plants' were carnivorous and more than a few were deadly to humans; unfortunately, more than a few were also delicious beyond description. Many groups around the galaxy formed to protect such plants from being poached, in all senses of the word. Poachers were incentivized by huge profits that could be made in the illegal trade of protected plant species. New grey areas emerged within which new boundaries needed to be drawn concerning the ethical use of plants. Distinctions needed to be made between levels of plant intelligence. Naturally rare wild plants needed protection. Decisions had to be made as to which plants were ethically sound to eat. These boundaries were fought over ferociously by special interest groups and vested interests. As it had always been, the grey matter of humanities brain always manages to find grey areas to fight over; usually only ending up with grey area's territory being enlarged. The argument over the eating of meat and the use of any animal product was long over. It had been a victory for the 'Ethicals' whose main weapon ended up being economic. Even cloned meat proved to be more costly and less flavoursome than advanced vegetable products; and when a poisonous spore found artificially produced meat and ideal breeding ground many thousands died. Finally determined meat eaters did not like meat unless it was off the bone. Once the breeding of animals for eating was outlawed the practice of eating flesh died out completely. The attentions of the Ethicals then turned to 'the rights of plants'. Many plants were found to have the ability to communicate with each other which created new divisions even within pro-plant groups concerning the welfare of plants. It was irrefutable that there was a significant proportion of plant life that could be considered to have levels of consciousness greater than many animal life forms. A very real and very militant plant rights movement was formed. It grew and spread as, rapidly as Japanese knotweed.

Welder took time to go back and view records of plants from the far-flung reaches of the ever-expanding explored galaxy being excitedly brought to the ever-expanding yet ever more hidden research facilities of 'the project'. Each heralding further leaps forward in the Keem but still along the guiding principles and foibles of Ben Crammer and Robby Green. Sometimes adherence to the original principles had become inspirational motivations, and sometimes, as the science took the family of researchers deeper into unknown territories, they were maintained out of a lack of any other obvious framework for decision making. Some guiding frameworks became traditions that no one understood but stuck to with almost religious fervour. The traditions were then kept going because it was believed that they might have significance that had long ago been forgotten but could be crucial. Some of the more unusual guiding principles related to 'Loony Tune' cartoons of the mid-twentieth century.

Welder realised he had no idea of how long he had been absorbing information from Milford's presentation and although he did not feel the slightest compulsion to rest *he paused out of habit. He paused the viewing just before learning of the project's first and perhaps greatest disaster. 'You haven't finished the story Welder?' mouthed the pink florescent face of a Keem looking down at him from ten metres overhead. It lay flat, halfway up the outside of Welder's cloche. The Keem's words were broadcast within the dome as if from an omnipotent presence. Welder regarded the childlike cartoon brightly coloured boyish-looking face and it made him smile. He was drawn to the pure bright yellow frock it was wearing; somehow the colour left him feeling inspired to think. He also marvelled at probably one of the least mind-boggling characteristics the Keem possessed, namely that from the most prodigious climbing and clinging plants the Keem had been bestowed the ability to adhere to any surface without effort. All twelve of the Keem were variously posed at unfeasible angles and points of the dome but all concentrated on Welder. Again their casual attentions seemed to have the menacing appearance of some sort of hovering alien vultures preferring to wait for their trapped prey to die rather than to put any effort into killing it. Welder noted this appearance but did not feel any genuine threat; it was more amusing than frightening but Welder did not trust any feeling he was experiencing. It was as if his rational mind was one or move levels removed from what was happening to him; like witness and participant.*

'I thought I would take a break' Welder finally replied. 'But you haven't come to the best bits' came a bright yellow female's amplified voice.

'Yes' said another Keem, 'the bit when Milford tells you how to destroy us' it completed. This was met with the collective tee-heeing of giggles from the Keem and bemusement and amusement from Welder.

'So I take it that you know everything that is on Milford's newsreel and that you don't approve of its ending'. Welder said in a questioning tone. No response came. Welder's mind had left the past as presented by Milford and his attentions came into sharp focus on his present circumstances. At that moment he noticed a smell very much like honey or Buddleia blossom. He closed his eyes and fell into a shallow sleep. His head did not drop; it somehow found a point of balance and remained upright. He entered a state similar to sleep but for the fact that he was fully conscious at the same time. It was as if he was sitting down on a couch watching the workings of his own unconscious or like someone conscious whilst going through brain surgery. Memory deduction and primitive fears melded into thoughts of giant Keem laughing and speaking with Milford's voice and getting drunk on 'steelberries'.

Welder pictured his father standing over him with the words Maintenance Welder on his overalls. He saw faces of familiar strangers reflected in the complex eyes of a giant fly called Louie. He saw a young Ben Crammer looking at him lovingly as a pet and Sally looking more than lovingly and telling him 'you had me at fuck off'. His dreaming self wondered what it all meant. The still conscious part of his self wondered what was happening. Whatever was happening he did not like it.

With the urgency, difficulty, and discomfort of a sufferer of sleep apnea, Welder roused himself into full consciousness.

'What's happening to me?' he asked with a soft tired wakeful voice.

He sat down surprised that he had been standing up.

'Don't worry Welder; Milford has taken care of everything. The vapours that you have smelled have been altering your metabolism and nourishing you. You are becoming like us Welder. Welder looked at his hands and was sure he detected a blue-green hue to his skin.

The Keem took it in turns to speak.

'It is not permanent'

'It just means that you don't need to eat'

'Or sleep'

'But you still need to dream so you do it while you are awake'

'Milford did it to you'

'He did it to himself'

'He did it for himself'

'So he could work and work'

'He wants you to work and work too'

'You have things to do'

'Milford wants you to decide'

'You will not sleep but you will still have dreams from time to time'

'That's what is happening to you'

'Don't worry Welder, you will be alright but you will have to stay here with us now'

'Until you have chosen'

'There are one or two side effects'

'You will occasionally need to release a little gas'

One of the central questions Welder needed to ask was forcing its way up into his mind. He had repressed it in an attempt to keep it from the Keem. Welder felt in enough control of his thoughts so that they could be heard by the Keem but not listened to. He had worked out that thought etiquette had similar principles to regular conversational etiquette. It believed it would be considered improper to listen in to people's private thoughts when not invited to, in *the same way, it can be considered rude to listen in on a private conversation. The Keem, it was clear from the outset, were extremely well mannered. He was whispering his thoughts. Once he had held the question in a private recess of his mind he was satisfied they were not listening in. Once satisfied he decided to test his skills of basic thought conversation by allowing the question to emerge and show itself publicly. He addressed his thought to all. 'What happened to Milford?'*

They did not give a spoken answer. They did not give a conversational thought answer. They simply all looked like one in one direction. They all looked at the plant Welder had unsatisfactorily relieved himself on earlier.

'That's Milford?'

'No that's Randolph. But that's what happened to Milford'

'At first'

'Is that what is going to happen to me'

'Oh no Welder, you will get to choose'

'You will get to choose what happens to all of us'

Chapter Twelve

Two flowers, one stem

Welder's desire and need to know more returned
and directed him to the Milford tapes with renewed vigour
and concentration. Despite the power of this compulsion,
Welder became sidetracked. He was struck with a question
he had asked himself before; only this time he allowed
himself the time to answer it, despite his certain knowledge
that time was not on his side. He trusted his instincts and
brushed aside the undergrowth of the circumstances right
in front of his face, to take a quick look at this sidetrack;
just a quick look he thought. Why are recordings of the type
he was about to recommence, called tapes? Not that it was
a widely used expression but it was one that the
researchers on the pet project persisted with; along with a
variety of archaic measuring systems. Certain terms
seemed to be held on to with a sense of tradition and
reverence. These traditions connected them with the spirit
of the past. Welder correctly suspected that as with the still
extant expression 'run out of steam', it related to some
ancient technology. The lack of any general interest in the
accuracy of such terms as 'tapes' did not prevent the
continuance of their use, whereas far more accurate
expressions died out. Welder put this down to some
expressive quality or perhaps powerful less obvious
significance in such terms and phrases. Or perhaps it was
the appeal of the words themselves. The unlikely survival of
certain words and phrases was something that Welder had
made note of before. Sometimes the etymology of words led
him to reassess an expression. When there was no
information about a phrase's history he came up with his
explanations. He had no idea where the expression, 'the
meek shall inherit the universe' came from but initially it
did not seem to be plausible, it seemed far-fetched. The way
the continued use of particular words even when they were

not appropriate gave him a way into understanding how the meek could end up on top. If something can remain inoffensive and under the radar of ideological, fashionable, intellectual and emotional scrutiny it may just survive whilst other dynamic and not so meek forces battle it out and destroy each other, and ultimately themselves. Welder notice that his sidetrack was opening out into a broader path but he allowed himself to wander further. In most cases, though accurate, terms and phrases are dropped from the store of collective phraseology because of their uncomfortable nature. The brief excursion of reflection ended with a sign in a clearing of Welder's thoughts. It read 'the route to the roots'. The side-tracking was a result of Welder drifting off into wakeful sleep. It was a little conscious snooze that had only lasted seconds. Welder rose out of his wakeful dreaming and gave the command 'play' out loud; out loud because he assumed the recordings were voice rather than thought activated. Nothing happened for a moment and he wondered whether he needed to give a thought command too. 'Play' he thought, 'now that's a word with roots'.

Welder had grown to like Milford from what he had seen of him on the tapes. He had known of Milford for many years but they had never met. The obvious love and admiration Milford's sister Sally had for him and the not so obvious but equally deep love Welder had for Sally played a part in Welder's good opinion of Milford.

It may not have been obvious to anyone else, and Welder gave no perceivable sign of his feelings, but his love for her was unmistakable to Sally. It was clear from the moment they met. Welder had no idea Sally knew. Equally unbeknownst to Welder, a mutual feeling had been growing like wildflowers for many years in a tiny patch of Sally's being. It was a meadow she had set aside; it was a meadow of wildflowers in her heart. He was there, in Sally's favourite refuge; Sally, a galactically brilliant, busy and pressured woman, with the added burden of humanity's evolutionary progression on her shoulders.

Her devotion to her part in one of the potentially largest steps in human development prevented her from acting on her feelings for Welder. What she sensed she was part of trumped her feelings. She felt and believed, she had a role in a giant leap for humanity beyond any form of words; beyond any formative intellectual principles and even her comprehension. But she knew it was right; she had surrendered herself to that knowledge.

Sally's poker face was inscrutable and even more masterful than Welder's. Being the more knowing party in the unspoken feelings that danced above both of their heads, Sally felt the shackles holding them back dig deeper and more painfully into her ankles. It had been many years since she had first noticed her feelings for Welder first emerge and many years before that when she noticed Welder's affection for her leaking out. In all that time she had never given him any encouragement, not even a sign that she had anything other than a professional relationship with him. That was until the very last moment before they parted after he had accepted his mission to Chippenham Five. Her obvious warmth was so unexpected that it did not register with Welder at the time.

Welder may have had a powerful and robust ego but when it came to love and Sally he was crippled by a feeling that had become a hard and fast belief; a belief that he was not worthy. The largest pennies of his life hung over his head waiting to drop and floor him. They were held securely in place waiting for the code that would trigger their release. Welder had not the foggiest idea that the information contained in the Milford tapes contained and his heady state within the dome would trigger the pennies cerebral release mechanism.

The awareness of Sally's deep love for him started in Welder as a growing suspicion at the same moment he was sure that Sally knew more than she was letting on regarding the mission. He had correctly assumed that he had been kept out of the loop so his assessments would not be prejudiced and his decisions not compromised, this was standard procedure. But there was something more; something different about the character of what she was not saying. Welder sensed there was something she wanted to tell him; something of huge significance and stretching beyond the mission. There was more than one thing on her mind waiting to burst out. He knew his mission had to be conducted out of sight and everything being held back was out of necessity. He was also correct in thinking that no one else they could have sent would have been more fully briefed beforehand than him. Trust; she trusted him and he felt it. He left it at that. Welder was used to the practice of being thrown in at the deep end. At least he was usually given the choice of using a gangplank. Whereas most operatives felt betrayed or insulted when they found out after an assignment that information had been withheld from them, Welder preferred it that way. He found that half the time the analysis and intelligence provided by the company would not be accurate and in many cases misleading and made his job harder, or a best longer. No Welder liked his briefings brief. Welder preferred the autonomy of ignorance and backed his deductive powers over those of administrators. He knew that they relied too heavily on data and information from other operatives, none of whom Welder had any faith in.

Sophie's attention shifted from the story of the Keem to her memories. She had not been aware of the

narrator for some time. For many years she had listened to
narrations of the greatest literature humanity had produced
and her mind was well used to losing awareness of the
teller when deep into a tale. She passed through the passage
to another space without paying attention to the quality of
the brickwork. When listening to a story being told she was
often amazed by just how many distinct characters could be
created through dialogue and minimal variations of the
same voice. But her engagement with what she had been
hearing, taking in and remembering reached greater levels
of experience than she had ever known in life. But she did
not feel alive. She was living through the story and reliving
through her memories. She occupied the infinite non-
physical reality of interpretation; she felt like an
uncontained flow of information, she had no physical body;
she was a body, a body of essential fluid data.

Sophie's memories began to string together in
coherent lines and the lines wove together like the fibres
encasing the flow of an electric current. The cables platted
and meshed like those of a suspension bridge. She was
suspended. None of this bothered her; she was more
interested in where she was going. She was eager to keep
going. Eagerness was how she perceived the energy of
momentum. She wanted to know which part of her life she
would pass through next; which part would join the stream
of threads. She could be delighted, or cringe with self-
loathing, or filled with joy, or gripped with fear; all from
the comfort of her own death. All washed over her as she
uncovered deeply buried forgotten passages of her life.
Landmarks were seldom on a familiar scale, and she drifted
simultaneously like a snowflake on a wind-swept mountain
and within a snow globe on her sister's mantelpiece. The
central threads that strung together her memories were not
always apparent at first. For example, she relived moments

with a string of different women from random points in her life. Then she realised the connection. One after another every child or adult called Rebekah she had ever known throughout her life came into her thoughts. The connection went as far as including every Becky or Becca, or any derivation or spelling of the name possible. One or two were secret Rebekahs and she had known by a different name in life, but not in death. In death, there was only the facts, only information. Every one of them she had ever known, friend or foe, came to her and in order.

Mostly Sophie's attentions were focused on extensive elaborate patterns of memories. The first memory was like a single small stone that had dropped to the ground and bounced about in irregular diminishing leaps and rolls before coming to rest at a seemingly random point. This would be followed by another memory, another dropped stone that did the same sort of random movements and landed some way from the first one. Then another stone dropped; another memory, only this time ending up near to the first. More and more would drop; each landing and rolling or bouncing away and coming to rest in no particular relationship to the previous ones. Some stones were larger but it was not until hundreds of stones had fallen, hundreds out of millions of moments relived, that the spiralling pattern began to emerge. Circular clusters along its uncoiling length were formed. Swirls and curls formed. As the pattern grew more distinct it grew like the pattern of one of the many crop circles she would seek out when she learned that a new one had formed in the summer wheat fields of the west-country where she spent the last years of her life.

The memories of Richard were widely spaced on her intertwining timelines but spanned a distance second only to those of her sister. Sophie had been spared the ignominy of public prosecution for embezzling from her employers and the distress this would have caused her and her family. Her unique mind was deemed such a valuable asset that she could have gotten away with acts that she could not even imagine and still been brought back into the fold. It meant that at what she thought was her lowest point, she could start a new life; a life where she could operate freely. Free even from her ambitions. It also meant leaving behind friends and the world she had inhabited. It meant leaving behind the lie she had been living to cover up her secret weakness. But she would not be entirely free; her leash was merely longer. But she decided it was long enough. It was longer than most. She would still be connected and beholden to her former bosses as they would also be her new ones. She thought briefly of being unleashed and completely free but it made no real sense. We are not free from the need to eat if we want to live. We are not free to choose where we are born or to live beyond the count of days available to us. She accepted the company's proposal before it was fully described and defined. She knew that if she thought too much about things she would never have managed to get her hair cut when she was thirteen and would not have fried bananas on that last morning. Choices she was pleased she made.

'What do you want to do?' asked Richard as he looked up at her between mouthfuls. Six weeks had passed since the pair had met at head office. He had given her a lift home after she had thrown her car keys down the drain. The door of Sophie's home had closed behind her that day, and she stood facing it blankly and listened to the sound of Richard's car disappearing down the road. Before the meeting, Sophie was preparing for the consequences of her actions. She expected them to blow her world away and to be all alone. She had been resolute but scared to her core.

In some ways; in the ways, she still had some measure of control over, she was already rebuilding her life. Her attraction to gambling that had started as a wonderfully random counterpoint to her fastidious life had taken control of her and deposited her at the edge of a deep ravine. The realization of what she had done, of the money she had stolen and lost dissolved away every lie she used to construct an image of herself. She saw every fallacy she had presented the world and was left with bleak withering shame. She wanted to confess to everyone the error of her ways; she was ready to lay her soul bare to those she had let down. One thing was sure in her mind; she would never be led to near self-destruction by anything or anyone ever again. So she went to the meeting ready. What she was not prepared for after groggily getting to her feet, straightening her back, taking in a draught of honest air and walking into that room at head office, was a relief. For whatever reason, the company would not be taking further action as long as an accommodation could be reached about how to use the genius for spotting particular patterns she barely knew she possessed. From the moment of learning of the company's proposal until the moment she was sure Richard had gone after being dropped off, she had remained calm cool and collected. She thought the neighbours must be very confused to see debt collectors at her house one day and to see her dropped off in a chauffeur-driven Bentley the next. She still found it hard to comprehend that Richard was sent to get to know more about her and not her worry lined, Line Manager. Was she that special? The tightly stitched and buttoned-down garments of cool, calm and collected had held together; just, only just. Once she was indoors and truly alone she tore of that restricting garb and went naked with relief and danced about the house with greater joy than any win the roulette wheel had given her. A point she

211

noticed and made a mental note of as she came to rest sitting on the top of the stairs. This point would always be a reminder to her of the things that mattered to her. She loved her family, her Mum, her Dad and her sister. She loved life, she loved the simple things. She had surrounded herself with things she did not care about and expensive clothes that did not suit her, despite looking good in them. She did not want the money she won or the money she lost. She had stolen just to keep gambling. She was truly addicted to gambling, she was addicted to being addicted because it gave her cause to feel, good and bad.

'Idiot, you fucking idiot' she said out loud as she thought of the madness of her addiction. She got to her feet and looked down the stairs. She turned with her hand smoothing the acorn-shaped head of the bannister post and stopped. She remained motionless for several minutes until she remembered that the company would be in touch. 'In Touch, out of touch, it had all been touch and go' she said still out loud but this time in a whisper without really knowing why. Then it dawned on her; what she had done and why. She had simply traded the control that a ruinous addiction had over her for the invisible control of a corporation that hinted at mysterious endeavours, perhaps even nefarious ones. Part of her trusted Richard though, in a way she hadn't trusted anyone before. That was the tipping point; she surrendered herself. Now completely naked, she lay on her bed and went through the meeting in every detail, remembering looks like sips of wine, and the tone of Richard's voice like a rich sauce. She would give her final answer to Richard that night over dinner.

'This is the most delicious pea soup I have ever had', she said almost completely distracted by it. As soon as she said the words she rewound to the question Richard had asked before the spoon met her lips. She answered it with another question.

'What are my options again?'

'You can walk away. There will be no charges pressed against you but, you will have to pay back the money and of course, no pension.'

'More than reasonable; almost too reasonable. Why so reasonable? And what are the other options?' Sophie had flipped from ethereal soup loving Sophie to savvy negotiator whilst looking at her contorted reflection in her empty soup spoon.

'The first option is so 'reasonable' to convince you to take the second one' responded Richard.

'Just two options Richard?' interrupted Sophie for Richard was obviously about to continue. Richard was not put off his stride. He merely continued serenely along, on his operational travelator without hesitation and without the option of deviation. He was used to distracting interjections; it was a habit his mother was well known for.

'If we made the first offer too unreasonable then choosing the second would seem to be made under duress, or at the very least, coercion. You would rebel against both and we would lose you' He spoke in quiet persuasive neutrality, except for the last bit, that came out well-seasoned with sentiment.

'Am I really that important, surely no one is irreplaceable' She said returning to marvelling at her soup and quite confident of her argument. She felt there must be some other explanation; they couldn't want her that much.

'There are those that are replaceable. As much due to the position, they hold as anything. There are those individuals that are harder to replace. There are a few that are so difficult to replace that they may as well be described as irreplaceable. And then there are those very rare individuals that are actually irreplaceable. You are smart enough to know that all of that. I am only surprised you are not aware enough to have spotted that you are one such rare irreplaceable individual. Our systems are supposed to be impossible to embezzle from, yet it seems with the wrong motivation you were able to. I know that by telling you this I am tipping our hand but as we are simply giving you choices and not negotiating, I am doing so to gain your trust.'

'Of course, I am one in a billion aren't I? Or am I one of a billion? Hmm'

'If you can come up with a better explanation of why we want you it would have to be convoluted. You can see flaws and irregularities in numbers without calculation and without prior knowledge. You are like someone who can mix and match colour without a formula and more importantly better than a machine. Surely you can see how valuable that is?' Still not convinced she assumed Richard was trying to come on to her. The brochures looked good. Was being offered a lake to build a home by? It looked grand in the advertising but was it a puddle on a rainy day, with hidden shallows of intent.

'I am not sure whether to be insulted or flattered', she said but Richard anticipated this possible misunderstanding and reassured her with such an authentic look to remove any hint of a sexual or other ulterior motives, that she suddenly sat up bolt upright and glared at him. He went on.

'We believe you have a unique mind. One we have been looking for, and for many, many years. All we want from you is for you to analyse our research. You can work from any location and it should only require you to work ten hours a month and you will earn ten times what you were earning before'

'So what's the catch' she knew that if there wasn't a catch then she could not agree to anything; a lack of catch wouldn't make sense. Any offer had to be understandable. In this instance, she saw the catch as one on a box that would lock down the deal and not one that would ladder her tights.

'The catch is that no one must know that you work for the company and that you can never discuss the nature of what you are doing with anyone. We need you to spot patterns in numbers, or anomalies, or links and we don't want anyone to know how we are doing it.'

'Why didn't you ask me before I took the money, surely if you have been looking for years I must have been on your radar? It would be very tacky if you waited to get some sort of leverage on me. Oh and that was two catches'

'No we had decided to make the offer before you embezzled the money; the fact you had a secret life of an addicted gambler only served to strengthen our belief that you were the one we have been looking for. I was sent by Mum to make a final appraisal of you and to get you onboard'. Richard hesitated somewhat nervously having referred to the relationship between him and Gillian Marston. 'And they are two parts of the same catch'

There was silence for a couple of minutes whilst they both ate and were digesting.

'We like to see how people operate. It may seem a little underhanded, but it is hard to completely avoid acting covertly'. He hesitated again and looked down at his empty soup bowl. He had come to the end of his travelator. He looked as if he was contemplating. But he was not contemplating; that's just the way he looked when he was bewildered. He was puzzled by his empty soup bowl. He could not, for the life of him, remember finishing the soup. Sophie was still enjoying hers. He dismissed his suspicions.

The atmosphere had changed; the steamy oppression of the negotiating cloche they had been under had lifted. Without any outward sign to indicate the change in his mood, Roger was relaxed. Now that the heat was off, they dropped any instinct to appear cool, calm and collected. They both suddenly took in their surroundings properly for the first time. The restaurant was a hemisphere of glass, a dome covered with fine shining chrome organic tracery of vines and carefully placed leaves of copper. They both followed individual vines back to the central column, and noticing their synchronicity, they silently chose to carry on the visual exploration of their surroundings together. There was a flavour of a French art nouveau train station about the place, interspersed with solid yet elegant beautiful wicker and highly crafted wooden furniture which added a sense of colonial hotel in the topics. Sophie did not like it. It reminded her of her own carefully crafted, tasteful interiors. She had been so pleased when everyone admired her choices, but her pleasure did not extend beyond theirs. Her insistence on functionality was her one way of convincing herself that it was not all a complete waste of money. She realised as she took in the scene and reflected on how she had felt when she watched her house empty of all her belongings, that she was more in tune to pleasing others than herself. She was not sure what she liked anymore apart from the pea soup she had just consumed. Oh, and one or two of the cheesy B and B's she stayed at to avoid bumping into anyone she knew from work when she went on secret gambling weekends. Richard and Sophie's visual stroll led inevitably back to the central column. It was a twisting swirling vine-like column. It yearned upwards towards the heavens until it met with the glass dome where it fanned out in all directions in controlled creeping. Each vine was the untwined thread from a cord, and each cord was twisted around others to form the massive rope-like trunk at the heart of the dome. Wrapped around the lower reaches of the trunk was cutlery rising from a circular pool of cutlery that formed the base. They emerged like huge glistening ants scaling the vine. The pair trailed the procession along the branching meandering vine until they were both looking directly overhead. The pain in their necks ended their diversion and their heads dropped like fallen fruit.

'You know we wouldn't have noticed the money was missing for some time if at all if I hadn't picked up the poker chip from out of your glove box when that car hit you.'

'That's was a souvenir' she said meekly 'it was worthless'. She had wondered how she had been caught out. In the turmoil that had ensued after it was obvious to her that she was busted, she had not bothered to explore that question fully, knowing the answer would reveal itself in time.

'So it was you'.

Milford had spent thirty years carefully studying, analysing and developing the project that so many generations of his family had devoted their lives to. His great grandmother Lisby, had literally laid down her life for the project. She physically fought off an attack from a crazed researcher that had gone berserk in the lab. She won the fight but died hours later. The brilliant young researcher, James Alright, had come in to contact with highly toxic spores from a recently discovered parasitic flesh-eating plant. The microscopic spores had evolved to transform just about any life form in the galaxy into an agent of death that would kill indiscriminately. The invasion of the spores and the deadly behaviour modifying toxins they exuded would lead to a painful frantic death for the host creature. New plants would feed on the carcasses of the slain and the assailant. One killing spree could nourish a colony of 'flesh-eating zombie weed' for hundreds of years. The plant would digest the bodies and produce a viscous jelly in pods the size of watermelons. The bright yellow jelly was how the plant stored the energy it needed to survive after it had harvested the corpses. The pods produce the most alluring and sweet-smelling blossom imaginable. The blossom of the plant produced no hint of pollen. The blossom had evolved its great beauty and intoxicating fragrance purely to attract higher life forms that had time enough to smell the roses. The colony of zombie weed would never be without at least one bloom. They weren't real blossoms; they were simply beautifully intoxicating spore cannons. The highly nutritious and captivatingly delicious jelly in the spore covered pods had a more basic attraction; the delicious jelly aroused a sexual pleasure unlike any other experience possible. The problem was stopping. Sessions would last weeks after a single teaspoon of jelly. Many died. But the spores were so fast-acting and so pernicious that the jelly was seldom successfully extracted. James Alright was fully aware of the plant's deadly nature but like so many hyper-intelligent beings, he was capable of doing what can only be considered the stupidest things. As a result of those who worked on the pet project having, an all-consuming and blinding sense of purpose, a slapstick sense of humour, a creative disregard for following the norm, and an appreciation of the value of a 'happy accident', they developed a deeply ingrained culture of complacency towards health and safety. An outside observer would consider the approach of many of the researchers over the centuries as being outright cavalier. Somehow they seemed to get away with it. Maybe it was because after all they were focused on getting results. That was until Alright. The 'devil may care' culture was coupled with the bravado of a *young man showing off in the case of James Alright. He was in his seventies, so old enough to have known better, but he was too charged with the vital energy of attraction to pay proper attention to the knowledge he possessed. He was smitten with Lisby. These factors combined to bring about the simple mistake by James that caused the catastrophic incident, which in turn caused his death and the death of the love he sought to impress. Flouting the signs all over the lab entreating workers to 'wear a safety mask' was quite common. The signs saying 'don't do anything stupid' were equally overlooked. James ignored both of these warnings and made a paper rose. The antiquated practise of writing on paper was a typical 'pet project' eccentricity. The love of such ancient ways played a part in some of the projects greatest achievements. It was the third warning that James chose not to heed that could have prevented the fatal danger. It was not a warning pinned to the wall for all to see. It was a warning that no one needed reminding of, 'don't sniff anything without 'mother's' permission. 'Mother' was an interactive computer. James lifted his death origami rose certificate and with a flourish called to Lisby, who looked up to see him give it an extravagant sniff. She smiled but before James could recite the poem he had composed for Lisby the effects of a single Zombie plant spore took hold of him. He had unwittingly transferred that one spore to the paper. He should have destroyed the paper earlier as part of safety procedures. That single invisible to the naked eye spore gripped him by the nasal passage. Lisby's smile turned to laugher when she saw what she thought was James doing a very authentic-looking zombie impression. She laughed till she was near to tears at the weirdly ugly expression that came over Alright's face. She continued to believe it was an act. If she had realized sooner that it was not an act, she would*

not have also been gripped, but in her case by a fit of the giggles. The fit meant she struggled to keep breathing and keep moving as James chased her slowly around the lab. She was a short dark-haired woman of a stocky broad hipped build. He was an athletic dark swarthy six foot six, and caught up with her easily with his two long, clumsy, zombie legs and got hold of her with his long extended clumsy zombie arms. She would have had the upper hand in getting away if she had cottoned on sooner. But he seized her and threw her across the room. There was a brief moment when what remained of James looked across at Lisby from behind the mask of the monster he had become. Her face was one of frozen incredulity. They looked deeply into each other's eyes fully aware of what was happening, and Lisby said the final words she would ever speak and the final ones that James would hear.
'You fucking idiot'

Urban and urbane myths grew about the properties and effects of zombie jelly and of the plant itself. These mainly surrounded the promise of unparalleled levels of sexual ecstasy with the unfortunate side effect of becoming a flesh-eating zombie; once the three-day-long orgasm ended. Humanity had long since turned away from eating flesh, but eating plants that eat flesh lay in a grey area; the grey areas of the grey matter of the mind to do with ethics and morality. There are, by the very nature of human thought, always those who seek to inhabit such grey areas. Some are driven, and others make their own way there. It is left to those who make it out alive, or those on the fringes, to generate the stories that act as a warning or enticement. These stories are the spores in propagating the type of legends that surround such things as 'Ombie weed'. The 'zombie weed' that was popular for many centuries around most of the galaxy, had nothing to do with the zombie plant, *but all who tried it, believed that it was, and all who sold it knew it wasn't.*

James had instantaneously become the involuntary accomplice of the zombie plant in its quest for prey. But apart from the tragic potential loss of James and Lisby, another great devastating danger to the project was posed by Alright's folly. It was something in its way, more dreadful than the loss of a uniquely gifted researcher like James Alright and more devastating and profoundly awful for the project than losing the talents and vision of a head of project like Lisby. It was the threat posed to the storage bubble. It was this threat that Lisby fought so hard to neutralise. The storage bubble held samples of every plant used in every adaptation the Keem had undergone. It was the stuff from which great numbers of Keem were to be propagated from.

At this point in their evolution, the Keem were about two foot tall and still looked very much like plants. Lisby's passion for the Keem and their future exceeded any compassion that she had for a brilliant researcher and it overrode any personal feelings she had for the man she had a growing love for. Once she realised he was a threat to the Keem's source material she knew he had to be neutralised; she knew she would have to kill him. She had to protect the source. It meant she couldn't leave the lab until the source was safe. After a violent struggle with the younger and stronger man she escaped his clutches and made sure the inner lab was sealed and could not be opened from within. Then she put her mind to the task of killing James. She chose her weapons and orchestrated her opportunity to strike. First, she threw the most toxic plant acid on the planet into his face, burning her own hands and arms in the process. His face and her flesh sizzled and smoked with the acids burning. He felt no pain but was blinded and she

221

fought off the pain to deliver the coup de gras. She jumped on to the bench and leaning over him from behind, she slit his throat with a scalpel. Even after the fatal blow was struck the surrogate slayer had enough strength to grab Lisby and hurl her towards the centre of the room and the vulnerable container of the source. She was fatally injured. The scalpel she had used to kill off her Zombie suitor was sticking perpendicularly from her left eye but it was her head cracking open that ended her life. She had saved the project by preventing James from leaving the lab alive. She had saved the Keem by containing the threat, but calamitously the genetic source material from which successive incarnations were to be cultivated and developed was destroyed.

Welder paused; after a slight stomach cramp, he belched a tiny bubble of gas that left the taste of strawberries and dust in his mouth. He deviated from the main line of Milford's guided tour wanting to know a little more about the story of the destroyed material called 'the source'. He tilted his head sideways making creaking and cracking sounds like a kung fu fighter about to engage in combat. He stood and straightened his back and was ready. He made a pinching movement as if plucking a toothpick and pulled out a file from a selection on the floating ethereal sidebar that came in to view whenever the recordings were paused. With the same miniature, martial arts movement he lifted his index finger and his selection came into central view and started playing.

The words 'The Source' appeared in large bold text with smaller text below it saying 'or sauce', see footnote 155532aln. Welder noted the footnote and proceeded. The source material was a green slime that was a conglomerate of every plant used in the development of the Keem. It was made up of the same constituent parts of organic matter as the Keem were in the exact same proportions.

The material was perfectly preserved and protected in a solution that itself was the product of years of refinement. The key ingredient of the solution was a gelatinous substance, similar to that of the jelly from the Zombie plant. This 'super sap' as it became known, from the Axil Melon also naturally formed a protective outer layer around the source bubble. The solution, and the transparent skin of great durability it formed, naturally regulated temperature and light. This 'super sap' was the key component of 'grass glass' of the kind Welder was under and the skin of the Keem. 'Super sap' was the plant extract which became the basis for the company's regenerative skin treatment that was cheap and actually worked. It was heralded as the 'solution-solution' in the fight against the effects of ageing on the skin.

There were originally three batches of samples; each containing the exact combination of material that made up the Keem. The batches were living material held in preserving solution. It was still early days, and the plan was to create vast quantities of the source material. The material would then be put into egg-shaped moulds and slowly dried to create a kind of bulb. Each egg would be put in a pot or 'birthing tub' of germinating soil. Water would then be added and, 'hey presto!' a pot pet would emerge and grow. This planned process was soon abandoned when the Keem's evolution through introduced adaptations advanced much faster and further than any means of propagation. It was always felt that once the Keem were fully developed than the means of cultivation could be found; as long as the source material was kept safe and up to date. Despite the batches supposedly being identical one batch slowly darkened into a viscous toxic *acidic oily mush. A generation of Keem was produced from the second batch but they grew too rapidly and only lived for three days. It was feared that all of the batches were contaminated, perhaps even deliberately by a saboteur. All hope was pinned on the final batch. Propagation was successful and the crop of Keem that Welder had encountered were the first and only one cultivated from it. Further adaptations were made directly on the Keem with the appropriate additions made to the source. But the nature of the pet project goals changed and any plan for mass cultivation of the Keem for commercial purposes was shelved. However, the source was considered to be a vital safeguard in the event of anything happening to the existing Keem.*

FOOTNOTE 155532aln. It is unclear whether the original material created by Robby Green was called 'the source' or 'the sauce'. Early records show it written and referred to in both forms.

Footnotes was another term that puzzled Welder, and he felt Milford's footnotes were rather lumpy to digest and lacking in flavour. For several minutes, since the delicious burp, Welder perceived everything as a flavour and as a texture in his mouth in preparation for being swallowed and digested. He thought of the Keem and had the sense that they would be very tasty.

The salient point for Welder was that source, or 'sauce' or whatever hysterically not funny, name the scientists gave it, was the store of all the genetic information gathered over the centuries from which the current Keem were cultivated. It was irreplaceable. The Keem had never been given the means to reproduce or even cloned. This was a precaution against what might happen if one was stolen. It was impossible to extract any genetic material of any use directly from them. This was done originally for financial-industrial copyright reasons. The Keem's physiology could not be used in any sort of attempt to reproduce or replicate them. They were one-offs. The thirteen Keem which were the seventh generation cultivated would be the last. If a scientist tried to create the Keem even with all the correct data at their disposal they would virtually have to start from scratch. Apart from that, at least three of the plants used to create the Keem no longer existed. If the brightest of all the minds in the company were given the task and access to the Sphere as Welder found it, it would be like a prehistoric human being given a band similar to Welder's and asked to recreate it. Even with all the information on how to use and make a band and all the time and means it could not be done. Certain things only happen once, even in a universe of infinite possibilities. The possibility of something only happening once is in itself a possibility that becomes a certainty in the flow of the infinite. Even with the right knowledge the right plants and the right conditions, the delicate balance of ingredients in the sauce would be impossible to match. The pea soup-like sauce was the focal point of the lab that James and Lisby were using. It was most researchers favourite lab; probably due to the presence of the sauce. It was contained in its own specially grown bubble of transparent skin. It kept itself in perfect condition in perfect conditions. The green orb floated on a bed of gas within an impenetrable clear super hard crystal cylinder. At first glance, it looked like a twice normal size floating green basketball.

As Welder looked upon the holographic image of the source suspended in its silo he froze the image and *approached it; it reminded him of something. It reminded him of a dream he had when he was a little boy, or perhaps a nightmare would be a more appropriate description. He was about seven when his father caught him picking his nose and then putting his harvest in his mouth. Welder remembered enjoying the smooth with crusty bits texture, and the salty taste of a large, fresh from the vine, bogie. To discourage his son, Welder's father asked Welder, 'would you eat a chip from my bowl if I offered you one' knowing full well he would.*

'Sure, have you got some chips Dad?' was the young Welders reply.

'Would you eat one of my bogies off my plate?' asked his father calmly.

'No way; that's disgusting' responded Welder starting to laugh.

'How about eating a big bowl of mixed bogies from hundreds of different people?'

'ERRR disgusting Dad' was Welder's reaction, laughing even harder and folding in the middle with his hands on the crease.

'How about a bogie ball this big?' he asked wrapping his large earthen hands around an imaginary ball about the size of a basketball.

Welder did not say anything as he had creased up further and was close to crying with laughter and vomiting.

'I tell you what son, I wouldn't eat your bogies and you wouldn't eat mine, so maybe we should agree as a general rule that we should not eat anything we couldn't offer someone else'

That night in his dreams, Welder dreamed of being forced to eat a bogie ball the size of a house, made up of at least one bogie from all the people on his homeworld. Welder went through life with a particular abhorrence to people eating their bogies. He also developed a very individual and distinct image of the bogie man.

Having realised where he had seen something like the ball of genetic slime, in a bad dream, Welder stood back and resumed the recordings. He was soon in the lab during the battle of James and Lisby at the point James sniffed his paper rose. It had been so long since any samples had been extracted from the source that no one noticed that the lid had not been put back on securely. During his plant induced involuntary rage and blood lust, James Alright jumped on a lab table and attempted to pick up the sauce jar with the intention of hurling it at Lisby. His handprint was all that was needed for the final removal of the already partly opened lid. Those who originally designed the security measures to protect the giant pea did not predict the scenario that unfolded. The crazed assistant then threw the freed lid at Lisby like a Frisbee which she managed to avoid by curving her body with extraordinary elasticity. Once the lid was off, the ball of green goo slowly started rising to the top of the cylinder on the gasses designed to lift it gently to the opening of the transparent tube. Lisby jumped on to the table armed with the scalpel and the jar of acid to do battle with James and protect the source. As the genetic slime rose slowly up and out of the

*cylinder the pair fought it out. Only the surgical steel used
in the lab for implements such as scalpels and the syringes
used to extract material could penetrate the bubble
protecting the source. Lisby managed to throw the contents
of the jar of acid in the face of her attackers and slit his
throat. At accomplishing this she hesitated for a moment in
shock at what she had done. But with one last burst of
energy Alright lunged at her and threw her across the lab
and she received the fatal blow to the head. The vulnerable
suspended sphere hung precariously. Lisby had dropped
the scalpel as she was being thrown. Alright picked up the
scalpel slashed the bubble and then through the blade at
Lisby. It was a direct hit in her eye. Covered in slime and
blood James finally collapsed. On the opposite end of the
lab lay the dedicated scientist Lisby, dead, still steaming
and smoking with burning acid and covered in blood.
Despite their horrible state they looked somehow noble to
the three other shocked and tearful scientists that looked
helplessly on from outside the impenetrably sealed lab.*

*Once Sally learnt from her father's orb about what
had happened she rightly surmised that from the moment
the sauce was destroyed, the current crop of Keem would
be the last.*

*Thankfully research into extending the life of the
Keem that watched over Welder as he learnt their story was
a total success. Welder learnt that they could live
indefinitely as long as they remained in their protective
environment; their bubble that was like the membrane
encasing the source.*

*The Keem within their bubble on a lifeless planet at
the edge of the galaxy only required light energy, moisture
from the atmosphere generated by other plant life in the
dome, and nutrients from the fragrant vapours of blossoms
of still more specially adapted plant life. The dome itself,*

darken and lightened as necessary to give the Keem the correct levels, day and night; it could store energy and give off light in response to the Keem. The expected life of the star whose energy shone down on Chippenham five extended so far into the future that it was not considered an issue. The Keem could be kept alive for as long as long can be; as long as they could be kept safe. Welder wondered what instrument could burst the Keem's bubble in the same way the scalpel slit open the membrane surrounding the source. He then considered who might want to, and who might do so by accident or design.

The project had become so secret that the administrative department of the company had no idea that Chippenham Five was anything but a dead rock. They saw no reason for it not to be sold for a huge profit when a buyer unexpectedly expressed interest. The right hand did not know what the left was doing. The left-wing did not know what the right one was doing more to the point. Sally had been fighting an internal battle with her company CEO counterpart Walbran Prawnshot for decades. She wanted to stop the sale and she thought she had succeeded. Unfortunately, Walbran used long-forgotten rules of sales and acquisition to give the go-ahead for disposing of the planet without her consent. It was only by chance Sally learnt of the sale, but she was too late to stop it. She was at least able to arrange Welder to be sent to deal with what needed to be dealt with before handover to the mystery party.

Welder belched again only this time he croaked like a frog as he let out a stream of gas that smelled like cream tea with a hint of a linen tablecloth. If he knew what a smart tearoom smelled like, he would have recognised the odour he was enjoying. He opened a file called 'Pooting and Prancing' in the hope it would inform him about the

Keem and perhaps throw some light on his worrying gas problem.

It turned out that as a bi-product of the processes that kept the Keem alive a little gas is produced. This gas was released in unison by all the Keem in small amounts each day and in a larger quantity once a month. So efficient was their conversion of nutritional vapours and water into everything they needed to sustain themselves that they only used less than five percent of what they took in. The expulsion of the used and unwanted gas was incorporated into a ritual dance. The release of the gas was called 'Pooting' and the ritual created to regulate pooting was, 'Prancing'.

Chapter Thirteen

Silly Billy

*By the time Milford had put together his
presentation for Welder, he had forgotten his initial
bewilderment at some of what he had initially learnt when
he watched the 'fob' his father had passed on to him for the
first time. The fob was one of the fourteen. Fourteen 'Info
orbs' specially created for the project generations in the
past and modified by Alfros. Alfros had applied his great
intellect and a relentless drive to turn the fobs in to 'super
peas'. Each fob was improved upon by successive project
heads; each time enhanced with many more lifetimes of
data storage capacity. But what Alfros added that made his
contribution so significant was a collating and retrieval
feature that patched into its user's thoughts when coupled
with their band. There was one for each Keem, and one for
the head of the project.*

*Welder continued to keep down, as far as he could,
any speculation as to why he had only seen twelve Keem.
He wanted to keep certain thoughts private by not paying
any attention to them. He let them be until he knew what he*

231

was going to do with them. It would seem that each successive generation of researchers became accustomed to the more idiosyncratic ways of the Keem. Somehow the bizarre characteristics they possessed soon seemed a natural part of their modus-operandi and intrinsic to their charm and therefore clever inclusions from past project scientists. In fact, the Keem's quirks were assumed to have an unspoken essential purpose.

Being bestowed with charm cuteness and lovability was a guiding principle in the Keem's evolution from the outset. In many ways, the focus of some of the greatest scientific minds humanity had ever produced had fulfilled Ben Crammer's seemingly impossible original vision of creating a loveable homegrown creature. Moreover, the level of consciousness achieved in the Keem was further advanced than anything Ben or the Booby could ever have imagined. However, there was one part of Crammer's original concept that was further off than ever. From very early on the research looked less and less at being able to replicate huge numbers of the process of cultivating the Keem. Instead, concentration was focussed almost solely on developing the attributes of the existing Keem. It was believed that as long as the source was in-tact, the material was there and a way could be found to replicate the process and create new crops of Keem. Each additional feature made this more and more unlikely until very quickly the prospect of making the Keem a product that could be developed for a mass market was so remote as to be unfeasible. The spin-off products from evolving the Keem had made 'The Company' a galactically powerful business entity. Research into the Keem became the exclusive pet project of Ben and Robby's descendants and hidden from the main body of research conducted. That main research body was like a giant twin that did not know it was

232

separated at birth but always sensed it's tiny double. The larger partner was commercially driven.

As long as the sauce existed there remained the thinnest thread connecting the project to the original idea of sea/space monkeys as a commercial enterprise. Once destroyed that thinnest of threads was snapped and it had a profound influence on the renewed and redefined objectives of the project. The Keem had become unique and irreplaceable. Keeping them alive indefinitely became imperative. The nature of sustaining life, the nature of life and evolution came into sharp focus. Possible implications for human evolution were beginning to be discussed in hushed tones. Ideas formed like a lingering mist from the sweaty vapours rising from the fevered brows of those who worked on the project. It was a fog of undefined possibilities and unforeseen developments. Attentions inside and outside the lab forced those involved to confront the moral and ethical grey vaporous cloud made up the countless whispering imaginations of great minds. It was a cloud where unpredictable consequences lurked.

Had Robby Green been born in the age of space travel with the eventual discovery of life, particularly plant life, on other worlds who knows what he would have made of it all? Would he have sought to go beyond using what was learnt from the Keem for more than anti-ageing products and procedures? The way the Keem converted energy had huge implications if it could be somehow adapted for humanity.

What if?, questions such as in 'what if Robby Roundway had greater means at his disposal to express his genius?' did not trouble Milford Lyme as much as the 'if only' statement when it came to his assessment of human progress. It pained Milford deeply to think of the many personifications of opportunity, advancement and human potential wasted through the destructive part of man-un-kind's nature. On the one hand as far back as he could remember he was amazed at advances in science, so much so he knew from early on that science would be the focus of his life. Nothing excited him more; nothing. And it was that science and technology that extended his life and made that life more comfortable and rewarding. But as amazed as he was with humanity's progress in understanding the physical universe, on the other hand, he was shocked at the lack of progress in the personality of humanity; its spiritual journey, the grim holding on to fears and self-interest and just the sheer numbers of assholes that continued to come in to being.

Science had met humanity's need for food and shelter with controlled environments. Food production and manufacture of necessary materials for shelter and long life were more than adequate to meet the galaxy's ever-growing populations. But still, there was conflict, greed and destruction leading to pain and suffering. Milford feared that there was something about the nature of human needs and having them met that prevented humankind evolving in any meaningful way. Rather than needs being met he believed they had to change.

Milford attempted but could not calculate the huge loss to the evolution of humanity when entire genetic lines with countless potential genii were wiped out in the barbarism of mankind's history. The maxim that 'what we learn from history is that we don't learn from history' was right often enough for him to carry its pessimism like a cold that never really gets better. That pessimism became part of the structure of Milford's core belief that mankind still had some catching up to do. Human progress had stalled and the project was part of his and his Sister's mission to give it a shove. With this at his heart, the project became stronger

234

than ever even though it was facing its greatest threats from quarters seen and unseen. The project had for some time been art for art's sake but Sally and Milford were heading for make or break choices. The responsibility the siblings felt was strangely liberating. Pre-race nerves ended with the prospects of going on the run. The project was free of constraints and led to undreamed of advancements in undreamed of directions.

  Welder decided to look again at the parameters Ben and Robby decided would define the Keem. His emotions may have been dulled by the dome's controlling vapours but his instincts were tingling and he felt like his whole body had been plucked from a warm bath, dipped in an icy plunge pool and sherbet dip. The oldest recordings were remarkably clear.

Robby started.

'They should not be able to reproduce; they should have no gender.'

Then it was Ben's turn.

'They should only display the characteristics of positive feelings'

FOOTNOTE; 1999.27b at this time the idea of genuine feelings being a possible goal was considered to be so remote as to not be worth considering. Ben was in this instance referring to the characteristics of feelings similar to a mechanical toy portraying an emotion. It was thought so unlikely to ever be possible for a plant to have emotions until, of course, the discovery of the Mude.

Welder thought the footnotes must have been written by someone quite involved with the project rather than a historian. Some may have been written by Milford himself but none seemed edited. The words Mude and Floaters came into the peripheral vision of Welder as a heading if he sought more information on.

The footnote continued. 'It was believed that if it were ever possible to incorporate actual feelings it would open up new territories fraught with ethical and moral pitfalls'
'Milford's words for sure' Welder remarked.
'Milford's indeed' responded an internal voice of a Keem Welder needed no reminding that he was still connected to the Keem's hive mind and was apt to have his thoughts buzzed.
The holographic image flickered at the point an upgrade of the original recordings started.
The projection from the past continued with Robby.
'The pets should be as self-sustaining as possible'. Then Milford's voice returned.
'This has many obvious advantages such as reducing the prospect of damage through neglect by those over-seeing, or the term caring would be a more accurate term, for them'
Then Ben again, 'The pets should never suffer'
'They should not be capable of harming themselves or others'
'They will be delightful'
'They should be brightly coloured and laugh'
Welder watched and listened like a spectator at a tennis match.

Ben and Rob went back and forth talking through what the Keem should be; with Milford's interesting but annoying footnotes pinned to them. Welder added what he was picking up from his direct encounters with the Keem to the history of their development and the parameters Ben and Robby initially set out for them. A feeling for who they are, rather than what they are, formed in his mind.

Ben and Robby went on to outline a funny loveable creature, a giggly creature that could make cute chit-chatty like sounds. Ben and Bobby frequently broke off with laughter at their shared imaginings unconcerned with the notion that they were laying down the guidelines referred to time and time again in the centuries to follow. Whenever there was a debate about which course to follow or a need for fresh inputs, the original outlines drawn by Ben and Robby were reviewed. Some of what they came up with sprang forth from the extra sense they often communicated through and so valued by the Mude; humour. As the pair went on describing the Keem they went into ever greater fits of laughter until eventually they both squeaked and rocked in their attempts to carry on talking whilst in the throes of their giggle fit. Only very few people, including Welder were able to watch without laughing themselves. This was despite, almost everyone not knowing what the pair were laughing about.

The scope of what Ben and the Boob believed possible and ipso facto their ambitions were limited to their knowledge of plant life that existed on earth. However, this was more than enough to get started with. Despite plant life being exploited for food, building material and purposes such as cotton for clothes, extracts for medicine and a myriad of other uses, Robby found that the potential uses of plant life remained huge.

'Very huge' as Robby put it. Robby made Ben aware of the fruit whose colour was the brightest colour of any kind ever recorded and the sophisticated methods plants employed for pollination. Some seeds only germinated with fire, plants that formed themselves into the female form of insects to lure males of the same bug so that they would serve their needs. Understanding the properties of the fruit with the brightest colour ever recorded led to the bright colours of the Keem from the earliest versions to the ones Welder was confronted with on his arrival. Welder put up with Milford's occasional, and occasionally not so occasional repetition of information knowing it to be a result of him leaving the central narrative and looking more closely into certain areas. He was impressed that Milford had created many new footnotes that he was drawn to. Especially as he was not sure what he was looking for. He ploughed on like a castaway gathering whatever looked potentially useful.

'Robby and Ben's early work led to cheaply produced wholly organic florescent fabrics that kick-started the company's fortunes; fabrics that used a reflective cellular structure with the inherent colour which in turn ended up with fabrics that generated warmth and light'

Welder watched an episode of the television program 'The Dragon's Den' on which Ben and Bobby's obvious investment potential caused an actual physical fight amongst the highly heated dragons. The show was never aired but went viral on the internet after Ben managed to get hold of a copy and leaked it. It was a virus that caused three of the Dragon's to withdraw from public life, so disfigured was their public image. It was a new fabric that Ben and Robby sought investment for and got; they did not let on that they would use profits to fund their pet project. Once the money starting to roll in Robby had the time to add new materials and products and most importantly in his heart and mind, he had more time to work on pet plants. It was not long before he came up with 'potted pets'. 'Potted pets' made very promising commercial beginnings and all was rosy in the company's garden. But it did not take long before a blight almost ruined their plans. Their pet pots were so convincing in their life like charm that further research and development was considered unethical, even immoral. But it was being wrongly connected with two near-fatal asthma attacks that change the public's affection for the product and its hurried withdrawal. So the pet project became exactly that.

'As new worlds were discovered so new and incredible plant life provided the Keem with ever greater levels of intelligence, longevity and cuteness.' No mention of the Floaters or Mude thought Welder. He had reached a dead end, but at least he had determined what he had a growing hunch about. He put that hunch on hold. Being in a mood conditioning dome meant he was not getting his usual range of hunches. He returned to the main text of the story.

His hunch was telling Welder that the Mude were important, perhaps in ways that Milford himself had overlooked. It was also telling him there was something else. Welder sensed that Milford's somewhat sententious yet compelling presentation was leading to something dramatic, something even more calamitous than the destruction of the irreplaceable source material.

Sophie looked forward to rendezvous with Richard. At least once a year they would meet up in the US, usually New York, upstate or city. One year Richard took Sophie to the Botanical Gardens in Brooklyn. There she learnt the sad tale of the nine hundred-year-old Bonsai tree that was donated to the Gardens by its Japanese owners. It died shortly after its arrival. The next time they met closer to home, in a Bed and Breakfast on the seafront in Morecombe Bay. Richard gave her a beautiful Bonsai tree which she tended with loving care. She paid particular attention to not overwatering it. One autumn or 'fall', Richard arranged a meeting at a Bed and Breakfast by one of the Finger Lakes, New York State. Sophie found the Victoriana furnishings pleasing, the antiques authentic and the breakfast tasty enough. But somehow it all added up to being too themed and too ordered. She felt the urge to visit the rather incongruous Greyhound track they passed driving out of the picturesque town. The only thing she liked was something Richard thought she would hate. There were many little hand-written signs phrased as though an inanimate object was talking. A painting had a note next to it written in elegant cursive saying 'Don't touch me, I'm very sensitive' and there was one on the mantelpiece saying 'Don't pick us up, we're delicate' referring to the collection of china dogs. And there was one on the hall stand next to a bowl of wax fruit saying 'Don't eat us, eat them' with an arrow pointing to a bowl of almonds still in their shells.

The work of running the 'Soft Sands' bed and breakfast dovetailed neatly with many of Sophie's anally retentive predispositions. Far from finding the notes she had seen at the Lakeside B and B in the US of A cheesy, she liked and employed them in her new business. Richard was surprised at some of her decorative choices for the B and B. They were bordering on kitsch but not in an interesting way. They did not seem to mesh with the good taste she normally displayed and even flaunted in her other choices. For her, such things as the notes, no matter how tacky, at least showed some individuality. Genuine heartfelt bad taste was better than formulaic soulless 'good taste'. She put one or two notes of her own around the place but stopped short writing directly on the toilet seat 'don't wee on me boys'. She had a number of illustrated notes that she had written without a specific place in mind for them such as, 'don't eat me; eat him' and 'I have good taste but not if you bite me'.

During those years of jointly running the guest house with Albert Sophie, by degrees, became a committed vegetarian. It started with the unusual decision of giving up chicken and fish and continuing to eat beef and pork. The reverse of many 'would be' vegetarians. Her rationale was that eating beef or pork constituted eating less of a whole animal. Many times more people could be fed from a single cow as opposed to one chicken or one fish.

Fewer living things, therefore, needed to die to feed twenty people. She felt that as long as she was convinced the animals she ate had had a good life and a good death, she would allow herself the occasional roast beef or pork on a Sunday. For a while she would occasionally eat roast lamb, once again, as long as she was convinced it had had a good life and a good death; despite that life being shortened. But she did not feel comfortable with this and widened the restrictive parameters to only eating large animals that had had a full and good life as well as the obligatory good death.

But it was the feeling Sophie had that it was contradictory to kill a different species in a way we would not treat our own, and to say it was done humanely. Eventually, she got to the point that she would have to witness the slaughter of any animal she ate a part of. She went to a local farm and prepared herself to be upset to the point of committing fully to vegetarianism; going 'the whole no hog' so to speak'. In fact, it was far less distressing than she thought it would be. It was not so much that she had detached herself from the process of slaughter, it was more as a result of being more attached to the organic farmer's compassion and understanding of the processes of living that meant she coped with witnessing an animal's death.

She was upset rather than disturbed, and rather than giving up meat she worked with the farmer once every few months and took charge of the slaughter process. She preferred to be in charge of the slaughter herself where possible. Verifying the restrictions on what meat she ate made it almost impossible to eat meat in all but a handful of restaurants. Mad cow disease, foot and mouth, the destruction of rainforest to make land available for beef cattle, and numerous other external factors combined with sheer inconvenience of her personal policy, sealed the deal and she became a committed vegetarian. Once she decided all arguments and constructs that rationalised eating meat collapsed, she cried at least once a day for a month.

The blank expression of surrender that she read into the face of the cows she had seen slaughtered came back to haunt her. The sticky wet smell of warm blood seemed to become lodged in her nose whenever she thought of meat. The quartered butchered carcass' hung in her mind. She could not console herself for taking so long to decide, even with the knowledge that battling with gambling addiction preoccupied her for many years. Her time at the Soft Sands allowed Sophie to stand her ground against what she considered her drifting self-neglect.

Sophie returned to memories of those years as if treading on a firm stepping stone in a slow flowing and safe part of a stream. It was not the first time she felt like she was hopping from rock to rock and stepping from stone to stone. What was curious to her was that with each careful step and brave leap she was making her way upstream and not across it. It did not seem like a memory and it did not seem to be part of the story.

'Bit of a corny metaphor for the source may be. Or maybe it's a memory that is harder to penetrate or I just don't remember fully?' Sophie's thought response waited for an answer from the narrator. None came. Sophie started to rationalise what she thought was happening to her. No image or sound and no sensations accompanied her thoughts.

'Whatever is happening to me, there is a 'me'. So surely I can't be dead. I can't see or hear, smell, touch or taste.

Surely I am not in a coma being read stories by, god knows who at my bedside. If I am in a coma or simply unconscious I hope I don't come to, because I know for certain I reached over one hundred years of age, and I was emotionally numbed from fighting off physical pain. If that's still the case I'd be better off dead; that's if I am not already. They'll know that. I better get ready to be sucked downstream when those hovering around my shell pull the plug hole and my skin and bones get flushed away. Then again maybe I am dead to the world and I am me without my dead body. Perhaps I am only my thoughts and memories on my way somewhere else. Perhaps I am like the light from a dead star, still being projected into infinite space. Death may simply be a transition from one state to another and I am in the passage between them. Somehow I know with as much certainty as anything else I know with any certainty, that I will not be reborn as a salmon swimming upstream, or a bear waiting to hook one out for lunch.

I know it but I don't know how I know it; it is not a knowledge that I arrived at. I don't know, but it makes sense that I was at the end of a chain, no not a chain, a branch that started with the first spark of life deep in the earth and that I share a common ancestry with every living thing. Just because I don't know my family tree more than three generations past doesn't mean I'm not still connected. It may be farfetched but my dreams of flying may be informed by sap rising from my evolutionary roots. It feels like a memory; all that flapping around, especially as it gets so tiring. I don't know why I'm trying to figure all this out; it is just as confusing as it was when I was alive! I've got to keep it simple. I have no awareness of a body because I am unconscious or dead. I am listening to a story which is either an internal voice or an external voice. It's either a creation of my unconscious or it's being prompted or directed by some outside agent. I can explore my memories in a way that I never could when I was conscious or alive. The only thing outside of the story and my memories is the weird channels with events, locations, and people and me with things that I don't recognise. Not unlike certain dreams, I used to have. There is also the stream; is it a memory or coarse I need to follow. Maybe if I reach the source. It's all part of moving on or getting out or getting up or something.'

Sophie returned to the Soft Sands Guest House and the feeling of being on a safe stepping stone returned. But rather than re-joining her past, she concentrated on the stepping stone and all else faded away. 'What if I step off the stone and into the water?' Sophie stepped off the rock and whoosh, she felt like she was being sucked up a hose pipe like a canister in a pneumatic-powered mail system. She could feel thoughts being stretched.

'Get out of the water you silly billy!'

With the sound of a strange adult's voice, she was pulled out of the water by her hair and the event or memory burst like a bubble.

'You'll never guess in a million years, my girl. Well not unless you got lucky. But you would definitely guess in one million and thirty-eight years, seventeen days six hours and four minutes; give or take a second. That's if you spent every one of those long stretched out seconds thinking about it. Eventually, you would have to hit the target. You could save yourself a lot of time if you didn't. The point is the death has released the arrow and it hit its mark. You are on the other side of the target' Sophie found the narrator's voice reassuring but what he was saying rather irritating.

'God you are annoying sometimes'

'No you are, and I am not God'

'I'd be better off alive' her words faded as she chose to let go and allowed herself to fall backwards on the bed in her room at the Bed and Breakfast.

The sheets had the freshness of a home wash. Most guests found that it was worth putting up with the shared toilet and Albert's and Sophie's orgy of decorative styles just for the smell of the sheets and the amazing breakfast. When Sophie put her mind to something she got as close to perfection with it as humanly possible.

Sophie would have loved to entertain Richard at the Soft Sands. Her ability to pretend the couple did not know each other was not in question but Richard saw risks where Sophie saw excitement. There was enough subterfuge in Sophie and Richard's clandestine rendezvous' to act as a perfect counter to her compulsive control-freakery around the guest house. Albert was more than happy to let Sophie get on with it. Sophie was his daily balm to soothe the pain of the loss of Mo and she held him back from walking into the huge chasm the mighty Mo had left in his life. He had lived in that gap for two years and it almost closed up on him.

Sophie bought the B and B from Albert when it got too much for her old friend. She did so with the proviso that he would stay on to help with the art classes for the children and to oversee the purchase of new and ever more exotic tropical fish for the collection.

Sophie's family were bemused when she left her high powered job at the company completely unaware of her continued relationship to it. They did not ask too many questions, they were so pleased with the change her new life had brought about in her. Her sister, however, knew that there was something decidedly fishy about the sudden change. She would close her eyes at Sophie's answers when she was being quizzed about her move to Weston Super Mare 'of all places'. When they stayed at the 'Soft Sands' and met Albert Sophie's family fell in love with the place and with him in particular. Albert had become Sophie's truest ever friend and confidant. She told him everything; everything, even about Richard. At first, she was worried that her Dad would be a little jealous of her obvious plutonic love for Albert as a father figure; all through her teenage years, it had been her Dad she had gone to for counsel. But her Dad was just pleased she had someone like Albert in her life, sticking to the belief that his Daughters could not have too many good people around them. Sophie was glad too, that her Dad did not expect her to be in a relationship or 'find someone special' as her Mum would often say.

'Albert's lovely but don't you want a proper partner'. Sophie many times heard her mother say those words when they had a private moment together. Once her sister had started having children her Mum eased off a little on Sophie needing a 'proper partner'.

Chapter Fourteen

Rhubarb and Rituals

Alfred or 'Freddo' as most people called him, pulled in to the allotted parking space for guests at the rear of the Soft Sands hotel, guesthouse slash bed and breakfast. Albert was already waiting at the back door to greet the expected arrivals.

Alfred was a tall man, much taller than the girls or their mother Alice. He was slim and his arms and face had the dark hue of someone who spent time outdoors; in his case, it was mainly in the garden. He had fine steel-grey hair and as he unfolded himself out of the car Albert could see Sophie in the features of his face. But as Alice got out of the car her resemblance to Sophie was so remarkable any similarity of appearance Sophie had to her father seemed to evaporate.

The garden of the Soft Sands, like many gardens of the houses and business' in the centre of town, had long ago given way to the concrete of much-needed parking spaces; concrete that covered every bit of bare ground. Albert's response to a lack of anything growing in the garden was to paint the parking spaces with flowers. Each space became a separate flower bed with different coloured flowers that matched the colour of the name and colours of the corresponding room; Sophie's idea. For Albert, gardening and painting were much the same things. They both involved the cultivation and arrangement of colour and texture to present the viewer an opportunity to relax, contemplate or possibly meditate. He spent many hours at his allotment but unlike the other patches, he grew very few vegetables. It was a composition of form and content that produced flowers for the bed and breakfast and a place for other gardeners to visit, admire and be part of. And like painting it left Albert's hands perpetually grubby. In the painted garden there were also two large wooden planters standing like sentinels at the entrance to the property, marking its extremities. They were close enough together to be like giant gateless pillars built to support a heavy iron gate. They were about a metre in length and breadth and two meters high. In them were the most splendid rhubarb plants imaginable. They were a rare large edible and decorative variety the size of large hydrangeas. Unbeknownst to Sophie, Albert had been secretly writing 'wacky' little signs of his own and hiding them for Sophie to one day uncover. He placed one at the base of the right-hand Rhubarb if one was to view the pair from the street. It read, 'don't eat me; eat him' and had a little arrow pointing towards the Rhubarb to the left. There was a matching sign at the base of the plant on the left, only pointing to the one on the right.

Freddo led the party through the back portal of the B and B. Sophie had been alerted of their presence by the sound of closing car doors and the distinctive deep tones of her Father's voice. His voice reassured her yet triggered a sense of anticipation as it always did. Sophie was all ready for them and had dozed off on top of the freshly made bed in the daffodil room. She came to and excitedly made her way down to greet them all.

'Hi Dad, where's Lily?' Sophie asked as she greeted her father with a kiss on the cheek.

'She's going to be an hour or so late. We all set out together but they forgot a bag of stuff in the fridge. You know what they are like.' He said with a resigned loving and wide-eyed smile.

It was the day before Lily's birthday which she happened to share with her second child, a little girl called Louise Sophie. Sophie had kept the B and B free of bookings for the weekend so her family could visit and celebrate the birthdays. She had a party planned for her little sister and her very little niece; her niece's first birthday party.

Under the cloche Welder felt no anxiety; he felt no fear. His animal instincts seemed to have deserted him, but his faculty for reason had not. He knew that his moods were being controlled; somehow he was able to keep his thoughts flying at speed slightly above them. Usually, it was his personal band that blocked feelings with a feature specially designed to control debilitating emotions, but when that was the case, he was in control of the blockers controls. In this instance, the controls were out of his reach. Welder's physical and emotional states were being monitored and kept in check by the sensors and a carefully balanced concoction of vapours in the atmosphere within the cloche cloud he was under. All of the vapours were purely plant-based excretion. Often there seemed to be a lag between physical and or emotional discomfort and achieving balance. Usually, there was a slight overcompensation and he would experience contrary feelings. Not long. but noticeable. There was a slight pendulum effect but each swing was shorter. The mood swings lessened. Most of the time, he was in perfect equilibrium and without any dulling of energy or concentration.

All but the entertainment functions on Welder's band had stopped working the moment he stepped out of the lift come decontamination column. The dome Welder was under was designed as a further level of quarantine and also as a means of allowing humans to acclimatise to the Keem's living conditions. Any more than a brief visit (up to three hours) to the Keem's large dome, or 'Keemdom' necessitated time in the cloche. The cloche was as vital to the rare visitors to the Keemdom as a decompression chamber is to a deep-sea diver. The Dome within the dome, or cloche, or smell-jar as it was variously called was used before and after longer visits to the home of the Keem. It was mainly used by maintenance workers and occasionally researchers. Welder had already been in and under the dome longer than needed for the usual researcher's extended playtime with the Keem. For this reason, he was being more than simply acclimatised. Researchers called the process acclimatisation but they knew full well that it required more than getting used to the climate to survive for any length of time amongst the Keem. The Keem were defended. They were defended by their environment. The cloche or steamer (yet another nickname) had only been used once since 'the incident' and it had not been tested at all since being modified by Milford. Welder decided to take the longer slower route through Milford's presentation sensing he was getting to the bit that concerned him personally. He was actually enjoying the process, or at the least, the vapours would have him believe he was. The use of concentration gas was widely banned across the galaxy due to its after-effects of verbal aggression and isolating introspection. Some individuals were either immune to these side effects or did not notice them. Welder slowed his progress a little like someone putting off reaching the end of a book whilst dying to come to it. Having made that choice, however, there was a sizable chunk related to the history of the cloche that he sped through on fast forward image mode. He reached the point he wanted. Milford was in full flow.

'Any attempt to stay beyond playtime requires another level of adjustment'.

Rather than allowing the human body to adjust and adapt through the use of 'fragens', the modified cloche brought about irreversible physical changes needed for the hemisphere the Keem called home. Those that called the cloche a steamer also called the 'Keemdom, 'the big platter'. The most tedious part for Welder in assimilating the salient points in the Milford tapes was the completely unnecessary renaming of things repeatedly by successive generations of those working on the project. If there was any humour there, Welder was deprived of the ability to appreciate it. Or so he thought. The dome was keeping Welder calm but when he heard the word irreversible, he knew he should be feeling more than a little anxious.

'You see Welder the cloche releases vapours that contain extracts which are derivations of powerful plant hormones. They are a delicate balance of chemicals such as those that trigger digestive enzy.....'

'Stop' Welder instructed, noticing an unusual noise and the tapes stopped. It was the Keem chanting. Welder figured it out as being part of their 'pooting' ritual. Welder would normally have investigated but he was compelled to continue with Milford's description of what was happening to him.

'....enzymes. We have developed a cocktail of vapours to act as a kind of catalyst for human beings to be able to convert energy directly from the sun and to absorb nutrients directly through the skin; much like the Keem. Can you imagine the implications of what the Keem have taught us? We could live as efficiently as plants! Wait till the pro-planters get to hear about it! That's if they ever do get to hear about it.' Milford had wandered off-script and Welder, unaware he was standing was suddenly overcome by his weight and melted down to his knees. From there he involuntarily ended up on his backside like a massive toddler or panda.

The projection looked paused but in fact, it was Milford contemplating what he was about to say. Welder was about to issue the instruction for the tapes to keep playing when he realised it was Milford that was paused.

'There is no going back on this one Welder' Welder had been thinking the same thing to himself. Without feeling resigned to it he knew he was not going to come out of this situation the same as he went in; that's if he came out at all. Welder's sense of fatalism kicked in but somehow he had faith in Sally and the importance of her quest, though he wasn't sure what that was. 'Sally, lovely Sally', the memory of the first and last embrace he shared with Sally took on a new poignancy. He rationalised it as being respectful rather than affectionate. He killed off a growing hope that she had feelings for him. He wrongly identified it as a weed and plucked it from his heart and mind. Welder's usually high scoring analytical hit rate missed the target once again.

An awareness of his vulnerability in regards to Sally made him wonder whether he would still have taken the job if he had broken from his usual pattern and gotten more information from Sally. 'No I would probably have gone for it anyway, just to please her; she is the only thing in the galaxy I truly love. Sally' he sighed like a small breaking wave on a beach of tiny pebbles. Emotion washed over him; not every feeling can be countered, he thought.

'All right Milford, let's hear it' was Welder's unnecessarily long command for the tapes to recommence.

'You have some very difficult choices to make Welder. Anyway, you will barely notice the changes to your physical being apart from...'

Welder paused the tapes once more, only this time with the jerk of his head and a thought. He realised he was still not quite ready. He remained in his Buddha pose whilst he took a moment to clear his thoughts. He knew from dealing with scientists before that on most things he could skip ahead and edit out most of what they took their time to explain, but when it came to matters of his welfare he should listen very carefully to the information they often liked to rush through; the bit that has to do with a few minor side-effects.

'And you will suffer no long term ill effects; at least none that I am aware of; you will simply be a little altered. To be amongst the Keem you must be a little more like them.'

Milford was indeed motoring along and Welder had to keep stopping. This time he chose to ask a direct question, to which the fobs interactive software 'May', was programmed to respond. As he spoke emotion rose in him. 'I didn't quite get what the side effects are, apart from being turned in to a fucking cumquat.'

'Do you have a question Welder' responded May in soothing neutral tones. May's lack of emotion seemed only to exaggerate Welder's. At home, he chose a highly-strung male interactive program prone to hysterical outbursts. MAY, which was an acronym for, Me, and You, was a system Milford developed himself.

'What are the side-effects of being turned in to a fucking cumquat? And I know you know what I'm talking about' Welder was experiencing mild annoyance.

'You will have an intense irresistible urge to urinate every twenty-four hours. You will excrete a small amount of bright blue liquid; much less liquid than your desire to urinate would suggest. One minute later you will expel a little gas through your lower exit point. It will sound a little like an old man clearing his throat and last ten seconds; approximately. It will have the odour of chips. Your skin will have a green tinge and may feel more waxy than usual' and with that, the programmed response ended.

'My skin doesn't ever feel waxy. I don't have a 'usual' level of waxiness. I am not a piece of wax fruit or an overgrown candle shaped like..' Welder ended his remarks unable to think of an appropriate celebrity that would be in a waxwork museum. Every quadrant of the galaxy had at least one planet which was solely dedicated to collecting

museums and collections. They were in effect, museum museums; or just in case we might want it later planets. It was bizarre and a bit of mystery to those who studied such things, that almost every civilization in the galaxy at some time or other made, or attempted to make likeness' of well-known people out of wax.

'Do you have another question Welder?'

'No. Piss off.'

Welder contemplated for a moment that the term 'piss off' would not have the same connotations in a world of human-plant hybrids. He mused that the world of human/plant, or human slash plant would have to drop the term slash all together from the colloquial lexicon when referring to urinating, whereas, taking a leak would probably be safe in whatever future may result from this mad undertaking.

Milford's voice was relaxed and Welder let out an exaggerated sigh as the feeling of relief that accompanied the emotionally balancing smell of pancakes set in. 'At least emocon is working'

In the few moments of anticipation before proceeding, images of having leaves sprouting out all over his body and having to eat dirt went through Welder's mind. As far as side effects go he had experienced worse but they were short-lived. Welder looked over at the palm-like plant in what would have been a corner if he wasn't in a dome.

The projections started up again without his initiation 'We found it necessary to neutralize emotions in the cloche; the adrenaline produced by any feelings of *panic or anger could have combined with the plant vapours to produce more radical physiological changes. I say we but I am alone now. Randolph is no longer with us; at least in a human bodily form that is'. Milford stopped for a moment as if to acknowledge and pay respect to the life of his assistant.*

'I am glad you are not able to panic; otherwise, you might do something wild before finishing the presentation. As I was saying, I am alone. Randolph had a terminal condition which we both knew would end his life in a matter of months once we detected it. We had been working on modifications for the cloche ever since the incident, which I will get to in due course. Randolph chose to risk losing a couple of weeks of his life in the name of research and offered himself as a human guinea pig to test the steamer's new functions. He was the only person I have ever met that had seen a guinea pig. He sacrificed himself but what we learnt enabled us to make the necessary modifications. I have not been able to test those modifications but I am sure the cloche is now fully functional and safe to use....' As Milford spoke a creaky sound like the rumbling of a giant's stomach travelled around the cloche. 'No one has ever attempted to go amongst the Keem for the extended periods needed to deal with the current crisis. I knew Sally would send you. By the time she gave you the mission I'll already be out of here; there's got to be no animal life forms on the planet when the buyer scans it in two days. This facility is mentioned in the inventory as an abandoned monitoring station with only a few house plants. Apart from them, it's a dead planet. Full decontamination of the facility is meant to take place before the imminent handover date' There was a pause as if Milford was turning a page in his head. 'In the past, we have managed to spend a day and once close to

two days in the main dome without any problems using the first cloche for acclimatising. We had never needed to stay longer, until now. Every scenario we can envisage for the removal of imminent danger to the Keem's future requires someone having to be amongst the Keem for an extended period; lengths of time that would necessitate taking in fluid and energy and being protected from the dome's defences. To adapt to the delicate balance within the Keem's rarefied atmosphere even for a short time means closing down the digestive system, and the reproductive system too, as it happens. Once in the dome to eat or drink anything could be fatal or at least leave you so unwell that you would be unable to function. Apart from that, the vapours would turn you, as it were into a vegetable, literally. As security against something ever getting into the dome the vapours in the atmosphere include a powerful appetite suppressant as certain plants are irresistible under normal circumstances. Many security measures were put in place when the lab was on planets where the threat of being eaten was very real though the risk of a break-in was slight. Still, we had to take precautions. Thank goodness we moved to Chippenham Five. Before the incident, we could not conceive of any reason to be in the dome beyond routine checks. The dome was designed to be self-maintaining, indefinitely. All bubbles and domes from the earliest days have been self-contained, self-sufficient and self-maintained, apart from the monitoring equipment. The dome has other plant-based defences which you will have to deal with later. Randolph was in the cloche for weeks and together we fine-tuned its workings. Here I'll play the tapes'. Welder watched and listened.

Randolph was a squat sturdy older looking man with ginger hair and a permanent smile that made people want *to hug something but to his great disappointment it was seldom him. He looked like an older man, but when pressed people found it difficult to pin it down any more specifically than that. He looked like an old man even when he was a baby; especially when he was a baby. Although the smile had no effect on Welder, he could tell somehow that this older looking man had genuine warmth. Randolph entered the dome completely naked and was free from the drugs controlling the symptoms of his terminal illness. Unfortunately, somehow, way back in the early years of galactic evolutionary history, a rare Trowbidian egg-monkey must have clambered its way into a branch of the human family tree, and somehow it left a rogue gene behind. The exact manner by which this occurred was never determined. And it was never really determined how exactly Trowbridian egg-monkeys mated. The most widely held theory was that it happened with a high five. The condition the rogue gene caused was difficult to spot for several reasons, one being that it was so rare in humans that it did not show up in the company's extensive genetic screening of every new employee. It was a gene which mimicked other genes and could only be detected if searched for and even then the chances of noticing it were slim. Only a handful of individuals such as Milford would ever think to look for it, in Milford's case simply for the hope of actually coming across an actual case. The symptoms were mild and caused no discomfort; another reason it was hard to detect and almost always went unnoticed. The subject would tend to smile for no reason and be more than averagely patient. The only real negative about having egg-monkey syndrome was certain death. After exactly, 29229 days all bodily functions would cease regardless of whatever state of health those carrying the gene were in. Every part of its victim's body would shut down and leave no sign of a cause of death. It appeared that the death was natural and completely painless, if not extremely pleasant. A careful study of galactic birth and death records would have shown that, of those individuals that died after exactly 29229 days, only one in a billion died of Trowbridian Egg Monkey syndrome. Randolph's life was on a timer from the moment he was born, just as ever ten-thousandth ginger-haired male in his family had been. It is worth pointing out that during Randolph's life, and for several hundreds of years preceding it, ginger hair with a freckled complexion was the most popular sort after look of fashionable 'creatives' and celebrities. Randolph had the hardest time convincing anyone that he was a natural G. Any benefit he could have had from being a natural G was therefore nullified. The fact that the timer of death had been counting down for just over eighty years meant any repetition of age at death of the past generations of ginger-haired males was not spotted in Randolph's family medical history. However, if anyone was going to spot it, Milford Lyme was the man, and spot it, he did. Milford wanted or needed to know a reason for everything and he was pretty good at finding one. When Randolph smiled, a smile broader than his permanent natural smiling expression and a touch more idiotic than usual, and when Randolph could not tell Milford why he was smiling after being asked, Milford, did not let it rest. Fortunately, Randolph's increased levels of patience helped him cope with the hours of interrogation and long drawn out processes involved in being tested for the egg-monkey syndrome. After the briefest of moments of excitement at coming across an actual case of egg-monkey syndrome, a wave of emotion swept Milford off his feet and he sunk back into his chair weeping at the prospect of losing Randolph. Milford's grief was tempered by the knowledge that there were plenty of worse mutant genes Randolph could have had the misfortune of being endowed with; much worse, unimaginably worse.*

Randolph had arrived on Chippenham Five-four days prior to Milford. The facility had been unpeopled for several months, though not unplanted of course.

Holborn Worlwipe, the predecessor to Milford at the sphere had manned the facility on his own for almost fifteen years, quite against convention. He had been left there by Milford and Sally's father Alfros who departed to instigate a much-needed root and branch review of the project following the consequences and fall out from 'the incident' also known as 'the peach-faced Loon affair'. An unprecedented meeting of 'R and B' was convened. Alfros' seat on the council had him seated amongst the unique gathering of all seven members of 'The Interplanetary Skittles League', a cover organisation used by R and B for meetings, of which Alfros was its most dynamic member. Welder watched as the league of five women and two men sat pontificating over the Keem's future. The gathering of venerable enlightened beings, all at least one hundred and seventy years old, all descendants of Ben and Robby were dressed in matching deep purple bowling team type tracksuits with 'The Hare and Hounds, Skittle Kings' embroiled in gold 1950's lettering on the back. They sat not looking at each other in Quaker like contemplation for what felt like hours to Welder and was indeed hours but cut down to three minutes. Finally, the baldest of the women looked up and spoke

'We need to put things on hold', and with that, the meeting ended and Alfros went off to prepare his fob for Milford.

260

Alfros completed the fob in five years and died shortly after in a climbing accident on the tallest of Mugwagger's ice peaks, Plop. Mugwagger was not a planet; it was the name of an artist and mountain climber, Mapworn Mugwagger. He created, with a galactic arts council grant, ten sculptures all precisely eight miles high. Each was the exact representation of ten mountains from around the galaxy. They were in a row on the ice plains of the frozen planet of Rop. Rop was bequeathed to the arts council by its original owner, the women who first arrived on the planet, Mo. She had been looking for an uninhabited planet to store her stuff. Rop was a huge planet, completely flat and completely covered in pristine white ice. It was like a huge cue ball slowly rolling in circles around a distant huge sun. Mo loved the planet from the moment she set foot on it. She was also a supporter of the ancient art of 'trying to come up with something different' and there were some tax incentives for her making a donation of such a magnitude as bequeathing a planet to the arts.

Alfros had left instructions the moment he finished the fob for just such an eventuality as Welder was facing. Sally was to activate the fob once Holborn had chosen to end his vigil on Chippenham Five or if that moment was chosen for him. Old Holborn kept an eye on the Keem and was instructed not to touch anything. His last act was to send himself into space so he could spend the last hours of his life where he had spent the first hours of his life, hurtling through space. He left a note for Milford which read.

'I'm taking off. I won't be back, so don't wait up for me. Everything has been left the way you want it. Peace Love and eternal cosmic wisdom'. It was a verbatim copy

of the oldest handwritten note in his family archives and as he couldn't think of anything else he used it. So off Holborn went in transparent capsule rotating slowing as he breathed his last. He knew the sphere and the Keem could survive hundreds, if not thousands of years in perfect environmental equilibrium but it was, in fact, the first time in their more than three thousand year existence that they had been left unattended. It was a risk Sally was prepared to take; she knew that anything other than the scheduled transport vessel making its scheduled detour to scan Chippenham Five could give the game away. And the stakes in the game were bigger than even she could have imagined before she activated her father's pea and learnt the true nature and potential of the project.

Milford had chosen Randolph as his assistant. He had known him since he taught him as a little boy at university. He had followed his progress and when he saw that Randolph was one of the three candidates for the position as his assistant he was delighted. Welder was intrigued but as the projection showed Randolph entering the dome a voice much like Sally's stopped the projection completely and announced.

'Adaptions complete, cloche returning to pod'

The dome did not lift like a giant lid being lifted by the mechanical equivalent of a huge waiter's arm; it shrank upwards towards its highest central point. It was like a controlled shrivelling. The rim lifted or more accurately shrank and condensed whilst it kept the overall original form. The retracting cellular rim reminded Welder of the rim on the nozzle of a balloon. The process also reminded him of a massive foreskin being pulled back over an invisible bell end and he chuckled and just as he was about to chastise himself for his lavatorial humour, he heard the tittering in the distance. Then the whole cloche shrivelled up into a giant pod that closed in on its self. It was a biomechanical device the like of which Welder had never witnessed.

Welder's attentions were then drawn away from watching the final stages of the cloche's retreat by the loud chanting of the Keem. He felt a little insecure once he was no longer enveloped by his metamorphosing dome. He did not feel prepared; he had not seen everything he wanted or needed to see from Milford's presentation. But his curiosity got the better of him and he made a moved judiciously towards the chanting. It was coming from somewhere behind the central column of the main dome. He noticed other pods like the one that contained the bell jar he had been in. They were hanging from vines of various lengths. The pods were light blue, white or pale yellow in roughly equal measure and ranged in size from a human head to that of an elephant. Welder stood still looking up and followed the path of a single vine from which a pod was suspended like a light bulb. Doing so drew his gaze ever higher. Once the vine reached the shell of the hemisphere it ran towards the domes highest point, as did all the other vines. They all ended up in the centre in a tangled, rooty, woven ball. It looked to Welder as if a jungle had invaded and abandoned disco and covered a massive mirror ball with creepers. Disco was reborn and survived as a political dance party. It was a movement based on movement. Dance proved an effective non-verbal means of negotiating and resolving conflict. From below the ball of tangled vines a single green stem about a metre thick hung. And from that stem, a huge red pod shaped like a dried poppy seed head *was suspended, though it was anything but dry. It oozed and sweated liquid. A steady dripping of a viscous orange solution fell into a fibrous collecting bowl-shaped trunk that looked like a giant coconut shell halve. The bowl was itself about halfway between the floor Welder was standing on and the total height of the hemisphere. It sat on top of the central shaft Welder had entered the dome through. Vines and creepers festooned the upper reaches of the shaft so that it had the appearance of a colossal ivy-covered column. It had just the right amount of foliage and archaic character to satisfy the sensibilities of a Capability Brown. Welder found it hard to judge the exact size of what he was surveying, but he knew it was big and presumed the liquid goo dropping from the pod went directly down the shaft as part of the spheres sustainable life support systems.*

Welder noticed emotional responses returning like blood flow forcing its way back into a part of the body that had fallen asleep and had become numb. This relinquishing of control by his environment subconsciously signalled that he was not in any immediate danger. He tingled all over. The first product of his restored emotional faculties was a feeling of the highest level of awe or 'omglob' that he had ever experienced. Omglob was a term used only to describe experiences of a profound spiritual nature. Welder knew he was hard to impress and a healthy cynic so assumed he would never experience omglob. The return of his emotions, his release from his 'dome from dome', the nature of what he had already learned from the fob and the cathedral-like magnificence of the vine ribbed hemisphere with its hanging pods, put Welder into a state he could only describe as omglob. The focal point of his awe was the giant red heart of the Keemdom, the huge central pod.

264

The sudden release of steamy cloud vapours from the 'forget me not' blue pods evenly dispersed overhead broke the spell. Welder was fully restored and his mind had never felt clearer and more focussed, though oddly enough he was not exactly sure what it was focussed on.

'What do I need to focus on?' he asked himself unhurriedly but still with a sense of urgency. 'I need to focus on what I need to do, and to make that decision I will need to know my options and I have not the foggiest what they are yet, apart from the self-destruct button which I am always presented with as a last resort. I will need more information, and not just from the fob'. He concluded his diagnostics as he peered and moved stealthily around the never-ending corner of the central column. He was light on his feet for a big bear.

'aye aye aluvi aye, aye aye aluvi aye'

The chanting of the Keem was louder than Welder expected; much louder. He knew it was a ritual during which excess gasses were expelled by the Keem in the process known as 'pooting'. The relatively small amounts of gasses were the only bi-product of their finely tuned metabolisms. The Keem were now in full sight and were not in the least disturbed by his presence so Welder stood motionless and watched. They were all wearing white gowns and it was impossible to affix a gender to them that they did not have anyway. There was no one Keem conducting affairs. They were equal in every respect. They stood hand in hand forming a circle around a spherical bluestone fountain which gurgled out a small spout of water at its highest point; at least it looked like water to Welder. The thin spout of liquid went up about six inches or *so from the globe which was about a meter diameter. Despite looking like a solid weighty lump of bluestone it appeared to hover or be held aloft by a single thread of water shooting upwards from beneath. The string stream on the blue balloon spread perfectly into a floret of liquid. Some fluid somehow dispersed upwards in tiny rivulets as if gravity had been reversed. The total height of the centrepiece was roughly twice as high as the Keem. As they chanted, their colours changed and Welder thought that they were growing and shrinking, or rising and falling slightly in time with longer cycles of changing pitch in their rounds of incantations. They were still repeating the same refrain.*

'aye aye, aluvi aye, aye aye, aluvi aye, aye aye, aluvi aye'

It started to get steadily louder and faster and louder and faster and louder and faster. until finally

'AYE AYE, ALUVI AYE, A NUCKI WOE FOREVER!' and with their climactic crescendo blasted out, silence settled upon them. They then released hands and filed off, stage left into a line of thirteen individual hemispherical enclosures. There was one enclosure for each Keem and one remained unoccupied. The enclosures looked like they were made up of banana plant shaped leaves. Welder was able to determine at a glance that the structures were living plants.

'Homegrown homes', he murmured. The Keem had not noticed or been uninterested in Welder's mumbled comment about their homes and Welder took it that they were otherwise occupied with their rituals and their telepathic functions were in neutral.

266

The concept of having living homes was not new to Welder. Most people lived within a plant that converted light to produce more than enough energy for the occupants. All that required was light and the resident's wastewater and solids. The structure was maintained itself, including the self-cleaning membrane windows and such homes looked very much like ones made from historically conventional materials. The company developed and grew many of the interdependent and symbiotic plants used for the grown home industry. Whole planets became vast landscapes of plant homes waiting to be picked. There was a dip in the market when somehow, genetic material from a zombie plant found its way into the mix and the inhabitants of the deluxe 'Melonette' homes were digested as they slept. There was a theory doing the rounds that there were powerful forces in the company that wanted to move away from an organic future and move into non-bio engineering and that it was someone in the company that had introduced the Zombie strain. It was certainly general knowledge that there were at the very least sharp tensions in the company between the administrative financial and investment side of the organisation, and those involved with the production and development of the company's huge catalogue of products. It was certainly also true that the part of the company which adhered to the 'organicistation not organisation' principle was at loggerheads with the part known as the 'fluid structuralists'. The organicists felt a strong allegiance to the spirit of the company's early pre-space days; those aims pursued by Ben and Bobby, or B and B as they came to be known. They were guided by principles such as money can grow on trees if you plant the right trees and look after them properly. The fluid structuralists were followers of the management genius and perhaps the company's greatest ever CEO, Malinda Page.

They correctly believed that if it was not for her vision and drive the company would never have got off the earth. Her genius was in inventing systems of management in response to need rather than adherence to systems born from theories, which proved problematic for those whose desire was the comfort of certainty. Such followers ended up overriding the organic nature of her core beliefs by sticking rigidly to them. She warned them that they had to look out for the times when she was wrong and act accordingly. Only very few were smart enough to appreciate such moments, fewer had the confidence to say so, and those that did were not believed. Malinda was admired and revered by all sides. Generations of management turned her creative organic management theories into systems almost as rigid as those that went before but with less chance of it ever becoming flexible again. Eventually, the word organic was dropped from the teaching of her ideas.

Sophie was more often than not her own worst enemy. She fought internal battles between different parts of herself over different regions of her emotional landscape. Her response, when faced with choices that had emotions attached, was inner turmoil. The inner pain that arose from her internal scratching and picking drove her mad at times; she drove herself mad at times. She would ride into those troubled lands and impose order but she was a reluctant ruler prone to fits of reckless spontaneity. Richard unwittingly triggered such conflict in Sophie. The brief and infrequent meetings she had with him would have presented many women with painful choices to make and in Sophie's case, the pain was acute. No more so than the first year at the B and B. She wanted to know as little as possible about the projections she made in accordance with the figures she was given. Her rare gift was in spotting patterns, almost mannerisms in calculations and sets of figures that were generated by seemingly innate algorithms. She was able to group, plot and analyse through characteristics that no computer or other individual could perceive.

Sophie did not want a quote-unquote, normal relationship with a man anyway, but most human emotion she believed was ambivalent, which undermined her confidence in her own. She preferred her own company in the day to day of her life but only with the knowledge that Albert was down the hall and Richard somewhere down the line. She did, however, love Roger and their meetings became physically passionate, but not always. Eventually, the pain subsided like a storm that had blown out as she accepted that the situation suited her perfectly. There were times when she longed to tell people of her love but the prospect of all that emotional uncertainty was a sturdy defence against such impulses. Those moments were fewer than the times she was with Roger. Sometimes, when her feeling of love for Roger was at its greatest she would part several hours before they needed to.

Albert was different. He was the central part of the equation that she had carefully balanced. With him, there was a magical irrational poetic view of the world that she loved. They were great housemates and he was a trusted confidante. Sometimes she would stare at the light coming through one of his favourite Bulgarian glassfish, making it glow and project bright swirls of colour on the wall and she would feel at peace. Sophie would not have had anything as tasteless as a glassfish in the executive home of her past existence. She was grateful to Albert for giving her the arena within which she was safe from the taste fascists and pseudo-intellectuals that made all the right choices and said all the right things and still whispered suggestions in her ear about changes that would have turned the Soft Sands into a uniform soulless supposedly tasteful but completely bland hotel. Mostly she was grateful for the simplicity of life with Albert at the B and B; a life she loved. At the height of the confusion in her heart over Roger, it took just one conversation with Albert to help her find resolution; to help her end her warring with herself. She ceased to be her enemy and found she had no others on her horizons. Things were the way she wanted; her life was not ever going to be conventional and that was the way she wanted it. The downsides, which she assumed existed in everyone's worlds, were 'no biggie'.

The conflict of emotions with her family and especially her sister were not as large but harder and slower to decipher and understand. She had even tested John's patience talking to him about them where she only mentioned Roger as a fictitious character and only once.

She was not sure, but as she looked in on herself sitting around the dinner table with her Mum and Dad, and Albert waiting for Lily to arrive with Tom and the little Rose, she remembered a sense of foreboding crushing her chest and throat. She could tell her Mum was feeling it too. They both kept it to themselves and put it down to a physical cause. The call came; it was Rose. She had been taken to hospital with Meningitis.

Chapter Fifteen

Family Tree

The idea that political power should be inherited and passed down along bloodlines, that someone should become the head of state with supreme powers because it was the position that their Dad or Mum, or some other member of the family held, was so ancient and anachronistic that it was all but forgotten. It made no rational sense that a national leader's offspring would necessarily be the best person to take up the responsibilities of the top job. When tribes were small and the gene pool shallow a particular bloodline may have produced the most worthy leaders but presumably they would still be the best leaders even if they had to demonstrate those qualities to get the job. Even the most consistent successive generations of the same family would experience the regular range of individual variance and free-thinking progeny who didn't want the job or were simply not cut out for it. Certainly, if a child wants to be a brain surgeon or pilot, like their Mum or Dad it was rightly believed that they should get some sort of training and attain that position through experience, ability and achievement. It made no sense to hand over the scalpel to someone because of their family name. However, it turned out when it came to systems of transferring power, most other systems ended up being just as arbitrary, flawed and vulnerable to corruption and nepotism. Vested interest, egomania, self-interest and tribalism managed to infiltrate almost every form of governance ever devised so that ultimately there was not much to choose between any of them. Some of the systems that looked the fairest on paper turned out to be the worst on record. Plans on paper and paperwork, though essential were also an excellent way of temporarily covering over many sins. No matter how they came to power, only rare leaders and governments put the long term interests of their people ahead of their short term popularity. It seemed that the very nature of power attracted entirely the wrong sorts of individuals for the job; whether they worked alone or in bunches. The issue of gaining and staying in power always seemed to take precedence over doing the job of governing properly. It was not ultimately the fairness of democracy that made it work to a fashion and be the, go to system, it was the arbitrary element in its nature that was its saving grace. It threw up enough variations of capable individuals to do less damage than some other systems. Throwing random elements into the pot to counter whatever potentially exploitable structure had been superimposed on humanity was found to be an essential part of maintaining stability. It turned out that finding groups or individuals being in temporary charge was not like brain surgery after all. It was the institutions set up to ensure continuity of governance that were the ones with the scalpels tucked out of sight in their portfolios. The leaders and politicians, those who had been given the power by whatever means, were the ones that got to choose the patients. Kings and Queens, Presidents and Prime-ministers were merely the face patients saw as they counted down from ten. A good deal of trust was necessary based on accurate diagnosis and information. Nine, eight, 'are you sure you know what you are dooo…'

No system of governing met the aspirations and high standards of fairness and equality sought by the greater populous or the great unwashed as they were smugly referred to by successive generations of Mandarins. What's more, rather disappointingly, individual aspirations and standards were all too often different to the ones demanded collectively and all too often similar to those they decried. Many individuals only discovered this gap between their private views and behaviour and their public persona when they too, took office. Some took the virtuous path, but most hid their true natures behind banners. After hundreds of years of study carried out independently of government authorities, it was proved that over the course of a thousand years, most systems of government performed as badly as another. It was the body of the masses that leaned and wobbled which provided the counterweight to keep those in power from completely messing things up. Sometimes the leaning of the people was too great and everything would come crashing down. Sometimes the shift from leaning this way and that would create a kind of speed wobble that bikers are familiar with, the kind that often leads to a complete loss of control. Following the 'They're All Shit' report, an attempt at total democracy overseen by a computer was attempted. Everyone's fobs gave everyone the ability to vote on every issue did not work as only a hand full of extremists seemed to make use of the opportunity. The computer shut itself down and nobody noticed for twenty-three years; everything carried on like a motorbike without a rider until a change of direction was needed. In the study, monarchy as a system for selecting a head of state fared only slightly worse than choosing one with elections but was cheaper to administer. It was eventually decided that no one individual was capable of enough, or had the breadth of vision to make decisions on behalf of vast populations, though the importance of the random element of having individuals was appreciated. So a kind of jury system was adopted. Three thousand and six individuals were chosen at random just as they would be for jury service. Along with the same number of elected representatives they collectively chose which patients got the treatment first with the proviso that everyone got treated eventually and were kept entertained while they waited. The ones wielding the knives remained more or less anonymous and rose through a system of talent spotting and a meritocracy that guaranteed the best people got the job. The three thousand and six were in power for up to thirty years at a time but were well rewarded. This system known as 'neo-mob rule' also proved far cheaper than most of its predecessors involving expenses claims. Even with very generous financial compensation, the bill for expenses was greatly reduced and far less resented. The system was tweaked over time but it seemed to work well enough to keep the masses from wobbling too much and the research that brought in neo-mob rule failed to get further funding ever again.

If the research had continued, patterns in neo-mob voting could have been detected and even greater fairness and equality could have been achieved. I was thought that a measure of disgruntlement was an important part of the balance of stability. It was decided that a small measure of believing things can be better was necessary.

It was more to do with the system of inherited wealth rather than any belief in its effectiveness that the company was owned and run by successive generations of the same five families. That seemed to be the right number of families to cope with most eventualities. The two most powerful families, but by no means the biggest, each controlled one of the two wings of the company. The two wings needed to co-operate to flap and keep flying. This was possible because of the unique natures of the family's two brains. One was given charge of both wings and the entire body for that matter; the other got to choose the flight path. Every leaf on every branch from every family tree was part of the same ancient woodland and they were all part of the same root system and they all drew from the same soil. The soil prepared and planted by Ben Crammer and Robby Green.

There was the Innaluci family that the whole galaxy knew about and the Lashmeres that virtually no one knew about. The Lucis as they were widely known ran the company. They were in charge and rewarded themselves well. They were the large brain in charge of everything and had all the power, or so they believed.

The Lucis may have been in charge, they may have run the company, but the Lashmere's owned it. Only the head of the company, which was usually a Luci ever knew this. Everyone assumed the Lucis owned the company including most of the Lashmere family. The Lashmeres were the more direct descendants of Ben and Daisy Crammer, and Robert and Rebekah Roundway, and they liked to call themselves 'Rounders and Crammeraliers'.

The Lashmeres had always worked within and had been in charge of, research. Maria Innaluci was the great-granddaughter of the great Malinda Page. She was the first of an unbroken line of Innalucis that ran through to Albran Prawnshot. Maria was succeeded by her daughter Lungstorm who was in turn succeeded by her daughter Sim, and the pattern of female CEO succession continued for twenty-seven generations. It was a period of steady growth for the company but the tensions between the families grew with the company's and family's fortunes.

By the time Albran Prawnshot took the reins to his reign, tensions had become enmity and mistrust became subterfuge. Albran made it his mission to find a way to take full control of the company. He wanted to crush the hidden power of the Lashmeres, he wanted to humiliate them and relegate those 'pompous smug grass lickers' to something, though he was not sure what, it would be something that brought him pleasure in their servitude. He knew the true value of the Lashmeres and their research to the company but he would relegate them to that something; that horrible something, horrible and dull, dull lucrative what they were told, research.

'I want them to work for me!' Albran said in exasperation on learning that his latest plans to sabotage the secret work

*of the pet project had failed. He wanted to scream out 'I
want to own the company' but he knew such an outburst
would set off a series of legal protocols that would leave
him and his family with nothing. Not that he was worried
that much about his family; he was a throwback to the hay
days of megalomaniacs.*

*'So what went wrong? No, don't tell me, the less I know the
better' he was staring intensely into the eyes of the target of
his question and could immediately see strength and
courage that he did not have and would not be able to
penetrate. So he turned his back mumbling to himself. He
had heard about the almost hypnotic power of Sally's gaze
and was wary of it even in his loyal minions. He trusted no
one, least of all his susceptibilities. After several operations
and intensive training with the Monks from the planet
Chipping Sodbury, Prawnshot rightly believed that he was
vulnerable to a gaze such as Sally's, but he wrongly
believed it was something he could learn himself. He
thought it was a trick.*

*He had barely been frustrated for a moment before
turning his agitated energy towards plan B12. Albran, a
name he hated once he learned its ancient origins was
somehow related to good digestion, had all the advantages
of the company's long list of regenerative procedures and
products.*

*He was able to pull off the charade of being a
strong almost spiritual leader. He never stood still and
never gave live interviews, which meant never actually
being in the same room as anyone other than with those he
had control over. His control came from corrupted fobs
given to chosen members of his own family at birth. The
power it gave him was subtle and fragile and took thirty
years or more to develop. Anything more and it would have
been detected.*

The woman he was speaking to, the one whose gaze he avoided was Edweener Malltredder. She was his second in command and in control of the day to day running of things, and she had her hidden craving for power. She exploited Albran's conceit to hide her intentions. Once Albran had overseen bringing the Lashmeres to heel, she would pounce and execute her plan, which would humiliate everyone around her and especially Albran. She had the courage intellect and drive of her Innalucci foremothers and wanted to re-establish a female dynasty.

'How far have we got with buying the planet?' he asked her staring out at the night sky and the planet his man-made spherical home and office floated high above. His was the largest of hundreds of spheres that slowly drifted over and around the planet. They were spread like hot air balloons at a festival. The Company Central was a huge planet and still growing. It was a living planet were the most sought after materials the company produced were grown and harvested. It was the brightest bloom in the Company's garden of achievement. It was a patchwork of amazing colour. It was thought to be so beautiful that it's sweet fragrance could be smelled from space.

'It's all done. We take possession in three weeks. They won't be able to escape. They couldn't even if they tried to do so openly. Our ships are underway and will get there in twenty days ready for the exchange. Someone called Welder will be handing over the keys' She expressed huge satisfaction with the tiniest smile possible. It was barely visible but she felt out of control with excitement.

'Welder, Welder, I know a Welder. He is thought to be an agent of the R and B. What the fuck is he doing there? It is the type of thing he does in his day job so it could mean nothing; would they send him if they were suspicious of something? No, they must know that we know him and they

278

would not send him even as a double bluff. None the less he might spot that we are not private buyers; he can sniff out a phoney in a vacuum underwater on a planet in a different fucking galaxy' the mention of Welder had heightened Albran's anxiety levels and all of his enhancements could not stop his contorted face from having an ugly countenance. His hair was unfeasibly black and cut into rows of cubes the size of sugar lumps. His skin had the slightly blue tinge that was popular at the time. His green eyes gave away the older nervous and manic individual that lay within.

'Bluff or not, we press on. Maybe there is more to this planet than an old research outpost with a couple of houseplants. Maybe we got lucky in our game of galactic battleships. Forget plan B12. Plan A is back on the table'
'Which plan A'. There were many plan A's
'The plan A. Who have we got on the job as backup?'
'We're not using our people we are using Pro-planters, the best they have. We told them that there was some seriously questionable plant research going on and that if our rouse works they get to lift the lid and expose what Sally and the Lashmeres have been doing all these centuries.'
'So it may be that we don't need to plant evidence. I get a feeling there is plenty already there and Welder was sent to tidy up before the mystery buyers arrive. I don't think R and B know it's us. It won't matter either way. Unless. What if the Pro-planters like whatever it is they've been doing?' he asked calming himself down as he spoke. Edweener continued the calming process with her deep laconic voice.

'Impossible they don't like anything other than free-range fruit and that disgusting ethical rock paste they eat. Besides, the fact that Root and Branch have been acting without permits will bring the authorities in to play. And if that

doesn't mess up the 'Rounders and Crammers', there is one more level to stoop to' Edweener was in full flow and on a roll; she was wearing her don't fuck with me expression. 'And what level is that' asked Albran whose crumpled angry face was re-inflating with Edweener's every word. 'Ultraplanters. If it all goes tits up Ultraplanters are waiting in the wings, ready to mulch anything that moves. They hate the company. They hate most things. They would do just about anything to those who are perceived to use or abuse plants. If they are sure there are no plants on board the hand over vessel, they'll blow it up and kill the lot of them. Based, that is, on the evidence we have been provided by the saps we sent in to infiltrate. All the Ultraplanters need is the final co-ordinates'

'Can our saps be trusted? Are they under fob control?' Edweener simply nodded confidently.

'But Utraplanters Weener? Isn't that a bit drastic?' his anxiety had continued to fall below calm and bottomed out at fear a started to rise again to arrogant disdain and mistrust.

'Are you sure this is plan A, the end game?' Edweener nodded again

'And Weener, I don't want to hear you mention Root and Branch or Rounders and Crammers in my presence again' 'Okay, I won't. Unless you call me Weener again' They both smiled and Edweener left the room thinking to herself, 'I'm going to make that fucker eat every smug patronising word he has ever said to me, and I'll use his forked tongue to serve them to him after I have pulled it out of his smug smiling disturbingly fascinating mouth.' 'I'll have to sort her out after this is all over' Albran said to himself as she left the room.

Sophie's attention left the room with Edweener and joined her Mother Father and Albert at the dining table. The artificially light conversation gave the impression of normality. How's business? did you see such and such a programme about some so and so banker, politician, policeman or priest? The quartet continued in unspoken collusion of denial until the spell was broken by Alice suddenly sobbing. Somehow at that point, Sophie knew what was coming; somehow they all did. Sophie remembered that feeling of foreboding, that certainty of the unknowing truth, that connectedness with those close to her and the events that engulf them. She knew because she was engulfed along with them. It was the moment of seeing something about to happen and being powerless to stop it. Alfred had taken the call in the passageway and he did his best to conceal the drama and dread of the situation. A jolt of cold pain near to panic gripped them all but their collective optimism pushed back. Within six hours all that was left of their defences against having their hearts torn out with grief was the thinnest veneer of hope. By then all but Albert were gathered at the hospital, powerless. Lily and David were on the verge of collapse. Rose was clinging to the thinnest thread of life. Jenny, Lily's eldest daughter was with friends. The group embraced in tearful pleading to whatever force in the universe could hear, 'save Rose'. Sophie's thoughts reconnected with her former self in imagining that thin thread of life growing stronger. Then she held an image of Rose's sleeping face in her mind. As she imagined Rose's eyes opening, and her own eyes opened too and the Doctor walked towards them in the corridor. Rose was passed the worst. It had been touch and go, but Rose would survive. The experience had changed them. As individuals, they had always struggled to find a home for their longing to believe. Together they found it, but they never found its name. All they knew was that it was rooted in love.

Sophie noted the truth of her experience and past experience and realised the memory had implications. The implications appeared to her as a fishbowl, not with water in but with hundreds of rolled up balls of paper the size of marbles. She reached in her hand and pulled one out. She unravelled it and read the message written in her handwriting 'you knew, and you know you knew'

Although Rose went on to fully recover Lily did not. The fright weakened her. Sophie knew it was that moment that caused the first crack in Lily's emotional and psychological defences. It was one of the great sadness of Sophie's life to watch her beautiful sister crumble. Lily frantically held herself together until Jenny and Rose got through University. She finally fell into a heap when Alice died followed three years later by her Father. Sophie watched on helplessly as Lily faded away and died before her time.

But as Sophie reacquainted herself with those dreadful feelings she did not re-live the pain. All of them, her Sister, Mother, Father, Albert and Roger were all dead; that much she was sure of. And in recalling events Sophie was even more certain than any thought or feeling concerning life external to her, that they were alright; especially Lily.

She had the sudden conviction that whatever was happening to her had happened to them. Whatever was happening to her would hold no fear for their good-natured souls. And that whatever transformation, transition or metamorphosis of being she was undergoing, even if it was living a stretched-out moment before finally dying, it would be straight forward for her sister. She sensed long life gives those who have the chance at it, greater opportunities and greater hazards. The hazards she was facing as she continued with the stream of memories whilst following the story. Those she had placed there when she was still alive. Louise would face no hazards and the other people she loved, very few.

'It wasn't a waste of time then, was it?' she asked not expecting an answer from the narrator.

'No, the clues were there, though you didn't like following clues that seemed too orderly. You didn't need to. You always had a feeling of knowing how the land lay. You trusted that instinctive belief that it was worth trying to understand, trying to be happy, trying to be good. And that good represented something beyond need and relative circumstances and subjective cultural or social criteria. You dealt with most of the obstacles that could have slowed you from letting go when you had a chance to do so during your life. You took your own good time but you kept moving. Those things that could have slowed you, could have done so indefinitely.'

Sophie felt contentment of thought in a way she had not quite done so in life. She had no needs. She let that contentment guide her back to her young self, lying on her back on the floor with her legs running up and resting on the wall like two tendrils of ivy. Her sapling body stretched and bent effortlessly. She let her legs drop slowly so her knees were on her chest. There followed a succession of intuitive yoga-like poses; each one finding some balance between and supported by different parts of her body. Blood enriched every part of her being with its invigorating payload. She felt like every part of her was pushing out from within to counter external pressure. She settled into a position in which internal and external forces were in such balance that she had no awareness of her body. She felt like the world had stopped moving her about, or about her. She felt like her thoughts were on a floating leaf or a boat in a pool of deep and clear, water, and that she was calm, spinning slowly looking skywards at the stars. Everyone had left the water. There were no waves. The leaf dissolved and she sunk back into the water and became part of the pool.

Sophie blinked forward. She had not thought of it before but it came out as if she had been thinking about nothing else. Roger lay deep in thought, looking towards the ceiling but looking way beyond it. His chest was rising and falling like ocean swells and the sound of his breath followed like the sound of waves on tiny pebbles. Sometimes Sophie felt dissolved and part of that ocean that filled Roger's lungs; an ocean of fluid souls.
'I want to donate my eggs'

Chapter Sixteen

The Peach Faced Loon

Welder had lost all track of time. After witnessing their chanting and 'pooting' ritual he knew that the Keem were free to hear his thoughts again, thus rendering any attempt to continue observing them unnoticed virtually impossible; so he joined them. They emerged from their upturned shell-shaped, plant-based homes back in their animated bright coloured combinations of shorts and tops or single frocks. They were quick to welcome him and explain that they entered home pods at random and emerged into a world 'fresh from the vine'.

'We don't look the same from one day to the next' one said out loud with an enthusiastic voice of a child. It seemed to Welder that when they were excited or at least well stimulated they could not contain themselves and spoke out loud.

'The pods are not homes they are more like changing rooms' said another

'Even our voices change', said yet another in a mock low voice which made them all laugh, including Welder. They explained that they liked talking about sensible things in silly ways and their own silly language and silly things in sensible ways in ordinary language. After that, they took it in turns to explain to Welder what they knew of their existence, much of which he did not understand as he was not used to their silly language. It was however terrifically amusing. They expressed no emotion or opinions about the nature of their lives but explained what those lives were made up of with infectious enthusiasm. They gave the impression that they knew the science that Welder had

*difficulty getting to grips with. They took their conversation
for a walk.*

*As they strode about the dome going from one
interesting plant to another, like a family of huge slow-
moving honey bees and one bumblebee, they started
communicating more telepathically. But for whatever
reason, either they could not broadcast in Silly language or
Welder could not receive it, or maybe silly language was
comprehensible in thought communication; whatever the
reason, Welder understood everything instantly and in-
depth. They showed Welder examples of plants that played
a part in their evolution. 'Marloo markoo, blip stom dillrus
purnumbum' explained the only yellow Keem wearing a
blue frock, as it pointed to a shrub the size of a football
with flowers flying on the end of fine vine lines, like
butterflies tied by silk threads fluttering about. Apparently,
it was called a 'Wally Woo'. Welder watched in awe as the
flowers flew about freely without getting in a tangle. After
about an hour of the Keem's 'nuky woe worbles' Welder
understood their general meaning even when they were
spoken out loud.*

*As a result of the distinction in approach to silliness
and seriousness, there was no hierarchy of thought;
silliness was as important as wisdom. Not that the Keem
professed to be wise, they merely cultivated it in the 'flower
bed of silliness to be appreciated by those who could
recognise it. Their ability to quote the wisdom of others at
the appropriate moment made it hard for Welder to not
believe he was in the presence of a profound balance
between, divine innocence and ancient wisdom. They made
Welder laugh with their ancient silly songs. The silly
language, which was first spoken by Ben and the Booby,
simply sounded funny and wise and made Welder happy
and content. They spent large parts of the day holding*

mock debates, mock philosophical discussions and speeches with 'question and answer' sessions afterwards; all in the ancient silly language. Welder lost track of time. He was mesmerized by their dialogues; they sounded pompous, profound and 'chit chats' were interspersed with just the right amount of winner jokes, but they did not mock. Sometimes they took it in turns to recite poetry that was made up equally of phrases Welder could understand and parts that were still in that silly sister of Latin, the ancient silly language. At one point they all stopped and looked at Welder. They were seated and reclining around the fountain-like students outside at lunchtime on a sunny day. Then they all got to their feet and surrounded Welder. They looked around at each other and one was silently nominated to speak. They spoke out loud.
'You are a lovely man Welder'. Then they all smiled and clapped their hands in applause that sounded like a rustling tree.

None of them had names or unique personalities. Traits were uniform. What variations there were in appearance and character seemed to shift about from one to the other in combinations that were a balance between them all. With their telepathic connections, they were all offshoots of the same plant. They were the same entity and thought was their sap. Love one and you love them all.

At some point, Welder went into a strange state. There was a misty edge to his vision and light-headed clarity of thought that he could not recall getting from even the strongest of natural or man-made cocktails, and he had tried most of them. His head was in his stomach and his heart was in his head. No part of him was separate; every part of him tingled with emotion and thought. He was one human being. He was in love. The Keem was every child, family member and friend he had ever known and never *known. He was at one with himself, and without effort, he was combining thought and regular conversation with them all. He was at one with them too. It was just as he remembered it was when he experienced being in love for the first time, it made no sense to do anything other than be together with that which he loved, to be in love, to be in love at all times. But as with the great loves of his life, the annoyance of the outside world and reality of need pushes its way in, making him get out of bed and go to the shops, and even to work! Separation occurs; you have to go to school and wave goodbye to your mother as you line up in the corridor. Then one day you wave goodbye to your children as they head off down the road in search of new life and love of their own. In Welder's case, the love spell was broken when the Keem started their pooting ritual once more. He had been with them for one full day (a human day that is) and it had been a lifetime.*

Welder with a new and renewed passion for his task, in fact with more passion and sense of purpose than he had ever felt for any task he ever undertook before began to assess the point he was at. But he was still unsure about where he was headed and indeed what his task was, other than the general one given him by Sally, 'take care of whatever needs taking care of'. Sally came to mind and he knew he would have no hesitation in telling her that he loved her, the next chance he got. He returned to his soft warm grassy living moss mound seat. It was comfortable beyond belief. To his surprise, the cloche descended. He did not resist his pending further level of captivity. Milford had it all planned. He trusted Milford, the brother of Sally, the woman he loved. Milford had become a brother in every sense that Welder understood that title to mean. As significantly as their love of Sally, they had been connected by the Keem. Whatever Milford had in store, Welder believed in.

'Welder my friend, now we come to it' Milford Lyme's recording addressed Welder directly. Milford had imagined Welder paying close attention to the story he was piecing together as he recorded it. In Milford's mind, the pair had become good friends, possibly even brothers. He had rightly guessed that Welder had spent time with the Keem. 'We come to it'

'The incident'. Milford's face grew visibly longer as he spoke. Then for the first time, Milford sat saying nothing. Welder watched Milford sitting in quiet reflection. He knew the look; it was the look of a man who was confronting his own death but had greater things on his mind. Welder had a brief and unusual craving to eat grass coupled with an even briefer but profoundly saddening feeling of guilt.

'You know Welder, only a hand full of researchers in the past three hundred years has ever left this place alive; one was Holborn who fired himself into depths of space to end life amongst the stars in a completely transparent capsule not much bigger than him. Another was my father. None of those who passed on here would have had it any other way. We have been swinging between excitement and anxiety, between profound belief in the greatness of what is possible, and doubt revulsion and contempt for the risk of so many disastrous, seen and unforeseen consequences. All we have ever strived for may end up being on a plague on all of the galaxies houses. We have been working on a project that has led us to the brink of understanding the very nature of the source and flow of all life in the universe. Not only that we may have found a way to link directly to it'. The passion in Milford's voice had risen and taken on the quality of a great orator with great conviction.

'I know because I have done it' Welder halted the tapes with a slight and swift jerk of his head. He needed a moment. He was allowing Milford's words to fall like scores of ball bearings on to and through a complex pattern of nails. He waited whilst the balls fell on the nails sending them bouncing and colliding madly about and eventually working their way down. Finally, they dropped, one by one into one of two pots. Pot one, Milford had lost it, he had lost his grip, and or his mind. Pot two, Milford had found it; he had found something he had not looked for. Maybe he had found something everybody had been looking for. The pots were at the two ends of the sensitive scales of Welder's reckoning. Milford had always sought the truth and the proof of that truth beyond his own experience. At some point that changed and he no longer sought verification of the truth beyond himself. He appeared that Milford was sure of the truth because he was the proof. 'He must have spent time with them too, or at least connected with them. And through them' Welder thought. The balls had all fallen and the scales had remained balanced, so Welder went on.
'Part of me is still a scientist with the need for empirical and irrefutable evidence. But I am also a product of science and there is evidence of my own experience. I am the test tube and the test. I have only my experience to guide me now and that experience may, of course, be a dream. And despite knowing how readily our understanding, our thoughts feelings and actions, can be manipulated and influenced to give the impression of knowledge, still, I know what I know, and I know what I know is true. I have gladly given most of what remains of this short life to know it. I tell you this Welder because you must make a decision based not only on the evidence indicating what might happen but on your instinctive belief of what will happen.

Your instinct is founded in imagination and experience. Sally tells me you are the best person for the job and I trust in her, I believe in her, I love her' Milford's voice stopped abruptly at Welders clapping command. He rubbed his eyes. 'What's he talking about? What the fuck is he talking about?' the question was directed at himself but the Keem heard and reassured him in silent communication, 'you'll see'. The calming influence of the Keem was short-lived. Soon it felt to Welder like there was a growing clamour of voices swirling around his whole body, not just his head. His mouth tasted like he was licking a steel bar. He felt like steel bars were weighing him down. He was weighed down with information and his whole body was feeling it. He felt pinned down in a rising of circumstances beyond his reckoning and control. His ability to lift himself was compromised. He was drowning in Milford's words. His senses were overlapping. He knew he had to make sense of the taste of hammering on the roof of his mouth. Then the voices were attached to people; the people gathered were filling the town square. The murmuring grew with the crowd then suddenly stopped. All as one they focused on something. That which silenced them passed unseen and unknown. Conjecture triggered further murmuring agitation. Their agitation created a rough texture of unified sound from grains of individual distress. It moved in waves across them all. Welder stopped the tapes to intervene before a mob formed and pulled him down from the podium. In effect Welder had been acting as the speaker of the lower house of the galactic neo-mob parliament and brought proceedings to order before they got out of hand. A house over stimulated by its machinations threatened to overrule, overturn and overrun, and even overthrow him at any point. Control of Welder's thoughts had been under threat of being mobbed before but he had always

291

maintained order. He had never once panicked in his life. He was an extraordinary individual. But the physical adaptations he had undergone to be amongst the Keem meant he felt the growing pressure to a greater than usual degree and in ways he had not experienced before. The coursing of emotion through his entire body had created strange physical discomfort and mental distress. He felt like his head desperately needed a shit and his stomach felt deeply depressed. He held fast and overcame. In the silence, his head stopped spinning and came to rest. Welder collected his thoughts that were left scattered around the now empty square and laid them out in a circle like the numbers on a roulette table waiting for Milford to spin the wheel and drop the ball. Each number on the dial was a possibility conjured up by Welder's astute mind. This was a form of visualisation that Welder had practised but never used before. As the numbers grew in number Welder did not like the odds and eliminated more than half based on intuition alone with greater confidence in that faculty given to him by the Keem.

In a silly discussion with the Keem on 'imagination and intuition being the basis for creative progression in science and pooting', Welder saw that the fusion of conscious and unconscious sources of analysis if allowed unfettered progress into action most often gave the most useful, though somewhat unpredictable outcomes. A thought momentarily swept aside his deductions and his attempts to make sense of what was happening and what was going to happen. The thought was 'how the hell, am I supposed to know?' A bubble of compressed gas suddenly developed deep in his gut. The irresistible gut feeling grew and the bubble began its steady quest for freedom. It stretched his throat beyond comfort to its limits. With his mouth open and his chin tucked in it was thrust out with a mighty contraction of his abdomen. It had the deep low powerful resonance of an electromagnetic pulse. He could almost see the shockwaves and he heard tittering Keem on the far side of the Dome. His mind, at least that part of it that resided in his stomach was clear and he asked himself the same rhetorical question.

'How the hell should I know?' Welder had once reflected that this question was as good a way as any of expressing Wittgenstein's seventh and final proposition in his own words. The proposition that 'about which we cannot speak we must pass over in silence' buoyed him and he was ready to let circumstances guide him. He instructed the interface controlling the tapes.

'Roll em'

'You see, Welder something has happened to me; it's getting harder and harder to think straight any more, my head and heart are one and they are leading me away. I'm dying and I want to die. The change in me is the result of something more significant than my death. The Keem are changing. Death is a change of state. I love the Keem'

Welder could see the change in Milford now that he pointed it out though he had taken subconscious note of it earlier. It had been taking hold gradually but Welder could see it clearly. He hoped Milford was able to finish his story. Welder knew Milford must be dead but Milford did not look like a dying man only a changed one. They went on together.

'We tried something; it didn't work and it had dire consequences.' Milford paused and wriggled in his seat as if he was suffering from stomach cramps.

'When I say we, I refer to the body of individuals simply known as 'researchers'. We wondered what would happen if the Keem had a pet. We thought it might continue their social evolution without any physical adaptations being *necessary. Without the source, we had stopped any further adaptations of the Keem's physiology. They could never reproduce or even be cloned. Our built-in, anti-intellectual property-right theft, self-destruct fail-safes made sure of that.' Milford's discomfort brought him to his feet which added a sense of drama to his delivery.*

'So we created the Loon. The peach-faced loon!' Milford's exclamation was followed by his chest expanding steadily as it filled with a huge draught of air in preparation for a long-winded explanation. His chest inflated upwards until full and he held his breath for a moment. He closed his eyes in the protracted exhalation of a silent sigh that followed then carried on as before.

'The name Loon was a shortening of the word balloon said the way a child may pronounce the word. It was meant to look like a beach ball rather than a balloon. Unity Lapwing and Loveluck Magoo were more like a double act than project coordinator and research assistant. They were in charge of implementing the programme and they came up with the name for it. They were twin sisters renowned for their dazzling intellect, great wit, and for being indistinguishable in looks and personality. But they did have very different voices and they were pretty young at eighty-seven when they were chosen to run things on Chippenham Five. From birth, they had a thirst and hunger for knowledge and an insatiable drive for discovery that only science and an interest in twentieth-century culture was able to provide them. They never used their astute minds and identical looks to fool anyone as to which twin was which. It was not in their nature to fool anyone; they thought all practical jokes were cruel and unnecessary and they never had any other reason to employ the potential of deception their looks gave them. They took the post together. It was thought at the time that the project needed

294

fresh impetus. One of the twins was an aficionado of ancient flat films and she came up with the creations form based on a creature from a science fiction movie; a creature that looked like a beach ball. They were drawn to the cultural era that Ben's grandfather grew up in. They loved the music, the films and television, and in particular, they loved cartoons of those times. They saw great wisdom in them. Far greater wisdom than the writings of intellectuals commentating on themselves and each other in a vain attempt to extricate themselves from any responsibility for the competitive, esoteric, self-serving, excluding and destructive cultural systems whilst milking it them for all its worth. Their favourite cartoons were 'Looney Tunes' which was the second reason for calling their creation a 'Loon'. The link between the moon and the Lune and changes in behaviour added further appeal through the twins considered it more of a poetic link. Although based on a beach ball rather than a balloon, they wanted to make the Loon like a balloon in character rather than a ball, in as much as it was intended to be skittish and flighty like a balloon and above all silly. They succeeded and anyone who saw the Loon could not help but smile. They added the prefix of 'peach-faced', not so much because it was peach coloured, for it was more a mad yellow with moving random pink patches like a Jersey Cow, no they called it peach-faced more because the texture of its faces skin. The Loon's face, and it had a recognisable face, was like a ripe peach to the touch, especially when you rubbed your cheek against it. The face was about the size of a dinner plate with large blue eyes made cuter by extra-large eyelashes, a button nose and a small thin-lipped mouth with lips of bright green. It reminded Welder a little of the face of his first steady girlfriend, Luda. The face was warm too as if it was a peach that had just been *picked on a hot sunny summer afternoon in Italy. The Loon's face was upright most of the time but it didn't have to be. It didn't have a right way up; the beauty of being a ball. It was not an issue for it to roll over its face when in motion with the ground. The eyes and nose had no function from a sensory standpoint. The whole Loon was sensitive to movement, light, smell, moisture and sound. The twins saw great potential of future Loons beyond being a pet. The rest of the Loon that wasn't the face, the all in one head and body, felt like a soft fake fur, like the texture of something you would throw over yourself relaxing on a couch; 'pho-fur for the sofa' as the twins called it. Welder was sensing the Loon's texture; he had activated the program that allowed him to sense the textures of various parts of the Loon as if they were squares of carpet samples.*

'mmm, so soft' Welder avoided wondering what the Keem felt like to the touch as he did not want them to hear but the thought was not far from his mind and he could see it hovering around him.

'The Loon seemed simple to create compared to the complexities of the Keem. It was not much more complicated than the original potted pets of Robby Roundway. It was in many ways harder to resist giving it too many characteristics and functions than it was to cultivate and activate. Our exuberance got the better of us; we took our eyes off the ball so to speak. We went too fast and did not spot the danger; though to be fair we may not have spotted the danger even if we went more slowly and judiciously. Here, see for yourself' Milford gestured swinging his right arm out to his side and behind with his hand-held flat with palm forward as if he was a master of ceremonies introducing the next act.

'Here's the Loon'

There followed a sequence of projections, images and observations of the development and creation of the Loon. Welder was impressed by Milford's montaging skills and tried to think what music would make an appropriate backing track. He decided on an abstract classical, planet and western, a punk track that lasted seventeen days called 'My Saddle Sore Days Are Almost Over'. He watched the early visualisations of the Loon and transparent prototypes the size of oranges floating across the twin's lab, overlaid with diagrams and formulas detailing the propulsion system. The Loon could inflate and deflate tiny cells all over the surface of its body without greatly changing form. It could hover or float and move up to five miles an hour in accelerated bursts that gave the impression that it was much faster. It could keep its face upright or roll over it on the ground.

'Very cute' Welder thought as he watched the Loon sit on Unity's lap making funny little squeaky sounds on the day it was ready to be presented to the Keem. It was about eighteen inches in diameter and perfectly spherical. A fitting tribute to Bobby's love of bubbles the twins thought. 'Thou art a peach-faced Loon' said Unity in a Shakespearean actor's dramatic fashion. She was standing and looking lovingly into the Loon's sweet little face. Then she threw the Loon with all her might across the room. It squeaked and squealed creating the impression of delight. It was only developed to react to feelings and give the impression of having them, nothing more. It flew into Loveluck's waiting arms.

'Shakespeare?' she asked tossing the Loon back to her. 'I'm not sure. It sounds like it could be' Unity replied catching the Loon whilst the Loon let out squeals mimicking delight.

Having seen no sign of the Loon since arriving Welder surmised that the demise of the Loon was central to the incident Milford was referring to but he did not attempt to guess how or why, and why it this was so calamitous.

Unity and Loveluck were noticeably crestfallen on the day when they first introduced the Loon to the Keem, even though the Keem's indifference to the Loon was expected. The Keem were not equipped to deal with anything outside of their range of responses. They had been told about the Loon's arrival and were given some suggestions for patterns of dialogue. Unity and Jealousy knew only too well that since 'the source' had been destroyed it had been determined that the only way to continue enhancement of the Keem was through circumstantial influence rather than physical adaptions. The destruction of the sauce triggered a debate that lasted two hundred and fifty years. The conclusion was that the independent plant-based life forms known as Keem had been refined far enough physically. The Keem's future lay in emotional evolution without substantive intervention. Whatever changes happen to the Keem's bodies would happen naturally.

'Just for the record Welder', recommenced Milford after his montage was over and only his seated projection remained visible.

'I have been talking to Sally much more lately' Welder detected a personal resonance to his voice. The montage had brought the story much further forward and Milford was building up to his final farewell. None the less Welder also sensed he had a 'ways' to go yet before that time came. Milford had the air of a coach addressing his star player or even a Father his son, knowing that the time that he could have any direct influence over his instrument of the future was getting limited. Milford noticed the closing window

and froze for a moment, then repeated himself. Events were taking over and time for the first time in Milford's life was noticeably running out.

'I have been speaking to Sally lately and she says you are capable of operating without the constraints of the usual arbitrary moral frameworks that societies impose on themselves. It is fascinating, I'm sure you will agree that there are some quite bizarre legal, ethical and moral frameworks grafted on to life around the galaxy. It is mind-blowing just how many variations there are, but they all have one thing in common, a motivation and a flaw. They seek, perhaps even need to explain, the unknown then base doctrine on that which at best is a theory and more often than not a guess. There is a compulsion to weigh ourselves down with theories to govern the one thing we do naturally anyway, be alive. Even those belief structures that focus almost exclusively on death do so only as a consequence of being alive. They see death as the path to a higher state, and by state they mean some kind of existence and by existence they mean life; so why devalue or relegate life at the outset, the life they know about. However having said all that, and however many flaws in the logic, I have never been able to completely dismiss the idea that death is a transition rather than an ending. I thought at one time that perhaps it was the route into a parallel universe. Or maybe our lives in our bodies are the chrysalis stage between two distinct states of being. Very different states perhaps, but even if we end up in different forms and maybe even different dimensions, these are forms of existence. A plant may seem to only exist and not much more for many people, but it is life, and all life is part of the same ocean. It is part of the function of humanity to progress towards a greater understanding, appreciation and reverence for all life. We collect and become information. That is our nature even

more deeply embedded within us than the need to eat with our mouths. At first, the thugs had their hands on the steering wheel of evolutionary progress and drove recklessly, almost killing us so many times. Thankfully pervasive, persuasive, positive impulses rose in humankind exerting some control. But that control can be wrestled away at any time. Maybe that's how it goes; round and fucking round. But I don't believe that to be the case. We just have no sure idea of where we are heading. We may just drive off a cliff but I don't think so. I don't feel that is the case. Humanity so far has been like rubble without a causeway to quote a miss-quote from the twins. Anyway, Welder let's proceed. Oh and one last thing you should be aware of, Sally says you don't have much time because Albran Prawnshot is behind the purchase of the planet and wants to humiliate Sally and take full control of the company. And of course, destroy Root and Branch which will be the end of the Keem. He had enlisted the services proplanters who will destroy the sphere; completely the wrong course of action born out of all of the right beliefs. It is a fail-safe. Oh well, onwards and upwards'
Milford's last statement was not a surprise to Welder and part of him wanted to be destroyed so he wouldn't have to decide what to do. On the flip side he believed in himself; because Sally believed in him. This gave him hope.

The montage ended at the point that the Loon had been successfully assimilated into the Keem's world. The story continued at a less truncated rhythm.

Unity and Loveluck were impeccable in monitoring, recording and collating data on the Keem's responses to the Loon. At first, the Loon would spend most of its time hovering and drifting about far above the Keem in the higher reaches of the Dome. The Keem paid no more attention to it than they did to any of the plants that

300

surrounded them. Every four hours bubbles were released for the Loon to chase. It was conditioned to act excitedly and give the impression of being happy when chasing and bursting them, and look as if it was trying to eat them. The twins decided to use the Loon's apparent love of bubbles to create a ritual of daily feeding modelled loosely on feeding the ducks and pigeons in the park, an activity the twins had enjoyed so much in their childhood.

Every day at the same time the sound of popping bubbles was broadcast in the dome. This was the signal for the Keem to let the Loon know that bubbles were on the way and to release the actual bubbles. The Keem would gather around the ceremonial tickler and when the sound of the bursting ended their role began. They would place all of their little plant hands on what looked like a giant plunger which was a large version of a standard acme cartoon plunger used by various cartoon characters to let off explosives. As they pushed it down together they would shout out in unison 'release the bubbles'. They were allowed to follow up with one of several choices of additional chants. What seemed to be their favourite was 'release those money balls'. Exactly twenty of the brightly coloured 'tuck bubbles', the size of tennis balls would be released, one at a time. They were pushed out from white blooms along a bubble vine especially grown for the purpose. There were several extra plants added to the Keemdom whilst the Loon was being cultivated. All of them were designed to trigger variations in the Loon's behaviour. Once released the Loon would chase the bubbles and burst them with a single shot of compressed air fired out at great speed from its open mouth. Similar to the shot of air Bobby talked about in his memoirs. The one he looked forward to every time he went for an eye test. His optician had never come across someone who liked anticipating and receiving *a shot of air in the eyeball before. Bobby was barely able to suppress his giggles.*

The released bubbles contents of 'tuck vapour', burst into a colourful puff and the Loon would harvest it like a whale gathering krill in its gaping mouth.

For safety reasons the Loon's mouth did not open wider than an inch and not much vapour was collected. This did not dent the Loon's apparent enthusiasm for trying. The twins would convulse with laughter watching the Loon chase the bubbles and would shout out like toddlers from their grass glass viewing orb, 'Loon Loon!' But the normally giggly Keem were nonplussed. The ritual had been formulated as a means of creating a connection between the Keem and the Loon, even perhaps a bond. But despite the huge leap forward in cognitive faculties that the insertion of floaters nuts had bestowed on the Keem's advanced plant brain, many subtle nuances of thought just went over their heads. Or maybe the whole thing just left them cold. Unity occasionally had mini-fits brought on by frustration. They lasted exactly ten seconds and involved a lot of shouting. After such outbursts, Unity and Loveluck both felt relieved.

'Why can't they see how fucking cute and fucking funny the Loon is?'

The ritual continued for every day for months but the Keem showed no interest in the Loon. The only satisfaction they got was the same as they did from following any ritual, purely superficial. They were encouraged to discuss the Loon but the programmed five minutes of discussion was silent. The twins wondered if the Keem resented or were threatened by the presence of the Loon, but extensive testing revealed that their only response to it was indifference.

302

Unity and Loveluck felt like parents that had gone all out on a Christmas present for their adored child, watched eagerly as it was unwrapped, and rather than exciting squeals were met with an unimpressed 'oh' and a reluctant 'thanks'. The Keem showed no sign of change, however, the Loon did. It would roll beneath a shrub in a little-used area of the dome as if sulking and only emerged at 'tuck bubble' time. The bubble chasing stopped making the twins laugh. The Loon spent part of each day rolling around following the Keem about waiting to be thrown around in much the same way a dog with a stick trails its master hoping they will relent and start throwing. Only in the case of the Loon, it was the dog and stick. The twins wondered if their unease at the response of the Keem to the Loon, and their anxiety that the whole project may be having a negative effect, was just them projecting their disappointment on the situation. The flight and rolling paths and every measurable characteristic of the Loons behaviour became uniform and the twins sensed an underlying change in the Loon. It no longer chased the tuck bubbles gleefully. There seemed to be a hint of aggression. Acting purely on that intuition they decided to remove the Loon from the Keemdom and the earliest opportunity.

Following the destruction of the source, all safety and security procedures were reviewed and the number of researchers and support staff was reduced to a maximum of four. There had been conjecture that the death of Lisby at the hands of her zombified assistant was some kind of deliberate sabotage from an outside agent. By the time the twins took up their posts all maintenance work was done by the one or two researchers overseeing the Keem's welfare. There were periods of up to a month during which the Keem were left unattended other than by remote monitoring.

Removing the Loon gained urgency when it did not respond to an initial scent trigger in the tuck bubbles vapour that should have mildly sedated it. The Loon did not want to take its medicine. The similarity between the Loon's behaviour and that of the fictional creature the twins drew inspiration from, profoundly worried them. Surely there was not something inherent in the beach ball form that they overlooked; that somehow being a ball or bubble form influences behaviour. Perhaps there was more to the saying 'as mad as a balloon', after all, they noted that there were not many examples of advanced ball-shaped life forms in the galaxy.

Unity was chosen to enter the dome and tranquilise the Loon with a harmless infusion designed for that very purpose and kept in the 'just in case' draw. The delivery method was an ancient one; the Loon would be shot; albeit completely unavoidable. It was done with a tiny soft tacky pellet that was designed to stick to the Loon's pho fur outer layer and the gently acting tranquilising vapour was released. As harmless as the whole operation was, shooting the Loon still felt like an aggressive act to the twins.

Unity entered the cloche to prepare her for spending time in the dome. It would only need three hours before and after being in the Keemdom to make the necessary physical adjustments. She was wearing her shadow. She did not like wearing a shadow but it gave Welder the clearest holographic projection he had seen to date. It was constructed from many more angles than standard shadow holographic recorders. It gave Welder the feeling of being a silent ghostly presence as events unfolded. Unity had on a slightly baggy set of company overalls similar to Welders but a bright blue. Emblazoned on the back was a large-headed cartoon canary that Welder did not recognise. Welder had not thought about his own inoperative shadow since it stopped working. He did note that it was not the conditions within the dome that determined it being shut down. Shutting off one's shadow was, of course, standard military procedure before an escape or surrendering.

The Keem were informed that Unity would be entering the dome and that the 'tuck bubble' ritual for that day was cancelled. The cloche shrivelled back into its husky shell and Unity headed for the usual laurel like shrub to which she knew the Loon had retreated. The pellet delivery system looked like a primitive TV remote control with a single red button. The retro-looking design was based on one of Ben Crammer's extensive collection of twentieth-century television remote controls. Some of them had seemed to have more buttons than functions. The twin's shooter was based on the popular all-in-one, one-button operates everything perfectly model, designed by Bobby's Mother that was thought to look too simple to be trusted and was never released commercially. Unity and Loveluck were expert shots with anything that could shoot. This was due to years of bubble shooting contests exclusively against each other during their downtime in various research facilities (mainly domes). Unity's shooter had a sensor set to detect the Loon and the red button would light up when it was accurately aimed and ready to shoot.

The 'tuck bubble' signal was sounded to draw the Loon out of its shrubby hideout. Unity approached the deep green-leafed clump and waited for the Loon to emerge. There was no sign of movement. Her first thought was that the previous days bubbles modified tuck vapour had done its job and the Loon was already neutralised. It was far more likely that she would find the Loon already dormant than her needing to shoot it with further neutralising agent. With this in mind, she pulled out the 'Bubblewrap' from one

of the many almost invisible pockets on her boiler-suit. She
had brought the wrap to transport the Loon back to the lab.
It was still compressed. It had the satisfying form of a
pebble that fitted neatly into the depression in her palm
with her fingers holding it tightly in place. She bent over
and pulled aside the outer layer of foliage and stuck her
head in the shrub. 'POP' the sound startled her but she
barely flinched. She sensed the fright but did not feel and
was still. The emotional stabilising effects of the cloche in
acclimatising had practically worn off and were only mild
at that point. It was her determination, resolve and instincts
that had kicked in and kept her feelings in check. Both
twins had cool heads and practised restraint by attempting
to scare each other at random moments. After a pause
Unity kneeled and moved forward on her knees. She passed
through the canopy of leaves and into the plants open
interior. She felt like she was entering the humble
woodland cave dwelling of a mythical creature. There, by
the trunk of the canopy, she was under; there looking like a
collapsed pumpkin many weeks after Halloween, was the
Loon. The pop she had heard was the final phase of the
Loon's immobilisation brought on by the tuck vapour.
Unity pushed down the rising sadness to concentrate on the
task at hand but a tear forced its way out and rolled down
her cheek at the sight of their deflated creation. She and
her sister had the rare condition of only crying with one
eye. After placing the wrap on the ground she gently lifted
the Loon and placed it on the circle of orange transparent
material that had unfurled itself from the compressed
pebble. She squeezed a bubble of liquid held between two
layers of the material and it inflated and wrapped itself
perfectly around the Loon's form like an inflatable splint.
The wrap formed into a hemispherical protective carrier
with handles. All of this, Welder had watched with

concentrated and increased readiness for something even worse to happen; something worse than the failure of the Keem's unfertilized feelings towards the Loon being germinated, and the Loon's recall. The recording went from within the shrub to without as Unity dragged the Loon out from its hidey-hole. It captured her appearing from behind a leafy veil holding the Loon in the inflated carryall. The organic gasses that inflated the bag gave it a degree of lift. The bubble wrap became a 'gasbag', which was very popular with shoppers. Only the company had perfected the mass production of the gasbag so that it could be affordable for everyday use. It used the genetic information gleaned from a vine that produced floating fruit. The floating fruits had evolved purely to provide the inhabitants of its native planet with target practice for the tranquilising phlegm they shot from their elongated blowpipe like mouths. Welder watched on.

Chapter Seventeen

Incident and Aftermaths

Unity carried the dormant Loon back towards the entrance of the Keemdom and the site of the cloche. She placed the Loon near the centre of the circle that marked out the area that would be under the organic glass dome as soon as it was stimulated into dropping down. Welder was not far from that point as he watched the holographic recording. But before getting started with the process of reversing acclimatisation, Unity went to check up on the Keem as she and her sister had planned. She still plenty of time left before she would have to return to cloche like a deep-sea diver returning to a decompression chamber. It made sense to make use of the opportunity and visit with the Keem especially in the light of the Loon. It was an unwritten unspoken ground rule that direct contact with the Keem should be kept to a minimum. This turned out to be a completely unnecessary and limiting approach.

Unity did not want to turn up with the deflated bubble wrapped Loon when hanging out with the Keem but she left it with a sense of unease. Even though they doubted whether the Keem would react adversely the twins did not want to take any chances. They had some thinking to do first. To her surprise when Unity rounded the column she found all of the Keem at the Loon's tuck bubbles release plunger. She assumed that they had mustered there on hearing the signal that had been given to get the Loon to come out from its lair despite being informed it was not necessary. That theory didn't quite gel though. Not only had the Keem been informed that they were no longer releasing bubbles for the foreseeable future but the alternative suggestion of a nature walk was not taken up.

'Why didn't you tell me that the Keem were gathered around the plunger Love?' to some the question Unity asked her sister back in the control room above her might have sounded like recrimination from a sibling or irritated colleague but it wasn't, and it wasn't taken that way either. If Loveluck didn't tell her there would be a reason and that's why Unity asked.

'They just got there, something's not right Nitty. There seems to be one not present' Loveluck's voice was only superficially calm. There was no point Unity asking if the tracking equipment was working correctly, Loveluck would be conducting a diagnostic and questions of that nature was not necessary.

'What's my move sis?'

'Count them off and if there is one missing they should know'

Welder was struck more so than at any other point just how much further advanced the Keem that he had just spent time with were compared to the ones the twins were engaged with. And in the scheme of things that was comparatively recent. He wondered why the researchers never used individual names or pet names for the Keem. Maybe he skipped that part of the presentation. Welder stopped to find out why, like someone stopping what they were reading to look up the meaning of a word that just won't be skipped. His mind then went back to the deflated Loon and he wondered if it was not quite out of it, and was about to make a dramatic re-entry into events.

'Why don't you use names for the Keem Milford? Wouldn't they be easier to keep track off?' Welder asked knowing the faceless interface would seek out an appropriate response from the data despite directing his question at Milford'.

'It goes way back' was Milford's response. 'Let me direct you to the relevant information'.

Milford had predicted Welder's question may be asked. A mini view footnote appeared about two feet away at eye level of the recently seated Welder. Welder was aware of time being limited but he was not one to rush things. He followed his gut thoughts.

'It has been decided that we should no longer use names for any of the Keem, or to number them, or to use any form of individual identification'. The voice was that of Geraldine Yurpturd, the scientist that oversaw the implanting of the Floaters central sensory processors into the Keem. It was Geraldine that first called the kernel like coordinating and processing pod a 'Hubnut'.

'We do not want to interrupt or influence the emergence of any individual's characteristics through associations connected with particular names; at least not names that we respond to emotionally. And it appears that our propensity to ascribe character to certain names is unavoidable. It has also been proved that such associations had an adverse impact on individuals of previous generations of Keem. And as we have found to our cost in the past, lose one and we lose them all. Somewhere along the line something got into the mix or resulted from it, which left them so sensitive to being treated differently

310

from one another that they must all be treated the same in every way. They are responsive to the slightest variations in our interaction with individuals that just the difference in the way we feel about names without even being aware of it is enough to possibly isolate an individual. An unstoppable wilting can occur; first with one and then, with them all. The potential hierarchy of numbers as a means of identification must also be avoided, even amongst ourselves. We must not project personalities or other aspects of ourselves on to individuals; we must not have favourites, consciously or unconsciously. As best as possible we will not refer to any individual Keem unless it is strictly necessary. When we do need to identify an individual we will use temporary random sound codes'

Welder asked to hear examples of such random temporary sound codes but the interface said playing of the codes in 'Domeland' could only be done with the authorisation of the Head Honcho.

'Well, I guess that isn't going to happen' Welder said out loud. The Keem seemed to be leaving Welder alone to wade through the swamp of data. 'Authorisation approved, go right ahead'. It was the same, man putting on a bad American accent voice as before. Welder was then able to listen to a description of the soft clicking clucking and bubbly notes that were the basis of the temporary sound tags given to individual Keem. It seemed somehow unscientific not to label something to monitor it. But he remembered the split vent experiment where one particle was shown to pass through two vents at the same time but would not do so if observed. Things behave differently when observed. If particles split, and or relocate when observed, he could understand the researcher's concern about the identification of individuals. The researchers had to be run and participate in blind testing. This neutrality

*was especially important if their fear that a lack of it may
have contributed to the loss of a previous generation of
Keem. Welder learnt that nearly all external features of this
generation were interchangeable and morphed daily; even
height.*

*'So a Keem might be slightly taller but only for a day; hmm,
resume'*

Unity's frozen form went into motion once again.

*'Ask them' came Loveluck's order from above. Loveluck
had assumed some measure of authority as she had the
most data at hand. Unity had already started looking for
the missing Keem without being too obvious she was doing
so.*

'Where are you?' she quietly asked.

     *The Keem looked back and forth between each
other and roughly at the same time moved away from the
plunger in a loose bushel. She saw the bunch move off and
followed. They made their way to the huts and all stood
outside one particular fond leaf changing rooms. The Keem
lined up and made a passage for Unity to walk along. She
entered the upturned green bowl through an arched
opening needing to bow her head and bend her back to do
so. Unity had forgotten just how hot and humid the interior
of a changing room was. It smelled and glowed oranges.
She was distracted for a moment by the matching colour
and odour. When her attention was back in the room her
worst fears were confirmed. She had prepared herself for
the worst but still, the shock overpowered her and she
dropped to her knees. One of the Keem was lying lifeless on
its back. It looked as if its body had been flattened by a
steam roller. Only the coordinut remained unharmed within
the head. The Keem's eyes and mouth were opened wide
and frozen in one of those expressions that could be crying
or laughter, or both. Thick sap, like that from a rubber*

plant, forming a thick even white line around the Keem's flattened grey-brown body. It was the most horrifying gory thing Unity had ever seen but she held herself together.

Loveluck was seeing what Unity was seeing as a partial holographic image in the open heart of the control centre.

'Don't show any signs of feeling to the Keem Unity. Take scans of all the Keem and leave the damaged Keem where it is for now.' Loveluck had the reassuring tone of someone who knew what to do and was ready for any eventuality. As Unity emerged from the changing room the Keem's normal blank expressions took on a mournful character to Unity but she did not react. She simply said thank you and goodbye. As she started back to the area to be covered by the cloche a Keem stated in a matter of fact way
'The Loon flattened us'
She did not turn around; as it was a not a question the Keem would not expect a response. The image of the Keem's flattened figure filled her thoughts. Welder was finally getting a sense of the mindsets that researchers had towards the Keem and the way they behaved towards them as a result. They served the Keem, they revered the Keem, and they loved them like a child. And they were children being, story or potential wisdom would one day inherit the universe. The researchers did not know how but one day the Keem would show them what to do. At the point in the story Welder had reached the Keem were not as he found them. Welder wondered how researchers of the past would have responded to the far more sophisticated Keem that he had become beguiled by. The Keem that watched on with him were informed of their history and happily discussed it with him only hours before. Back then, Welder thought, they did not seem to be able to read the thoughts of Unity when she was in their presence. Now he believed they had

read his thoughts even before he entered the Dome. Back then they seemed to be a series of conditioned reflexes whereas the Keem that greeted him seemed to have their thoughts possibly their ideas.

Sophie woke to find Paul from the coffee shop already dressed in his barista's uniform, sitting on the end of her bed and bending over to tie his laces. As he stood with his back to her she was reminded of at least one reason she had been attracted to him. Her sleepy little smile was the tip of a smile as big as a mile. It was a smile dancing in satisfied triumph. She reproached herself with what some people might say about having sex with a younger man, but more so as he worked at Weston Super Mare's newest coffee shop. A place she could have been a regular at. But to say her self-recrimination was half-hearted would be to massively underestimate the denominator in the expressions equation. She was not even one-sixteenth hearted. But she was shocked to find how easy it had been once the fancy took her. She was smart enough to deduce that something that may happen only rarely or even only once can happen with greater ease, like a mistake. As Paul turned to greet her he smiled and he gave the impression of knowing what she was thinking. His eyes and warm expression went partway to reassuring her that her intuitive mental situational calculator had not veered off the track too far.

'Bye Sophie, I'll see you in the coffee shop' and with that, the young man, who knew exactly how Sophie liked her coffee, left. She pondered that either he was a smart likeable person who would probably have a good life as a result of those qualities, or the standard of service training in the country had hit new heights. Funny that she once so fervently riled against constant civility yet as the years rolled by she could see that it had unforeseen benefits. 'He even dispensed with the awkwardness of a parting kiss, 'unless he didn't kiss me bec… Don't finish that question Sophie' she suspended her thoughts whilst she looked down from her attic bedroom window at the back of Soft Sands and watched Paul make his exit from the building and across the floral car park. He stopped for a moment as if he had forgotten something, or possibly he was enjoying the paintings of flowers on the ground in the grounds. He moved off and Sophie's ego led her to think she had made his steps look so light, 'the equation is balanced Sophie, don't stick in any more numbers with more questions'. And with that, all of her feelings were parked in their allotted bright flower painted spaces. She looked down and as if she had just arrived at the office and left her private life in the glove compartment of her car, she was ready for work at the R and B. Oops, that's meant to be B and B.' Sophie had not been aware of the narrator or their voice and the slight error did not throw her off, but she did notice it.

'Sophie went downstairs and picked out the post from the wire basket attached to the inside of the front door, just below its mouth. Light passing through the art deco stained glass of the top half of the door painted coloured patterns on her bare arms. She was in the moment. She paused and enjoyed the slight anticipation she got every morning from picking up the mail. It was an excitement based on the against the odds belief that there could be a mystery letter from an old friend or news of good fortune that depended on her going on an adventure. She explained her more than averagely heightened appreciation of this feeling as being a result of the physical warmth she was experiencing. But she was also aware of the other side of the equation; the dreaded letter that could send someone's life into a tailspin. The anxiety of anticipation and imaginings were an accepted part of the balanced tension that was the constant undercurrent to her daily life. She was used to it. But something was different and it wasn't anything to do with what had transpired earlier. And it wasn't a premonition either; she simply knew that something was lurking amongst the bills and offers of cheap broadband. It was the response to a request for information she had written off for six months before that was the unconscious source of her sense of anticipation. She interpreted this increased wakefulness as a kind of calculated premonition. And in a sense, it was, for it was always below the surface waiting to emerge and announce 'I knew it'. It was nearly the summer solstice so despite it being only six-thirty in the morning the sun had risen almost an hour earlier and the approaching sun had started lightening the sky an hour before that. The coffee machine was set for 06.15 and was ready with Sophie's special blend; selected as much for aroma as taste. She flopped the post on the kitchen table poured herself some coffee in her favourite large mug with 'keep calm' crossed out and 'you keep fucking calm and make some more coffee' written above it. She never opened the post in the hallway or before she was sitting down with a coffee. When she saw the letter with markings that gave away that it was what she had been waiting for, her unease remarkably disappeared. Her cool self had woken to smell the coffee. Once, when Sophie was being berated by a disgruntled manager over her pernickety but highly effective ways from a jealous underachieving line manager who told her she should 'wake up and smell the coffee'. It was her cool self that replied, 'I like the smell of coffee, so I will be only too happy to wake up and smell it'. Not the wittiest thing she had ever said but enough to make her inadequate superior throw an ornamental paperweight at her. It was a plastic sphere with tiny trapped coloured bubbles and it did what all parents warned it would do if thrown recklessly and took someone's eye out. Sophie felt sorry for her out of control boss and realised that trying to play it cool did not diffuse the heat of others. She decided to be more selective about when to play the cool hand in future. Her cool self speculated on whether her subconscious was capable of calculating to the day when the letter in her hand would arrive. If any person's subconscious was capable of such a calculation hers was, but her conscious mind told her the odds made it unlikely. She was distracting herself but was aware that the time to start preparing the guests breakfasts was approaching. She knew that the letter would contain two numbers of significance, 'x' the number of procedures and 'y' the number of successes. It was her relationship with Roger that had made access to the information possible through discreet channels. Permutations went rushing through her mind with the same intensity as those that preceded her taking a big bet in her 'crazy days'. This time she was not trying to predict a number on a wheel, or the face that would be revealed on the turn of a card. She was trying to predict her emotional responses to numbers on a page. The calculations were less random than which number will come upon a roulette wheel but if anything harder to predict, 'at least in my case' she said out loud in a clear but quiet voice acknowledging that very point. She deferred back to her original decision to request the information and opened the letter. She read them, the numbers, and tears sprang forth. One fell into her black coffee and she sobbed for the full five minutes she had left before cooking commenced. More emotion was released than she expected and she 'knew it'. John came down at seven as it was his turn to serve; it was always his turn to serve. None the less a timetable with a column indicating whose turn it was to serve and whose turn it was to cook was held by souvenir magnets of Blackpool on the fridge. Sophie had composed her self by the time John reported for duty. The news wasn't bad. Deep down it registered as profoundly good news but desperately sad too. The good won out. John connected Sophie's noticeably good spirits to the young man that he had seen leaving at what would have been the dead of night six months before. He thought of saying 'you're in good spirits' but with the discretion of a thoughtful teacher or sensitive father he didn't. He knew Sophie well enough to know that the good spirits she was in ran deeper and longer than anything she would want to discuss before breakfast and only after breakfast if she initiated it. The number thirteen was writ large on the inside of her forehead.

Milford looked fully concentrated with his legs flapping open occasionally like unfastened stable doors flapping in a steady breeze.

'It was the Loon that was responsible for flattening the Keem and the twins were able to work out exactly how, but not completely why. The Keem have ticklish tummies. The Loon was developed to follow the Keem for a short time each day like a puppy wanting to play. It would roll away at a lack of response to it, or any number of signs signals or commands would trigger the same action. The Loon would roll away at the slightest sign of distress. Conversely, it would stay and play in response to the appropriate behavioural indicators from the Keem, such as laughter. The Loon must have followed the Keem into the changing room. The Keem would have been lying down as part of its routine to ensure structural renewal and integrity. The back was weakened during this process and lying down was necessary. The Keem would have stayed on its back once the procedure began even if it had seen the Loon approach. It would be incapable of movement but would

have still been able to give oral commands. The Keem stick to their routines religiously. The Loon must have rolled on to the Keem's stomach causing it to giggle. A cycle of rolling and giggling must have started. The Loon would not have recognised the Keem's distress, indeed the giggling would have encouraged it to continue and go on for as long as the Keem appeared to be happy. The real mystery was why the Loon exerted so much downward force; more force in fact than it was supposed to be capable of. The twins were devastated as you can imagine but they could not find the source of whatever gave the Loon its added downward thrust. They were convinced it was sabotage and my personal feeling is that they were right.' Milford appeared physically uncomfortable and started wondering about. So much so that he was compelled to comment. 'Don't worry Welder; plants in my pants. Where was I?' He continued to move about but in controlled pacing back and forth with his hands behind his back and his head slightly bowed, in the manner of a lawyer pacing back and forth in front of a jury during a long summing up. Now and then he would look up with a jerk and release his arms and flap them around for a few seconds uncontrollably. 'I believe that our cultivation of the Loon or something similar was predicted some time ago by agents or a rogue element that wanted the project to end. There was a plant deeply embedded; someone way back was a plant, if you take my meaning. Someone fears we are focusing on producing some kind of product for popular consumption to shift the balance of power in the company back to organicisation. And that someone believes we are doing so outside legal constraints governing plant research. There are more rules Welder than there are stars in the night sky. You can understand why though. Whole star systems have been wiped out by the humble introduction of the most basic life forms. You know the *stories. I am also convinced that whoever was responsible for the incident was also somehow responsible for the destruction of the sauce. And whoever it was, they were acting as covertly as us. The fact that they did not simply expose us to the galaxy indicates that they were afraid of the negative impact on the company. So our enemy must lie somewhere within and most likely floating like turds on the top. After all, our work has provided countless innovations and bi-products that remain the bedrock of the company, so this is about power and not law, ethics, morality and definitely not a virtue. No, it was an inside job and they have not finished their work yet. They have no idea of the magnitude and significance of our work and we can't tell them and if we could they would not listen. Sally figured all of this stuff out long ago. She believes that Albran Prawnshot is the turd and that he wants to take the company in a totally different direction. He has been overseeing secret research of his own; research into organic machines; machines that grow. Sally says he has taken viral battery production technology into new realms. He is operating within the law but the destruction his research could cause is incalculable, I should know because I tried to calculate it, whereas the only danger of our research is to the Keem, yet we must hide our work from the authorities and even our organisation. The Keem are the opposite of a threat. In many ways research has been secondary to caring and protecting the Keem for the last five hundred years. The introduction of the Loon was as much aimed at preparing them for a potential forced relocation that could bring them in to contact with many more individuals. We wanted then to be able to adjust naturally; on their own. Their garden is under threat and it was thought they would need to get to know the gardeners that would be in charge of transplantation and* transportation. Some clever bog on the other side figured this scenario out and planted the seeds of the weeds of destruction years ago. The twins left' as he said this, his arms went briefly into helicopter motion and then returned into the position behind his back where he clasped them tightly. 'They did as much as they could to uncover the mystery of the Loon's behaviour. But it was the change in the Keem after the incident that they were most concerned about' Milford's whole body began to twitch and began to sweat profusely. 'Here are the twins again' he was speaking through clenched teeth and Welder could see his skin was turning that green a field goes when millions of tiny verdant shoots first appear in springtime.

'There are ten short recordings of the twins each making a salient point in their investigations' Welder could see that Milford wanted to get through his material as quickly as he could. After an obvious edit, Milford was slightly restored and he proceeded with deliberate calmness.

'It was decided that the flattened Keem should remain in situ. The shock of removing it could have had unforeseen consequences. The Keem did not appear to be suffering from its presence; they simply went about their business and avoided the changing room that contained it. The twins visited the Keem as often as they dared to monitor one and all. Here are just some of their more important findings'

'Clip one'. It was not Milford's voice; it was Milford's assistant Randolph's voice speaking in an exaggerated attempt at neutral tone; exaggeration that ended its neutrality. His voice ended up expressing his loyal resolute nature, better than any deliberate attempt would have. Clip one was a format that the other clips would roughly follow. It was made up of important dialogue between the twins around what looked like an antique solid round kitchen table about six feet across and made of wood. Welder noted

321

that the twins had stopped dying and playing about with the style of their hair and looked more similar than they had before. Concern and intensity had washed away any superficial applied differences. At first, there was a holographic projection of the flattened Keem hanging above the centre of the table. It had neat sections cutaway; some sections were completely removed and others were cut on three sides and peeled back like a museum model revealing and identifying its hidden internal workings. In this case, there was no need for labels; the twins knew all there was to know about the physiology of the Keem. As the conversations between the women peeled away the external layers and dissected the incident, projected scraps of writing, formulas, sections of the Keem and models of complex chemicals filled the space above the table. Now and then one of them would clear a space for new speculations like a chef clearing their chopping board. Heaps of peel and detritus piled up around the fringes of their work stations as their chopping got ever finer.

The first point established was that the flattened Keem could not be pronounced dead. The main fabric of its body showed no signs of living cells but the co-ordinut, though void of any activity was not degrading. The outer layer of the nut dried and a formed hard protective covering of the soft centre. The inner core remained moist in the same way a planet's core remains molten. It was like a cross between a seed and a dormant root of a plant that could start growing given the right conditions; not cloned but regrown. The Dome's sophisticated sensors meant that an accurate virtual autopsy was possible and the squashed Keem remained intact and in place as it was found. There were long debates over whether to remove the remains of the Keem and freeze it in the condition it was in. They wanted to protect it, preserve it and possibly care for it

322

within the lab. But understandably their instincts pointed them towards a path of non-intervention.

Welder was only shown the conclusion of the point which was revisited many times but he could see it had been taxing on the twins, though they never got heated or irritated with each other in the slightest way. Their view was to leave it alone and let it do its thing. Interference often has the reverse effect to its intentions. Besides, they decided it would cause the least disruption for them all, especially the other parts of the Keem.

'Second clip'. Randolph was announcer again. Welder was able to cut off his impulse to work out Randolph's accent but he was not able to ignore it. Ancient Scottish accents had a familiar ring to him but he had no real knowledge of them. Time had passed before the starting point of clip two. It showed the nut unchanged but the body of the Keem was withdrawn like a tadpole's tail rather than withered like a corn husk. The twin's anxiety seemed to have shrivelled up with the main trunk of the flattened figure still hovering in holographic form above the lab table. Most to the projected workings had gone. The twins had tidied up the place. They were surer of their instincts. They saw the deterioration they were witnessing as part of a process. Though not physically connected they believed the flattened Keem was still part of the flow of energy that bound them all.

Clip three showed examples of the changing state of the Keem's shell formed a ring around the table. The twin's spirits were buoyed by developments. They were also frantically trying to determine the nature of what was happening to the co-ordinut. Was it like a seed that could be germinated, and if so, how?

'Clip four'. Welder found a strange comfort in Randolph's voice. Clip four saw the twins in full flow. They looked even more similar if that was possible. This time it was

enthusiasm and purpose that homogenised their appearance and actions. Their attentions turned to all the Keem. They too were changing. Not physically, but their manner and communications were changing. They stuck religiously to their rituals but their silly language debates, recitals and discussions began to follow regular patterns. They appeared to be giving new meanings to words and then, three months after the incident a new word became used regularly, 'clewpot'. They were forming their vocabulary or perhaps slang.

Clip five focussed on the co-ordinut. It had changed very little whilst the body it was attached to slowly recoiled. It was the only completely un-flattened part of the Keem. Once it was fully exposed it changed colour from deep burgundy to burnt orange. It ended up looking like a butternut squash in the form with a tough leathery shell.

'Clip six'. The Keem's vocabulary grew but laughter and silliness levels were the same as before the incident. Then at about six months post-incident, or PI as the twins had started referring to it and BI for before the incident came the first silent meeting between.

The seventh clip was a simulation of the incident. It started from the moment the Loon entered the changing room. It was as realistic to Welder's eyes as the recordings of Milford and the twins. It was hard to watch for all of them. Clip eight and the twins worked out the meanings of several of the words used, invented or adopted by the Keem. 'Clewpot' referred to the flattened Keem. 'Marpoo' was the name they gave to their language and 'Blorp' was the name of the Loon. The Keem were starting a new language from scratch. The silences grew and it became obvious that the Keem were communicating telepathically. The twins learnt what they could of the new language when it was spoken out loud.

324

'Clip Nine'. Welder looked quizzically at the projection of a lab. The flattened Keem in various states of reduction were gone. The central hologram of the Keem that hung over the round table was gone. All material relating to the twin's investigations were gone. Loveluck and Unity were standing on the table dressed exactly the same in every detail and impossible to tell apart. They were silent and still. They were communicating with the Keem.

Clip Ten was simply large text suspended where the Keem's holographic body once was. The twins too were nowhere to be seen. It read as follows. 'The incident with the Keem has triggered a change in Keem; a mental and physical change. This change cannot be stopped. This change was always meant to be and must be assisted. You will know what to do Alfros'

'The twins were the only researchers in the long history of the project that just up and left. No clue as to where they were going or why.' There was a tone of bemusement in Milford's voice. 'They knew my father and Holborn were due to visit and I'm sure they would not have gone if they had any fears about the welfare of the Keem resulting from being left alone. It is my belief that they left to protect the Keem and that they decided the less said the better. My knowledge of what they are up to, even if they are alive or not would be pure speculation on my part at this point so I will refrain. Speculation thrives in a vacuum and can be better than out and out misdirection when not wanting to be found. Misdirection is the clue. I digress. The short and long of it is, I plead Wittgenstein's seventh' and he brought that particular mental detour to an end, with a single puff of laughter acting as a full stop. It appeared to Welder as if Milford loved speculation or at least the imaginative process of coming up with theories. There was an undertone of nostalgia in Milford's voice. Nostalgia he had *for the many decades of his life he enjoyed idling along meanders of thought drifting merrily, merrily, merrily, gently down the screen.*

'My father was no researcher and Holborn thought a great biological scientist was needed; his area was cosmology. But they were chosen and willingly responded to the call of duty as long as their positions weren't permanent.

Once Father left to seek a replacement for himself, Holborn decided that he preferred being on his own and rather liked the dome. He realised it was the perfect place and conditions for him to be. He was given the post as sole overseer of the project rather than working as a part of a pair of researchers. He observed the Keem with the bare minimum of input into their world. He watched as the growth in their mental faculties levelled off. The Co-ordinut, or Kernel Bogie as Holborn liked to call it, remained dormant and unchanged. I suppose coming up with silly puns is a natural consequence of a self-amusing mind' Welder thought he heard a collective 'hear-hear' in the distance.

'So Holborn, the Kernal, and the twelve other Keem existed happily in their bubble whilst 'Root and Branch' sat in contemplative silence glad not to need any immediate decision on anything. Holborn and the Keem spent many hours reciting silly poetry together. They took nonsense verse to new levels, depths and roundabouts. All was going well enough for the Keem to be left to go through whatever changes they would. It was believed that the Keem would all become Kernels and be safe in that condition until they germinated. Mostly 'Root and Branch' were glad not to have to worry about what to do for a while. The results of their last decision, of introducing the Loon was far too

326

confusing, although it was believed that everything turned out exactly how it was meant to. R and B were convinced that the decision was possibly a crucial one but unfortunately they were not sure how they came to it. It was Holborn that determined through his observations and communications with the Keem that they would all naturally go through the same transformation that was forced upon the flattened one. There was the added advantage that once the Keem became Kernels they would be easy to hide. Plus they would provide scope for infinite speculation as to what life form would emerge from them, or well enough. So, all was well; until Sally and R and B, were unable to prevent the sale of Chippenham Five to Walbran's proxy. The twins are an unknown quantity. It is believed they may be starting a new facility in case things don't end well here.'

Chapter Eighteen

Transplant

One of the attractions of her niece Jenny's house was the wonderful trees in the long garden that led down to the river. She never imagined that she would one day move in with her niece and enjoyed seeing those trees every day. And every day she would remember Albert and with the bursting of blossoms, every spring Roger would re-enter her thoughts. Her remembrances of them did not fade any more than the mighty Copper Beech or the Yew tree did; they simply had their seasons. The freshness of her feelings was no less bright than the blossoms of the Cherry trees from one year to the next.

She had easy access to the garden from her 'Aunty Annex'. She was still able to get herself up in the mornings but had no qualms about using her high tech retro mobility scooter. The French doors from her bedroom to the garden responded to the sound of her quiet commanding voice and opened. She liked to try different voices to see if she could catch out the voice recognition software. She tried grandiose flourishes, quiet as mouse welsh, and dry nasal Australian accents. She tried monotonous choked burbled garbled and pinched and clipped tones, and even Donald Duck impressions but nothing audible as words from her mouth got by it. There was something immeasurable but unique about her voice that could not be disguised.

She persisted as it gave the routine of opening the doors a sense of a repeated mental challenge to replace the physical one. She had a file of music befitting a grand opening ceremony; her daily opening ceremony. Her favourite was 'two thousand and one a space odyssey'. Without fail this never witnessed ritual fortified Sophie and made her tingle with anticipation for the brief moment before guiding her 'chariot' out of the house with maximum acceleration.

The soft rumbling sound, of her four-wheeled electric powered mobility scooter's rubber tyres as they rolled over the shallow ribs of the boards on a specially built runway down the garden, reminded Sophie of the first time she crossed the Brooklyn Bridge in a cab. Of course, she could have used the hover feature but she never got on with it and preferred the reassurance of feeling the wheels beneath her connecting with the ground. She was old school. Her favourite part of her slightly downhill plank path was a sweeping curve around a glorious Horse chestnut tree. From there the path led through the arch of a Yew hedge across a bridge over the fish pond and ended up on a spacious deck by the river. On the other side of the river were flood meadows used for grazing and beyond that were fields given over to wheat and barley that provided a calendar of colours.

Sophie liked to switch off her chariot and coast the last twenty yards of her daily pilgrimage to the water's edge. There was just enough momentum to carry her up the slight incline and on to the decking. In the forward corners of the deck were the two grand Rhubarb plants still in their pots. Sophie brought them with her when she left Soft Sands. It was twenty years since she sold the B and B after Albert's death.

One morning Albert did not turn up for his duties of serving breakfast and it was, of course, his turn. On this occasion, there was no sense of foreboding or premonition at this rare occurrence. She presumed he had overslept. There was no reply to her knocks on his bedroom door, so she shouted out a warning that he 'better be decent' and walked into the room.

Nothing in Sophie's life was more shocking than the sight that met her when she walked into Albert's bedroom. Blood; blood sprayed on the walls and on the floor and there, lying on his back on the bed, covered in blood, was Albert. In his hand was the old fashioned shaving razor he used every day. Sophie fell to her knees, bowed her head and wept unable to lift her eyes and look upon Albert's lifeless cadaver in his striped blood-soaked pyjamas. The sound of someone on the stairs did not break the grip of pain, shock and sorrow. The guest knocked gently on the door before pushing it open, just far enough to poke their head around it, just far enough to see what lay within and scream and release Sophie's frozen being. She sprang to her feet and into action. She ushered away the young female guest who had come in search of her breakfast. Sophie went on to autopilot with one independent nagging thought clinging on, 'why like this?'

It was Milford's way to mull over things; especially negative feelings. He knew this of himself and avoided such things. He had spent much of his life alone with his work and he liked it that way. Too often people and his feelings towards them confused him and that confusion demanded attention. And that attention took up time; time away from his work. He found balance and creative exhilaration in his work akin to the sublimation of a sculptor forcing and caressing form from clay with their hands or a surgeon wielding a knife to save a life. Work was his life, work brought him balance. He neither wanted nor needed a work-life balance. So anything extra on the life side of the equation of those not driven as Milford was driven could cause the loss of focus and was to be avoided. He loved weighing things up and finding equilibrium, albeit exclusively within the parameters of his work. The balance he sought and found was between two divergent aspects of his character as expressed through his research. It was no different than the challenge of finding life-work or head-heart balance. For Milford it was work one way and, work another way balance. It was the methodical and the spontaneous, the intuitive and the rational, the spiritual and the physical, the saver and the gambler that Milford sought to accommodate. He had to. And he did: aged nine. Even so young he had already seen great rational and emotional minds torn apart by two or more divergent motivational impulses pulling in different directions in an attempt to put all their conviction and energies towards one end. Milford saw that sometimes you need to change the route and sometimes the choice of destination. And for him, the balance worked. Understanding himself was not directed towards being popular, finding someone to share parenthood with, financial gain or even the admiration of his peers. Milford sought to understand his internal world with the same sense of purpose as he did with the external one. So self-improvement was a subject of interest for him as well as the desired consequence of what he chose to do. He believed that the positive interplay between reason appetite and desire directed by positive individual co-incidence between universal positive evolutionary impulses such as compassion and equal respect for all life would make him happy as well as contribute to life's forward momentum and its ability to cope with, and possibly even overcome the end of the universe; or something like that, he wasn't sure. His was a balance enabled and strengthened by a third component. This third component was one of his making as many solutions and problems were. Finding the right problems was essential. He constructed a third point, a third leg for his stool rather than constantly living between the two stools he found himself at any given time. This balance broadly worked for him in relation to the success of any given project but not so when it came to his happiness. What he found was that no matter what changes he made in his thinking, feelings or actions the proportionality between being miserable and happy remained the same. The intensity apart from occasional spikes on the graph also remained unchanged and lasted for about the same amount of time. He calculated that he was annoyed about fifteen percent of the time and angry less than one per cent. This was regardless of whether he was alone or in amongst others; it was just that he noticed his moods more around other people which gave the impression that they were somehow responsible. He finally decided that he was as happy as he was going to get and there was no real need, on a personal level to pursue trying to improve the percentages. Until that point, the processes of self-improvement he attempted had, at times, been exhausting. The variables other people introduced were too great for any further progress anyway, he decided. Once he got on with his work and was guided by his conscious thought, conscience and intuition rather than playing the percentages, the percentages improved on their own, but without him noticing of course. He made a peace treaty after the last time he was at war with himself aged eleven. He was glad that the time he had spent analysing what arose from reflection and greater awareness had not been a total waste of time. He knew it was something he needed to go through rather than dwell on. He wanted to be more like his sister and it was her love and acceptance of him that helped him let go of what ended up as a distracting phase of self-obsession. Her love and that of his parents was part of his stable core being.

He was left with an unfortunate legacy from his past obsessions, a war wound if you like from battling with himself. He called it his 'double whammy'. It occurred during those diminishing percentage moments of annoyance. When he got annoyed frustrated or angry about something he would then get annoyed, frustrated and angry about getting annoyed, frustrated and angry. He would feel annoyed about feeling angry and frustrated with anything he felt was not in accordance with parameters of feeling he believed acceptable.

Fortunately, such moments lasted less than a second and produced a nauseous shiver and tiny foul-smelling burp. So when Milford's interaction with the Keem led to a shift in his century-old internal emotional and intellectual balance it made him sit up and take note. It was no small thing; it was huge. He had to get to the source of the changes he was experiencing as it was part of understanding the Keem. Thus he became the focus of his attention once again after so many years.

Welder took a break from the presentation. He simply needed to take a stroll in the garden, stretch his legs and clear his mind. He needed to enjoy a few quiet moments before learning what he would be asked to do. He calculated he had at least one more full day to learn and then finally to choose. The Keem joined him one by one and suggested the best blossoms for him to smell to reinvigorate him and to increase his capacity to take in information. He wandered and wondered. Then he was ready once more. Milford watched Randolph's naked sturdy and incredibly hairy frame enter the dome with a powerful mix of strong emotions; not the least of which being love and admiration. Once the pair had recovered from the shock of the test results showing he had Trowbridian Monkey Syndrome, Randolph calculated the exact moment, to within an hour, of his death. And Welder watched Milford who had gone from the purely scientific at the start of his presentation to unashamedly emotional as it was drawing closer to its conclusion. The clips were not always in sequence at this point but Welder got the gist of their collective meaning and significance. The tapes jumped back to the conversation between Milford and Randolph that led to Randolph entering the dome.

'I will die on the twenty-seventh of March somewhere between the hours of nine and ten in the morning'. Randolph gave Milford the information as if he was reading it from a chart. Then after a pause, he added 'I will definitely be getting up early that morning' with that the pair laughed. The laughter ended up in a giggle fit that in turn ended up in a tearful embrace that lasted as long as it did

'Ever since one of them was flattened by the possibly adulterated pet loon they began to change'. Milford sighed with a sense of devastating acceptance at what had come to

333

pass and what would inevitably follow. Randolph responded

'An awareness of death may have released an enzyme that acted as a catalyst or spark to an evolutionary process that has no bounds. The Keem are only held back by their biology for now. They are not territorial, competitive, driven to reproduce or fight over resources. They are not shackled intellectually or spiritually by need. Who is to say what contribution they could make to our spiritual evolution?'

'An awareness of death as a point on a longer timeline; a timeline they did not know of is a possibility for the leap in development the Keem has undergone since the incident, but it is my belief and that of the twins that the flattened Keem is not dead. It, at least the information that made it what it is, is still all there, locked in the kernel waiting to be released. They could have lived indefinitely as they were, but we had our part to play. I have no doubt that we were the random element that the Keem, in full partnership with the Floaters, needed to bring about change. And it is a unifying change. It is more than a mutual survival strategy it is a preprogrammed evolutionary leap of which we are a part, just as much as the winds blowing seeds or ocean currents are. We are the changing seasons, the late summer sun that dries the poppy's head that releases its seeds to scatter. Now we must blow. But from what we can tell, what remains of the flattened Keem is not so much a seed as it is a cross between a seed and a chrysalis. I don't lament the change I only fear the uncertainty of it. There are so many variables out of our control. I'm not used to it. I fear the fragility of the future but there is no time to indulge in weakness. So much could be hanging in the balance. I believe humanities destiny and future is somehow tied in to whatever comes of all of this. The Loon accelerated the

334

process for one, and now all will follow. They will all change and we must help them. It is the vital and not only physical and spiritual evolution of the Keem Randolph; we could be talking about our physical evolution too. We are natural beings capable of understanding the nature of what makes us what we are, and how we became this way. Being smart enough to choose is where we're heading. We can be the conditions that determine, and the one impetus and guiding principle to select'

'Are you suggesting we change our physiology to be more like the Keem?'

'It can be done. Over time through a series of adaptations made possible from the knowledge we have attained through our work with the Keem, we can change. We can adapt to process energy from the sun like a plant. We would be a new species no longer dogged by animal needs. I am not suggesting humanity should all change; I am suggesting we branch off. We will branch off just as animal and plant life branched off nearer the source. We will be the gardeners and the garden. We will grow towards the light. We will move forward in the direction that our own nature's selection's guides us. Humanity will have to take its chances; we will go our own way'

'Who is 'we'?'

'Well there is only me and Sally so far and you by default. The 'we' will be those who come to know the story of the Keem and choose to follow. It is a root and branch change and Root and Branch have been readying the organisation for this step. And it is the first step of many in a new direction. The Keem carry all that is needed to start a new line. They must be protected in whatever form they emerge as. Sally will see that their fobs get to a safe place. It is like the Keem will be the seeds of some unknowable universal future. The fobs, with the knowledge they contain, are the

*pots of knowledge for us to use. We must find fertile ground;
a hidden valley on a remote planet on the other side of
nowhere. Sally and I are two of the twenty. The twenty are
the sap running through 'Root and Branch'. We have risen
first. The others will act slowly at first but they already
sense where we are headed. The long winter is coming to
an end and they will rise to a springtime of possibility. The
twins have made their move and we must make ours. If the
twin's calculations are correct the Keem would have all
undergone the final stages of their change unaided into
Kernels in six years. The other parts of the Keem will have
a much less dramatic and potentially traumatic
transformation than being flattened. The question is
whether we will have enough time to oversee the process
before outside forces crash the party. The twins showed
that the process was triggered by certain chemicals
released during the flattening. We don't know whether that
was through a moment of realisation concerning the
fragility of life or due to a signal sent from the disrupted
Keem. Either way, we have isolated those chemicals and
we can use them to force the pace. We can give the Keem a
course of chemicals and calculate the exact hour of their
transformation. I don't want to intervene in this way but I
don't see that we have any choice. It is a little like inducing
labour. The only way the chemicals can be administered is
two sets of injections. The chemicals must be injected right
into their co-ordinuts. It's the only way. The first jabs must
be given very soon. We must introduce the chemicals slowly;
it could take weeks. The second series will be only one final
jab but must be administered in the final hour before
transplantation and evacuation.' Milford stopped at that
point knowing that both of them knew what such a course
of action meant. One of them would have to stay in the*

dome longer than any human had done so in the past. It would mean a stay too long to return from.

A footnote appeared in anticipation of Welder's question. The footnote was both spoken and in a translucent white text, a foot high scrolling passed a metre away from Welder's face. Welder did not recognise the voice.

'It was decided after the destruction of the source, that any intention to strive towards cultivating Keem as some kind of pet was to end immediately and once and for all. Greater attention was then directed to the welfare and protection of the existing Keem. At that point, the specialised atmospheric conditions developed to support Keem and the plants that supported them were designed to be hazardous to non-plant life as the first line of defence. The Keem live within a self-sustaining sphere; a careful balance of the life and processes contained within. But it is not a fragile balance as one might expect. It can defend itself; it is designed to do so. It is designed to assimilate all living things into the existing order. Powerful enzymes and hormones; the most powerful in the galaxy will be released in vapour, harmless to the plant life within but deadly to any intrusion or even invasion. Humanity lives very much on the external surface of the atmospheric bubbles surrounding planets; humanity lives in its bubbles, far more fragile than the dome. And it seems humanity loves to pop bubbles.'

Welder got what he needed to know and moved on leaving the footnote in a silent sock.

'So the plants can fight their corner. That's good to know' Welder heard a combative whooping like that of a Jerry Springer live audience coming from the Keem on the other side of the dome.

'Oo oo oo!' Their whooping was remarkably deep and guttural.

Milford and Randolph's plan was hatched and initiated. Welder reviewed the situation in his mind, safe in the knowledge that if it had succeeded the Keem would know all. It turned out that there were no secrets in the Dome. Welder launched into a soliloquy as a way of summing up in his mind.

'So there is a convergence of circumstances, threats that forced Milford's hand. And his hand is connected to the body of 'Root and Branch' the true authority behind the company and the protectors of the secret life of the Keem. They believe the Keem may hold the prospects of a new branch of life that either we can be part of or swing from; whatever, whatever way you shake the tree some marvellous fruit will fall. We must plant the seeds, we must plant the flag; we must take action. One thing for sure, one thing I know for sure, the Keem are radiant beings of great innocent wisdom. They still possess something we lost a long time ago, a connection with each other and all life. Competition made one part of us stronger and almost destroyed that part of us where the future lies. Thank fuck for the reaches and influences of the human mind that operates separate to our egos and conscious fear and fallibility.' Welder had not heard the word fuck until he listened to the recordings of a conversation between Robby and Ben. He rather liked the sound of it and it felt good to use it. He did not know its meaning, only its use in emphasising what he said. He did not know what sort of a face a cuntface was so held off on using it, though it sounded interesting too. 'So telepathy is just a minor consequence of your connection to all life. When I was with you guys, I felt that connection; and so did Milford.' There was a ripple of applause from the Keem like rain in a

338

puddle. 'The sale of this planet could not be stopped. There are forces from within the company; forces personified by the slimy Walbran Prawnshot. He is hell-bent on gaining full control of the company. To achieve this he is prepared to destroy the project and turn 'Root and Branch' into a bonsai tree to adorn the desk in his office. There are the well-intentioned radical proplanters that may see the work of the project as an abomination and vaporise it as some kind of service to the greater good. They usually underestimate nature's ability to create its own balance. Anyway, then there is the Keem themselves; you that is.' this time the sound of far off tittering. *'They are undergoing a change; a type of metamorphosis. They will all become Kernels, seeds, nuts or whatever. This was the result of the Loon flattening one. That incident was the trigger. Some seeds need a fire to germinate; a Keem needed to be flattened by a genetically constructed crazy beach ball. All to become seeds or Kernels or organic fobs with generations of genetic history stored. It should make them easier to get them out of here if that's the plan. After that, well after that, I hope Sally has the answer. For now, Milford has a plan that starts with Randolph spending his last days with the Keem and giving them their first set of jabs. One way or the other it looks like we are going have to get the fuck out here. But there is bound to be an alternative.'*

Randolph did not even bother with the cloche and Welder watched as he explained to the Keem what the plan was. Their faculties were already increasing exponentially since the incident and they understood and trusted. They had no difficulty identifying the truth when expressed through authenticity. Randolph barely had to explain all the darker reasons behind the need to move. They had reached the point of knowing they had to protect their *innocence for a greater purpose without losing it to do so. The domes defences started acting on Randolph immediately he entered it. The Dome sought to incorporate all living matter into its controlled balance, including Randolph who was fully aware of what lay in store for him.*

At first, Randolph's skin took on a green hue and then his hair dropped out almost in an instant, like petals from a faded withering tulip in a vase. Then a clump of stems the size of a tea coaster started to sprout from the top of his head and the green hue was revealed as tiny leaves all over his body as they grew bigger. By the time he administered the last jab, he could barely walk. His head was like a green medusa of snaking vines. He was truly the green man. Randolph tried to disguise his slight squeamishness about getting the Keem to hold open the slit in the backs of their necks whilst he shot them in the Nut. The chemicals were shot into the Keem with a powerful needle of air. A light would come on when the angle of the shot was good. The Keem seemed to enjoy the procedure and rigmarole; they were great enthusiasts for rigmarole, which eased Randolph's discomfort. Once completed the changes in his physiology had reached a critical point like plaster in the final moment of being workable before suddenly going hard or 'going off' as it was called by sculptors of old. At this point, he moved with the urgency and awkwardness of post-crash track debris clearers at a Grand Prix during the race with their shoelaces tied. He headed back towards the ring of the cloche. The Keem excitedly surrounded him, took his hand and helped him on his way shouting, 'make way, make way, coming through; mind your backs, man needs planting'. Randolph made it to the ring and managed with stiffening limbs and the assistance of the Keem to climb into a large plant pot.

Welder watched as the Keem retreated to the ring. Randolph started laughing and the Keem joined in. Then his laughter became interspersed with babbling, a kind of speaking in tongues. He did indeed grow many tongues of bright green; at least five emerging from the widening orifice that once was his mouth. What were words became sounds growing louder and higher in pitch. His head tipped back and the squealing became a single beautiful note that faded away. With the beautiful disconcerting squealing ended a matted texture of gurgling and creaking and occasional cracking was far more noticeable. Welder watched the whole transformation close in, for a better look at the amazing metamorphosis. He was close enough to the holographic recording to see into the pot as roots burst from Randolph's feet and spread like writhing snakes. The roots filled the pot, but not beyond the lip. Once the pot was full they stopped. Then his legs began to fuse into a single fibrous trunk. Welder looked on in a calm yet disturbed fascination. The change accelerated, rising up his legs. At the same time, Randolph's head had finished tipping back and splitting at the point where once his gaping mouth had been. It turned completely inside out. Randolph's legs were soon completely fused and covered in a furry bark, like the trunk of an Australian tree fern. The process continued passed his waste. The gurgling noises began to sound more like a blend of gibberish and laughter. It matched the rising tide of 'plantification' and rose in pitch. The word 'plantification' hung to the side of the scene with a helpful arrow pointing at Randolph. Rather unnecessarily it was in a decorative floral font. Proof Welder thought, of Milford's affection for the man Randolph was and the plant he was becoming. It also indicated a level of appreciation for Milford's own changing state whilst making the recording. Randolph's arms had lifted as the sap rose; it was as if he was being inflated and his arms forced up and out. The change continued up his trunk. His arms shortened, thickened and stiffened and the change progressed to the ends of what were his hands. Leaves started sprouting where fingers once were. As the rising tide continued and reached his neck, the burbling became higher and higher like the rise in pitch of a wine bottle being filled with water. Where his head had once been, green and red variegated leaves sprouted. They almost popped out instantly like a magician's bunch of flowers. Silence and stillness followed. The brief silent pause was followed by reverential applause from the Keem and ended with a collective 'PING'. The plantification had only taken a few minutes. Milford's voice came in from behind Welder as if he had been standing behind him during the whole procedure. It only sounded that way because Welder had gradually moved in closer and closer to the projection of Randolph

'Randolph chose that form. He designed it himself'. Welder backed up through Milford's projected image face him. He had a childlike drawing of a pot plant in his hands; Randolph's handy-work. Milford looked at the drawing and Welder looked at the plant that was once a man, the same plant he had urinated on two days before, albeit a small amount of blue liquid that smelled of popcorn. He had wrongly thought that the plant may have been Milford when the Keem looked in the direction of it in response to a question about Milford that rose in Welder's mind. If the plant was Randolph the question remained, 'what happened to Milford'. Milford's hologram welled up looking at the only example in the known universe of a Randolph Rhubarb Fern. Then as if deliberately timed that way, two large buds opened out revealing a hairy red interior and an aroma akin to fennel. Milford put aside the drawing and snapped out of reflective melancholy and into focussed urgency

342

'Now it's just me left to tell you about, and then we can get down to what your options are. I have made my choice. After Randolph went through his change it was up to me alone to develop the necessary modifications to the cloche so that you carry out your chosen task. You needed to be amongst them, to be with them and to know them. You also needed to be able to leave rather than end up another flower pot man like our noble Randolph. I did not have time for our usual rigorous testing to find the correct balance of chemicals to counter the domes defences but I believe I have come up with the right mix. From the grass glass of its exterior shell to what appears to be stone used for the fountain, the ground you are standing on and even the cloche; all of it has grown and fused as one entity. The whole sphere is one living organism. All that is protected from the Keemdom is the control room. The living quarters and lab are within the lower hemisphere. The bubble is not a perfect sealed sphere as you know. The ant farm as we like to call it is below and accessible through an open tunnel like a wormhole in an apple. And of course, there is the main entrance through which you arrived. In effect, both of these are part of the exterior of the Sphere, as the surface flows into the opening. They are like an underwater chamber connected to the surface by a pipe. The column is part of the exterior like a huge finger pushing into a bubble without popping it. The insertion process you went through delivered you into the dome, rendering you, and all other extraneous material safe for about three hours. That's how long you would have had before the sphere's defences would have kicked in; and when they kick in, they kick hard and fast. The cloche normally acts as a kind of airlock. The chemicals needed to prevent plantersising could only be produced by Randolph consuming a special formula and allowing himself to be plantersised. In his case, due to the

343

formula he drank, he only had half an hour to perform his task. Welder looked down at his wrist and noticed his band had changed. It had become rooty looking. He tried to take it off but it wouldn't open. He tried pulling it off but it was too tough. He was sure that it would be a problem later. 'Don't worry about your band, the Keem removed it during your nap and replaced it with an organic dummy. We used to have protective suits when we first upped the domes defences. They were living plants that were meant to resist the Dome. They were effective for a while but soon they failed. The development of the Dome's defences was successful beyond our wildest expectations. No material, organic, synthetic, mineral or biological can resist the dome. The true and awesome wrath of the dome is deeply rooted and as yet undisturbed. Turning people into plants is its party piece; it has the potential to do much worse. All the time we were working on the Keem we were also creating a world; a world that lives. It is a world that lives to serve and protect the Keem. Since the defence of the Keem was written into the genetic make-up of the Dome it has evolved beyond our control. Any protective suit or chemical infusion absorbed in the cloche is only temporary. We lost three researchers to the dome, four if you count Randolph even though he only had three hours and two minutes to live. The first was taken by the vines and the other two dissolved into mulch' Welder paused the tapes and looked around. The Dome looked as idyllic as before but now he felt the presence of something else looking at him from the jungle beyond the clearing; it was as though watchful eyes were waiting for him to make a wrong move and wander off the trail. There seemed to be more vines than before as he looked overhead. They were like a net of sleeping snakes that could drop into angry wakefulness on to him at any time. He gestured for the tape to continue. He was nearing its end.

'The only way to enter the Dome at all, even for limited periods, is with personalised regenerative organic overalls or naked. Fortunately, you were given one of only a hundred sets of such overalls ever produced outside this place. Someone must have been thinking ahead. The admin men at the company cancelled commercial development of personalised fabrics saying, producing a fabric that grew back like skin would not be profitable; you know like a drink that replenished itself, that's what they said anyway. Your overalls and the twins offer as much or as little protection as the skin they cover. Randolph never had overalls of his own, and for that matter neither do I. It seems I am and Randy are two rare individuals for whose natural skin rejected their 'grow baggies'. We're more or less allergic to onesies. Randolph's last visit gave me vital data to improve the cloche and buy you some more time, but not so much more that we can hang around. You are safe for now. Randolph was truly a rare individual. His hidden condition may well have been the reason for his reaction to the fabric. Why I am allergic, who knows; I don't have a flight licence either' Welder stopped again to let out another EMP belch. The Keem tittered as they usually did when he burped.

'So that's why Randolph was naked and Unity wasn't' Milford once again anticipated and answered Welder's question. This gave Welder the impression of having a conversation with someone from the past.

'The twins also detected worrying signs that the Dome was taking its laws into its branches. I did not tell you about some of this stuff earlier because that would have meant telling you about the Dome and we suspect that it may somehow be able to listen in, indirectly. Since the incident

345

and the rapid evolution of the Keem's cognitive powers and the emergence of their ability to connect through thought, a connection has also developed between the Keem and the Dome. A channel of communication of sorts now exists from you, via the Keem to the Dome. Your knowledge of the Dome's nature could be communicated and act as a trigger. I am estimating that you still have forty hours before the Dome will perceive your reaction to the knowledge as a threat and the penny will drop followed by the snakes of Damocles over your head'

      Sophie was independent of her memories and her thoughts strengthened and what's more, she noticed.
'My thoughts are growing stronger. But is that me growing stronger or just my thoughts. Is there a me or am I now only my thoughts?'
'When the Keem came to life with the insertion of the Mude's plant minds we did not create a monster; quite the opposite. Nothing monstrous has ever entered a single cell of their bodies. From their creation, nothing, no desire or need, corruption or contamination has been part of their cultivation and now they are ready to leave home. When we created the Keem we did not create a monster, but we did create a monstrously powerful agent to nurture and protect them. The Keem and the Dome have been inseparable with the Keem in their current form. And the Keem in their current form could not survive without the Dome. Metamorphosis happens for a reason; a tadpole grows legs and hops out of the pond and a caterpillar grows wings to fly high and seek nectar. The Keem are changing because they need to move on. You see Welder the incident forced the pace of change that may not have occurred for centuries, or even longer. The twin's work has revealed however that the change was inevitable. Their work has also shown us that the metamorphosis the Keem will

346

undergo will be as great as that of any living thing the universe has ever known. What were the brains of the Mude and became the brains of Keem which became the kernel of the flattened Keem is both seed and chrysalis. Propagation and individual transformation in one process; they will be many and one. They will not need to learn lessons anew with each generation. Butterfly's need to fly from tree to tree to propagate and Sally has found a world for the next step. In reality, we believe the transformation of the Keem will be more like the tadpole and frogs but perhaps in reverse. Whatever adaptations they are acquiring and need from their new environment we know they are preparing for life in water. We went back and analysed all of the colour shifting communications of the Floaters before their world ended. It may be that the Keem are more a part of the Floaters metamorphosis than the other way around. What will come from the fusion, it is hard to say precisely. Maybe all of what went into the Keem will be only be a fraction of the life to come. Our only fear is that the Keem are only the hosts. I don't believe that but I have no evidence either way. I only know that the Keem will become the seeds and larvae and we must be the birds that carry them to fertile new earth or waters in this case. It is hoped that even in the worst-case scenario the seeds of life will survive and lie dormant but according to the twin's theories, it should be a case of 'just add water' for germination. Much of this will depend on you. You will also have the power to terminate the project rather than risk contamination of the Keem and the future they represent. That will be your decision and you MUST take it if there is no other way. For my part, I have no options. I have already initiated phase one of the release of the sphere. As I speak I have broken the seal and the vapours and protective forces of the Dome are creeping into every nook

*and cranny of the lower hemisphere. As you stand there,
the entrance and exit to the sphere are closing, or more
accurately, growing over. The Dome will spread its control;
it will become whole sphere. Nothing will exist separate to
it. All traces of the labs and living quarters will be
composted. By the time you make your move, I will already
be mulch. I have sent the pea to Sally. She knows my
decision to stay and my reasons why. I don't have much
time now so I will tell you your options. A word of warning
first: the dome sense of a threat will grow and reach a
tipping point. It senses the Keem and it won't want to let
them go. It is their living motherland and it bites.' A classic
digital countdown clock appeared.
'The central column you entered the dome through and the
big apple's wormhole, and it's not an actual wormhole in
case you are getting excited, anyway the exhaust pipe you
must exit by will be the last inorganic material to be
ingested. Your adaptations through being in the cloche will
mean you will be safe from detection till the very end, as
long as the dome does not perceive you as a direct threat to
the natural order; its natural order and the life of the Keem.
Your connection to the Keem should help matters.'*

Chapter Nineteen

Dumdum, dum daa da dumdum

Welder was ready to find out his options, weigh them up, and choose. He had literally set the countdown clock counting down, by confirming for the third and final time that he was ready to make his choice. If he did not make his wishes known the emergency protocol would automatically kick in. As Milford pointed out, 'once it kicks in it can't be kicked out and within five minutes all living things within the sphere will be happily dead. The Dome is no more; now 'the sphere' is the boss. It is receptive to a trigger I have cocked that will begin a process of complete meltdown baby; all will be resolved and dissolved'. Welder expected Milford's emotional levels to fluctuate leading to the use of uncharacteristic words and phrases, and more besides as he drew closer to his end. 'The most powerful anaesthetizing and rapture inducing chemicals known to human and plant-kind will be released followed by a cloud of the galaxy's most powerful digestive enzymes. And I am the catalyst amongst the pigeons, ducky. I have given myself the gear; I have shot up and opened the flood gates. When the Sphere reaches my cactus carcass and absorbs me it will be swallowing a suicide pill. I will be in a protective bubble baby, and you can burst my bubble by pressing the button in your head. But don't worry Welder, the sphere will believe, in so far as it can believe, it will believe, and it will be correct in believing, that it is doing what it must for the sake of the Keem. Within half an hour all that will be left in the sphere will be noxious slurry.

Welder often used a method of choosing where he forced his hand. He used it when he was with a group of friends in a restaurant. When asked by the waiter if the group was ready to order he would say he was ready despite being undecided. He used the strategy of declaring readiness whilst still choosing between two or three equally

*enticing choices knowing any choice would be a good one.
He would nod his preparedness to order knowing that by
saying so he was setting a time limit and he could then
relax knowing he was not holding proceedings up for other
people. He also knew that the others would have to say
whether they were ready which would effectively buy him
time. When his turn did come he would simply say one of
the options he was considering or occasionally choosing
something he had forgotten he was considering. Sometimes
such a commitment would reveal that in his heart of hearts
he knew that choice was the wrong one; not a luxury his
present circumstance would allow. But mostly this
considered spontaneity seldom let him down even when the
buffer of time was limited to being the first to order. He
never had this problem when eating alone as he would
always choose what he wanted before leaving the house
and then go to the restaurant best able to provide it. He
was also aware of his tendency to take on the duty of
expediting the ordering process for the good of all and his
stomach's grumbling impatience. Now Welder found
himself within a living globe, which was but a tiny dot on
the surface of a greater dead globe, which was orbiting a
still far greater one, in a calm moment looking towards an
approaching storm. He would face a menu choices that on
this occasion were all equally unenticing. If he didn't force
his hand he knew it would not have been long before
circumstances did; the kitchen was about to close and it
was time to give his order. Welder knew his mind, he knew
how it worked. Somehow by starting the countdown clock
just a few minutes earlier than it would have on its own
made him feel more in control. It somehow relieved the
pressure. There was nothing more he needed to know; he
just needed to remove barriers between his rational and his
intuitive faculties, between his conscious and unconscious*

and between the two hemispheres of his brain. This way he knew the right answer would come, it would come through him rather than from him. The combination and balance of practical and spiritual energy that powered Welder's thoughts were rare enough, but Sally saw something more in him besides. She saw something profoundly stable despite his non-allegiance to any particular theology or philosophy; he had basic goodness.

Before Welder there were four buttons on the top of four plinths marking the four corners of an invisible square. The cylindrical columns had risen from below ground level once Welder had confirmed to the interface he was ready to choose. They looked like marble with frozen swirls of colour from deep beetroot and cabbage red to regal purples and deep blues. And like a sliced open cabbage there were veins of white running through them. Just like everything else in the dome that looked like stone, they were of course forms of plant life. The buttons were as sensitive as the interior of a Venus Fly-trap. The corners of the square were all on the circular boundary describing the reach of the cloche. 'Eternity and reason' Welder thought to himself as the plinths had emerged and he saw them defining a square within a circle. 'Oooo' followed by tittering was the just audible sounds that came from the Keem in response to Welder's thought as if to suggest 'well aren't you the clever clogs' in mocking tones. 'Not that helpful guys' Welder said out loud but chuckling to himself as he did so. 'Or maybe it is' The laughter had burst a toughening bubble of anxiety Welder was becoming enveloped in, in response to the pressure of the decision he had to make. The effect of the Keem's laughter and remembering the chants of the ancient silly language 'life is silly' left Welder's mind completely free to choose. He stood in the centre of the square at the point where the *square's diagonals would have crossed. The glowing buttons were all different colours atop their marbled columns. They were turquoise, egg yolk yellow, rose red and apple green. They were all different and far enough apart to avoid mistakes and accidents. Welder had initiated the process from the centre where he had to stand before making his final declaration of readiness. He stood there motionless with his head back and his eyes closed. He had ten minutes to make his up his mind rather than the seventeen that he would have had available if he did not start early. Being reckless had given Welder the edge before. Better to have ten minutes focussed time than seventeen of faffing. Irresponsibility in small measure had been a useful tool in cutting through layers of irrelevance during Welder's career.*

With the entirety of the tapes consumed and with full knowledge of the options, after ten seconds he had narrowed the choice down to two; two options diagonally opposite each other, but the other two options were still in play. So there he stood with his eyes closed, not even looking at the clock or counting down in his mind.

Three minutes were left on the clock when he opened his eyes feeling as if he had had no life before standing in the centre of the four choices. The Keem were present. They had made their way to regular points around the circle but did not disturb the calm of Welder's pool of thought. He had stilled the murky waters and they were clear. Welder looked to be at the heart of one of the Keem's many Silly rituals.

The choice triggered by the turquoise button would happen automatically anyway if no choice was made by the end of the countdown; the entire contents of the sphere including the labs and control rooms in the lower hemisphere would be liquidised. The gas produced within

352

the sphere would give it enough lift to float it off its cuboid base. The base would collapse into a pile of rubble as the sphere drifted upwards like a child's wayward helium balloon. It would float to the edge of space. A waiting transport vessel arranged by Sally would be at hand to reach down and retrieve the bubble of powerful liquid compost. Such a procedure was within the bounds of normal operating procedures for moving off a planet and would not attract unwanted attention. A little like a mate turning up with a van to pick the last remaining black bags of personal treasures and rubbish. Nothing would survive within the sphere. Milford had already taken the necessary steps to begin sealing off the wormhole, the column and his fate. The only hope of retrieving anything to do with the project would lie in the hands of future scientists dipping into the soup and seeing what they could pull out. Button number one was not an option Welder wished to take or allow to happen as he would be an ingredient in the mulch.

It was designed to leave no trace of anything useful to outside hostile agents. It would be a last resort if there was a danger of the wrong parties getting hold of anything to do with the Keem. He had not fully assessed those dangers but at the very least telepathic power could become a tool of control and manipulation; every megalomaniac's wet dream. Welder was in no doubt that serving up soup to Sally would be infinitely preferable to presenting Wallbran the project on a platter. Welder correctly sensed that Wallbran's corruptibility had not reached its full potential. Until he heard the coded message directly from Sally he was to assume Wallbran or other and greater dangers lay in wait. There was however one persuasive highly personal reason for Welder to press button number one. Doing so meant Welder would have comfortably enough time to make his escape. Milford

*planned it that way and no one would have blamed Welder
if he chooses button mushroom number one. The terminal
procedure would not begin immediately; the countdown
clock would be reset. An opening would appear in the
column and Welder would fall like Alice down a rabbit hole
and out of the sphere and make a cushioned landing in the
cube. He would jump aboard his hopper and make his
getaway. The escape chute would seal over and the exterior
of the globe would be sealed once again and harden
rapidly as the interior turned in to homogenised slop.*

*He had the option of launching 'liquidation' at a
later moment but any delay meant he would become an
ingredient as well as sous chef. Despite the risk to himself,
Welder felt he still had enough options not to choose button
number one, the 'leave and liquidise' button.*

*Diagonally opposite option one was button number
three, the red button was simply to release the gases to
launch the bubble intact to be caught by the waiting Sally.
Up until that point Welder had not heard from Sally but he
trusted she would be there when it mattered. It was up to
Welder alone to decide if the coast was clear, the coast and
the immediate space surrounding Chippenham Five. And
Welder did not have enough information to make that call
just yet. It was too great a risk to take off with everything in
tack. Milford had convinced Welder that although the
project would be set back for centuries or longer that there
would still be hope soup. Postponement, even indefinitely,
of the project's potential in the form of slurry in the hands
of R and B was infinitely better than it falling into the
wrong hands in its current state. Without the pea which
was now with Sally, anyone trying to extract knowledge
from the slurry would be like Cromagnon man making
sense of a bucket containing a computer that had been
ground to grit.*

Welder could hit the red button in hope rather than expectation that Sally would be there and he could set off the self-destruct at the first sign of trouble. The sphere would seal and through the efforts of all of its plant life, gasses would lift the inside out world of the Keem to the stars. The Keem would be left to undergo their transformation without further intervention. Sally would be waiting, the mirror of his hope. Up, up and away from snow globe to beautiful balloon. He could always hit the self-destruct even if it meant his demise. But there was a hitch; if he fell asleep or dropped dead whilst drifting skywards in his bubble, he would not be able to activate the self-destruct. The red button was a gamble Welder was not prepared to take, but it represented the hope of the best scenario and outcome; the 'up, up, and away' option.

Welder watched the huge red numbers counting down. There were the hundredths of a second madly flashing outnumbers almost passing too quick to make out and the minutes' column with the static number two. Just over two minutes to go when Welder turned and faced the amber option. Milford had been beginning to show the first signs of being absorbed when he started to explain the third choice for Welder to consider.

'This option has the most variables Welder' Milford's voice sounded moist as if he had a salivary lisp. 'You would have to accelerate the Keem's transformation. Once they are kernels you will need to place them in the case provided and get them and you out of the Dome and off this rock. The globe and the base were built over a particularly deep pothole. On leaving you would trigger defoliation and deflation of the sphere and then the collapsing of the base. The entire remnants of the facility, globe and all will drop into the depths of the planet and leave no trace visible from above. The hole would be indistinguishable from any of the *tens of millions of holes around the planet. There are hazards and drawbacks to this plan of course but I can't quite remember them now. No need to sleep on it. By now you will not need to sleep or eat.' Milford paused to collect his thoughts.*

'Welder you have a difficult decision to make. We have tried to leave you enough options to accommodate variations in the events that may unfold'. Milford's eyes were slowly sinking into his head. 'You are due to arrive soon, so not much time for me in this state.' A sense of relief was still discernable on Milford's stubbly green visage. He had been slowly slumping into his chair, which itself was changing; it looked like it was turning into a giant malformed sweaty potato. Milford deliberately stiffened his trunk and head upright in his potato, as he refocused his mind, perhaps for the last time.

'It did not happen as a result of a meeting of minds or from the findings of a galactic focus group but somewhere early in the pet project's past the word pet was dropped. The nature of the Keem themselves gave the project a new direction and purpose. The Keem showed us that it is possible to have an advanced form of life that only requires the direct energy of the sun for survival. We believe that the evolutionary life force within humanity is directing us towards incorporating physical adaptations that will enable us to do the same. We will one day be as much like plants than animals. We have been behaving like animals for too long. I say this to you now because the project has strayed into areas greyer than the colour of the human brain or my hair. Each new generation of researchers has questioned and had misgivings about the nature of what we are doing. There are many safeguards built in to prevent our work falling into the wrong hands and also against external contamination resulting from accidental release of

356

anything produced by us. You need to know what's at stake here. I have looked upon our work. I have done more that look, I have connected with the Keem. I know what we do here to be good. The nature of our animal life has been blighted by fear and aggression; a primitive deeply ingrained fear of being prey, of being eaten, and aggression borne from a need to compete for resources, a mate and eventually just to compete for the hell of it. Imagine if we could walk free and stand tall like a tree and live like plants drawing all the energy we need from the fire of a star. Yes, I was scared too once, and when I looked into the soul of the Keem and asked that despairing rhetorical question that scientists have asked through the millennium, 'what have we done?' But I need not have feared. Rather than create a monster we have done the opposite, we have created a radiant being that will shine a light on the fruits of a new branch of evolution. We have reactivated a line that connects us near to the base of the tree of life. Like the giant curtain fig, we have grown our roots from the highest branches and let them grow back towards the soil. Now we have reconnected nearer to the roots that have nourished us all this time. We are connected with the earliest of divergent branches from the trunk. Back before Australopithecus and before we split into species of man and apes, back before reptiles took to the branches of the tree of life they would fly from as birds, even back before coelacanths emerged from the sea. All the way back to one of the earliest forks, back to when plants and animals diverged.' Milford was sweating profusely and beginning to chuckle as foam was appearing in the corners of his mouth.

'I don't have much time left. Your transport will be coming into scanner range soon. And when it does those scanners will show no sign of animal life forms. I have already

detailed the third way, getting you and the kernels out of here, 'the great escape'.

So study the supporting documentation and instructions carefully. It just remains for me to tell you the final option on offer to you triggered by the green button, or is it the red button. Anyway, the important thing is that it is called, 'hiding in a hole'. Welder was not sure why the name was the important thing and wondered if Milford's mind was going green too.

'All you have to do is press the amber button...' When Welder heard Milford say amber his concern heightened as to whether Milford had held himself together long enough to label the buttons with the correct colours. It was an added complication. It was a random element that he was aware of but it didn't worry him that much until he learnt the full details of the fourth and final option. The fourth touch of his hand on the sensitive button would mean the sphere would harden and the base collapse. Everything in the sphere would remain intact gently sank to the bottom of the bottomless pit. The energy stored in the sphere's shell was enough to sustain life contained within for hundreds of years. The energy of Chippenham Five's sun was held in transparent barnacle-like cells on the interior of the outer shell. The luminescent light-sensitive plants had grown as part of the domes self-sustaining nature.

'Before I let you go and make your choice when you stand at the centre to start proceedings pause for a moment and remember. Remember what it was like being with the Keem. That is your evidence. It is all the evidence you need to know that the Keem and the floaters are more enlightened and connected to the source than humanity will ever be in its present form'. With that, the Milford started laughing and a frothy foam started to rise up around him. 'It's like being a slug and someone pouring salt on me, yippee!' and

with that, his laughter grew louder. There was a crackling and the tape ended. Welder wondered for the briefest of moments what his own last words would be. Not those of Milford even if they came to mind, he was sure of that. Before declaring himself ready to choose, Welder examined the details of the third and fourth ways and after deep contemplation and an element of guesswork he fixed each choice to a colour.

The final recording Welder watched was a brief message from Milford. He had recorded his last message first and Randolph was pottering about in the background. 'I am sorry not to meet you and that the task of making such an important, a galactically important decision has been placed on your shoulders. I will live on in the sphere. What form I take will depend on your choice. Timing is crucial. I must get things moving. I wish I could be there to see the outcome, but I am happy to be an ingredient. Give my love to Sally.' A single large tear rolled down Milford's cheek as he contemplated his fate with every emotion possible.

'Goodbye Welder'.

'So there we have it' thought Welder, 'one; 'liquidation'. Everything gets turned to soup and drifts upward for collection, hopefully by Sally. This will happen in the event of my not choosing. Two; 'up, up and away'; we drift up intact into the waiting tractor beams of Sally. I will need a word from Sally for that one. Three; 'the great escape'; I complete the Keem's induced metamorphosis and high tail it out of here with the Nuts. Four 'take the plunge. We simply get sealed up and drop down the bottomless pit this ball is sitting above. Maybe someone will find us and get us out or maybe they won't. More like 'the kid down the well' scenario really'.

Welder allowed himself ten seconds to make his way to his chosen target; that ten-second was forty seconds away when his head began to spin. The calm meditative waters were no longer so calm. Each option went through his mind followed by the next and the next and the next and then the first again. The circular motion had gradually been gaining momentum and his head was in a spin. Any attempt to concentrate on any one choice made him dizzy. Thirty seconds left and he felt like he was going to pass out. He wondered if he could physically make it to reach any of the buttons. If he did not reach he would be sealed in the bubble and be liquidised like leftovers to make a broth. Twenty seconds to go and he made a choice. He moved like a child that had made themselves dizzy by spinning. The feeling made him cry with nostalgia and worry. He spiralled around heading to the circumference and the corners but did not make it. He passed out and just as he lost consciousness he heard the Keem counting down from ten and the image of a sunflower came into his mind and he knew the yellow button would have been the right choice.

Welder started to come to but was still in a dream. He could hear wind blowing and the rustling of leaves. He was on his back and was looking skywards and could see patterns of light through the leaves of a pear tree. He could see a single pear hanging above him. It dropped. It was falling towards his head. He woke in a start and instantly sat bolt upright just in time to avoid a dropping vine. It took root and grew towards him. He jumped to his feet and took in the scene. He was still near the centre of the circle and the Keem were still at all positions of the clock. He assumed that the default option of the sphere being sealed in preparation for mulching and lift off was underway but then he looked at the rooted vine and he began to doubt. 'Yellow' said a Keem.

360

'You chose yellow' said another at three on the clock face if the first speaker was at twelve.

Welder got to his feet but did not face either Keem as he was still giddy and wanted to avoid getting into another spin. He focused on his feet. The giant worm of a vine segment that almost landed on him, had stiffened a few inches short of his the toes of his foot pod boots.

'Sorry about that Welder. We were chatting while you were sleeping and a vine slipped passed us.' said four o'clock.

Next, the Keem at seven o'clock spoke.

'You chose yellow and we pressed it'

'Yes, but which yellow?' Welder asked.

'The yellow one' answered one o'clock Keem followed by giggles.

Welder played out his hand of clockwork patience to the end when he got all the answers he needed. He had passed out and the Keem, who had gathered specifically to carry out Welder's wishes, if he was incapacitated for any reason, had pressed the yellow slash amber button. The Keem being at intervals around the circle like numbers on a dial meant they were on hand to press any option Welder chose right up to the last dying second and possibly his last dying breath. The vine had dropped because Welder's intuition was correct. Whilst asleep he was still in the Keem's telepathic net. The yellow button was the 'great escape'. This meant Welder would have to get himself and the Keem out of there. The dome was just beginning to sense something was up, hence the first tentative dropping of a vine to feel Welder out. He would increasingly become the target of the dome's defences so he would have to act quickly.

The main worm-hole tunnel that led to the facilities in the lower hemisphere was blocked. Everything below Welders feet was now mulch, including Milford. The only *way out was the escape-chute in the central column that would close and seal up in three hours. That's how long Welder had to induce the final stage of the Keem's transformation into their avocado seed like kernel form. Then it would be time to pack up and get out; quickly. It would be a straight forward procedure but not one Welder was looking forward to.*

The Keem knew everything and resisted no more than a tadpole resists absorbing its tail and growing legs. They were already slowly changing and Welder was the accelerating agent, an elemental component. He was there in service of what was to be. But they could not resist having a little fun with Welder. They decided, like a toddler that is meant to be getting ready for going out that they wanted to play 'touch and go'. What the Keem were unable to grasp was that by doing so they were putting their escape, their transformation and the future the new dawning of their new life at risk. Events and the atmosphere surrounding physical change had the same unpredictable side effect as hormones do on teenagers. The Keem started running around.

'Okay guys, let's get this done. How about we stop running around and go over to the fountain?' Welder had reverted to verbal communication as the Keem seemed to be in a skittish mood. There was a pause but to Welders surprise the Keem all ran off laughing and shouting 'CATCH US!' They were unimpressed at Welder's attempt at be authoritative. He had to accept what parents of teenagers have had to accept from the dawn of time; drastic physical change and the chemicals that make it possible can have side effects, not least mood swings. The impulse to have fun had overridden any sense of urgency which the Keem felt. Having to do something became a mild abstract compulsion to be resisted. Welder twigged and could think

of no other course of action other than to go along with the
game and hope they tired of it; quickly. 'Touch and go'
meant that Welder would have to tag the Keem one by one.
Once he had tagged one the tagged Keem had to freeze on
the spot, something they enjoyed doing in the most
elaborate comic positions imaginable. Welder had to shout
out 'stone'. Once 'tagged and bagged' a Keem could be
unfrozen by an untagged Keem tagging them and shouting
'touch and go'. Welder took up the gauntlet but got off to a
poor start. It took ten minutes to tag his first Keem after
that fatigue limited his strategic options to playing possum.
He had tried to reason with the Keem but they resisted
believing it to be a game ploy to catch them. The longer the
game went on the more Welder despaired, and the more
Welder despaired the more the Keem in their mischievous
mood seemed to be enjoying themselves. The dropping
vines were increasing in number and when one fell on
Welder's back it started to eat away at his overalls like a
huge deadly leach. He brushed it off in less than a second
but not before it left a steaming darken stain.
'That's enough you guys, game over we have to leave'
Welder's voice had a rigid brittle precise construction that
barely held back a rapidly rising tide of impatience. He
was losing the game and losing his temper. Finally, he sat
on the edge of the fountains pool thinking through what to
do. He could not escape down the chute without the Keem.
He was already identified by the dome as a threat. The
escape chute was a hollow vine; it was part of the central
network of vines that were dropping more acidic segments
every minute. If Welder attempted to go down the chute
without the Keem he would more or less be jumping into
the belly of a giant snake. It would grab him before he got
ten feet down. Milford was gambling that the Keem, even as
Kernels would be Welders shield as he made his way down

363

*the chute. Two snake vine segments dropped in quick
succession into the fountain with a steaming hiss as they hit
the liquid. They swam about seeking something to attach
themselves to. Welder made for one of the Keem's half-
shell shelters and had to brush off several vines before
making it safely inside it. He had to dive in through the
opening that was only just big enough for his ample girth.
He sat on his behind with his legs crossed like a panda or a
naughty toddler in a time out pod. The vines dropped on to
the shelter and Welder felt like a tiny creature sheltering
from a deadly acid snake rainstorm. The raining down of
the vines was got heavier and the shelter was beginning to
buckle under their weight. The vines did not enter the pod;
they stuck on the part of the roof they landed on. Instead of
entering they rooted themselves around the pod and
reached down to the threshold. They began to seal up the
entrance. Welder decided that he would have to make a
move. He looked around just as a hole formed in the shelter
above him and the tale of a vine flopped in, wriggled for a
moment then stiffened. He started pulling at a loose part of
the pod in the hope of fashioning some kind of a protective
shield. The raining down of the vines went from downpour
to torrential downpour. The shelter was collapsing and
Welder summoned up all his strength and energy intending
to burst out. Just as he was about to make his move he
heard a chant. 'dumdum da da da dumdum, dum dum da
dumdum da da' The chanting grew louder dumdum da da
da dumdum, dum dum da dumdum da da' and the falling of
the vines slowed. 'DUMDUM DA DA DA DUMDUM..'
The Keem came to the entrance of the pod. Welder
managed to squeeze his way out through the stiffened
curtain of vines flanking the entrance. If Welder was as
much an aficionado of the twentieth-century cultural
backdrop of Ben Crammer's grandfather Poopah, as Unity*

and Loveluck were, he might have identified the Keem's chanting as the theme tune to the film 'The Great Escape'. That knowledge may have reassured him. He would have appreciated the appropriateness of the tune as a musical accompaniment for his escape from the vines and the escape attempt he and the Keem were about to embark upon. It would have also indicated to Welder that the twins had played more of a part in the planning of events after their departure than Milford had let on. The Keem had been drilled. Their strict adherence to procedures and protocol with the prompting and fortification of timely releases of stimulants and audio triggers meant that Milford was able to build a failsafe. The vines themselves released a strange vapour that had the faint odour of singed hair. This was the signal for the Keem to focus on Welder. Implementing the escape plan was the last card in the deck. The 'Great Escape' theme song was not strictly necessary but was included because the Keem like a good sing-along. Milford had predicted Welders near absorption by nasty acidic snake vines.

As Welder emerged from the pod he entered a circle formed by the Keem about ten foot across. The Keem's attentions were fully focussed on the task at hand. They showed no fear and no pleasure. In the centre of the circle was the open container about the size of a long weekend suitcase. The Keem had followed their instructions to the letter and retrieved the case from the column and brought it there. It was oval-shaped and hinged giving it the look of giant locket or a giant cockle shell. The interior of the case was as white as the centre of a coconut and the outside was as hard and deep brown, also like a coconut though smooth and shiny. All available space within the case was a solid spongy white material. There was a circle of twelve concave receptacles on one side for the kernels and matching indentations on the other side to fully enclose and protect them. In the centre was the kernel of the flattened Keem.

'A baker's dozen' Welder said quietly to himself and the Keem did not react. Looking at the kernel in the case seemed to put the Keem into a sombre mood; if that was possible. They snapped out of it and back into the line of steps laid out for them to follow.

'We're going to be Kernels' said a Keem

'We are going to all be the same again'. That was the closest the Keem came to registering any sense of missing the flattened Keem.

'We are going to be kernels like colonel bogie' said yet another. But the giggles that always accompanied the word bogie and anything slightly silly were half-hearted.

'Are we scared Welder' asked yet another Keem looking up at Welder dolefully.

'You might be. What did Milford tell you?'

'He told us we are going to change, that we have changed slowly before to become what we are now.'

'We are going to change into what we will become'

'Only this time the change is going to be quicker'

'And you are going to help us'

'Thank you, Welder'

'We love you'

Also in the case, a little further out from the centre like the dots on i's of the recesses for the kernels were bright orange balls like gumballs. The Keem had seated themselves cross-legged in the circle in readiness for the next stage. The Keem knew all the instructions and Welder had to catch up with them. When Milford spent time discussing with the Keem all the options that Welder would have, including the 'pea soup' option, it was the Keem that comforted him rather than the other way around. They reassured him that with Sally's help even being part of the liquidized contents of a soup bubble would not be the end of the story. 'All the information will be there', they reminded him. By the end of their final chat, Milford was at ease with the choices and outcomes they had worked out; remarkably at ease, he thought. As he signed off for the last time he was filled with optimism and resolve. He stopped in his tracks in a moment of awakening when he realised that it was the Keem that had led him through formulating the plans but stopped short of initiating them. He felt in service to them more completely than he had ever done and it contented him more than he had ever been contented. He did not look back at the Keem after his pause for thought and appreciation; he smiled to himself and walked away.

The little spheres reminded Welder of fobs. He took four out at a time and handed one to each Keem. When all of them were handed out the Keem reached out their left hands and placed them on their neighbour's shoulder and held the spheres in the palms of their right hands.

Above them, there was a sudden loud creaking of vines and the multifarious blooms dotted about the highest reaches of the dome began to swell. The final stages of the outer shell of the organic globe's hardening was complete. And those blooms were building up to something Welder did not want to be part of. He became instantly aware that they were running out of time before the escape chute would heal over and they would drift down into the deep dark hole below.

'Okay folks, you know what to do. Happy trails', Welder had no idea why he chose those words for such an important moment but he did, and so be it. The Keem popped the balls into their mouths and begun to hum. The Keem had no digestive system and did not produce anything approximating to saliva. The vibrations from the *humming would stimulate the release of the accelerant that would trigger the rapid completion of the Keem's transition. Welder watched anxiously but nothing seemed to be happening. For the first time since arriving on Chippenham Five, he began to have doubts. Maybe the catalyst was impotent.*

His doubts were initially centred on whether the escape plan would work but they grew like the rapid growing vines in the dome. They grew into one hideous doubt of writhing individual tendrils; was he doing the right thing after all? Maybe Milford had lost his mind and Sally had sent him on the mission to spot that very problem. 'Ah', Welder realised with blinding insight that what he was experiencing was separation anxiety. The connection he had with the Keem was about to be severed, they were no longer hearing his thoughts; he was alone. This fact encouraged rather than disturbed him; it showed the process was working. Sally flashed into his mind. Before his eyes like time-lapse film welts formed on the skin of every part of the Keem. They quivered and vibrated producing an accompanying note in harmony with the Keem's initial hum which was still resonating strongly. The hum shifted from one made by vibrating what was their mouth and welts to a hum made from the quivering of their whole bodies. The change accelerated and the hum grew louder. They all melted into a humming fluorescent green jelly. Quite different to the flattened Keem, thought Welder and not that attractive. Twelve stems sprouted and buds emerged at the points where the Keem had been sitting. The bud opened and roses bloomed. The roses filled out within a minute to the size of a human head. They looked similar in shape to an unopened courgettes flowers but were deep red. Without pause, they blossomed forth and revealed their blood-red petals and released a fragrance of wordless beauty. Welder was momentarily intoxicated but the smell faded and so did the flowers, as quickly as they bloomed. The speed reassured Welder. The induced pace of change did not abate and as the petals withered and fell away the kernels were revealed.

Before Welder could reach the edge of the circle in readiness to pick up the first kernel all that remained of the supporting foliage was a ring of dead and darkened dried petals. Any sign of the Keem as they were was gone.
One by one Welder moved the kernels into their soft spots in the case. They were about twice the size of a dried avocado heart but similar in looks once dried. Vines had started dropping once more but nothing fell within the ring of withered flowers.

As Welder placed the final kernel in its housing he noticed the central kernel looked as if it was not sitting comfortably. When he went to readjust it, to Welder's horror it burst. The force of the kernel bursting sent hundreds of tiny seeds flying in all directions. They were light enough to be easily propelled with the aerodynamics similar to sycamore seeds. Welder was able to field many of the seeds and keep them within the case but several bakers dozens escaped and flew upwards like little helicopters on the warm current generated by the Keem's transformation. They had been coiled springs and when the kernel split they were propelled into the open. Welder hurriedly closed the case. Above the sound of the sphere preparing itself for the big drop that would follow Welder's departure, Welder could hear what sounded like moths beating against the inside of a light shade as the seeds inside the case sprang into futile motion. Welder shelved his concerns about any damage that the seeds could be causing themselves or the unopened Kernels. The case itself had built-in buoyancy which was activated as soon as

Welder closed the lid. He lifted the case effortlessly above his head like a makeshift umbrella and dashed the chute. The opening was at about three o'clock on the column to his position of six o'clock. He had thirty seconds to get himself and the case into the tunnel. Vines began to rain heavily all about him, fizzing, whipping and thrashing about, but even in an altered state, the Keem protected him. Welder trod briskly and gingerly across the ground not covered with writhing vines as their digestive enzymes began to eat away at his boots. He hot-footed it towards the entrance of the chute which soon came into sight, as Milford said it would. But it looked like it had already started to heal over. Welder's body had already begun to prepare for the feet first leap he was going to make in the last seconds he had left before the opening sealed over completely.

'Here goes...ahhh...'

Welder's weight helped him burst through a membrane that had begun to form within the large green and white fleshy slit of an opening. To Welder's surprise, the chute went vertically down. As is the way in such escapes the case got stuck in the opening and Welder was beginning to lose his grip under his weight. But his weight became the solution as well as the problem. He was heavy enough and strong enough to pull the case into the tunnel with him and down they went. At first, he and his luggage went at great speed down the pipe which was a little wider than his girth but as he progressed downwards the pipe narrowed and he slowed. The lining of the tunnel was shiny and a dark green like the leaves of laurel. It was padded and shiny and slippery as a water slide but dry. Welder had no choice but to keep the case above his head as he continued feet first. He slowed to a near standstill as he the chute tightened. A claustrophobic sense of panic was engulfing him and he felt like he was in the stomach of a sleeping snake. Gripped by fear and seemingly gripped by the intestinal botanic tube he made his passage along by concertinaing his body and bearing down. He thought he may have a better chance of making it out if he let go of the case. The tube contracted and gripped him tighter. It felt the Domes defences had located him and seized him like a trapped insect for digesting at its leisure. He determined that the squeeze on him was too tight to continue down and out under his weight even if he released his hold on the case.

Welder was stuck. He could not move and he was being gripped ever harder. For the first time in his life, he was both physically and mentally stuck. He could not think of a way out. He resolved to meet the end of his long adventurous exciting life stuck in the gut of giant plant dome along with a case of nuts and seeds. He prepared to be dissolved and hoped that there was some kind of humane anaesthetizing even rapture inducing solvent for him beforehand. His feet felt stinging heat and he drew in a deep breath; possibly his final. He figured that Milford was not himself at the end otherwise he would have foreseen the dilemma he was in. But Milford had foreseen almost every detail of the escape apart from the bursting kernel. What Welder did not realise was that the tube had grabbed him to slow his descent and ease his exit. Welder felt himself being gently forced along the tract and let out the breath he thought was going to be his last. He and the case were extruded gently into the block base of the facility. He felt a sense of exhilaration and relief at being laid like an egg rather than being shat out like a turd of humanity.

Within minutes Welder was on his way at great speed across the pitted and potholed plain towards the gap. He watched the rearview screen showing the scene he had

371

departed dispassionately; his mind was concentrated on what lay ahead. But almost as a mark of respect he bore witness to the sphere dropping into the base it had rested on, and then the whole box of wonders sunk like a golf ball into a bottomless cup. Welder knew before he emerged from the chasm he had first passed through not that long ago that Sally could be waiting for him, and she was. 'How many days had it been?' he asked himself but he couldn't figure it out. 'I wonder what Sally will make of my slightly waxy, slightly green complexion?'

Chapter Twenty

Plan Plant Planet

'Are you ready Sophie?' The voice of her niece Jennifer came from an intercom speaker built into one of the posts of the wooden railings on the decking by the river where Sophie spent the first hours of most clear mornings between April and October. She had been retired for more than thirty years; ever since the death of Roger. She reflected that when she was growing up that a man dying in his mid-sixties did not seem that unusual. But when Roger died at sixty-five comments like, 'that's not that old nowadays' and 'he went too soon' were part of the safe network of conversational pathways taken in the oft avoided landscape that is, 'the subject of death'. Sophie agreed with such sentiments if the truth be told, and found said, scripted dialogues irritatingly predictable and strangely comforting, in equal measure. After Albert's death, Roger came out of the shadows. He accompanied Sophie to the funeral and though he remained a mysterious figure to Sophie's friends and family, he was a known mystery. Roger was trampled by galloping cancer. Until its onset he was a vital and even quietly charismatic man; he was unobtrusive but everyone noticed him. He did not reach old age, his dotage, his golden years of quiet contemplation and reflection. The ones Sophie had been living in for twenty years. As much as she loved Roger it was not his name that was projected on to every object and scene Sophie surveyed. And it was not John's her soul mate, her Mother, Alice or Father Alfred. And it was not her first and constant love Lily, her sister. All of these loved ones were gone, but despite the feeling that all of them had more life to live, Sophie knew they had all lived long enough to experience most of what life had to offer, sometimes twice. After decades of meditation, Sophie experienced memories with almost hallucinogenic qualities. The name that was printed on a transparent film overlaying her mind's eye so that it was projected on every object she saw and every scene she surveyed was Paul, her son. He had died shortly before his ninth birthday. It was his loss that was the chasm that could not be filled. All Sophie was able to do was build a swaying rope bridge over it to cross over and carry on living. She wanted to live for him because he would not have forgiven her if she did not embrace the gift of life he was denied. He would have been sad if she died too young. It was not easy but she felt it was her duty to him to find contentment; somehow. So she visited that bridge over the chasm every day in her mind; the gaping hole of loss. Each day tears fell, and she spoke of her love for her dead son. Then one day, as she walked back from the centre of the bridge, she realised that she had shed no tears; no tears had fallen into the chasm on that day. And no tears fell for the next several days that followed. After that, she crossed the bridge and sat on the far side as a new day broke. The morning sun cast light on to a beautiful gorge that grew from a magnificent waterfall. The clear burbling stream from the waterfall flowed far below in the narrow cut through dark grey-green rock. It was a gorge that would have taken millennium to carve out. Once the stream left the gorge it coursed out of the highlands and on to the open plain where it meandered its way to the distant ocean. Every day after that she left her room celebrating the new

374

day and went down to the river and watched it flow past. Every day she crossed the bridge and every day she would pause. Some days tears fell most days they did not, but every day she smiled and carried on. This way she showed her love for her son. A love that did not fade; somehow it only grew brighter.

From her deck Sophie watched a resident Kingfisher's flashing iridescent blue flight dip and into the river a pluck out its breakfast.

As Sophie listened to the narrator, part of her continued to dip into her memories as they flowed passed. She would often be back at the river where a day was a single breath and her shadow left its mark. Sophie was recalling meditations of reflection on memories. She lost herself as she drifted downstream floating like an insect on a leaf as it made its way through the delta whilst listening to the story.

Sally had it all planned; not only had she been in contact with Milford during the last weeks leading up to Welder's arrival in the Dome, she had been in touch with the Keem. Sally was the only one in the galaxy with the natural telepathic faculties to communicate, albeit in the vaguest sense, with the Keem, and she happened to know and love, practically the only man in the universe suitable to rescue them. The great escape from the sphere was a fortuitous alignment of circumstances. Coincidence yes, but life on earth, created so many billions of years before relied on many more things coinciding to spark into being. The more variables there are, the greater the coincidence, but within the stream of infinite circumstances flowing through the universe, such things are inevitable. As inevitable as an alignment of galactic bodies that only happens once in the history of the universe. Yet everything happens somewhere, at some time. Eventually, everything happens at once. The numbers of things in the right place and the wrong time, or the wrong place and the right time, are vast, but tiny compared to the numbers of things in the wrong place and the wrong time. These things must be for exciting things to have the remotest chance of happening. To be in the right place, at the right time is only right if it is recognised as such. There are only a place and a time waiting for something to decide it is right. And that something was Welder. Sally had the extended life needed to develop the extremely rare, in the first instance, and usually dormant in the second, capacity to truly know the minds of others. She did not read minds the way you would read a book or hear thoughts the way you would listen to the radio. Her mind was connected to the source as all life is, but she was able to interpret information that passed along, that connection, her connection or her point of viewing. She understood and perceived data and through years of meditative analysis and interpretation began to understand this language that nearly all of humanity had neglected and forgotten. Some people catch bits and pieces of the information coming down the line in their hats, and others get glimpses of things through windows made by numbers or pieces of music; a little like you did Sophie, so a little bird told me. Most people are no more aware of this connection than they are of the part of the brain that receives it. Nor are they aware that part of the brain is part of a network that runs through the whole body. Yes, the whole body is a receiver; it's a psychic satellite dish centred on the stomach. For the first time, Sophie sensed the narrator was offering up the story like a garment for her to wear with all of the extra accessories. The narrator was a tailor laying out a heavily embroidered coat hoping that even if Sophie didn't find it particularly appealing to look at, she would find that it fit her well. That it fit her so well and comfortably that she would wear it regardless of how outlandish it looked. Sophie began to feel her resistance. She liked to choose her garb.

Sally was connected to the source in the way the Keem were. The Keem never lost their connections and neither did the Floaters. All life is part of the source; good bad indifferent or unseen. The source is the collective data stream of the existence of all life rooted in time. We are all part of it and what we affect it and counts. Sally's great achievement was reading her mind; the part most people are not aware of. She knew what the Kernels of the Keem needed. She knew it, and she knew where to find it; a planet made up almost entirely of warm salty water. There were of course limits to her understanding of what she sensed. She did not, for instance, know what would emerge from the Kernels. What she was sure about was sunlight and oceans. Most of the time she did not tap into the source that ran through her; she was happy and operated better responding to the external world. Tapping into the source was disorienting and the longer she was hooked in the more she felt like she was going to be dragged under.
'Where are we going Sal?' Welder had no idea why he called her that and expected to be rebuked. He was relieved to see her smile approvingly.
'To the back of beyond; to a little place I know. It's the moon of a toxic planet out of bounds to all; at least that's the status we gave it; we being R and B. We, and now I'm talking about me, and you, and the Keem, and a few chosen others; it is a place where we will all be safe for generations.' Sophie reflected, 'and who knows how many generations will end up living'. She continued, 'R and B woke up just before I headed to Chippenham Five and decided to ditch Walbran once and for all. Edweener has taken the helm; she ought to be good for a hundred years at least. She came over to our way of thinking. She was happy

enough without the power she did not know about and had never imagined, once we offered her the power she had known about and had always dreamed of'.

Welder noticed Sally regarding his green hue. The ship was a small four ways pick up called 'Igwack' and was taking a roundabout route to their final destination. For now, the pair could relax after the drama of the mad events that had just transpired.

'I guess I am a little green when it comes to Roots and Branches' Welder said sheepishly addressing the elephant palm in the room; his greenness.

'I find it oddly alluring.' Sally spoke in a soft somewhat bewildered tone. 'A green man'

Welder had already put Sally in the picture concerning the Keem and what had taken place in the big bubble, which was now in the depths of Chippenham Five. The planet would have to be monitored as no one was sure what might emerge from the sphere planted in the depths of a planet. From Milford and the twin's data, R and B scientists had determined that all the Kernels would burst open into flocks of seeds just like the one in the case Welder shut the lid on. They were not sure of the trigger and assumed that it was the job of researchers long into the future to work that out. It did not occur to them to tell Welder of the prospect of a bursting. Being right almost all of the time can make it difficult to spot minor mistakes or an oversight but Milford would have been furious with himself for not spotting one.

Everything was in order and there was nothing left for Sally and Welder to do other than settle back and prepare for a long journey.

'Is there a bar?' asked Welder unconsciously enjoying the smooth texture of the skin on his forearm with strokes of his hand.

378

'Deck C' replied Sally. Welder nodded his appreciation and turned towards the lift.

'Welder, before you go there is something you should know.' She took a contemplative pause, 'I know you feel' Welder went a little blue with an embarrassment which made Sally pause once again. After looking for a moment at the floor he looked up and was immediately put at his ease by Sally's warm smiling eyes, and her smiling lips which parted and added 'I feel the same'. Less than a second later, 'MARP MARP MARP' the ship's systems detected a hostile vessel approaching. It was Walbran, intent on revenge for being ousted from the Company. He wanted to expose R and B but without evidence, he would only be exposing himself. He no longer had the resources or authority to explore Chippenham Five. He was right in assuming that whatever remnants of the project would lie buried there. He was wrong in assuming that if he did find any leftovers they would be useless as proof. He believed his only chance was to track down Welder and he did. Wallbran Prawnshot's oversized visage and a manicured voice came to life on the several screens on the bridge of the Igwack. Two-way visual communications had been established.

'Sally, well I didn't expect to see you here. What a bonus. I see you have joined Welder or has he joined you. He is looking a little green around the gills I must say' as Wallbran spoke four more vessels joined the party. Igwack came to a dead-holt and was encircled.

'That's my pro-planter friends' announced Wallbran

'Friends Prawnshot?' enquired Sally sarcastically.

'Allies then', answered Wallbran with a hint of subservience and deep, deep resentment detectable in his speech. He recovered himself and continued.

'These guys are going to present more evidence to the galaxy's fobs than even I could have hoped for. All they wanted was the pleasure of seeing the company hit by scandal and the pleasure of eliminating you. They were on a leash when I still had a stake in the company's future but now, well now I can let the vegetarian sausage dogs loose. All I had to do was track you down. So my work here is done. Goodbye Sally. Don't forget to water your friend', with that Wallbran's image disappeared and the stern female face of the Proplanters chief of operations took its place. To no one's surprise but Welders the face was that of Loveluck. The twins had infiltrated the Proplanter organisation as a single entity, Rose. The plan was to present enough just enough evidence to the media for Prawnshot to be convinced. Wallbran's ego wanted to be convinced. The company would ride out the storm. The company would take a hit from the press and appear to move away from bio synthetics and towards financial services and the dry economy. The Proplanter movement would be vindicated in its belief that secret projects involving unnecessary harm to plants had been taking place. They exposed that experiments took place as part of the project 'Loon'. 'Loon', they proposed, was also the name of the group originating and protected by the company. The deflated Peach face Loon was their evidence, given to them by Loveluck and Unity. In reality, no plant had been harmed in the development of the Keem for centuries. It was the discoveries of plant's sensory life that provided the Proplanter movement with the information they used to put the case for plants. R and B was the anonymous financier of the organisation and had been feeding them all along; though none of its members knew, except Rose. Rose was able to assure the leaders of the movement, whose ranks she was rising through that all

research on plant life had ended. As part of the plan, Rose escorted Igwack to the moon of an out of bounds toxic planet known as Melksham 828765, Ben crammers landline number, one of the last landlines ever used on earth.

There was only one island on the watery moon of Melksham 828765, 'Tartatarta', that was big enough to settle. Melksham 828765 was not, in fact, a toxic planet. It was a gas giant called 'Alan', and those gases of which it was made up of were in no way harmful to life. Indeed they could have been considered strangely fragrant.

There was a small community of R and B members settled on the island wishing to retire from the hubbub and pressure of making decisions. The five-year deadline for decisions regarding logo design was the final straw for many of them. They had in no way got things ready for the arrival of the Igwack. Welder's metabolism was never restored to the way it was it continued to evolve. He was the first human being able to metabolise the energy of the sun. He needed only one hour of sleep a month and any food or drink he consumed passed unaltered through his system. He ended up only eating socially and could never make up his mind what to eat. The love between him and Sally blossomed but children were not possible from their union in the usual way but many cuttings were taken. One month after arriving on the island of Pondor, they ceremoniously released the seeds of the Keem, which had all burst out their nuts inside the case. Sally and Welder stood alone on a specially commissioned platform that hovered twenty metres above the moon's watery surface. The former R and B members could not decide whether it was appropriate or not to join them so they didn't. The pair opened the floating on air case together and watched as the helicopter seeds scattered on the four winds that all blew at once over the ocean called 'See'. As the seeds spun out of *sight like a dispersing swarm of flying ants, intermittently one would drift downwards and land. Welder followed individual seeds downward trajectories and mused that 'land' was an odd term for something settling on the water. The flakes rose and fell on the surface swell, and would then suddenly, sink. Welder thought of the germinal impulse of Ben Crammer that led to the cultivation, development, evolution and eventual liberation of the Keem. Welder thought of the original packets of sea monkeys. He imagined Ben's grandfather Poopa, sprinkling the flakes of life into a bowl of water. He wondered what form of life would grow from the seeds he and Sally had just sprinkled into the ocean of 'Tartatata'. He was sure they would be much the same as the floaters, but some part of the Keem would enhance their being. Maybe they would be shrimp-like. He went on to speculate whether the Mude had been running the show all along, and were just looking for a way to cast their seeds on the wind and die and be reborn in peace. They had been seeking conveyance; a host to hitch a ride with. What would Ben and Robby have made of the Floaters, having set out to create life that looked like what was shown on the packet. Sally suggested that they would have changed the images of the packaging. They would certainly have been content that their 'pet project', was complete.*

Milford had been right in thinking that the evolutionary future of humanity lay in physical adaptations that enabled it to directly convert the energy from the light of the galaxy's billions of stars; that being more like plants would give humankind hugely extended life spans. He was also correct in foreseeing that there would be a great evolutionary leap forward, one initiated by our intervention. He knew in his heart of hearts that the fate of humanity would be determined by our natural evolutionary impulse to 'fuck around with things' and that our best hope was to 'fuck around with the right things'. Once that happened the rest of the universe would be free to get on with things unfettered by humankind. There would be tens of thousands of years before it arrived but the first naturally evolved hybrid did finally sprout into existence. It was the first of many competing hybrids that negotiated and unfortunately had to fight for their place in the Governmental offices of the Greenhouse. They fought politely with words, chants and liberal use of silliness. All life in the universe moved slowly away from the need to eat and the inherited376 historical fear of being eaten, all but disappeared. The Mude of Pondoor flourished and their sentient powers grew beyond anything that could be imagined. They reached a maximum viable number but their capacity to incorporate others thoughts and knowledge knew no bounds. 'Pondooring' was a communal meditation that enlightened all that joined in.

Welder and Sally and those who came after them remained connected to the Mude and the Mude were connected to the flow of all life which stemmed from the source. Their thoughts and passages of words music and feelings became the passages through which all living creatures could walkthrough to join them and connect to the source. So this is where the story ends and our conversation begins. It's time to give yourself a good talking to.

Printed in Great Britain
by Amazon